# Mr. Darcy's Enchantment

## A *Pride & Prejudice* Variation

## Abigail Reynolds

White Soup Press

# Part One

# Mages and Magic

# Chapter 1

Elizabeth Bennet leaned over the injured boy lying in the narrow bed. "What happened to you, Tommy?" She did not expect a useful answer. No one else had been able to tell her what had attacked them.

"Don't know," said the boy sullenly.

"I saw it." A girl of perhaps five peeked out from behind the door. "It was a fay. It jumped out of the bushes, grabbed his leg, and bit him."

Finally, someone who could confirm her guess! "What did it look like?"

The child considered. "It was one of the little ones with the red stocking hats."

A redcap, as Elizabeth had suspected. "Thank you. That is very helpful."

"Only babies see the fay," Tommy sneered.

Elizabeth gently touched the skin around his wound. Hot. Too hot. "All children can see them when they are very young, but I know a few lucky people who have kept the ability to see fay folk all their lives."

The little girl crept forward to stand by Elizabeth's skirt. "I hope I can. I like the fay folk. We have a brownie."

"I can tell," said Elizabeth. The cottage was sparkling clean, inside and out, unlike many of the neglected cottages at Hunsford. "She does excellent work." She nodded to the short, stocky creature who stood outside the window, polishing each pane. The brownie glared at her.

"Is this going to hurt?" asked the boy suspiciously.

"A little, but it should not be bad. Your mother was clever to rinse it out so quickly." Elizabeth unpacked several vials from her satchel and handed one to Tommy's mother. "Put two drops of this on his temples and rub it in slowly." It would make no real difference, but it served as a good distraction while she performed her magic.

She sent her consciousness through her fingertips into the gaping maw of the bite. The fay poison had not traveled far, but the bite was alive with sparks of malicious magic. One by one she stubbed out the sparks and drew the poison to the surface.

"That stings!" the boy cried as she wiped a damp cloth over his wound to collect the poison.

"I am sorry." Elizabeth folded the cloth over itself twice and handed it to Charlotte.

"Will he live?" Tommy's mother, Mrs. Miller, asked, her voice trembling.

"I see no reason why he should not." Elizabeth wrapped a thick bandage around his leg. "He is young and healthy. You should put a deadly nightshade vine around his leg above the wound, but not touching it. That will draw out the rest of the poison." The nightshade would do nothing for the poison, but it would catch any sparks of malicious magic she might have missed. If only she did not have to hide her use of magic! "We will come again tomorrow to check on him."

Mrs. Miller wrung her hands. "Why are the fay folk attacking us? They never used to hurt anyone. Now it isn't safe to cross a field."

"I wish I knew." Elizabeth surreptitiously pinched out a stray spark of magic. "I remember when redcaps never bothered people unless they were attacked."

The woman lowered her voice. "Is it safe, living in a house with a brownie?"

"Your brownie will not hurt you. I have only seen injuries from redcaps and elfshot. Staying away from trees and bushes may help to keep the children safe from redcaps." Nothing could protect against elfshot, the terrifying projectile that seemed to come out of nowhere and ate its way to the victim's heart. It was no wonder the villagers were frightened. "If he worsens, send for me at the parsonage."

Tears filled the woman's eyes. "Thank you. I will."

Elizabeth followed Charlotte Collins out of the cottage. "Could you wait for a minute? There is something I need to do." Beside her a fluffy white cat yawned and stretched.

"Of course," said Charlotte.

Elizabeth walked around the outside of the cottage to the window where she had seen the brownie. The stocky fay was still there, scrubbing industriously at the window frame with a worn rag.

She scowled at Elizabeth. "What is it ye want?" she demanded. "I've work to do."

"The bandage on the boy's leg has iron shavings in it. I did not wish for you to burn yourself by touching it."

"Iron shavings, forsooth," grumbled the brownie. "Mortals are nothing but trouble." With inhuman speed she reached out and scratched the side of Elizabeth's neck with the pointed nail of her little finger. "Now be off wi' ye, and take yon bit of bad luck with you." She pointed at the white cat.

The cat hissed at her, turned and stalked away. Elizabeth followed her.

"What was that?" asked Charlotte. "Who were you talking to?"

"The brownie. I warned her about the iron shavings." Elizabeth rubbed her skin where the brownie had scratched her.

Charlotte peered at her neck. "What happened?"

"The brownie marked me. It is a message, I think, to tell other fay that I helped her, but I could do without it."

"I wish I could still see fay folk. I do not remember much about them from when I was little," said Charlotte wistfully.

"And I wish I understood why they are attacking innocent children," grumbled Elizabeth. "I hope the boy improves. Once Mr. Darcy arrives, I cannot afford to use magic on him again."

"I doubt we will see much of Mr. Darcy. Lady Catherine will have less use for our company once her nephews are at Rosings," said Charlotte.

"Her nephews? Is there another one besides Mr. Darcy?"

Charlotte nodded. "Lady Catherine told Mr. Collins yesterday that Mr. Darcy will be bringing his cousin, Colonel Fitzwilliam, the son of the Earl of Matlock. That should work in your favor; Mr. Darcy will be spending his time with him. He may not even notice you are here."

Elizabeth stopped short in horror. "The Earl of Matlock's son? That is even worse! Lord Matlock is the Master of the Collegium of Mages. If Mr. Darcy confides his suspicions to his cousin, I am lost." She tried to still her racing heart. "It is too dangerous. I cannot stay here."

"Don't be foolish, Lizzy. Leaving would be even more likely to draw their attention. Besides, you do not know that Mr. Darcy suspects you."

"I cannot prove it, but why else would he always be watching me? He suspected me in Meryton and he wished to catch me in the act." She had been so frightened of making a slip during those days at Netherfield.

"I remember, but I think he watched you for a completely different reason. He finds you attractive, Lizzy."

"Nonsense. He finds me tolerable, but not handsome enough to tempt him. He said so himself." One more reason to dislike Mr. Darcy.

"Why are you so worried about Mr. Darcy? You never fretted so much over any of the mages near Meryton discovering you."

"The Meryton mages have known me all my life and would likely be forgiving if they discovered my magic. Mr. Darcy disapproves of me. I was so relieved when he finally left Netherfield."

"How could he have found you out? You are always careful not to let anyone see you use magic."

Elizabeth closed her eyes. "Because I was foolish. I employed an illusion that first night at the assembly in Meryton, just a tiny illusion to cover a stain on my dress where Lydia spilled tea, but he must have noticed it. I risked everything for vanity."

"Perhaps he noticed and did not care. Have you ever considered that?"

Elizabeth shook her head. "He paid too much attention to me for that. I will not be so foolish now. Oh, why could they not have waited to visit until after I left?"

"How clever of you to be acquainted with the new parson's wife and her friend," said Richard Fitzwilliam. "It gives us a good excuse to escape from Rosings. I always forget just how much I dislike the place."

"You hide it well." Darcy's step was light. Soon he would be in the same room with Elizabeth, after all these dark months believing he would never see her again.

It had to be an improvement over the empty months of longing. Perhaps he would discover she was not as bewitching as he remembered, and she would stop haunting his dreams. Or perhaps he would once again experience the sheer delight of being in her presence, the shiver her low laugh sent down his spine, and the freedom of spirit only she could bring to him. Or perhaps when she saw him, her fine eyes would burn with a sultry look, and she would take him by the hand, lead him somewhere private, slide her hands under his coat and caress him as her lips feathered along the line of his jaw, sending a jolt of awareness and desire straight through his body as he finally captured those tempting lips with his own... Well, perhaps not that, but a man could dream.

How often had he awakened from fevered dreams of Elizabeth

Bennet, dreams of pushing aside the fabric of her dress to reveal the untouched flesh below, dreams of her dark curls spread across his pillow as she moved beneath him?

Richard continued, "I can ignore Her Harridanship easily enough, but Anne would be a blow to any man's pride. Not that she is any prize, but what man likes being around a woman who swoons in fear whenever he comes near her? What did I ever do to produce such terror in her? Jasper was the one who put crickets in her bed, not me." He snorted in disgust. "The servants are the worst part. God knows I am accustomed to servants who spy on me, but the ones here are so, well, servile. All that abject boot licking turns my stomach, just like eating jellied eels does. Ugh. I would not be surprised to discover that they actually clean my boots by licking them."

"Wait until you meet Mr. Collins, the parson. He has taken toadying to a high art. He cannot stop praising our aunt even when he is three counties away."

Richard groaned. "I hope he is not at home, then. I do not need another dose of jellied eels."

It was a constant mystery to Darcy why Richard could face Napoleon's charging army without turning a hair, yet there were certain everyday people whose presence he could barely tolerate without feeling ill. They were never the people one would expect, either. Usually it was just some harmless busybody. But he could not deny that the abject, cringing behavior Lady Catherine demanded in those around her could be stomach turning. "Collins's wife is a good enough sort. I cannot imagine what induced her to marry such a ridiculous man."

"Money will make women do the strangest things. For example, Anne does not swoon when you approach her. I do not think it is merely your pretty face, cousin. Do you suppose that could be why she fears me? Perhaps she thinks I will try to compromise her for her money and snatch her and Rosings out of your hands."

9

It was Darcy's turn to groan. "Please do! I would be in your debt."

"That would be a novel experience," Richard grumbled. "Just think, I could spend every day of my life among servants who make my skin crawl. Delightful."

They had reached the parsonage, so Darcy did not trouble himself to point out that Richard could hire new servants. His heart began to beat faster as he rapped on the door with the gold knob of his cane. Elizabeth was behind that door. He could tell she was there because the constant pressure of the elements around him was already starting to fade.

The maid showed them into a small sitting room where Elizabeth and the former Miss Lucas sat near a tiny fire. Darcy somehow managed to introduce Richard to them despite his every sense being overwhelmed by Elizabeth's light and pleasing figure, the tiny dark curls along her neck that escaped from the restraint of her hairpins, the movements of the long, slender fingers on her small hands. Oh, to have those delicate fingers caressing his skin! If he did not restrain his thoughts, the direction of them would become all too apparent.

How was it that the air around Elizabeth seemed brighter than everywhere else?

Her dark eyes were every bit as fine as he remembered, although the expression in them was not sultry, but wary. It was natural, he supposed. He had singled her out for attention at the Netherfield ball and then he had abandoned her. She must think he had deliberately toyed with her feelings. But she seemed well enough; her complexion was still rosy, and she did not appear to have lost weight, as he had.

Charlotte said, "It is a pleasure to meet you, Colonel. Lady Catherine often tells us about you and your family."

Richard assumed an expression of mock dismay. "Pray permit me to guess." He pressed his hand to his chest and said in falsetto, "My dear brother, the Earl of Matlock."

Charlotte laughed. "To be fair, she has mentioned him once or twice without reminding us he is an earl – but only to remind us he is also a powerful mage."

"I am all astonishment that she should ever forget!" said Richard.

Darcy felt pressure against his leg and looked down to see a white cat turning mismatched eyes to him. "Miss Elizabeth, did you bring your cat to Kent, or is this simply a close relative?"

Elizabeth smiled. "That is indeed my cat. She hates being separated from me. Since she does not mind curling up in a basket on the stage, I brought her with me."

"I recall how she followed you across three miles of fields when you stayed at Netherfield." Darcy reached down to scratch the cat's head. Normally he did not care much for cats, but he had felt so peaceful when this one sat in his lap in the garden at Netherfield. Or perhaps he liked her simply because she was Elizabeth's cat.

"I am impressed you remember her," said Elizabeth.

"A white cat named Pepper is rather memorable." Darcy could hardly say he had not forgotten anything about Elizabeth during the months since he had seen her at Netherfield. He had tried to forget her and failed, and now he could not stay away from her.

"You named a white cat Pepper?" asked Richard in surprise. Hearing her name, the cat sniffed at his boots.

"I cannot claim the credit," said Elizabeth lightly. "She was given to me by a friend with an unusual sense of humor. I am fortunate she did not name her Bluebird or Elephant or something even less appropriate than Pepper."

"Good God! Her eyes!" exclaimed Richard. "One is blue and the other yellow. I have never seen such a thing."

"Pepper is an unusual cat," Elizabeth said archly.

Pepper abandoned Richard's boots and jumped onto Darcy's lap. Her fluffy tail tickled his chin as she turned around, curled up, and started to purr. Darcy's muscles relaxed as he stroked her back. The purr grew louder.

Mrs. Collins handed Richard a cup of tea. "Are you a mage like your father?"

"Of a sort," said Richard. "My magic cannot compare to his. A good thing, since otherwise

I would have been forced to follow in his footsteps at the Collegium of Mages, and I am much happier in the Army."

"It must be exciting to grow up with a father who is a mage," said Mrs. Collins. "When I was a child, Mr. Bennet would occasionally create an illusion to entertain us, and I thought it the most marvelous thing in the world."

A shadow crossed Elizabeth's face so quickly Darcy thought he might have imagined it. She said, "My father no longer practices magery. For all I know, he may have resigned from the Collegium."

Richard shook his head. "He would not resign. People would suspect he was dabbling in sorcery."

"Surely that is no longer the case," said Mrs. Collins. "There has not been a sorcerer in England in more than a century."

"Only thanks to the Collegium, and the watchful eye it keeps on all mages to keep them from being tempted into sorcery." Richard sipped his tea with the elegant grace his mother had instilled into him. "Good Lord, I sound just like my father. Heaven forbid!"

Mrs. Collins shivered. "Tempted into sorcery? Who would want to become a monster from our nightmares?"

"I doubt any of them set out to be evil. But have you never wished you could make someone do your bidding? For a mage, that is the road to sorcery, so we have outlawed casting spells on people."

Elizabeth's eyes flashed. "At least on men." Her normally smiling lips had a bitter twist to them.

Oh, no. Darcy wanted to kick himself. He should have seen that coming.

Richard fell into the trap. "Mages don't cast spells on women or children, either."

"Except for those unfortunate women who have magic," Elizabeth said with finality.

Before Richard could reply, Mrs. Collins said firmly, "Lady Catherine was gracious enough to send us one of her cook's delicious almond tarts. Lizzy, would you like a slice?" Her tone held a warning.

"I thank you, no." Elizabeth sounded subdued.

"Mr. Darcy? Colonel Fitzwilliam?" She cut a slice for each of the gentlemen. "I hope Lady Catherine and Miss de Bourgh are in good health."

"Indeed they are," said Richard a little too heartily. "Lady Catherine is very pleased with the state of Anne's health. She has told us that at least four times since we arrived yesterday."

As if being in good health meant someone who swooned twice a day and could barely complete a thought before being distracted by something else! Darcy would much rather be with Elizabeth, even though he would pay for it later with tortured dreams.

But Elizabeth did not seem to have recovered her spirits. She had not even touched her tea. Had she missed him as much as he had longed for her? Was it painful for her to be thrown into his company, knowing there could be no future? Poor Elizabeth! If only he had the right to make her smile again.

Absently he continued to stroke her cat. It was as close as he was ever likely to come to touching her.

"Lizzy, what were you thinking?" exclaimed Charlotte in exasperation. "Were you trying to expose yourself?"

Elizabeth looked away. "I know. I was not thinking."

"You most certainly were not! Two mages, and you immediately inform them that their treatment of women with magic is unfair. They are not stupid, Lizzy. What if they tell Lady Catherine what you said? It could bring trouble for me as well."

As if she did not feel frightened enough about her slip already! "I truly am sorry. I just could not bear it when the Colonel went on about how the enlightened Collegium will not permit spells on people's minds – at least when it suits them. I stayed out of the discussion until then. Perhaps I should return to London early, and you can tell Lady Catherine you sent me away because of my behavior."

"Don't be silly. It will come to nothing. Colonel Fitzwilliam seems to find Lady Catherine a subject for mockery. I doubt he would consult her on anything."

"If you change your mind –" Elizabeth wished she would. It would be so much easier to leave all of this behind, but she had promised Charlotte a long visit. Besides, the injured villagers needed her.

"I will not change my mind. I am happy to have you here." Charlotte picked up Elizabeth's full tea cup and placed it on the tray. "Was something wrong with the tea?"

Elizabeth shook her head. "No. It was simply not as hot as I like it. I had best accustom myself to it. I will be drinking a great deal of lukewarm tea until Mr. Darcy leaves Rosings Park." Noticing Charlotte's worried look, she added, "I do not mind lukewarm tea, to tell the truth. It simply made me angry that I could not heat it with magic as I usually do."

"And then you did not want it at all, because you were so busy resenting Mr. Darcy."

"How well you know me!" Elizabeth turned to her cat. "And you have turned traitor, Pepper. When did you become such a great friend of Mr. Darcy?"

"Mrowr." Pepper nonchalantly began to wash herself.

Darcy took the path through the grove towards the parsonage. He had planned to call there with Colonel Fitzwilliam later in the day, but the thought of Elizabeth drew him in, moth to her flame, and he could not wait to be in her presence. She had seemed unhappy at the end of their visit yesterday, and he ached to relieve her distress.

He stopped in mid-stride. The elements were growing weaker, so Elizabeth had to be near, probably here in the grove. Darcy went still and listened. Yes, there were sounds from over to the left. He hurried to reach the path in that direction.

There she was. He could see her light and pleasing figure past a clump of trees. A smile curved his lips. Elizabeth! She was looking down at something and seemed to be talking to it. Her cat, most likely. How very like Elizabeth to have conversations with her cat!

But as he rounded the curve, he discovered a little girl was skipping beside her, a tenant's child, by the look of her. What was she doing on the private grounds of Rosings? Tenants were only allowed there if they were doing work.

He bowed. "Miss Bennet, this is a fortuitous meeting. I was on my way to call on you at the parsonage." It came out sounding too stilted and formal.

Her cheerful expression faded. "You would have found no one there. Mrs. Collins is helping at a parishioner's cottage, and I am assisting her by distracting young Meggy."

Darcy examined the girl. Her clothes were clean and mended, at least, but her hands were grubby. "This is Meggy, I assume." She certainly did not belong on the private estate lands.

The girl buried her face into Elizabeth's skirt. "Am I in trouble?" she whimpered.

"Not at all," Elizabeth said firmly. "Mr. Darcy, Meggy knows she is not supposed to come onto the Rosings grounds, but I told her it would be acceptable for her to come into the grove this one time with me. Her brother is very ill, and I wanted to show her something here." She gave him a pleading look.

Ordinarily he did not approve of bending rules of this sort, but clearly Elizabeth had done it out of a charitable impulse. "You are not in trouble. As long as you are with Miss Bennet, you may come here."

"You see, all is well." Elizabeth smiled and mouthed the words 'thank you' to him. "Meggy, this is Mr. Darcy, Lady Catherine's nephew, and he will not eat you up like the wicked wolf."

The girl's face emerged, but she kept hold of Elizabeth's skirt. "Promise?" she asked Elizabeth shyly.

If being kind to the little girl meant smiles from Elizabeth, he intended to make the most of it. "I promise on my honor as a gentleman not to eat you up."

"Oh." The girl ducked her chin. "Or tell her ladyship?" Her tone made it clear that telling her ladyship was a worse threat than being eaten by the wicked wolf.

"Or tell her ladyship."

Elizabeth said, "Thank you. Lady Catherine is an intimidating figure to some of the children here."

Darcy chucked. "I can imagine. She intimidates many adults, too."

"I was not going to say that," Elizabeth said pointedly, but with a smile.

"I cannot imagine that you allow yourself to be intimidated by her," Darcy said.

"Of course not," Elizabeth said gravely. "It would be most ungenerous of me to let her intimidate me."

This was much better. She was about to tease him, he could tell.

"I fail to see why it would be ungenerous." He awaited her riposte.

She opened her eyes wide in mock innocence. "Why, if I were intimidated, I would be afraid to reveal my character flaws and the deficits in my education, and that would deprive Lady Catherine of the great joy of informing me of my failings and those of my parents. I do not think I have ever seen her as happy as when she is informing someone of their inferiority to her and instructing them on how they might improve."

He tipped his head. "A veritable hit, Miss Bennet. I cannot deny Lady Catherine's pleasure in correcting others, although I cannot believe she has found you in any need of correction."

Her musical laugh sounded freer and more genuine than he had heard from her since arriving in Kent. "I beg to differ! I would be happy to list all the faults she has found in me, but I imagine Meggy might become impatient after the first hour or so."

He raised an eyebrow. "Very neatly done! If I now suggest you cannot possibly have so many faults, you will ask me which faults I believe you do have."

Elizabeth dramatically pressed her hand to her chest. "You have spotted my devious plan. Alas, that I should be too clever to please your aunt, and not clever enough for you!"

"Miss Bennet!" The girl tugged at Elizabeth's arm, her face suddenly ashen.

Elizabeth bent down to speak to the girl. "What is it, Meggy?"

Meggy whispered something, a tear running down her cheek.

Elizabeth straightened and looked past Darcy with an odd, arrested expression. She reached surreptitiously into the reticule pinned to her waist.

"Is something the matter?" Darcy asked. There were no dangers in the grove, but perhaps this was a game.

"Mr. Darcy, I pray you to listen to me very carefully," Elizabeth said levelly. "Remain still. Do not move a muscle."

She darted around him, and he heard thrashing in the bushes. "You wretched little creature! You may not bite him," she scolded. "Besides, he would taste sour."

Shrill keening was followed by a squeaky voice shrieking, "Let me go! Let me go! It burns!"

So there really was something. Judging it now safe to move, Darcy turned to see Elizabeth holding up a creature no more than two feet tall by the back collar of its shirt. The fay's tiny hands clung to his red stocking cap and his legs kicked wildly.

"Now listen to me," said Elizabeth sternly. "This is my place and you cannot come here. If I find you anywhere nearby, I will do worse to you than this."

"It burns! It burns!" the redcap squealed, displaying a mouthful of pointed teeth.

"Go, and do not return!" Elizabeth flung the creature into the bushes. Shrill howls echoed as it ran away.

"You can see redcaps?" Darcy was stunned.

She smiled ruefully. "I suppose I gave myself away. He was about to bite you. You see the fay as well, then?"

"Guilty as charged, although I have never spoken to one. What did you do to him?"

She held up her hand, showing a few iron filings clinging to her palm. "I put iron shavings under his shirt. He will not forget that quickly."

"Do you always carry iron shavings?" he asked. Few people worried that much about encountering the fay.

She gave him an impudent smile. "Only when I think they might be useful."

The little girl quavered, "Is it gone?"

"He is gone, Meggy, and he did not bite anyone." Elizabeth

looked up at Darcy. "Her brother was bitten by a redcap and is still very ill from the poison, so she is frightened of them now."

Darcy frowned. Usually redcaps avoided people unless they were attacked. "Was your brother teasing the redcap?"

Meggy wiped away her tears, her grubby hand leaving a dirty streak across her cheek. "He wasn't doing anything, just sitting by the hearth. He's too old to see the fay, but I saw it."

Darcy recoiled. "In your house? Do you not have wards to keep out malicious fay?"

Elizabeth made a face. "Lady Catherine has deemed it unnecessary to have the old wards renewed, except at Rosings itself, of course. She says fay folk will not come near a good Christian. Therefore, if anyone is troubled by the fay, it means they are not good Christians and unworthy of her protection."

Darcy snorted. "That is ridiculous."

"I know." Elizabeth dusted the last of the iron filings from her hands. "Unfortunately, Meggy's brother and the two other townsfolk who have been bitten are paying the price."

"Three people have been attacked by redcaps?" asked Darcy in disbelief. "I have heard of recent fay attacks elsewhere, but here they always left people alone unless they were threatened."

"No doubt that was true once. Something has changed, but I do not know what." She wiped Meggy's face clean with her handkerchief.

"Lady Catherine has said nothing about fay attacks," he said, half to himself.

"I cannot think why. Even if no one has told her about the redcap bites, a man was killed by elfshot last month." She sounded irritated.

"Meggy, I will make certain the wards on your house are renewed so you can be safe inside it." What was Lady Catherine thinking to let the wards lapse?

"What do you say, Meggy?" prompted Elizabeth.

"Thank you, sir," the girl whispered.

Elizabeth said, "I would appreciate it, too, especially as there is no wisewoman here to treat illnesses caused by the fay. The poisoned bites would not have become so serious if there were one, but Lady Catherine forced the last wisewoman to leave. Charlotte and I gave the boy some herbal simples, but it is not the same."

Darcy's mouth twisted. "A wisewoman? You mean a hedge witch?"

Elizabeth stiffened. "You may call them that if you choose," she said coolly. "Meggy, perhaps we should go on instead of bothering Mr. Darcy."

He did not want her to leave, especially not when she was unhappy with him again. "Wait! I did not mean to offend you."

She thawed a bit. "Wisewomen are insulted by that term. Most of them have spent a lifetime learning their craft, and if they do live in the hedges, it is because mages have left them no other choice," she said defiantly. "The wisewoman near Longbourn is very knowledgeable about healing and she has saved lives."

"You are perhaps under misapprehension. I have no objection to hedge – to wisewomen as long as they do no sorcery."

She eyed him suspiciously. "That is very generous of you." This time there was definitely irony in her voice.

He did not want to be in conflict with her. Perhaps it would please her if he talked to the girl again. "Meggy, have you seen anything interesting here in the grove?"

The girl shook her head and buried her face in Elizabeth's skirt again. Why was she frightened now?

"We might as well confess, since I have already been caught out," said Elizabeth with a rueful laugh. "Meggy wanted to see a dryad."

Darcy eyed her doubtfully. Was she teasing him? "I have never seen a dryad here."

"They are probably shy of you." Elizabeth absently rubbed her neck just below her ear. "I see them here most days, tending to the trees."

Was this a fanciful story she was weaving to amuse the girl? "I am sorry if I have chased away your entertainment. Is there something I can do to make the dryads more comfortable?"

She drew her brows together. "Will you promise not to hurt them?"

"Of course. They are doing no harm, are they?"

"No. Perhaps if you and Meggy sit on the bench, I can convince one to come out."

Now she was definitely pretending. How could Elizabeth Bennet draw out the fay? "Very well." He walked to the stone bench and sat down. Meggy timidly joined him, careful to sit as far from him as she could. At least the girl seemed to know her place.

Elizabeth went past them, off the path, and into the trees. "If there is a dryad here, I would count it a great kindness if you would permit yourself to be seen by my friends. The little girl is very worried about her ill brother, and she has always wished to see a dryad, even if only for a moment." She returned to sit between the two of them.

Now Darcy appreciated the little girl's presence, since it meant Elizabeth had to sit close enough to him that he could feel the pressure of her arm against his and catch the aroma of sweet lavender she wore. He would believe any faerie story she wished if she would stay this close to him.

"Will they come?" whispered Meggy.

"Perhaps they will, and perhaps not," said Elizabeth kindly. "They are shy around mortals."

"Look!" Wide-eyed, the girl pointed at a large oak, where several strips of turquoise silk fluttered in the breeze.

How had Elizabeth managed to set that up so quickly? It was clever, though. Now the girl would go home happy, thinking she had seen a dryad.

Then Darcy caught his breath as half of a pale, elongated face with tip-tilted eyes and high cheekbones peeked out from behind the oak. An unnaturally slender arm, half hidden by floating silk, reached out and beckoned to the child.

"Go to her," urged Elizabeth, who did not seem surprised by the apparition. "She will not hurt you." Her hand descended on Darcy's arm, warning him not to move.

Meggy's mouth hung open in shock as she hesitantly tiptoed towards the dryad. The fay creature stepped out from the oak, dressed in filmy silks that only half concealed her delicate legs. She took the child's hands and leaned down to press a kiss on her forehead. Then she disappeared behind the oak again.

Elizabeth called out to the empty air, "I will not forget your kindness and generosity."

"How did you do that?" asked Darcy in astonishment.

A gentle smile lit Elizabeth's face. "Just good fortune. I am surprised she did so much, as they never approach me. Perhaps it was because I asked on behalf of a child."

Meggy returned to them, looking half mesmerized. "She was so beautiful," she sighed.

Darcy said slowly, "I have never been so close to one of the fay. Usually I only see them at a distance."

Elizabeth's lips quivered. "Perhaps it is because you are a mage," she said archly. Then she looked away. "But usually that is all I see as well. Come, Meggy, I should take you back to your mother now that you have seen your dryad."

He did not want her to leave, not so soon after that magical moment. "May I walk with you?"

"If you wish," she said guardedly.

"I would like to see the location of these cottages that need their wards renewed." That would please her, would it not?

She seemed to relax a little. "Very well."

The boy Tommy was feverish today, a bad sign, but Elizabeth felt none of the tingling sensation of magic when she laid her hand on his ankle. Unwrapping the bandage revealed red, swollen skin above the wound and two red streaks traveling up his leg. She laid the back of her fingers against one of the red streaks. Burning hot.

"Infected," she said quietly to Charlotte.

"Can you do anything to help?"

Elizabeth grimaced. "Very little under my current limitations." If only Mr. Darcy would go away! Then she could use her magic to give the boy a fighting chance.

"It's bad, isn't it?" asked Mrs. Miller.

"It isn't good. How long has he had the fever?" asked Elizabeth.

"It started last night."

Elizabeth bit her lip. "I had best clean the wound. Is there a basin of water?" She took out clean rags and some herbal simples from her satchel, more for something to do than because she thought they might help.

If she did nothing, the infection might improve on its own, but more likely it would progress. The leg would have to be amputated – most surgeons would be suggesting that already – and even then Tommy might die. If she used her magic, he would have a better chance of recovery, but there would be no guarantee. But if Mr. Darcy caught her using magic, he would put her under a binding spell, and she would lose everything that made her herself. She had seen Mrs. Goulding after she was spell-bound. It had made her slow-witted, nervous, and fretful. It was a choice between her mind and Tommy's leg, if not his life.

If only she knew more about the abilities of mages! They were half a mile from Rosings. Would Mr. Darcy be able to sense her using magic from that far? Perhaps she was worrying too much. If mages could sense magic half a mile away, they would have caught every woman with magic years ago. But Mr. Darcy had been watching her so closely. Did that make a difference?

Perhaps she could wait until late tonight when Mr. Darcy and Colonel Fitzwilliam would likely be asleep. But how would she explain to the boy's mother that she wished to treat him in the middle of the night rather than now? The infection could be much worse by then, too.

"This is going to hurt." She dipped a rag into the water his mother had brought and began to gently cleanse the bite wound.

The boy moaned. "Make it go away!"

"Not much more now, Tommy. You are being very brave." It hurt to see his suffering.

She had to do it. If she did not take the risk, she would never be able to look at herself in a mirror again. Magic was the only thing she could do to help him, so she would use magic and hope that the distance from Rosings was enough that the mages there would not notice.

Elizabeth placed her fingers on Tommy's ankles and felt for his life force. There it was, a little weak, but it was enough to work with.

A knock at the cottage door broke her concentration. As the boy's mother answered it, Elizabeth lifted her hands. Better to wait until they were alone again.

A familiar voice said, "I am Darcy, the nephew of Lady Catherine de Bourgh. I am here to renew the wards on your cottage."

Elizabeth jumped backwards, her heart pounding. Thank God she had not truly started yet! Her stomach churned at her narrow escape. She surreptitiously pulled the blanket over Tommy's wound.

"Oh, come in, Mr. Darcy," said Mrs. Miller. "We would be very grateful to have the wards renewed."

Darcy ducked his head to step inside the cottage. "I did not realize you had callers." He bowed to Elizabeth and Charlotte.

"Young Tommy is very ill," said Charlotte. "We came to see if there was anything we could do to help."

"I am sorry to hear it. Is this the boy who was bitten by a redcap?" he asked Elizabeth.

"Yes." Oh, why had she told him anything about the boy?

Charlotte appeared to reach a decision and stepped closer to whisper something to Mr. Darcy. Elizabeth took advantage of his distraction to fade further back into the shadows. She could hardly believe he had almost caught her in the act of using magic.

"I have no particular talent for healing, but I know the basic spells for treating common problems," Darcy told Charlotte.

"Would you condescend so far as to see if Tommy's injury is something you might be able to help with?"

Darcy moved to stand at Elizabeth's side. "Do you think it is a fay spell?" he asked her quietly.

She somehow managed to find her voice. "It started that way, but now the problem is infection."

"There is a spell for drawing out infection. It rarely solves the problem completely, but it often improves matters. I could try that."

Why was he looking at her? "Mrs. Miller, Mr. Darcy is a mage. Would you like him to use magic on Tommy's wound?"

"I'd take help from the devil himself," said Mrs. Miller, her eyes filling with tears. "It's that worried I am."

Elizabeth carefully drew back the blanket to reveal the injury.

Mr. Darcy studied Tommy's leg, looking at it first from one direction and then another. With a pained expression, he pushed aside the deadly nightshade vine. "What nonsense," he muttered. He began murmuring in Latin, dipped his forefinger into the water and put two drops side by side above the wound and two just below. Elizabeth felt the tingle of building magic as he passed his hand over the wound.

Nothing seemed to happen as Darcy finished reciting the spell. He said, "Now we must wait for the poisons to flow out of the wound. It may take some time." But a cloudy fluid was already beginning to fill the bite. "I can check the wards in the meantime."

He paced along the wall and stopped near a corner. He turned his back on the others to begin the warding spell. Elizabeth could not make out the hand gestures he made, and he was apparently careful not to speak the spell itself loud enough to be overheard. Elizabeth curled her lip. Typical mage behavior, making certain no one else could learn their skills.

She refused to stand there and gawk at him. Instead she tended to Tommy, wiping away the fluid trickling out of the bite. The red streaks running up his leg were already beginning to fade. Nothing she could have done would have worked so quickly or so well. It should have relieved her, but instead anger surged through her. It was not fair. Darcy had the opportunity to study magery and to learn skills and spells instead of having to fumble to discover how to use his magic. Not fair at all.

Elizabeth was still seething when she and Charlotte left the cottage, long after Darcy had finished renewing the wards. "I am glad for Tommy's sake, but the Millers could never have afforded to pay a mage to heal him. Darcy happened to be feeling charitable, or more likely he wanted to look charitable, and so he deigned to help out. I would help boys like Tommy without charging money, but I am not permitted to learn how to do so, and I can be punished if I even dare to try. It is infuriating!"

"Still, it was kind of him to help when I asked," said Charlotte reasonably. "He need not have obliged. And it is not his fault that women cannot receive the same training as men."

"No, but he is content to be part of the Collegium that enforces those rules," Elizabeth muttered. "I cannot forgive him for that."

Darcy hurried through the gate to the formal gardens of Rosings Park. It was faster that way and would give him a chance to change his clothes before calling on Elizabeth. Would her warm smiles be back now that she had seen him help the sick boy?

He had just reached the Italian Garden when he felt her presence, that subtle relaxing of the pressure of the elements, and his yearning hunger for her began grow. Then he saw her, perched on the edge of the fountain, her gloves beside her and her fingertips trailing in the pool. It made an enchanting picture, one that took his breath away, at least until she spotted him and pulled her hand out of the water.

Darcy halted and bowed, pleasure in every breath now that he was in her presence. "Good day, Miss Elizabeth. I had not realized you were fond of these gardens."

"In general, I prefer the grove, but today I was in the mood for flowers planted in straight lines. Lady Catherine told me I might walk in the gardens whenever I pleased so long as I was in no one's way." She added archly, "I hope I am not in your way."

It would be unwise to tell her just how much he liked having her in his way. "Not at all. I am on my way back from the village, and this route is more direct than the road."

"It is kind of you to renew the wards. I would not have imagined you would take that kind of work on yourself." There was a slight edge to her voice.

Was she implying it was beneath him? Of course, he would usually think so, too. "The villagers need protection during these fay attacks, and I have a certain responsibility for the tenants of Rosings, including the village."

She tilted her head. "Is that not Lady Catherine's duty?"

"She does much of the day-to-day estate management because she prefers it that way, and I have seen no reason to interfere, but the estate belongs to Miss de Bourgh, and I am her guardian." If only he could kiss her rosy lips instead of making nonsensical chatter!

"You are? It must be challenging to be guardian to a woman your own age."

"My father was originally named as her guardian. I inherited the responsibility after his death." It was a nuisance he would generally prefer to avoid, but it was that same guardianship that had forced him to come to Rosings each year, and without that he would not have seen Elizabeth again.

"I hope Lady Catherine has not objected to the wards being renewed."

"I did not discuss the matter with her. It needed to be done, and so I have done it. Unless she wishes to dig each ward out of the walls, she has little choice but to tolerate it." He did not want to waste his time with Elizabeth talking about his aunt or the wards.

Elizabeth reached behind her to trail her fingers in the fountain pool again. It was at once innocent and sensual, the movement exposing the curves of her body. She could have been a water nymph sitting there, and he was the Greek god desperate to possess her. How could he keep himself from touching her, twining his fingers with hers and then moving on to stroke her shapely arms, his body demanding more and more from her –

With a cry of surprise, Elizabeth yanked her hand out of the water, staring at it in shock.

"What is the matter?" Darcy asked.

"The water! Only my fingertips were in it, but the water crept up my hand and wrist!" Her disturbance was evident. "Did you cast a spell?" she accused.

"Not a spell as such, but it is my fault." How could he have lost control like that? He wanted to sink into the ground. "My magic is elemental, and water has a particular affinity for me. When I am this close to a body of water, it can misbehave unless I make an effort to keep it quiet. I failed to pay sufficient attention to it, and I apologize for that."

Elizabeth continued to stare down at her hand. "Water is not alive. How can it have an affinity for you?"

"Lodestones are not alive, either, yet they turn to point to the north. Natural philosophers have argued about water's affinity for centuries. Some would say that my presence agitates the aetheric vibrations which keep the water in place. Others would say it is a relic of some fay traces in my blood. I have yet to see a convincing explanation of why I can do this." He pressed his palms together and slowly separated them by a foot or so. The water in the fountain obediently retreated to each side, leaving a dry space in the middle.

Elizabeth eyed him warily. "That is uncanny. And it is not a spell?"

"No, although there are spells which could do similar things. I simply concentrate on the water and what I wish it to do. Left to itself, without my efforts to keep it quiet, it would do this." He crossed his arms and withdrew from the constant calming refrain in his mind.

The water inched towards him, splashing over the edge of the fountain and running in rivulets towards his boots. It was slower than usual, most likely because Elizabeth's odd ability to suppress some of his effect on the elements. "That is why I say it has an affinity for me." He resumed his calming thoughts and the water stopped splashing out of the fountain. "My moods can affect water, too." He never told people these things, but she ought to know what she would be facing if he offered for her.

Elizabeth touched one of the rivulets. "Not an illusion, then," she said, as if to herself. "But I have never seen that happen to you before."

"Usually I am telling the water not to do that."

"All the time?" She sounded disbelieving.

"All the time. I had a very wet childhood until I learned to control it."

That seemed to amuse her. "I suppose it is a useful skill to have."

"No. It is not useful at all." He had not meant to sound abrupt, but the subject rankled. "Apart from parlor tricks like these and telling people the best place to dig a well, I am forbidden from using it."

"Forbidden? By whom?"

"The Collegium. It is a dangerous ability and easy to misuse. If there is drought in my lands and I draw water to my wells, someone else's wells go dry. If I divert floodwaters from my doorstep, another house is flooded as a result. And while water is my primary affinity, I can also set fires with a thought. I am forbidden that, too."

She nodded slowly. "They are afraid of you."

"Rightly so. I could wreak havoc if I chose."

"So they are willing to trust you to follow their rules, but not to use your powers wisely."

And that was why it rankled. "More or less."

She turned her hand palm up and looked down at it. "I do not understand one thing. Why did the water go up my arm instead of moving towards you?"

Of course Elizabeth had seen that one flaw in his explanation. How could he extricate himself from this predicament? Perhaps he should simply say he did not know. Or perhaps it was a sign that he should stop fighting the inevitable. "I was thinking about your arm. The water must have followed my thoughts."

She stood, color rising on her cheeks. "Mr. Darcy, I believe it is time for me to go."

He held up his hand. "Wait, I beg you. I meant no disrespect."

"You were respectfully thinking about my arm? I am not a fool, Mr. Darcy. Good day."

He dodged around her to block her path. He could not allow her to leave him in anger. "I assure you my intentions are honorable." The words had spilled out before he had known what he was saying.

She turned slowly to face him again, her eyes wide. "What did you say?" she asked dubiously.

He had started, and now he must go on. "I had not meant to speak today, but apparently I must, since my feelings will not be repressed. You must allow me to tell you how ardently I admire and love you. I have wished to make you my wife since shortly after we met, and my feelings have only grown stronger since then. I have fought against them. I cannot deny that I have tried to avoid this connection. Your father's position in life is acceptable, although lower than mine, but your mother's birth is otherwise. More importantly, the inappropriate behavior of your mother, younger sisters, and even occasionally your father caused me to hesitate, and had my attraction to you been any less intense, I could not have –"

"Mr. Darcy, I pray you to say no more," interrupted Elizabeth firmly. "While I am honored by the great compliment of your attentions, any connection between us is impossible. In addition to the obstacles you have mentioned, I resolved long ago never to marry a mage, and nothing will induce me to change my mind. I am sorry for any disappointment it may occasion you. For our peace of mind, let us say nothing more on the subject."

Darcy stared at her incredulously. "That you would refuse me comes as a surprise, I admit, but that you should do so because I am a mage? Because I was born with powers I did not request and have spent years learning to suppress? You might as well refuse me because I have brown eyes."

Elizabeth's eyes narrowed. "Pardon me. I should have been clearer. It is not because you have magical powers, but because you are a member of the Collegium of Mages. If you belonged to a society of brown-eyed men who were determined to subdue all blue-eyed men by means fair and foul, then yes, I would refuse you for having brown eyes. But it does not matter, since I have other reasons as well." She tried to move past him.

This time anger made him stand in her way. "Oh? Will you be so kind as to enlighten me as to my other faults?" He bit out the words.

Elizabeth paled. "All of us have flaws, and I do not think a recitation of them would reflect well on either of us. Suffice to say that I must refuse your very flattering offer."

"I wish to know why." He spoke through gritted teeth.

She kept her silence for a moment, and then the words began to pour out. "Very well. I do not like your proud and disdainful attitude to anyone beneath your station. It is abhorrent to me, especially your carelessness towards the devastation it causes. Need I explain that you have ruined the happiness of my beloved sister, who still suffers from heartbreak because you thought she was not good enough for your friend? If that is still not sufficient reason for my refusal, Mr. Wickham told me how he lost his ability to earn his living as a mage since you had him expelled from the Collegium because of his low birth."

Darcy clenched his fists. "George Wickham is a liar. He was expelled from the Collegium for using his magic to cheat at cards. It had nothing to do with his station in life. If you do not believe me, I suggest you ask Colonel Fitzwilliam, who can tell you the entire tale."

Elizabeth took a step backwards, clearly struggling to contain her own feelings. "I grant you I have no proof as to which of your stories is true, but you yourself showed your disdain for my low connections just minutes ago."

"Could you expect me to rejoice in the inferiority of your connections? To congratulate myself on the hope of relations, whose condition in life is so decidedly beneath my own?" He could not stop himself.

"You should be relieved I refused you, then, since you have no idea how low my connections go. I can help a boy who is attacked by redcaps because for years I served as the assistant to a wisewoman, or as you would say, a hedge witch, a crone whose father was nothing more than a tenant farmer. She was going blind and could not do her work without someone who could see fay and their traces, and I was the only one she could find. And I admire her, even though she is far beneath me in birth. Now you see why I cannot marry a mage, a man who would imprison her with a binding spell merely because she is female. You should be grateful for my refusal. You are the last man in the world I could be prevailed upon to marry."

Each of her words hit him like a dagger. That she should think so ill of him! There was nothing to do for it but to retreat and hope that someday this agonizing emptiness would fade. "You do not know me at all. Pray forgive me for having taken so much of your time." He turned and strode away, his shoulders stiff.

# Chapter 2

Elizabeth turned away from Darcy and hurried off, lest he look back over his shoulder and see her standing there like a lost waif. Had that truly just happened? Mr. Darcy making her an offer of marriage – and in such an insulting manner! And she had been just as bad, saying horrible things back to him. Charlotte would be furious with her if she knew.

She pressed her hands against her hot cheeks. Charlotte's wrath was the least of her worries. She had put herself in danger. If Mr. Darcy had not known of her magic already, he certainly had enough evidence to realize it now. After all, who would resolve never to marry a mage unless they were afraid of mages? And there was only one reason she would be afraid of mages.

Why had she not simply said it was because of Jane? He had not contested that point at all, as he had regarding Wickham and the Collegium. Oh dear, his explanation for that made more sense than Wickham's, and Darcy would not have told her to ask Colonel Fitzwilliam if it were false. Wickham had seemed so honest and open. Or perhaps she had just been gullible. Now she had made a fool of herself on top of everything else. What did it matter? Darcy had plenty of reasons to think ill of her besides her gullibility.

Tears ran down her face. She could not return to the parsonage like this, so she stopped at the stone bench in the grove and finally allowed herself to sob into her handkerchief, overcome with shame and wretchedness. That Mr. Darcy had cared for her all this time, while despising her and her family! She had always seen her mother and younger sisters as an embarrassment, but to hear him describe how their behavior reflected on her was beyond humiliation. How many other people felt the same way?

A cold shiver ran up her spine. Her humiliation did not matter. She was in danger now. There was no time to dwell on anything else. Once Mr. Darcy realized she had magic, he would put a binding spell on her. She had to get away before that happened, but how? The coaching inn was five miles away, and by the time she arrived there, the last coach of the day would have departed. She would have to delay until tomorrow. But would Mr. Darcy wait that long? He was due to leave Rosings the day after tomorrow, and he would want to resolve this right away.

Tonight she was to dine at Rosings along with the Collinses. She would have to plead a headache to avoid going. But that might make him suspicious that she was trying to escape, and he would act even more quickly. Better for her to go to Rosings, uncomfortable as it might be, and make him think he had plenty of time to deal with her. After all, he could hardly place a spell on her at dinner. No, he would want to wait until morning when he could get her alone.

She was not safe even now. What was she thinking to sit in a place he knew was one of her favorites? Barely able to see through her tears, she hurried away to the hidden deer path leading to the center of the grove. He would not know to look for her in the glade. She was safe, at least for the moment.

She would have to sneak away from the parsonage during the night if she wished to arrive at the posting inn for the first stagecoach. Once she reached the Gardiners in London, they would help her find a place to hide. Too many people could guess that would be her destination, though, so she needed to lay a false trail to delay Mr. Darcy.

She could leave a note saying she could no longer live with herself and that she would find peace in the millpond. Charlotte would be distraught until she discovered it was untrue, but it would delay Mr. Darcy until they dredged the millpond. By then she would be in London.

She gazed across the glade. If she could not reach the stagecoach, there was still one last option. She fingered the smooth stone in her reticule. It would be risky, but better than being bound. The tightness in her chest eased a little.

But even if she escaped and avoided being bound, nothing would ever be the same. She could never return to her home because Darcy would know to look for her there. For now, she could not afford to dwell on that future. She had to be strong, and she had always known this could happen someday. There was even a certain comfort in having an end to it.

She waited until she thought the signs of tears would have faded from her face before starting off for the parsonage. When she came to the gate at the edge of the grounds of Rosings, she peered up and down the lane. No one in sight.

She had not gone far when she encountered Colonel Fitzwilliam walking towards Rosings. After a brief jolt of fear, she realized he could not yet have spoken to Darcy. But he might still be aware of Darcy's feelings for her, and that made her unaccountably nervous.

"Well met, Miss Bennet," he said jovially. "I was just at the parsonage hoping to see you."

"Now you have found me." She forced a smile to her face. "I am on my way back there."

"May I have the honor of walking with you?"

"It would be a pleasure." Or at least a distraction. And perhaps she could take the opportunity to confirm Mr. Darcy's story about Mr. Wickham. It would answer at least one of the million questions swirling in her head. "Colonel, I would like to ask you a question, if that would not be impertinent."

"You may ask a question, and I will do my best to answer it."

"Recently a troop of militia was stationed in the town where I live. Among them was a man who claimed acquaintance with Mr. Darcy, a Mr. Wickham. He told me –"

The usually affable Colonel looked thunderous. "Whatever Wickham told you is likely to be a lie. He is not to be trusted."

She flushed. Now he would know how gullible she had been, too. "He said he had been a member of the Collegium, but that Mr. Darcy had him expelled because of his low birth."

"Because of his low morals would be more accurate. Darcy should have reported him to the Collegium years before he did, but he kept giving Wickham warnings and hoping he would change. I could have told him that would never happen. Wickham is a gambler. He used illusions to change the appearance of his cards so he could win. He is a blackguard. I urge you to stay well away from him."

Wickham, who had seemed so sincere in his attentions to her. How utterly humiliating to discover what a fool she had been! "Thank you. I had been wondering if there might be more to the story than he had told me, and you have confirmed it."

"I commend you for your perception. Wickham has such a charming manner with ladies. I have never yet known one who could see through his masquerade before it was too late."

She looked away from him and said in a low voice, "You give me credit where none is due. I believed his blandishments until I was given reason to suspect him. I am mortified to discover I was so gullible."

"You should not be. I have known experienced, sensible women who have fallen for his charm. I sometimes wonder if he uses magic to blind ladies to his failings."

"That is a frightening thought." But it made more sense than she cared to admit.

"Frightening indeed. There are very few mages who can cast

glamour, but I suspect he may be one of them."

"I thought only the fay could cast glamour," she said.

"They are the masters of it, if the old stories are to be believed. Most mages are limited to illusions which can be easily detected by touch."

Which would be worse, that he had fooled her with false charm or with magic? Time for a change of subject, or she would start crying again. "I hear that illusion has become more popular as decoration at society events in London."

"True. It is amusing to attempt to pick out which one of the guests has cast the spells. At Lady Atherton's ball last month, one wall appeared to open onto the desert and the Great Pyramids. It took two mages all day to weave that one."

"Was it convincing?"

"From a visual standpoint, yes, unless you attempted to walk into it and hit the wall instead. Since I could still smell the hothouse flowers, perfume, and candlewax and hear the orchestra playing, it was difficult to convince me I was in the Egyptian desert. It is tiring work, maintaining a large illusion for so long."

It was even more tiring to maintain the illusion that she had no magic. How would the colonel react when Darcy told him she might have magic? She would rather not know.

Darcy rested his forehead in his left hand while he dipped his quill in the inkwell. Only a little more now. He had already written an explanation why he had separated Bingley from Jane Bennet and laid bare the entirety of his connection to Wickham, from their childhood to Wickham's expulsion from the Collegium to his attempt to elope with Georgiana as revenge. If Elizabeth was fool enough to trust Wickham after that, her downfall would not be on Darcy's conscience.

Only one more section and he would be done. Once he was finished with this letter, the stabbing pain in his chest and the nausea of humiliation would end, and he would be free again. He needed to say all the things he had been too angry and hurt to tell her in person. After that, their entire acquaintance would be over.

He had to hurry. He would be expected downstairs in less than an hour, and that might be his only opportunity to give her the letter.

*Lastly I must mention the matter of the Collegium. I am not in agreement with all Collegium policies. Many mages would prefer to see an end to the restriction on women's use of magic, but change comes slowly. Perhaps you will still condemn me for any association with the Collegium, but if those of us who disagree with the rules depart, those changes will never happen.*

How could Elizabeth, his heart's own Elizabeth, have simply assumed the worst about him? He had never said a word to her about women and magic, though he had long since guessed she had it. Did she think him so detestable that there was not even the possibility he might have his own opinions on the matter? And he had thought she cared about him. Wretched, wretched mistake.

Now she would know better, and she would see what her prejudiced view of all mages had cost her. She could have been Mistress of Pemberley, and instead she would be nothing.

Why could she not simply have accepted him as any other woman in England would be delighted to do? But he did not want any of them. He only wanted Elizabeth.

He still hesitated to sign the letter. Once he did that, it would be done, and he could walk away from Elizabeth Bennet. Still, there was something so final about signing his name. That would be the end of everything.

What was the matter with him? Was he the Master of Pemberley or a puling schoolboy?

*I will only add, God bless you.*
*Fitzwilliam Darcy*

He was going to be late. He sanded the letter quickly and called for his valet to help him dress for dinner.

He had written the letter and said everything he needed to say. Why did his chest still hurt, making him feel as if he could never stand up straight again? If anything, the agony was worse. The agony of not only losing the woman he loved but discovering she had never existed in the first place. The one woman he thought would understand all he had suffered and teach him to laugh again. The one woman who would make him feel as if his struggles were worth something.

Elizabeth. Ah, Elizabeth.

"Are you certain you are well enough to go to dinner?" Charlotte asked Elizabeth as they approached Rosings.

"It is only a headache, and I would not dream of disappointing Lady Catherine over such a small matter," said Elizabeth. There was no point in pretending nothing was bothering her. Charlotte would see through that at once.

Mr. Collins said, "An admirable sentiment, Cousin Elizabeth. Lady Catherine's wishes must come first."

"I cannot hope to match the depth of your regard for Lady Catherine, but I do my poor best." She could say what she liked, since Mr.

Collins would not recognize it as a barb. The man never thought of anything except Lady Catherine's desires.

Elizabeth was determined to avoid drawing any notice to herself. She would stay in the background as much as possible and avoid looking at Mr. Darcy. She might sit with Miss de Bourgh, since Mr. Darcy rarely went near her. Besides, she felt sorry for Miss de Bourgh's loneliness, especially since she had a good sense of the subjects that provoked that lady's frequent fainting spells.

Thankfully Mr. Darcy was not present in Lady Catherine's drawing room when they arrived. Relieved, Elizabeth smiled at Colonel Fitzwilliam and sat next to Charlotte, turning half an ear to Lady Catherine's usual monologue.

"Where is Darcy?" demanded Lady Catherine. "Does he not know how I particularly detest tardiness?"

Colonel Fitzwilliam said, "He was just finishing a letter and said he would be down shortly."

"I hope he is writing to Georgiana with my advice that she cannot expect to excel at the pianoforte if she does not practice a great deal. Anne would have been a great proficient had her health permitted her to learn."

How could Miss de Bourgh be proficient at anything if she could barely manage to complete a sentence before being distracted by something else?

"There you are, Darcy. You are late."

Painfully self-conscious, Elizabeth kept her eyes on the floor after her curtsy. Her anxiety grew with every breath.

"Pardon me," said Darcy coldly. "I wished to find a particular reference in a book to show to Miss Bennet, and it took me longer than I expected."

Elizabeth stiffened. What was he about?

"For Miss Bennet?" Lady Catherine sounded displeased. "Why would you be concerned about finding reading material for her?"

"It is something I wish her to read. We had a minor disagreement over methods of land management. She felt her father's methods were superior to the ones I proposed. I thought it would benefit her to learn the truth of the matter," he said with no trace of warmth in his voice.

"You are very kind, sir," said Elizabeth hastily without looking at him. "I am certain you know far more about the matter than I do, or than my father does, for that matter."

"Darcy is certainly correct," said Lady Catherine. "He is showing great condescension by pointing out your errors. Is it a long passage, Darcy?"

"Just a few pages."

"Then she may sit over by the piano as she reads it. She will be in no one's way there."

A pair of shiny boots appeared on the floor by her feet, forcing Elizabeth to finally raise her eyes. Mr. Darcy's expression was cold and disdainful as he held out a leather-bound volume to her. His fingertips were ink stained.

She took it in numb hands. "I thank you."

"You may start on page 36." He turned on his heel and strode over to Colonel Fitzwilliam. He could not have said more clearly that he was done with her.

She swallowed hard. At least this gave her an excuse to sit on the other side of the room. She chose the chair where her face would be hidden by an ornate statuette of a shepherdess. Why did his coldness hurt her so much?

She opened the book to the page he had indicated and found three sheets of letter paper, written quite through, in a close hand. She took a deep breath to calm herself, reminding herself of the abominable things he had said. Did he think he could offer some excuse? This letter was likely to make her even angrier than she already was.

Elizabeth hardly knew how she had made it through the rest of that nightmarish evening. Somehow she had managed to return the book to Mr. Darcy, who merely nodded acknowledgment as he accepted it. Apparently he had already dismissed her from his acquaintance in his own mind.

She could not decide what to make of his letter. His excuses for separating Jane and Bingley seemed weak, but she kept returning to his words about the Collegium. Did he truly disagree with the Collegium view on women and magic? If so, she might not have to leave behind her family and friends to live with strangers. But what if he said it merely to lower her guard? The risk was frightening, but so was the thought of leaving her family and friends. It would be so much simpler if she could accept his assurances. She disliked many things about him, but deceptive behavior had not been one of the faults she had observed. His weak fib about wanting her to read the book had not been the work of a practiced liar.

She passed a restless night haunted by dreams of Mr. Darcy's disdainful face and cold dislike. In the morning she walked out for the sole purpose of re-reading and brooding upon his letter and the humiliation of his words. She had always prided herself on her judgment of character, and now she knew how wanting in it she was. She was as much a fool as Lydia or Kitty. Mr. Darcy's criticisms of her family left her spirits lower than they had been in years.

On her return to the parsonage, she discovered her walk had saved her from the mortification of meeting Mr. Darcy and Colonel Fitzwilliam when they called at the parsonage to say their farewells before departing the following morning. Even this fortunate timing could not relieve her oppression of spirits.

The next day, knowing that Mr. Darcy had left Rosings Park, she attempted to put on a brave face with Charlotte. She suspected her friend was not fooled, though Charlotte did not question her. She had always been good about respecting Elizabeth's privacy.

In the early afternoon, the maid brought a piece of folded notepaper to Charlotte. A look of concern crossed her face as she read it.

"Charlotte, is something amiss?" The last thing Elizabeth needed was more trouble.

"Lady Catherine has taken ill. Mr. Darcy is requesting my presence at Rosings. I suppose her ladyship must want me to read to her."

Her stomach seemed to turn somersaults. "Mr. Darcy? I thought he had left!"

"Apparently not yet. He asks specifically that I bring you with me."

Elizabeth's heart twisted in her chest. "Me? Why would he want me there?" Was it a ploy to do a binding spell after all, or only to berate her, or to show her he no longer cared for her by the cold and disdainful look on his face? *You must allow me to tell you how ardently I admire and love you.* And now she would have to see him again, with the shame of everything he had said in his letter fresh in her mind.

Charlotte shrugged. "Perhaps Lady Catherine wishes to listen to you play. I am sorry to impose upon you this way, but we cannot afford to offend her ladyship."

Her dismay must be showing. "Of course I will go with you." Somehow she would manage to keep her composure with Mr. Darcy. Somehow.

The tingling sensation from crossing the Rosings wards only worsened Elizabeth's queasiness. She would have to see Mr. Darcy and converse with him. Perhaps she could hide behind Charlotte and leave her to do all the speaking. That way she could concentrate on being ready to run away if he spoke even one word in Latin.

At least Darcy did not keep them waiting long, appearing in the drawing room not five minutes after the butler had showed them in. "I thank you for coming so promptly, Mrs. Collins."

"I am happy to be of service," said Charlotte demurely.

Darcy looked past Charlotte, his lips tightening. "Miss Elizabeth, may I speak freely in front of Mrs. Collins?" he asked abruptly.

Elizabeth inhaled sharply. What in heaven's name was he thinking? "I have not discussed, er, recent events with her." The disaster of Mr. Darcy's proposal was none of Charlotte's business.

He shook his head impatiently. "Not that. I speak of your activities in visiting the sick."

Relief rushed through her. "Charlotte knows I do the work of a wisewoman, if that is what you mean."

"Good. Lady Catherine's illness appears to be otherworldly. She was found unconscious in the garden. Nothing I have attempted has had any effect." He bit the words out, as if he hated admitting to any weakness.

Was it possible his summons had nothing to do with his offer of marriage or her magic? Elizabeth said cautiously, "If you would like me to see if there is anything I can do, I would be happy to do so. However, there are much more experienced wisewomen available."

"No. We must keep this private."

Elizabeth glanced at Charlotte. "Very well. Could someone be sent to the parsonage to collect my satchel? There are supplies in it I may need."

It was hardly surprising that Miss Elizabeth hesitated just inside

Lady Catherine's bedroom. Lady Catherine lay pallid and utterly without motion, looking more dead than alive.

Elizabeth asked him, "Are you certain this is not an apoplexy?"

"It stinks of fay mischief." He lowered himself into a chair, watching her intently as she approached Lady Catherine and felt her wrist. He should be worried about his aunt, but the sight of Elizabeth brought back too many painful memories.

Richard looked in the door questioningly. Darcy waved him inside.

Elizabeth did not seem taken aback by how Lady Catherine's eyes stared straight up, regardless of the movement around her. She laid the back of her hand on her forehead. "No fever. This illness is different from the redcap bites I have been seeing. Charlotte, would you assist me in examining her clothing? I am looking for a small tear or cut in the fabric."

"Elfshot?" Darcy asked harshly. Elfshot was a death sentence.

"It is too soon to say." Elizabeth ran her fingers up and down the fabric of Lady Catherine's dress.

"There is a small rip here," Charlotte pointed to Lady Catherine's forearm. "I see no blood, though."

"Elfshot does not cause bleeding, although no one knows why." Elizabeth hurried to the opposite side of the bed. She pressed her fingers into Lady Catherine's arm beneath the shoulder and began to palpate her flesh. She moved her hands along her arm until her fingers halted just above the elbow.

"There," she murmured as if to herself. Straightening, she brushed back a stray lock of her hair and looked up at Darcy. "I am sorry to say it does appear to be elfshot, but it is still in her arm, so all is not yet lost. I can attempt to remove it if you wish, but it is a difficult process which may well not succeed."

"And if we do nothing?" asked Richard.

"The elfshot will continue its journey to her heart and kill her."

Richard turned to him. "Darcy? What do you think?"

Why did it have to be his decision? It was hard enough just to look at Elizabeth, much less speak to her on such matters. Darcy cleared his throat experimentally. Good; his voice still worked. "We would be most appreciative for whatever you can do."

She hesitated, biting her lip. "It might be a wise precaution to fetch a surgeon. If my attempt to remove the elfshot fails, the next choice would be to amputate her arm, and time is of the essence."

"Will that save her?"

"Logic says it should do so, but elfshot does not always follow the laws of logic."

Darcy nodded to Richard, who left the room. He did not even want to think about how his aunt would react if she awoke without an arm. She might prefer to be dead.

Elizabeth glanced down at Lady Catherine and then back at Darcy. "If I am able to remove the elfshot, do you have the ability to destroy it? Otherwise it will seek her out again."

"Naturally," he said, stung by the doubt in her voice. "What else will you need?"

"Everything I need is in my satchel, but perhaps I can start without it. A sharp knife and a tourniquet to begin with. An unstarched cravat and a stick will serve admirably as a tourniquet. Forceps, if there are any at hand. Rags for when the bleeding starts. Perhaps her maid could cut away the sleeve of her dress."

"No servants." If word got out that he had employed a wisewoman, he would lose the last vestiges of trust from the Collegium. The same would be true if Lady Catherine died suspiciously in his presence, or he would never have resorted to this. "I will fetch what you require."

Elizabeth looked surprised. "Very well. Charlotte, dear, will the sight of Lady Catherine's blood trouble you?"

By the time Richard returned with word that the surgeon had been sent for, Elizabeth's satchel had arrived, and she had set the tourniquet in place on Lady Catherine's upper arm. She rummaged through the satchel and removed several objects, including a small metal tin. Her movements were efficient and competent.

Despite himself, Darcy could not take his eyes from her. This was a side of Elizabeth he had never seen before and hardly even guessed at. The stories he had been told of wisewomen always portrayed them as crones who were more than half lunatic, scattering herbs and drawing signs in the air. No one had ever mentioned they could be bewitchingly beautiful with fine eyes. Standing beside her was torture.

Elizabeth stripped off the wire holding the tin closed. Could that thick lining inside the tin be iron? She gingerly lifted out a stone arrowhead. Perhaps this was the start of the lunatic bit.

"What is that?" Darcy asked.

"Inert elfshot." She did not look at him.

He reached past her. The stone tingled at his touch, and he snatched his hand away.

"Mostly inert," she said with a slight smile. "Otherwise it would not help me." She slid the arrowhead along Lady Catherine's arm until it abruptly stopped as if of its own accord. "Yes, definitely elfshot. It seeks out its own kind. But I suppose you know that."

He could almost hear the echo of her voice. *I resolved long ago never to marry a mage, and nothing will induce me to change my mind.* "No. We learn other things in the Collegium."

She raised her eyebrows at him and then returned the arrowhead to its iron box. She took up her scalpel and wrapped the handle in a scrap of cloth, but then stopped short. She held out the candlestick from the bedside table to Mrs. Collins. "Charlotte, could you light this, if you please?" Her voice was oddly flat.

Darcy flicked a finger. "*Ardescas.*" The wick caught with a steady flame.

"Thank you." The words sounded forced. Elizabeth held the scalpel in the flame until the tip of it glowed.

"Why do you –"

"Elfshot dislikes fire," she snapped. "It is difficult enough doing this with a mage in the room without having to explain everything."

Mrs. Collins asked timidly, "Should I hold her arm down?"

Elizabeth shook her head. "No need. She can feel nothing while she is under the influence of elfshot."

Darcy sucked in his breath as Elizabeth made a deep slice in his aunt's arm. She did not hesitate, though, poking deeper with the scalpel as blood welled around it.

"There," she murmured. She held out her hand. "The inert elfshot, if you please. Mind the edges of it."

Darcy hastened to obey. Elizabeth took it without a word and set it directly in the wound. Could that possibly be safe? But there was nothing safe about any of this.

What was happening? She did not seem to be doing anything. But suddenly she had two arrowheads in her hand. She pulled the second one off using the forceps and held it out in his direction. "Do it."

He murmured the words of unmaking, and the elfshot dissolved into ashes. "Is she safe now?"

Elizabeth shook her head. "There are still traces I must remove." She leaned over the wound and covered it with both her hands, one on top of the other. Mrs. Collins wiped away the oozing blood.

Since it seemed there was nothing further he could do to assist her, Darcy stepped back. It was safer that way. The immediate crisis was over, and being near her just reminded him of all he had lost. He had offered her everything he possessed, and she had disdained it. He was the last man in the world she could be prevailed upon to marry. And while he might be seeing a new side of her today, his desire for her was unchanged.

He ached for her, and she wanted nothing to do with him.

But he could not stop watching her. He settled in a chair where he could see her face. Her fingers were moving near the wound, but her eyes were closed. It must be part of the wisewoman show, but he was surprised Elizabeth would indulge in such theatrics.

As silent minutes passed, a look of strain came over Elizabeth's face. Her body grew rigid and beads of perspiration began to form on her forehead. Her eyes were tightly shut.

Could something have gone amiss? Were the traces of elfshot affecting Elizabeth? Dear God, he could not bear it if something happened to her! Perhaps he should put a stop to this.

Mrs. Collins asked, "Lizzy, are you unwell?"

Elizabeth shook her head almost imperceptibly but remained silent.

Finally, after what felt like hours, she lifted her hands and opened her eyes. "Charlotte, would you bandage the wound? I am too..." Her voice trailed off, and she collapsed into a nearby chair, her hands still covered with blood. She sighed heavily and looked straight at Darcy. "You might have warned me she had magic of her own." Her voice was accusing. "She fought me every inch of the way."

"Magic?" Darcy bristled at the implication. "My aunt has no magical abilities."

"You may believe that if it gives you comfort." She sounded exhausted. It was unlike Elizabeth to give in so easily.

Richard frowned and laid his fingertips on Lady Catherine's throat. Surely he was not taking this ridiculous allegation seriously! He straightened, his face losing its color. "Miss Bennet is correct. Ice cold Fitzwilliam power."

How could it be?

His cousin shook his head in disbelief. "I apologize, Miss Bennet. We had no idea. Either she herself is unaware of it, or she disguised it very well." He crossed to the side table, poured water from the ewer into the basin, and carried the basin and towel to Elizabeth.

She seemed confused by his offering. Richard knelt beside her, dipped the towel in the water, and began washing the blood from her hands.

"Thank you," she murmured, as if too tired to speak aloud.

Richard was staring at her hand. "Darcy," he said evenly. "I don't suppose you can do anything for burns."

That was enough to rouse Darcy from his stunned state. He hurried to her side. Her fingers, her beautiful fingers that he had admired as they moved across the piano keys, were covered with red, angry blisters. Gently, reverently, he took her hand in his own, careful to touch only where the skin was intact.

"What are you going to do?" she asked wearily.

He could not give the answer that sprang immediately to his mind, so instead he said, "I cannot heal the burns, but I can encourage your skin to grow quickly." Taking her lack of protest as consent, he muttered the words to spur healthy growth. It made no visible difference, but he could feel it working, the throb of growth, the rush of healing blood under her skin. It was dizzyingly intimate.

"That does feel better." She sounded surprised – and more alert. How had she recovered so quickly?

Of course. He should have known. Richard was on her other side, his fingertips on the inside of her wrist. He must be feeding her power, replenishing what she had exhausted.

Mrs. Collins said, "Lady Catherine is stirring!"

Elizabeth's expression brightened. "Good. That means all the elfshot is gone."

"She will be well again?" asked Richard.

"Eventually. The other person I know of who survived elfshot babbled meaningless nonsense when he first awoke, and it was more than a week before he was himself again. Some residual influence of the elfshot, I assume."

Richard's lips quirked. "But how will we know if she is babbling meaningless nonsense or is merely being her usual self?"

Elizabeth started to laugh and covered it with a cough, but her eyes sparkled.

And Darcy still cupped her hand in his. He said huskily, "That is the limit of my ability to help. I am sorry I can do no more."

Elizabeth tentatively stretched her fingers and then closed her hand. "It hardly hurts now, and I feel much better. I thank you."

Darcy looked away, already missing the touch of her hand. "That is Richard's doing, not mine. Restoring strength is his gift."

Richard took his fingers from Elizabeth's wrist and straightened. "You seemed in need of it." His cheeks bore a telltale flush. "And now we should feed you. Between what you did and Darcy's healing, you must be hungry enough to eat the counterpane."

Elizabeth gave a half smile. "I was thinking of starting with the bed curtains, actually. They look more appetizing."

What had she done?

The colonel had been correct when he said she would be hungry. Elizabeth had never been so famished in her life. Of course, she had never used so much magic at once, either. It was all she could do not to attack the tray of pastries and cold meats with both hands. Picking delicately at her food like a lady was out of the question, so she settled for eating at a steady pace, even if in an unladylike amount. The colonel ate just as heartily. Fortunately Elizabeth could leave the care of Lady Catherine to Charlotte for the moment.

Colonel Fitzwilliam kept up a steady stream of conversation

between bites, but Mr. Darcy had excused himself as soon as the food arrived. At first it was a relief not to have to worry what he thought of her at every moment, but now she feared where he might have gone. Was his willingness to tolerate women with magic not as great as his letter had implied? Perhaps Colonel Fitzwilliam was merely keeping her here while Darcy took steps to prepare a binding spell. Oh, she could not bear it, especially not from him!

Why, oh, why had she done it? She could not have exposed herself more completely if she had made a deliberate attempt. He already had reason to believe she might have magic, but now she had shown it without a shadow of a doubt. Why had she not told Mr. Darcy there was nothing she could do? She could have stopped her efforts rather than use her powers when Lady Catherine's magic had attacked her. Lady Catherine might have lost her arm or even her life, but Elizabeth would not be at risk of losing everything she cared about. If she had stopped, Darcy would have thought her no more than another harmless wisewomen employing charms she did not understand.

And to expose herself to Mr. Darcy, of all people! The man she had insulted gravely only two days ago, the man who had no reason to think kindly of her or to protect her. She might as well have thrown herself off a cliff.

To make it worse, she could not even claim that the cause of her downfall had been a desire to heal Lady Catherine. It had been her pride, her ridiculous, dangerous pride. Mr. Darcy had insulted her abilities, her family, and herself. When he had needed her help, she could not resist the chance to show him her skills were not useless. And then, after it was too late, she had not known when to stop.

But Colonel Fitzwilliam had been so kind to her. He had shown no shock or dismay and had treated her as if it were a natural thing for a woman to have magic. Was there a chance he would defend her?

She swallowed down a bite of pastry. "Colonel, you do not seem troubled by what I did."

"Saving Lady Catherine?" he teased. "No doubt I will regret it someday when she is chastising me for breathing improperly or some other sin, but I could not have left her to die."

"But you did not expect how I would do it, and I am a woman."

"A very lovely one at that!"

She hesitated. "The Collegium of Mages takes the position that women cannot be trusted with magic because their weaker characters and lack of reason would make them too susceptible to the temptations of sorcery."

The colonel's lips twitched with amusement. "I believe there is also something in there about women's poor moral judgment and inability to tell right from wrong, but you are in general correct. I do wonder how the men who think that way permit such deficient creatures to raise their children! As for your use of magic, well, I have a sister. I am aware many women have the ability. It appears you use your powers for healing. Why should I object?"

"Many mages would already have put a binding spell on me."

He shook his head. "Many mages still have their heads in the Middle Ages. I take a more scientific view. All the Fitzwilliams do. We have seen how power so often goes from parent to child. It does not favor the eldest son nor the youngest daughter."

Relief trickled through her. "That is indeed modern thinking. I had not realized anyone held such views."

"If you look at the evidence, it is clear. Your father is a mage, is he not?"

"Yes," she admitted. "He rarely uses his powers, though."

"Even so, as soon as I knew that, I assumed you were likely to be gifted with magic. Darcy confirmed it when I asked him after our first visit."

Shock riveted her in place. "Mr. Darcy *knew*?"

Colonel Fitzwilliam chuckled. "You thought he did not?"

"I was terrified he would guess! How did he find out?" And he had proposed to her anyway!

"Something about your effect on his elemental magic. I do not remember the details."

Her magic affected him? Then he must have known all along, all those months when she had been so frantically worried he would discover her secret! "I had no idea."

"Even without that, he knows magic is often inherited. My grandfather noted the pattern, and when he realized my father had unusually strong abilities, he made a point of marrying his other children into families with powerful mages. Darcy's father was an expert at manipulating the elements, and my grandfather hoped his daughter would produce a son with both elemental powers and the ability to create spells. Alas for Darcy, he got only the elemental powers, but with the strength of the Fitzwilliam magic. The poor fellow cannot create even the most basic spell, but he always has to be careful not to inadvertently cause a flood or set a fire. Lady Catherine denied having any magic, but my grandfather married her off to a strong mage anyway. Perhaps he knew she was not telling the truth. I myself have only the abilities that run in my mother's family, not my father's."

Elizabeth's tea had cooled. But now that there was no need for secrecy, she might as well have hot tea. She wrapped her hand around her teacup and willed the temperature to rise. "If Mr. Darcy cannot use spells, how did he heal my hands?"

"He can employ spells designed by another mage. He simply cannot create his own."

"If it is not improper to ask – if he can heal, why did he not offer to mend Lady Catherine's wound?"

The colonel shook his head. "Healing a blood relative is dangerous. Too often it turns out badly, usually in some unexpected way."

Was that why her remedies always seemed to make Jane sicker instead of restoring her health? If only she had known! "What sort of power did you inherit from your mother?"

"Me? I am a source. I can provide power to another mage. I can sense spells – what they are, who made them, that sort of thing. Most mages can do a bit of that, but not as easily as a source. Nothing dramatic, I fear."

"But very useful on occasion, I imagine. I certainly appreciated your confirmation about Lady Catherine's magic."

"Yes, there was that." He tapped his finger on the side of the table. "What troubles me is how it has gone unnoticed for so long in a family like mine. Why have I never sensed it from her before?"

Elizabeth considered. "Might she have a way of covering it up? She was unconscious when you checked her. Perhaps if she had been awake, you would have found nothing."

"That, my dear, is an interesting thought. I must ask my father about it. Lady Catherine's hatred of being touched may play a role. I cannot remember the last time she offered me her hand."

"Truly? She does it frequently with Mr. Collins."

The colonel's eyebrows shot up. "Does she, indeed? She allows non-mages to touch her, knowing they will learn nothing from it. How deviously clever she is! Still, it is a good thing you saved her. If she had died magically when Darcy was here, some people might have suspected he had a hand in it."

"Mr. Darcy? Why would he want her to die? He tried to save her."

"I know, I know. But some people might suspect he wanted Lady Catherine out of the way, so he could marry Anne and have complete control of all the Rosings assets without interference. But, as you may know, Darcy has no interest in marrying Anne, even with Rosings as her dowry."

Elizabeth smothered an urge to laugh. So Colonel Fitzwilliam did not know Darcy had offered for her. That was a relief. "I have never seen him show an interest in her, despite all of Lady Catherine's hints."

"And my father's. He is even more set on Darcy marrying Anne than Lady Catherine is. Poor Darcy. But that reminds me – might I examine that inert elfshot of yours?"

"Certainly. Here it is." She paused eating just long enough to remove the tin from her satchel.

"Thank you. I have never seen such a thing before." He opened the box and set his fingertips on it, his eyes taking on a distant look.

"Really? Every wisewoman has one."

He raised his eyebrows. "The procedure you did today is common, then?"

"No, not at all. If elfshot hits anywhere but the arm, it reaches the heart too quickly for any hope of stopping it."

"Yet all wisewomen carry these?"

Elizabeth smiled. "Not for that reason. We use them to determine if someone's death was caused by elfshot. That way we know whether to bury them with iron over their heart to prevent it from escaping and seeking a new target."

"Interesting. I should talk to wisewomen more often."

She was tempted to laugh. "Good luck. It is unlikely they will want to talk to you. Wisewomen have good reason to fear mages."

"I suppose so. But how did you become one? I was under the impression wisewomen were usually, er, older."

"They are. It is considered ill luck for a woman with young children to do this sort of work, so mostly it is spinsters or women whose children are grown."

"So how did a marriageable young lady like you become one?"

She laughed. "I am a fraud. I am not really a wisewoman. I have just been present when a wisewoman was working often enough to have learned her ways. The local wisewoman sought me out when I was twelve because she thought I could be of help to her."

He raised an eyebrow. "With things like lighting candles and destroying elfshot?"

"You saw through my deception! Yes, that sort of thing. She had lost her vision, and with it her ability to do magic. I went with her whenever she was called to see someone, and I paid attention."

"Your parents permitted it?"

Elizabeth flushed. "They did not know. They thought I just liked to take long walks alone. But I would have had to stop when I turned eighteen because the wisewoman said it was unsuitable work for a marriageable gentlewoman, but then there was a rash of fay-borne illnesses this last year and the work was too much for her. I saw the easier cases myself, the ones where a half-trained student is better than no wisewoman at all." She paused and said ruefully, "Your aunt was not an easy case. I am surprised I succeeded."

"But you did succeed," the colonel said with a smile. "How did you learn to light candles and destroy elfshot?"

"By experimentation. When I was a child, my father amused himself by making illusions for me, and one time he showed me how he did it. I could not remember the spell, but once I knew it was possible, I somehow found my own way to cast illusions, little ones, mostly so I could hide things from my mother. When my father caught me doing it, he refused to show me anything more. I learned a few more things by watching him. I was determined to master unmaking so I would never be made to eat food I did not like. I detested fish, you see. I can unmake small objects, but I never became quite good enough to unmake fish."

He chuckled. "Living things and things that have been alive resist unmaking. It would take a powerful mage to unmake a fish."

"Is that why it did not work? I was so frustrated by it.

Fortunately, our cook eventually left us and I liked the new cook's fish dishes much better."

"What else can you do besides unmaking and illusions?"

"Mostly healing, since I avoid doing unnecessary spells for fear of being caught. I can heat up lukewarm tea. I can see fay folk and tell when they have been present, like finding the elfshot traces, and I can perform a few fay spells - how to make milk curdle and that sort of thing."

Colonel Fitzwilliam straightened abruptly. "Good Lord! You are full of surprises. How on earth did you learn fay spells?"

"When I was small, a fay child befriended me. Well, not exactly a child, because they do not have children as we know it. Just a very new one who had only recently come into being and had little experience of the world. She said she would be a dryad when she was ready, but she was very mischievous. I never knew what to believe because she could make up elaborate stories." Elizabeth smiled in recollection. "She tried to teach me to shape-change, but needless to say that was not a success."

"Good Lord. But I just said that, did I not? Well, it deserves saying again. Do you have any idea how rare that is?"

Elizabeth shrugged. "I have no idea. My friend took me to Faerie a time or two, so it seemed natural to me."

The colonel's jaw dropped. "You have been to Faerie, too? Astonishing! Does your friend still visit you?"

"No. Even though I can still see fay folk, my friend and I drifted apart. She would visit me from time to time until about two years ago. The last time she told me she could not come again because their king was declaring war on all mortals and had forbidden any fay folk to aid mortals on pain of banishment. And she gave me a cat to remember her by – the white cat named Pepper, if you recall."

He held up his hands. "Wait, wait! Their king has declared war on us? Are you certain of this?"

Taken aback by his intensity, she said slowly, "That is what she said. Whether it is true or not I cannot tell you. She is fay, after all, and she had named herself Bluebird because she was neither blue nor a bird, so I would not put much credence in anything she said. Except that it does rather feel as if Faerie is at war with us, with all these attacks by the fay."

"But why? Why would they be at war with us?"

Elizabeth shrugged. "Bluebird said it was because of the trees. She was never particularly literal, so she might have meant anything by it."

"The trees? That makes no sense."

Before he could continue, Darcy returned, looking frustrated. "I have been trying to explain to Anne what has happened to her mother. I cannot tell if she simply does not understand what I am saying or whether she is refusing to listen. In the end she just stared at me as if she had no idea who I was. Perhaps she is upset about her mother, but I have never seen her so confused. Richard, perhaps if you –"

"Oh, no, not me. She is terrified of me. You know what will happen. I will walk in and say 'Cousin Anne' and she will swoon. Or run away. Or run away and then swoon. Perhaps Miss Bennet..." The colonel turned hopefully to her.

"I barely know her," protested Elizabeth, her self-consciousness returning with Darcy's presence. "We have scarcely exchanged a dozen words. Oh, very well, I will try, but I have little expectation of success. Perhaps Mrs. Collins can join me. Miss de Bourgh knows her better." She paused. "Colonel, is it possible Miss de Bourgh is afraid that you might touch her?"

"I would never hurt her! Or do you mean....Hmm. What do you think, Darcy?"

Darcy eyed him thoughtfully. "If she will not permit you to touch her, we are unlikely to find out if she has reason to avoid you."

"I am not surprised Miss de Bourgh did not understand Mr. Darcy's explanations," said Charlotte. "Unless one is very patient with her, she becomes confused."

"I am unsurprised as well," Elizabeth replied. "But my reasoning is different. Have you noticed that Miss de Bourgh's spells of confusion and swoons usually occur when the subject of magic arises?"

"How odd. I had not made that connection. What could have made her so frightened of magic?"

"Perhaps she is not frightened of it at all," said Elizabeth darkly. "The only reason I can think of for someone to grow confused when magic is mentioned is more magic."

Charlotte caught at her arm. "Surely you cannot think she is under a spell?"

"That is precisely what I think, and knowing that Lady Catherine has magic, it is not difficult to guess why her daughter is bespelled."

"A binding spell," Charlotte breathed.

"And now you can see why I fear them. I would rather die than be like her."

Miss de Bourgh was in her sitting room, looking distractedly out the window while Mrs. Jenkinson read to her. She stopped at the sight of them.

Charlotte nodded to her. "Mr. Darcy asked us to explain Lady Catherine's indisposition to Miss de Bourgh."

"Oh!" exclaimed Mrs. Jenkinson. She lowered her voice to a whisper. "You must be very gentle. Miss de Bourgh is not having a good day. Not a good day at all."

"We will be gentle," said Charlotte soothingly. "Miss de Bourgh, did Mr. Darcy explain to you that your mother has been injured?"

Miss de Bourgh rose to her feet. "Injured? I must go to her. She will expect it."

"It will be better if you wait. Lady Catherine is unconscious and is likely to remain so for some time."

"She swooned?" She smiled unexpectedly, a mischievous smile. "She swooned!"

"Er, yes," said Charlotte. "She is in no danger at present."

"Oh." Miss de Bourgh looked back out the window, her fingers picking at the fringe of her shawl.

"We believe she was attacked by one of the fay folk. She was struck by elfshot, but it has been removed."

Miss de Bourgh's brow creased. "Fay folk? There are no fay folk at Rosings. I..." Her forehead suddenly smoothed. "What was I saying?"

"Your mother's injury was caused by elfshot," prompted Charlotte.

"Elfshot? How odd." She paused. "The sun has come out, I see."

Elizabeth leaned forward to be ready to catch Miss de Bourgh. "We believe Lady Catherine's injury is magical in nature."

As she had expected, Miss de Bourgh's eyes turned up, and her head fell to the side. Elizabeth eased her back into her chair.

As Mrs. Jenkinson bustled around Miss de Bourgh with vinaigrette and pillows, Elizabeth laid a hand on the young woman's wrist and extended her senses. Yes, there was a spell, no question, but it did not have the same flavor as either Mr. Darcy's magic or Colonel Fitzwilliam's. It was a relief to know neither of them were responsible for it.

Richard strolled in and stopped short at the sight of Darcy. "I had not expected to find you here. I thought you would be keeping Miss Bennet company."

Darcy scowled. "I doubt Miss Bennet wishes for my company, especially after I disrupted her visit by bringing her here. And I might point out you apparently decided not to remain with her either."

Richard sat down in the leather armchair and stretched his legs out in front of him. "I was writing a letter to my father. Since it was about Miss Bennet, I thought it better done in privacy."

Darcy stiffened. "You wrote to your father about her?"

"Of course. He will want to meet her."

"Why?"

"No need to snap at me, old fellow! Because she has information about Faerie. He may or may not already be aware of the practices of wisewomen, but you know how anxious he is to learn anything about Faerie. She has only been there very briefly, but that is more than anyone else we are aware of. And..."

"And what?" A weight settled on Darcy's chest.

Richard leaned forward and spoke quietly. "She knows the fay spell for shape-changing. She cannot do it, but she knows the words. My father would sell his soul for that spell."

"Even though it does not work?"

"Come now, Darcy. Just because an untrained girl cannot make it work does not mean my father cannot. If there is a spell that has defeated him, I do not know of it." Richard rubbed his hands together.

A bitter taste stung Darcy's mouth. While Lord Matlock might not sell his soul for the spell, he would certainly sell his son. Richard had made no secret of his admiration for Elizabeth, but her pittance of a dowry had put her out of his reach. That spell alone would be an enormous dowry. "Elizabeth is unlikely to wish to meet your father. She has made it clear she wanted as little as possible to do with the mages, much less the Master of the Collegium."

"She need not fear him. You know that as well as I do. I will say nothing of it to her for now. If he is not in London, that letter might take a week to reach him. I told him I could not bring her to him, so he would have to come here. Once she meets him, she will understand he would not hurt her."

It was better not to answer that. Let Richard learn for himself that Elizabeth did not like to be coerced.

"Still, this means I must remain here until I hear from my father. I know you were eager to leave before any of this happened, so if you wish, you can return to London tomorrow while I manage matters here."

An hour ago Darcy had been cursing the fate forcing him to stay at Rosings, subject to the agony and the humiliation of being in Elizabeth's company. But Richard's plan to manage things might include managing a ring onto Elizabeth's finger. "I prefer to remain for now. I am Anne's guardian, and I do not wish to face our aunt's righteous wrath if she discovers I abandoned my duty." Did it sound like a good enough reason?

"Good. If you are still here when she recovers, you can be the one to explain why we allowed a wisewoman to treat her and that we discovered her secret. She will take it better from you."

The butler brought in a calling card and silver tray. Who would be calling at this hour? Darcy read the card and snorted. "Collins. You had best receive him, Richard. I would end up saying something I would regret." Darcy headed for the door.

"Oh, thank you so very much, my dear cousin!" Richard called after him in a falsetto voice.

A quiet knock at Lady Catherine's bedroom door made Elizabeth snap shut the lady's magazine she had been paging through. She had not been reading it, anyway, only using it to disguise her discomfort. She kept hearing Colonel Fitzwilliam telling her that Darcy had known about her magic all along. That one fact turned everything she thought she knew of him on end. He had sought out her company, even offered her marriage, knowing she had magic. It sounded as if his family would even expect him to marry a woman with magic. If only she had known! She would have given anything to find a mage who supported her use of her abilities. She would have been beyond grateful for his attentions, no matter how proud and disdainful he might be. But how could she have guessed that his beliefs were in opposition to the Collegium?

How could she face him now, after the accusations she had made to him when he offered her his hand? She had misjudged him so badly. And now she could not stop thinking about him.

Charlotte rose from her seat by Lady Catherine's bedside and opened the door. "Mr. Darcy, do come in."

Heat flooded Elizabeth as she stood and curtsied. Oh, why must she be so embarrassed by his very presence? He had no doubt only come to inquire after his aunt. Most likely he was not even thinking about her. After all, he had shown no interest in her earlier apart from her treatment of Lady Catherine, and had left as soon as that was done. He could hardly have made his wish to avoid her company any clearer, and she could hardly blame him for it.

"Has there been any change?" he asked Charlotte, his face impassive.

Charlotte gestured towards Lady Catherine's bed. "No improvement, but no worsening either. We have been dabbing her lips with essence of feverfew. Some say it may be helpful in treatment of elfshot."

"Pray inform me if there is any change. Mrs. Collins, might I have the honor of a private conversation with Miss Elizabeth?"

Oh, no. What could he possibly want to tell her that he could not say in front of Charlotte? Could he possibly wish to return to the subject of his offer of marriage? No, that was impossible. Not after the way she had treated him.

His mouth twisted. "There is nothing to worry about, Miss

Elizabeth. I merely wish to share a piece of information with you." He did not trouble to keep the irony out of his voice. He must have guessed what she was thinking.

Charlotte looked concerned, as well she might. "If Lizzy wishes to speak to you, I have no objection."

Darcy tilted his head. "Miss Elizabeth, perhaps we could speak in the sitting room with the door open. Mrs. Collins would be able to see us there." There was no warmth in his voice.

She could hardly refuse, so she walked ahead of him into the sitting room. "Yes, Mr. Darcy?"

He paced across the small space before turning back to her. "You told my cousin that you know the fay shape-changing spell." He did not sound pleased.

Why was she longing for some sign of softening in his face? He had every reason to dislike her. "I know the words, but I cannot make it work."

"Miss Elizabeth, those words, whether you can employ them or not, would be worth a great deal to certain people. A very great deal indeed. I would suggest that you do not give them away."

She moistened her lips with her tongue. "I do not understand what you mean."

If anything, his expression darkened. "You should not tell them to anyone without extracting something in return. You could get almost anything you like. An estate which is not entailed away to Mr. Collins. A dowry. A guarantee that no mage will ever put a binding spell on you."

"I see." Was it possible he was trying to help her?

"But once you tell anyone those words, you give away that power."

Why was he telling her this? "Am I to assume mages are the ones who would seek the spell? Will they attempt to trick me into giving it to them?"

"I would hope not. My concern was more that you might freely offer the spell, unaware that you could purchase your own safety with it. Your other knowledge about the fay is valuable as well, but that spell particularly so."

She looked down at her hands for a moment and then deliberately met his eyes. "I thank you for telling me this. Especially since you could have simply asked me for the spell and I would have told you it."

His throat bobbed as he swallowed hard. "I know what it is like to be threatened with a binding spell. I would not wish it on you or anyone."

Her mouth dropped open in surprise. "You know that fear?"

"It is nothing now," he said dismissively. "Someone went to a great deal of trouble to make it appear I had been abusing my abilities, and the punishment for that is binding."

"Oh. I am sorry you faced that." She meant it. It would break her heart to see his pride and cleverness brought down by a binding spell. How could anyone think he would do such a thing, or that he would allow himself to be caught? "It is a silly idea."

Now he looked furious. He must have misunderstood her.

She said quickly, "Oh, your expression! I meant only that if you were to misuse your powers – and I by no means intend to suggest you would – but if you were to do so, you would cover your tracks so carefully that no one would ever dream of connecting it to you. You would never do it in a careless, obvious manner. That is all."

His anger seemed to vanish, replaced by a slight smile. "Very perceptive, Miss Elizabeth. It is a pity you were not on the Board of Inquiry."

Hesitantly she smiled back.

"Lizzy!" Mrs. Collins's voice interrupted the moment of connection. "Her ladyship's eyes are open again."

"Excuse me," Elizabeth murmured as she hurried back into the bedroom.

Lady Catherine's eyes were indeed wide open and staring straight up again, the pupils dilated. Elizabeth waved a hand in front of her face, but she showed no awareness, just as she had not when the elfshot was in her arm. "I wish I could tell you what that means, but I have no idea," Elizabeth said.

Lady Catherine's eyelids slid closed.

"How odd," said Mrs. Collins.

Darcy said, "Mrs. Collins, I forgot to mention your husband is downstairs with Colonel Fitzwilliam. I imagine he is curious about your presence here. While I greatly appreciate your assistance, I can hardly expect you to stay longer."

Charlotte glanced at her. "And Lizzy?"

"That is up to her," he said in a level voice.

"I would think it wise for her to remain here. If something should change in Lady Catherine's condition, it would be difficult to explain why you would come to the parsonage in the middle of the night to fetch Lizzy."

How could she stay the night in the same house with him? But she had no excuse for refusing. "Very well; I will remain here."

"Will Mr. Collins object?" Darcy asked Charlotte.

Mrs. Collins shook her head. "I will tell him Lady Catherine, in a brief moment of consciousness, expressed a preference for Lizzy to tend to her. He will accept that. I will stay here with her tonight, if that is not inconvenient."

Darcy bowed. "Thank you. We would be happy to have both of you. I think it would be safe now to allow the maids to assist you. We have explained to them that Lady Catherine hit her head and has not yet regained consciousness. The surgeon should be here shortly, and we will ask him to use the same story."

"Very well. I suppose I must speak to my husband before he

annoys Colonel Fitzwilliam past his endurance," said Mrs. Collins. "Would you accompany me, Mr. Darcy?"

He inclined his head. "I will be happy to."

Elizabeth let out a breath she had not known she was holding. Suddenly she did not want him to leave, not until she had managed to thank him properly. By all rights, he should be bitterly angry at her after the acrimonious manner of her refusal, but somehow he had overcome that in an attempt to help her avoid her greatest fear. Surely that required some sort of acknowledgment, and if she did not say something now, she would never find the courage to do so.

But he was already following Charlotte out the door.

She had to stop him. "Mr. Darcy, may I ask you a question?"

He turned immediately. "Of course, Miss Elizabeth." Was there some gentleness in his tone?

She bit her lip. A question. She needed to ask a question that showed he had earned some of her trust. "My cat, Pepper. Did you notice anything unusual about her?"

He shook his head. "Not apart from her name and her eyes."

"She is fay, or at least part fay. Is that something other mages might notice?" She watched him anxiously.

He stiffened, his eyes wide, and paused before answering. "It is not something I have ever considered. Richard is very sensitive to magic, and he did not seem to notice anything, so I would suspect no one else would. But I will give the matter further thought."

"Thank you. I would prefer it if no one recognized her true nature. She is very important to me." Would he understand that this was her apology for distrusting him?

"I will certainly do anything in my power to distract anyone's attention from Pepper."

She smiled in relief. He had understood. "I thank you."

He hesitated. "I hope I will have the opportunity to meet Pepper again now that I know this."

With a playful look, she said, "That will be up to Pepper. Like any other cat, she makes her own decisions."

# Chapter 3

Darcy looked up from his book as Elizabeth entered the library. His heart lurched at the sight, even as the pressure of the elements receded.

She stopped short as soon as she saw him. "Pardon me. I did not mean to disturb you. I was looking for a book to read." She stood poised like a doe preparing to flee the hunter.

How could her presence disturb him when he could hardly focus on his book for thoughts of her? He had not spoken to her alone at all yesterday, only a brief conversation in front of the servants about Lady Catherine's health. Otherwise she had stayed in Lady Catherine's bedroom all day. Since there had been no change in his aunt's status, he could only assume she had been hiding from him, a bitter disappointment after the amicability of the end of their discussion of Pepper. "Pray come in and take your pick. I imagine it must be dull watching Lady Catherine sleep."

She seemed to relax a bit. "I do not mind. It is a novel experience to be in her presence for so long without earning a reprimand of some sort."

"Rosings does seem unusually quiet without her." Clearly he still made her nervous. Perhaps he could remind her of their moment of agreement. "I have been hoping to ask you more about Pepper. I cannot recall ever noticing anything unusual about her apart from her eyes and her willingness to travel with you. She seemed like any other cat."

"I am glad to hear it."

He decided to push his advantage. "If she is part fay, what is the other part? A normal cat?"

"I do not know. I have assumed she is not fully fay since everyone can see her, not just children, but she is not an ordinary cat. She can disappear when she wishes. Even I cannot see her if she does not want to be seen." Elizabeth crossed to the window and opened one pane.

"Some fresh air?" It was a chilly day for it.

"Not exactly." She studied the view briefly.

A white bird flew past the window and then settled on the ledge. Elizabeth whispered some words to it and held out her finger like a perch. The bird hopped onto her finger.

Astonished, Darcy said, "Is that a white raven? I have never seen one before, much less a tame one."

"Look closer." There was laughter in Elizabeth's voice as she carried the bird towards him. "Pepper dear, do you remember Mr. Darcy? I have been telling him about you."

Surely she could not believe this bird was her cat!

The white raven stretched its wings, showing a wider wingspan than Darcy had expected. With a soft caw, it took to the air, circled the library once, and landed on Darcy's shoulder.

Darcy stared at the bird. He had never seen a live bird at such close range. How tiny the feathers on its face were! It tilted its head as if studying him. Was one of its eyes yellow? With a sudden move, it caught a lock of his hair in its beak and tugged it. Hard. Darcy winced.

"Be kind, Pepper. Mr. Darcy wants to help us stay safe."

This was altogether too strange for Darcy's comfort. "Are you telling me your cat changes shape?"

Elizabeth smirked. "Actually, I thought I was showing you."

The bird pecked at his nose. Quite distinctly it said, "Mrrow."

"Good God!" cried Darcy. Birds were not supposed to meow!

"Pepper, do take pity on the poor man. He has never conceived of a creature as astonishing as you."

The white raven hopped onto Darcy's leg and began to preen itself. Somehow it blurred around the edges, and suddenly became the familiar white cat. Pepper licked her paw and rubbed it across her face as if this were a perfectly normal occasion.

In a strangled voice, Darcy managed to say, "I grant you this is not an ordinary cat."

"No, she is quite extraordinary," said Elizabeth with some pride. "And vain of her beauty. She likes to be scratched under her ears."

Darcy followed her instructions, though it took more courage than he cared to admit. "Does she turn into other animals?"

"Not that I know of, but she seems to understand what I say, at least when she chooses to. She often ignores me as well. She knows when I want her. It was not mere chance that she flew to this window. But most of the time she is like any other cat, except that she happens to turn into a bird."

Pepper began to purr.

He tried to gather his scattered wits. "Is she a phouka, then? In the old stories, cat and raven are two of the shapes phoukas can take, but I thought all phoukas were dark."

"I have no idea what she is, and she is not telling. I only know she is a very beautiful kitty, aren't you, Pepper?" She leaned down to pat the cat's head.

How was he to think clearly with her body right in front of his face, her scent of lavender tickling his nose? "I do not think other mages would suspect her. I cannot imagine anyone thinking to test your cat with iron."

The cat narrowed her eyes at him, as if to suggest anyone who did so would regret it.

To his regret, Elizabeth straightened. "I hope not."

Think. He needed to think of something to say that was not related to the neckline of her dress. "I suppose this explains how she could come to Kent with you."

"As far as I know, she flew. The basket she was supposed to be in held a loaf of bread."

The cat stood and arched her back in a stretch. She reached one paw up to touch Darcy below his left ear. Without warning she dug in a claw and scratched him.

"Ouch! What was that for?" Darcy demanded, as if the cat might answer him. And he had liked the creature!

Elizabeth held up her hand. "Wait. Do not move."

Now the dratted cat put both front paws on his shoulder. Did she expect him to let her scratch him again? But Elizabeth had told him not to move.

Instead of a sharp claw, a raspy tongue rubbed over the scratched spot. How very strange! As he held still, he felt a tiny prickle of power. "She is using magic!" he said accusingly. "What is she doing?"

"The fay call it marking. It tells other fay that she trusts you. Pepper marked me when she first came to live with me." Elizabeth turned her head and pushed aside her ringlets to reveal a tiny scar beneath her left ear.

The sight of her exposed neck made him dizzy. "It makes no sense."

"No, but do the fay ever make sense? They seem to delight in being illogical. I do not claim to understand Pepper. I do not even know why she chooses to live with me rather than in Faerie."

Pepper seemed satisfied with her work and curled up again on Darcy's lap, but he no longer found it relaxing. He did not like unpredictability and things he could not understand. At least the scratch no longer hurt. Darcy reached up to touch the spot where she had clawed him. The flesh was not even tender, and he could feel no more than a tiny ridge. "Could it be healed already?" he asked Elizabeth.

She peered at the spot beneath his ear, torturing him again with the sight of her chest. "It appears to be. I am sorry she hurt you. She does like you. It is rare for her to sit on anyone's lap but my own."

Richard strode into the room. "Here you are. That cat is going to leave fur all over you, Darcy."

That was the least of Darcy's worries about Pepper.

"Miss Bennet, the sun is finally out, and I wondered if you would care to go for a stroll in the gardens," said Richard.

Darcy glared at him, but before Elizabeth could even respond, a familiar hearty voice came from the entrance hall. "Never mind. I'll show myself in."

Elizabeth quickly rose to her feet. What man would dare to march into Rosings uninvited? Neither Darcy nor the colonel appeared particularly surprised, though.

A stout older gentleman with long sideburns strode into the room, his gloves in one hand. "There you are, my boy. And Darcy, too, I see."

Pepper jumped off Darcy's lap and ran behind Elizabeth's skirts.

Darcy bowed. "Welcome to Rosings, sir."

The man tossed his dusty gloves on a side table, apparently oblivious to the fact that a servant would have to clean it as a result. "Catherine has got herself in a spot of trouble, I understand. How is she?"

"Improving slowly," said the colonel. "She awakens briefly but speaks only nonsense. Sometimes she throws things."

The older man guffawed. "Sounds like typical Catherine to me! I thought I had best check in on her myself. And is this the young lady who provided such signal assistance when my dear sister was taken ill?"

Pepper hissed softly.

"Yes, it is," said Colonel Fitzwilliam. "Miss Bennet, might I have the honor of presenting my father, Lord Matlock?"

The Earl of Matlock, the Master of the Collegium of Mages. And someone had told him about her. Elizabeth caught her breath, her shoulders stiff. Somehow she managed to curtsy and murmur, "It is an honor, my lord."

He advanced until he was standing directly in front of her. "Well, well, well. You have certainly managed to impress my son. He mentioned you in his letter. It seems we all owe you a great debt of gratitude."

She could feel goosebumps rising on her arms. "Lady Catherine has been very gracious to me. I was happy to assist her in my own small way."

Why was he looking at her so expectantly? Surely he did not expect her to offer him her hand. She would never take such a liberty with a peer of the realm! But he had raised his own hand, so she had no choice but to offer hers. What odd manners he had!

His hand closed around her fingers. The tingle of magic prickled her skin. The flavor of it was different from Darcy's or the colonel's, or even her father's, but it was still familiar. It was like –

"You!" she cried involuntarily, pulling her hand away and wiping it fiercely on her skirt. She jumped behind a chair. It would not offer her any protection from a mage, but it was all she had. Her heart pounded with terror.

"Miss Bennet, I assure you that I intend you no harm," said the earl. "I am looking forward to knowing you better."

The colonel said, "It is true. He will not hurt you."

Elizabeth stared at the colonel in disbelieving horror. "I trusted you. I trusted both of you. I could have let your aunt die instead of taking the risk of exposing myself. I believed you when you claimed not to support using binding spells on women, but that was not true, was it?

Neither of you could perform a binding spell, so you sent for someone who could. And I trusted you!"

Darcy looked stricken, as well he might. Had he thought she would never learn the truth? And she had told him Pepper's secret as well. What a fool she had been! And now she would pay the price.

Colonel Fitzwilliam came up beside her. "I did not deceive you. I assure you my father can be trusted. I only told him about you because I knew he would want to hear your story."

Lord Matlock wore an air of saintly patience. "This is all a misunderstanding. I give you my word as a gentleman that I will not perform a binding spell on you. I never do them. I find them unnecessary. My own daughter has magic, and she is unbound."

Elizabeth felt trapped. "But you put one on your niece! I recognize your touch. Tell me, was Miss de Bourgh once able to speak in complete sentences? Did she always become lost halfway through a thought? Did she know how to have an everyday conversation before you made her into half a person?"

The colonel was shaking his head. "Anne is not under a binding spell. That is the way she has always been."

Darcy said slowly, "Miss Bennet was correct about Lady Catherine's powers. If she says Anne is under a binding spell, I have to wonder if that may be true as well. I do not know who might have performed it –"

The earl held up a hand to silence him. "You are correct, Miss Bennet. I congratulate you on your perceptiveness. The binding spell on my niece is of my making, but it was because of an extraordinarily dangerous situation, quite unlike your own, and there was no other choice short of imprisonment. I did it with the utmost reluctance."

"It is always with the utmost reluctance, is it not? I would rather die than be bound." Desperate, Elizabeth glanced from side to side. Escape was impossible, but she had to try. She darted around them, but before she could reach the door, an invisible net halted her in her tracks. She struggled against it with all her strength, but it made no difference.

Darcy cried, "Let her go, I implore you! This is not the way –"

A blur of white fur flew across the room. Lord Matlock gave a roar of pain. "Get this thing off me!"

The invisible bindings holding her slipped away. Elizabeth fled.

"Darcy, help me here!" Richard called as he tried to pry off the white cat wrapped around his father's head. Lord Matlock's hands flailed at Pepper, but with the cat's body across his face, he could not see to use his magic – no doubt why Pepper had chosen to attack him there.

Darcy tore his eyes away from the sight of Elizabeth racing across the lawn away from Rosings. He made a perfunctory effort to grasp Pepper's flying paws. After all, if a shape-changing fay cat was determined to attack his uncle, Darcy doubted anything could be done but to wait for her to stop of her own accord. Richard certainly seemed to be finding the cat's strength unusual.

"Dammit, Richard!" his uncle swore.

"The more you fight to pull her off, the harder she will dig in her claws," said Darcy. "Let her go and she will likely run off." He surreptitiously opened the window behind him.

"Worth a try," Richard grumbled, releasing Pepper's fur.

"Ow!" cried Lord Matlock.

But Pepper had taken Darcy's hint and leapt off. She ran straight for the window, as if aware of what he had done, and jumped out.

"I'll have that cat shot!" snarled Lord Matlock, blood running down his face from multiple scratches.

"No need," said Darcy. "She may not have survived that fall." He leaned his head out the window to watch a white raven winging its way in the direction Elizabeth had fled.

Lord Matlock mopped at his scratches with his handkerchief. He growled at the bloody evidence on the white linen. "That animal should never have been allowed inside this house!"

"Pepper is usually quite friendly," Darcy said. "She must have thought you were threatening Miss Bennet. She is very protective of her."

"She is as mad as her mistress! Richard, you did not warn me the girl was a lunatic."

Richard shrugged. "She has always been perfectly calm until now. She is terrified of binding spells, though."

"Justifiably so," said Darcy coldly. "It was a misunderstanding, but I can see why she would misinterpret your intentions. If you give her a little time, she will be able to discuss it rationally." He had never spoken this way to Lord Matlock before. Now that Elizabeth was safe, he could give way to the simmering anger. How dare his uncle bind Anne and then have the gall to try to force Darcy to marry her?

Richard poured a glass of port from the decanter on the sideboard and handed it to his disgruntled father. "Did you truly put Cousin Anne under a binding spell?"

Matlock tossed back an amount of port that would have made Darcy choke and held out the glass for more. "Had to."

"Why?" Darcy tried to keep his anger from showing.

"She is too strong. Unnaturally strong. Stronger than me. Stronger even than you, Darcy. Never saw anything like it. Even worse, her affinity was for unmaking, and she was a temperamental child. She unmade half of the east wing in a tantrum. Sir Lewis caned her for it and she unmade him. Yes, you heard me correctly. I can barely unmake an apple, and she unmade a man! She was only nine years old and completely untrained. We gave out that Sir Lewis was lost at sea, buried an empty coffin, and I put her in the tightest binding spell I could manage. No point in trying to imprison her; she would just unmake the walls.

Terrifying child."

"But surely now she is an adult and could understand the consequences –"

"If you had done as you were told, Darcy, and married her years ago, I could have loosened the bindings. You are the only one with the training and the ability to keep her in line if something went wrong. Catherine would have been helpless on her own."

There was some logic to it, but his uncle would not have come up with the marriage plan out of charity for his niece. It must have been one of his experiments to breed stronger mages. Damn him!

Without a word Darcy strode out of the room.

Richard called after him. "Where are you going?"

"To look for Miss Bennet. Where else?"

The parsonage was the obvious place to begin. The Collins's maid admitted that Miss Bennet had been there, but only long enough to fetch something from her room. No, she had not taken her luggage. No, she had not seen which direction Miss Bennet had taken. Yes, she would send word to him when Miss Bennet returned.

It was hardly surprising Elizabeth had gone out again. She would not have wanted to be easily found. But where could she have gone? His first impulse was that she might have sought out the grove where he had often found her walking, but he could not imagine she would choose to be so close to Rosings Park.

Had she made other friends in Hunsford? She had cared for several ill parishioners, but he did not know whom or where. Did he truly know so little of her daily life? He checked the church, although it seemed an unlikely refuge for her. Finding it empty, he set out for Rosings again.

He skirted the study where Richard and Lord Matlock were deep in conversation, instead seeking out Mrs. Collins in Lady Catherine's rooms.

Mrs. Collins put her finger to her lips when he entered the sitting room. "She is finally asleep," she whispered.

He had practically forgotten Lady Catherine's injury in this last chaotic hour. Darcy gestured at the open door. Mrs. Collins followed his direction and he joined her at the top of the stairwell.

"Her ladyship is sleeping peacefully," she said. "I have had all the fragile items removed from her rooms and replaced them with the old mismatched china used by the servants. That way she can still break things if she wishes, but nothing valuable will be lost." She obviously assumed he had come to check on his aunt's condition.

"I thank you for your forethought. My uncle, Lord Matlock, has recently arrived and will no doubt wish to see Lady Catherine at some point." Darcy hesitated. "He managed to inadvertently frighten Miss Bennet, causing her to flee the house."

"Oh, dear. That is most unlike Lizzy."

"It is, but he is the Master of the Collegium of Mages. It is perhaps understandable that he would seem intimidating. I do not believe he meant her any harm, but I can see how she might jump to that conclusion."

Mrs. Collins said, "Perhaps if you try speaking to her alone, without your intimidating uncle, she might be more willing to listen."

"That had been my thought. I went to the parsonage, but she had already been there and left, so I will have to wait until she returns. When you see her, would you be so kind as to tell her I spoke to you?"

"Certainly. Perhaps Lizzy should stay at the parsonage now. Lady Catherine is well enough that I do not think Lizzy's presence here is needed at night."

"I suppose not." It would be easier if she had fewer dealings with his uncle, but it would reduce his chances of seeing her. It was the first step to going on to a life without her. An empty, hollow life without her.

And Elizabeth thought he had betrayed her. His stomach clenched into a knot, his throat so tight he doubted he could force out even a word more. He bowed to Mrs. Collins and left. Alone.

"Darcy, do come join us," Richard said genially. "I was just showing my father the spell for curdling milk Miss Bennet taught me. He is going to try it as soon as the girl brings us more fresh milk. Not that being able to curdle milk is particularly useful, but it proves we can perform fay spells."

"If Richard can do it, that proves almost anyone can perform them," Lord Matlock said repressively. The scratches on his face were less vivid now. He must have done a healing spell.

"The next time you need a power source, you will not be complaining about my limited ability with spells," retorted Richard.

Darcy added, "Your talents were very useful when Miss Bennet insisted Lady Catherine had magic, and I said that was ridiculous."

Lord Matlock harrumphed. "It only goes to reason that she has some magic. Everyone else in the family does, after all."

"No one else always denied it vehemently," said Darcy.

"How is Miss Bennet? Any calmer?" asked Richard.

"I could not find her. Most likely she has gone for a walk to compose herself. The servants will send a message when she returns."

"Good," growled Lord Matlock. "I need to talk to that girl. Have you found out more about what she knows?"

Richard shook his head. "Very little. She spoke freely about it the day Lady Catherine was injured, but afterwards she became more reticent. Perhaps she is embarrassed by it."

"Or perhaps she realized her knowledge had value and should not be given away for free," Darcy said. Apparently she had taken his suggestion.

"We can find some way to recompense her, if necessary. Richard, how powerful is her magic?"

"Middling," Richard responded. "She has done well at learning to use it in the absence of spells."

"Middling power or not, she can see fay and communicate with them," Darcy said. Why did he care what they thought of Elizabeth's powers? "There are few enough of us who can do that."

"True, but she will have to demonstrate her abilities before I believe it. It is easy enough to say she can see fay."

"I can attest to it," said Darcy. "She spotted a redcap coming up behind me. She got between us and scolded it until it fled. Later a dryad showed herself at her request."

Lord Matlock's eyes narrowed. "Could she be a changeling?"

Darcy shook his head. "I saw her hold iron shavings in her bare hand." He had wondered the same thing briefly, especially since Elizabeth was so unlike her mother and younger sisters. "Her father is a mage, and his father before him."

"What of her mother's family?"

"They are in trade, so it is unlikely they have any magic."

"I have wondered if magic powers might be more common than we think. If the stories are true, many common people have some fay blood. A pity there is no way to tell."

More of those ridiculous theories. "On the subject of breeding, I wish to speak very clearly. I will not marry Anne. That is not negotiable."

Lord Matlock waved his hand in dismissal. "You are the perfect choice for her. You have the skills to manage her, and it will keep Rosings in the family."

Darcy spread his fingers on the table and leaned forward. "Anne does not like me. I do not like her. I do not want a wife with the mind of a child, and I most especially do not wish to be my wife's jailer. If you want her to have children, marry her to someone with lesser powers. Otherwise you risk having a child even more out-of-control than she was. I will not do it."

"You would have her remain under a binding spell for the rest of her life?" demanded Lord Matlock.

"That is not my responsibility. Why do you not take her into your household? You could control her as well as I. I do not understand why you did not do so years ago."

"I had duties to the Collegium, and Catherine insisted she remain here. She had lost her husband and did not wish to lose her daughter. She asked that Anne remain bound all her life."

Darcy snapped, "You may be certain I will give her my opinion on that when she regains her wits."

Darcy watched the clock hands creep forward. Mrs. Collins had returned to the parsonage after answering Lord Matlock's questions about Lady Catherine's health. It should have taken her no more than a quarter hour to reach the parsonage, perhaps another quarter hour to greet her husband, and one more to allow her to send him a message saying Elizabeth had returned. It had been nearly two hours, and dusk was approaching, but no word had arrived. Darcy had even asked the butler if a message had come and made it clear there should be no delay in delivering it to him when it arrived.

Then it was two and a half hours, and only a little light left in the sky. Darcy sent a kitchen boy to the parsonage to ask after Miss Bennet. When he returned without any news apart from Mrs. Collins being worried, Darcy's stomach tied in knots.

Unable to keep a calm demeanor with Richard and Lord Matlock, Darcy ordered a lantern and set out for the nearest posting inn. He could not imagine she would flee without a word and with none of her belongings, but it was the only way she could have left the vicinity. But no one had seen her at the inn.

Darcy returned to Rosings empty-handed, after making certain every stable boy knew they would be well rewarded for sending him word if Miss Bennet did appear.

He could not sleep. Elizabeth would never stay away at night, no matter how frightened she was. It would ruin her reputation and stain her for the rest of her life. Not that he cared about any of that, but he knew she would.

Dawn found him at the parsonage door. It was a completely inappropriate time to call, but what did that matter?

Despite the hour, Mrs. Collins herself opened the door, her face lined with worry. "Is she at Rosings?" she asked.

He shook his head. "Nor here, I take it."

"No, not a word from her. I have searched her room, but if anything is missing, I cannot recognize it. I have put together a list of everyone I have introduced her to here, both parishioners and tenants. I plan to go to each of them. Perhaps she spent the night caring for someone who is ill."

They both knew Elizabeth would have sent word if that were the case, but Darcy would grasp at any straw. "How may I help? Should I accompany you?"

"That would only draw attention to her absence. If you could arrange a search through the grounds at Rosings –"

"It is being done now. She did not take a stagecoach from the inn, but if she managed to leave the area – perhaps someone offered her a ride? – where would she go?"

Mrs. Collins chewed her lip. "Her uncle in London is closest. He lives on Gracechurch Street, but I do not know the number. Meryton is another possibility. I can think of nowhere else. But she would expect us to look in those places."

"Does she have other relatives? Friends who married and moved away?" He had spent the long night trying to think of possibilities.

"Her family is all in Meryton, apart from her uncle. As for friends, there was a girl who married and moved to Ware, just a few miles from Meryton. Her name was Emma Swift. It would be Emma Lazarus now, but I do not know how to find her."

"I will send men to check all of those. Discreetly, of course. Do you plan to notify Mr. Bennet?"

For the first time she looked uncertain. "I started a letter a few minutes ago, but I wonder if I should wait until tomorrow. Lizzy would be furious if I worried him unnecessarily."

"I would not wait. If we find her, you can send a second letter, but if there is a chance the Bennets would know where to look... She cannot have much money and no extra clothes, so time is of the essence." His words echoed in his ears: if we find her, if we find her.

"You are right. I will send it immediately. And I will let you know what I discover today, even if it is nothing."

Darcy knelt by the edge of the lake that bordered the grove at Rosings Park. Fear made him hesitate, but he plunged both hands into the cold lake, letting his magic reach out to the water, gathering it together, and letting it flow past his fingers. His senses followed the magic into the murky, half lit depths, searching, always searching. His magic sifted through the silt at the bottom, inch by inch and foot by foot. His nerves were rattled by each obstruction he encountered, and his heart almost stopped when he found a long thick form. But it was only a large tree limb, and somehow he forced himself to keep going, checking and rechecking until he was certain there was nothing that did not belong.

Finally he sank back on his haunches, a nauseating sense of relief filling him. She had said she would rather die than be bound, and while he did not think she would act upon it, he could not be certain. At least it had not been here, in the lake they had walked next to together while he dreamed of their future. Yesterday he had been bereft by the knowledge she would never be his; today he would be grateful just to know she was alive. He covered his face with his cold, wet hands.

"Mr. Darcy! Is something the matter, sir?" It was one of the servants combing the grounds for any sign of Elizabeth.

He dropped his hands. "No. There is nothing in the lake."

"Oh, well, that's good, isn't it?" Fortunately the man seemed not to need a reply as he meandered away, his eyes searching the ground.

Lord Matlock took his leave later that morning, seeming more concerned for the knowledge he might be losing than for Elizabeth's well-being. Darcy was glad to see him go. Richard had gone riding, hoping to cover ground in neighboring estates the searchers on foot would not reach.

Darcy was alone when he received a note from Mrs. Collins. She had found nothing. No one had seen Elizabeth.

How could she have vanished into thin air? The only possibility left seemed to be that she might be hiding somewhere under an illusion, but how long could she keep that up? The nights were still cold. What would she eat?

How would he survive not knowing what had happened to her?

Unable to sit still, he tried something he had never done before. He sought out his cousin Anne.

She did not seem surprised to see him, but then she rarely showed any sign of emotion. Darcy carefully explained about the search for Elizabeth, noticing for the first time how she would lose the train of conversation whenever the subject skirted on magic. The evidence had been there; he had simply never bothered to look for it.

After the fifth or sixth time Anne failed to finish a sentence, he asked, "Does it ever feel as if you are thinking something and the thought is snatched out of your head?"

She leaned forward and grasped his hands. "Yes. Yes, yes, yes." It was as if she turned into a different person, one he had never met before.

She did feel the loss.

Now how could he respond? He could not offer to fix it. Finally he said, "Miss Bennet wants to help you."

Her vague look was back. "You like Miss Bennet, do you not?"

He tightened his lips to keep the words inside, but what was the point? "Yes. I like Miss Bennet very much." It was a relief to say it.

She nodded. "Then you must... You must..." Her face screwed up as if in pain. "You must throw grass. In the air."

"Green grass? That is just an old wives' tale."

"No, no, no." She pressed the heels of her hands against her temples. "Promise me!"

"Oh, very well. I promise."

Her face relaxed. "What was I saying?"

Darcy hoped no one could see him. He must look like a complete fool, plucking blades of grass from the manicured lawn like a lovesick peasant boy. It was ridiculous even to attempt this. But he had promised, and even if he had not, if there was the tiniest chance it could lead him to Elizabeth, he would happily make a fool of himself.

He stared down at the grass stems cupped in his hands. How was this supposed to be done? Was the old children's rhyme a spell of sorts? He raised his hands in front of his face. "Elizabeth," he whispered to the grass. "Elizabeth." Elizabeth of the fine eyes, the light and pleasing figure, the bubbling melodious laughter. Elizabeth. "*Green grass, green grass, floating in the air, Green grass, green grass, lead me to my true love fair.*" He tossed the grass into the air and waited as it fluttered down, knowing full well it would fall randomly all around him.

His breath froze in his throat. The blades of grass formed a straight line starting at the toes of his boots and leading a few feet away. Towards the grove, the sheep fields, and the road to Tunbridge Wells.

He took off at a run.

The winding paths through the grove made it impossible to keep his direction precisely straight, but finally he reached the sheep field. He clambered over a tall stile and hurried across the pasture. Frightened sheep raced away at his approach.

When he reached the far side, he stopped to look back at the roof line of Rosings. Had he followed a straight line? How could he tell? He grabbed two handfuls of grass, an easier task here than in the closely trimmed lawn, whispered to it, and tossed it into the air, waiting for the blades to align in front of him.

Nothing.

Was hope to be snatched away so quickly? He slowly turned in a circle. Perhaps he simply could not see it among all the other grass. No, there it was – pointing back in the direction he had come.

Was the magic toying with him? Or was Elizabeth hidden in the grove, somewhere he had not looked, perhaps even up a tree? He retraced his steps.

He followed the path until he judged himself to be near the middle of the grove, stopping to collect grass again and throw it in the air. This time the line led off the path. He cut between trees, pushing past saplings and into an area of dense undergrowth that tore at his boots and the tail of his coat. It did not matter. The only thing that mattered was following a straight line.

The woods opened into a small glade. Odd; he thought he had explored every inch of the grove, but he had never seen this clearing before. Could Elizabeth be nearby?

Gather grass, whisper her name, toss. This time there was no line. The grass settled into a neat pile in the center of the glade. But if this was the correct spot, where was Elizabeth? He stood beside the pile and turned around slowly, looking up and around, trying to spot the odd bits of reflection that were the telltale signs of illusions. Nothing. He tried again, forcing himself to examine everything, trying to keep despair at bay.

"Elizabeth!" he called frantically. "Elizabeth, can you hear me? I beg you to show yourself. We have been desperately worried."

Nothing. The green grass had been a false hope.

He sank to his knees, covering his face with his hands. The grass must have led him to a place Elizabeth loved rather than to Elizabeth herself. It had been a forlorn hope at best, but now even that small hope was gone.

No. He would not give up. Anne had been trying to tell him something; he was sure of it. He would examine every inch of this glade, no matter how long it took him. He would not fail Elizabeth again.

Sitting back on his heels, Darcy studied the hillocks of grass, woodland plants, twigs sticking up from the ground, a line of mushrooms –

A line of mushrooms. His breath caught in his throat. Yes, the line continued until it disappeared under some of last year's fallen leaves. Carefully he brushed the leaves away. The mushrooms continued all the way around him, a circle that enclosed the greater part of the glade.

He was in the middle of a faerie ring.

He gasped for breath. How had he failed to see the answer? Elizabeth had not run off to someone's house, nor had she harmed herself. She had gone to Faerie, the one place she knew Lord Matlock could not follow her. He could not begin to guess how she had done it, but it made perfect sense. She had taken her fay cat and gone to Faerie to see her fay friend.

Now he could feel the subtle thrum of fay spells surrounding him. There must be a way to find her. He would go through every book of magic ever written if that was what it took. And in the meantime, if he could not reach Elizabeth, at least he knew she was alive.

She was alive.

Mrs. Collins clapped her hands to her cheeks. "She is in Faerie?"

"I believe so," he said. "My cousin Anne suggested a spell I could use to find her, and it led me straight to a faerie ring."

"That would explain how she could vanish without a trace, but how did she manage it? Faerie rings do not work for mortals."

"I cannot say. Perhaps her fay friend assisted her, but that is just a guess."

"My poor Lizzy! Will we ever see her again? Will she be able to return, or are the old stories true about men who spent a day in Faerie and return to find a hundred years had passed?"

He had forgotten about that. The elation of his discovery drained away as if it had never been. "No one knows for certain how time works in Faerie except that it is different from here, sometimes faster, sometimes slower. But Elizabeth would know of that risk, and she did not mention having a problem when she visited Faerie before. She would be careful of time passing, would she not?" As if somehow Mrs. Collins could answer his question and reassure him.

"I hope so." She looked down at her hands. "I always wondered how the old stories could be true. If the fay dance on Beltane and All Souls Night, and a day in Faerie is as long as a hundred of our years, would that not mean they would be dancing at a hundred Beltanes and a hundred All Souls Nights each day?"

"A good point. Any difference of time between our world and faerie must not be large. That would relieve one worry." Darcy refused to consider any other option.

Mrs. Collins said, "Should I tell the Bennets about your theory? I would rather not mention it to my husband. Lady Catherine equates the fay with the devil, and he has adopted her attitude in this, as in so many other things."

As if his aunt had not already caused enough trouble! "I am aware of Lady Catherine's prejudices. Perhaps it would be best to keep this to ourselves for now."

"I will. But I thank you for telling me. It has relieved my mind of my worst suspicions." Mrs. Collins wiped away a stray tear.

"Her chatelaine. Her keys. Where are Lady Catherine's keys?" Darcy tried to keep his anger in check. His aunt's nonsensical shouting from the next room did not help.

"Yes, sir. I know, sir," the maid squeaked. "They are in the table beside her bed. The drawer, but she says we are never, ever, ever to touch that drawer. Ever."

"I am not asking you to touch it." Darcy opened the bedroom door and strode in. A teacup flew at his head, but he ducked it without missing a step.

"Gardenias!" cried Lady Catherine. "Nettles and gardenias, all of them!"

"Nettles and gardenias," Darcy agreed as he opened the drawer. The chatelaine with its dangling keys sat atop a pile of old papers.

A bony hand grasped his wrist. "No!" shrieked his aunt. Of course, the very first word Lady Catherine used sensibly would be 'no.'

Darcy pried away her fingers. "Yes. Elizabeth saved your life, and now I am trying to save hers." He held the keys out of her reach. "You should rest."

"Oak and ash and thorn, they are all thieves born," she said in the singsong of a nursery rhyme.

Dear God, now she sounded like a fay. He would have to ask Elizabeth if that was typical after elfshot.

No, he had to find Elizabeth first.

The maid still looked horrified at his presumption. Darcy moved past her and started up the stairs two at a time.

Sir Lewis de Bourgh's library and study were at the far end of the wing. No doubt Lady Catherine had thought it safer that way. Now it was abandoned. The housekeeper had told him no one was permitted near the room, and Lady Catherine kept the only key. The heavy layer of dust outside the door seem to confirm her story.

He tried the keys one by one. When he finally found the correct key, the lock was too stiff to turn. He had already tried the usual spell for unlocking doors without success, so he leaned his forehead against the lock plate, picturing drops of oil running through the mechanism. Finally, with a piercing squeal of metal on metal, the key turned, and the door opened.

A cloud of dust made him cough as soon as he stepped inside the room. He wrenched open the closed curtains to allow enough light in to see. A long workbench stood against one wall, its surface cluttered with flasks and bottles of all sizes, stones, and unrecognizable wizened things. Darcy raised his eyebrows. Sir Lewis must have been mixing alchemy and magic. He would have been expelled from the Collegium of Mages if anyone had ever found out.

Darcy did not care about the past, only about Sir Lewis's books. They were in a locked bookcase, but this lock responded to his spell. The top shelf held musty books in Italian and Latin, so he started on the second shelf where the books were in English. They were all locked with standard Collegium spells to keep the books closed to any non-mage, but that would not stop him. He chose several to take downstairs to read in less unpleasant surroundings.

Bleary-eyed from examining the centuries-old book, Darcy looked up to see Richard in the doorway, his clothing covered with road dust.

"Nothing," said Richard gloomily. "I found plenty of things, mostly dead rabbits and the remains of poached deer, but no sign of her. Has there been any word here?"

"None," said Darcy. "But I do have a theory, one that I do not want to come to the attention of the Collegium or your father, at least not until Miss Bennet is safely back."

Richard grimaced. "I will tell no one, and I pray your theory is correct, since otherwise I see little hope of finding her alive."

"This may not be much better." Darcy closed the tome in front of him. "I cast an old finding spell, one I did not expect to work, but I had already tried everything else. It led me straight to a faerie ring, one I have walked past a dozen times and never noticed. The trail stopped in the center of the ring."

Richard whistled. "You think she went to Faerie?"

Darcy nodded.

"Faerie," said Richard reflectively. "That is perhaps the most preposterous theory I have heard, but it makes more sense than any other."

"My thought exactly. And she has gone to Faerie before, which makes it slightly less preposterous."

"Good Lord. Faerie. I need a drink if I am going to digest that." Richard crossed to the sideboard and poured a generous glass of brandy. "Any for you? Remind me next year to bring my own brandy to Rosings, or better yet, some of yours. Even mine would be better than this swill."

"It would not take much to be an improvement."

Richard set a glass on the desk where Darcy sat. He peered at the spell book. "That does not look like enjoyable reading."

"I raided Sir Lewis's library, hoping to find something about Faerie. I never paid much attention to the subject at Cambridge."

"Nor I." He took a sip of his brandy and made a sour face. "If that is where she is, is there anything we can do besides wait?"

"That is the question. I plan to write a letter to her and leave it at the circle for her to read on her return. If she returns." He also planned to spend as much time as he could at the faerie ring.

"If she returns there, you mean. There are faerie rings all over England. Would she not be more likely to appear somewhere else, perhaps nearer to her home?"

"That is one of the answers I am trying to find, whether the stories tell of anyone who disappeared at one ring and reappeared at another. In the meantime, since we cannot be at every faerie ring, I can but hope she will return through this one."

"I suppose so." Richard gazed moodily into his brandy. "What spell did you use to find her? I do not recall any spells for finding things out of sight."

Now was Darcy's turn to stare into his brandy. He had hoped his cousin would not ask that question. All his possible answers were bad. He did not like to lie, and if he refused to answer, that would only make Richard more curious. He said in a low voice, "Green grass, green grass."

"Green grass, green grass, floating in the air? *That* green grass?" Richard's voice was edged in disbelief.

"Yes, that green grass."

"That is just an old nursery rhyme! And it is only for finding your true love, not a missing girl."

"I am well aware of that," said Darcy sharply. Surely Richard did not need him to explain.

"But she... Oh." Richard fell silent. "I'm sorry, Darcy."

"I would prefer not to speak about it," Darcy said stiffly. "But I do wish to tell you about a very interesting conversation I had with Cousin Anne."

Darcy spun in a slow circle. Where would Elizabeth be most likely to notice his letter when she returned through the faerie ring? Placing it in the thorn bush beside the ring was as good as anything. Perhaps he should write more letters and hang them from every tree like Orlando in *As You Like It*. He snorted at the image.

He balanced the letter on two branches. That would have to do. Now for the embarrassing part. He crouched down beside the ring and rubbed his hand over his mouth.

At least no one would ever know about this. A good thing, as any sane person would think him ready for Bedlam. Still, the grass spell had been ridiculous, but it had worked. And last night's muddled dreams had been haunted by white cats and white ravens. It might have been some sort of fay sending, or more likely his fatigue-addled brain trying to tell him something. In any case, here he was.

"Pepper," he called softly. "Pepper, can you hear me? I need your help, Pepper. I am here beside the faerie ring." Yes, he was beside the faerie ring begging for help from a fay cat who was not there. How far the mighty mage had fallen!

He pictured the cat in his mind and called again. Nothing. "Pepper, if you can hear me, I beg you to come to me. I am worried about Elizabeth. Help me, Pepper." This was ridiculous. He rocked back and sat on his heels, covering his eyes with one hand. How would he ever find Elizabeth if this nonsense was the best he could manage?

"Mrrow."

Darcy's eyes flew open. "Pepper! You came! Where is Elizabeth? I have been out of my mind with worry. Is she in Faerie? Is she safe?"

Pepper began to groom her already immaculate white fur.

Darcy said ruefully, "Perhaps the correct question is why I am asking questions of a cat who may be able to turn into a bird, but who has never given any evidence of being able to speak."

Pepper stopped washing herself and gazed at him balefully.

"Yes, I am a very stupid mortal. I do not know what to do. Can you help me?"

The cat stretched and ambled towards him. He reached out to pet her, and she bumped her head against his knee.

"What is it? Do you want me to stand up?" Feeling utterly foolish, Darcy stood and allowed the cat to herd him into the center of the ring. "Pepper, I think you want me to go to Faerie, but I do not know the spell. I have no power over faerie rings."

Pepper meowed and gave him an assessing look.

"Yes, I truly am that stupid. I do not know what to do." And he probably did belong in Bedlam.

The cat crouched down, wiggled her hindquarters, and launched herself at his chest. Sharp claws hooked into his lapels.

"What?" Darcy grabbed at the cat before she tore the fabric. She immediately relaxed in his arms and began to purr. The ground melted under his feet.

# Part Two

# Faerie

# Chapter 4

Had he lost consciousness in the faerie ring? What had happened after Pepper jumped up at him?

Darcy was no longer in the glade in the grove, but wherever he was, it did not match his expectations for Faerie. None of the old tales had mentioned a forest so misty he could barely see twenty feet in front of him. There was no path or sign of habitation. Pepper had vanished.

This must be some wild part of Faerie. All he needed to do was to find his way out of the woods.

What had his father always said he should do if he lost his bearings? Find the nearest water, and follow it to civilization. Darcy reached out his senses and found...nothing. No water. No fire. No elements. It was as if he had suddenly gone deaf, disconnected from the world around him. Was this what ordinary people felt like?

But he still needed to find his way out of the forest. How did people without elemental powers find the nearest water? Go downhill, that was it. Downhill would lead to a stream, and a stream would lead to civilization. At least it would if there was any water in this strange world. The ground here seemed level as far as he could see in the mist, but perhaps he could find a slope.

He set off, choosing the route that seemed clearest. Occasionally he stopped to call Pepper's name. He trudged for what seemed like hours, until his feet were sore and his legs were tired, but when he checked his watch, he found it had stopped around the time of his arrival in Faerie.

Surely there must be a hill somewhere. Perhaps he had been

walking in circles all this time. How could he rescue Elizabeth if he could not even take care of himself? Would he wander in this mist forever?

Hunger gnawed at his belly. He had a little food in his pocket, but he did not eat it. He might need it more later if his strength began to fail him.

Perhaps a little rest might restore him. He sat down by the roots of a tree, leaning back against its wide trunk and stretching out his legs. What a relief to be off his feet! His boots had not been meant for a walk of this duration. He closed his eyes.

He awoke with a start, tree bark digging into his back. How long had he slept? He had not meant to fall asleep. The mist was still all around him, and silence was everywhere.

Silence. Complete silence. No animals rustling in the underbrush, no bird calls. He picked up a twig and snapped it in half. Still no sound.

It must be glamour. What a fool he had been not to see it! He closed his eyes and passed his thumbs over his eyelids, reciting the spell for clear vision.

When he opened his eyes, the sun was shining, and he stood beside a country lane. The grass was a little too green, and the air seemed to sparkle. A cluster of oddly shaped dwellings sat further down the lane. There was something not right about the horizon. The fragrance of gardenias was everywhere. This was more like the stories of Faerie.

Pepper clawed at his leg. She looked larger here, more like a small wildcat than a mouser, but otherwise she was unchanged. He felt an absurd gratitude at the sight of the familiar cat in this strange place.

Darcy detached her claws from his trousers. He had already wasted far too much time. "Pepper, can you take me to Elizabeth?"

With a swish of her fluffy tail, she rubbed against his boots and sauntered off behind his back. When Darcy turned to see where she was going, he spotted Elizabeth on a nearby hillock, sitting on the ground with her arms wrapped around her knees.

Thank God! The rush of relief robbed him of words and the ability to think. His pulses thrummed as if to say *she is alive, she is alive.* Darcy's legs had already started carrying him forward before he consciously decided to move.

He ran to her side. "Elizabeth!"

She did not react, not even looking in his direction. He waved a hand in front of her face. She continued to gaze off in the distance.

He knelt beside her. With his fingers on her temples, he drew his thumbs slowly and lightly across her eyes, repeating the clear vision spell.

Elizabeth started, her gaze suddenly meeting his. "Mr. Darcy! What are you doing here... And what are you doing?" Her last words were pointed.

He snatched his hands away from her face. It must have looked to her as if he wanted to kiss her, and for once that had not been foremost in his mind. If he ever had the chance to kiss her, he wanted her to be an active participant.

"Forgive my presumption. You were trapped in glamour, so I put a spell of clear vision on you."

Her lips pursed suspiciously. "A spell?"

"Were you trapped in a forest? It was glamour, and my spell allowed you to see through it. That is all. There is no binding attached, nor any other spell. I will swear to it on my mother's grave if you wish." The words poured out of him. What if she ran away from him as she had fled Lord Matlock?

The corners of her mouth turned up. "That will not be necessary. I believe you."

Now he did want to kiss her.

"Pepper!" Elizabeth stretched out her arms to the cat. "I am so glad to see you!" She tried to hug Pepper, but the cat was more interested in chasing some invisible object. Looking up at Darcy, Elizabeth added, "I was afraid Lord Matlock might have caught her."

"Or that I might have told him about her?" He could not keep all the bitterness from his voice.

She flushed and looked away. "I did not know what to think, after learning you had told Lord Matlock about me."

"Richard was the one who told him. I warned him you would be upset."

"I wish you had told me." Elizabeth looked around her. "So I did make it to Faerie. I thought I might not have. How did you come here?"

"Pepper helped me." Somehow it no longer sounded like a silly idea.

"Then I do not need to fear Lord Matlock will appear next?"

"Not unless Pepper helps him, and that seems unlikely after she did her utmost to scratch his face off."

She gave a delighted laugh. "What a clever cat she is! Although I suppose I should not say that to you. He is your uncle, after all." Her smile faded away.

"He deserved it. But he would not put a binding spell on you. I do not defend his decision to put one on Anne, but her situation was very different from yours. She had killed a man with her untrained magic."

Elizabeth's eyes widened. "I think you believe he would not bind me, but I have my doubts. He was very free with his attempts to bespell me. I felt it as soon as he touched my hand."

"I do not know what he was doing, but it was badly done on his part. Still, if nothing else, he has selfish reasons not to bind you. He wants to study you, and he cannot do that if you are bound."

Elizabeth sighed. "I suppose I cannot disbelieve selfish motives."

"In any case, he left Rosings yesterday morning." If it had been yesterday morning. He had no idea how long he had walked through the glamour.

Her brow screwed together in puzzlement. "Yesterday morning?"

"You have been gone two nights and a day. Mrs. Collins has been frantic."

"Poor Charlotte! I could not tell day from night in the glamour. I suppose I must return quickly, then. It did not seem quite that long although it was very long indeed, enough to leave me exhausted and famished."

After all that time with no food, she must be ravenous, far hungrier than he was. Thank God he had not eaten what little he had! Darcy rummaged in his pockets and produced a waxed fabric pouch with two ginger biscuits, a piece of cheese, and a twisted paper filled with dried fruit. "It is but poor fare, but if you would like it, it is yours."

She snatched it from his hands and began to eat. Between bites of ginger biscuit, she managed to say, "Pray forgive my manners. I was afraid I would die of starvation in that awful mist."

"And so you would have, like those who came before you. We do not like uninvited guests here." The speaker was a squat fellow who came only to Darcy's shoulder. His wide mouth, tilted eyes, and leathery skin marked him as fay. His clothes were of a nondescript color in a style that might have been worn in the Middle Ages.

Elizabeth swallowed a bite of cheese and drew a stone out of her reticule. She held it out to him on her open palm. "But I was invited."

The small man examined the rounded grey stone. "So you were," he said grudgingly. He grabbed Darcy's chin and turned his face to the side. "And you. I see the mark of the phouka here, so I suppose you will be allowed to live, at least for now."

Darcy forced himself not to react. He was an invader in a strange country here, not the Master of Pemberley, and only allowed to live because Elizabeth's cat had scratched him.

"We do not wish to trespass," said Elizabeth apologetically. "We will leave immediately."

"I think not," said the gnome. "You must go before the laird and be judged by him first."

"Very well," Darcy said, trying to establish a balance between confidence and submission. "Can you direct us to the laird?"

"There are many roads a man may walk, but none of them are for you."

Elizabeth looked as bewildered as he felt. "Should we wait here for your laird?"

The fay put two fingers in his mouth and whistled. An elegant white mare trotted up in response. "She will take you."

Darcy eyed the horse. No saddle, bit or bridle, and too small a horse to carry two people.

Elizabeth pointed to the horse's face. "Look at her eyes." One was blue and the other gold. Elizabeth tangled her hand in the horse's golden mane. "Pepper, you beautiful thing, is that you?" The horse nuzzled her ear.

The gnome spat on the ground. "'Tis bad luck, a white phouka."

Could horses look offended? This one certainly did.

Elizabeth kissed the horse's cheek. "She has brought only good fortune to me. And what a lovely horse you are! The King himself would be proud to have you in his stables."

Elizabeth had said the cat was vain, had she not? Darcy added, "The ladies in London would fight over who could ride you." It was also true. He turned to the gnome. "But how can we ride her? I do not wish to overburden her. Perhaps I should walk beside her."

"You have dirtied the ground with enough mortal footprints already. You will ride."

Bareback, with no reins, and double. Darcy hoped Pepper's gait was very steady indeed. Could Elizabeth ride sidesaddle when bareback?

Pepper obligingly turned her flank to Darcy. No stirrups, either. With trepidation he placed his hands on her back and vaulted onto her. Clumsily, even he would admit that, but successfully.

He held his hand out to Elizabeth. "If you put your foot on my boot, I should be able to bring you up in front of me. At least I hope so."

Elizabeth took his hand. "I cannot believe I am doing this. I am no horsewoman, even when there is a saddle and reins."

Darcy smiled down at her. "We will learn together." Perhaps the air of Faerie was intoxicating. He certainly should not have agreed to this.

He managed to wrestle her up to sit sideways in front of him across Pepper's back. Her perch was even more precarious than his. "I believe you would do best to hold on to me," he said huskily.

After a brief hesitation, she linked her arms around him. "If I fall off, I suppose I will simply have to abandon all dignity and ride astride."

"It might be safer." Darcy made a valiant attempt not to imagine the sight of her exposed legs. He was having enough trouble pretending he was not intoxicated by the pleasure of having her arms around him.

"I trust Pepper." She patted the horse's neck.

Darcy turned back to the gnome. "How do we find the laird?"

"She knows the way." He spat again and ambled off, muttering, "Mortals and a white phouka in the same day. Fah."

Pepper turned her head back to look at them with her blue eye, as if asking whether they were ready. Darcy nodded at her resignedly.

It could have been worse. Neither of them fell off when the horse took her first steps, although it was a near thing. Darcy had to grab Elizabeth around the waist to keep her in place. He hoped it was not far to the laird's...house? Manor? Castle? No, on second thought, he hoped the trip would take forever. Then he need not ever let go of Elizabeth.

Faerie was a very strange place indeed. Darcy was riding bareback on a horse who was also a cat, and Elizabeth was pressed against him, two impossibilities at once. At least Pepper was superbly smooth-gaited, and she appeared to bear the weight of them both easily.

"Do they always ride bareback?" he asked Elizabeth.

"The Sidhe use saddles and bridles, I believe. I had forgotten how hard it is to think clearly when you first come to Faerie."

"I thought it was only me." At least that was reassuring.

"Fortunately, it passes after you have been here for a time."

If she were to write a book of advice for young ladies, Elizabeth decided, she would devote an entire chapter to how one should behave after refusing a proposal of marriage. Do not stay under the same roof as your rejected suitor would be high on the list, along with not allowing him to perform magical spells on you, and do not reveal to him – or to his cousin – secrets you have kept all your life. But the top spot on the list would have to be this: do not spend hours in close physical contact with him by sharing an unsaddled horse.

The list of words she could apply to this experience was extensive: mortifying, humiliating, embarrassing. With his arms circling her waist and the side of her body pressed against his chest, how could she pretend to forget how recently Darcy had been professing ardent love for her? A few days ago she had been shocked when he touched her ungloved hands to heal her burns, and now this!

There were other things it made her feel, too, strange and exciting new feelings like butterflies inside her, but she did not want to admit to those. Resting her head on his shoulder would not help her stabilize her position, so why did she have to keep fighting the urge to do it? Perhaps it was because she felt as if she had just awoken from the nightmare of the glamour forest.

That treacherous, frightening forest. Had she truly spent days there? The agonizing pain of Darcy's betrayal of her had made the forest a nightmare long before she realized its dangers. Since learning he had known her secret all along, she had discovered the side of him she had always ignored, the part of him that could be generous, clever, well-educated, and all too attractive. He was still proud and occasionally disagreeable, but that could not outweigh the fact that he had been willing to accept a wife with magic. She had never dared to dream of such a future. But no sooner had she started to trust him, and even to have a few regrets about refusing him, than he had betrayed her in the worst possible way. How could he have said he understood her fear of binding spells and then exposed her to Lord Matlock? Had Colonel Fitzwilliam lied when he said they already knew about her magic to make her lower her guard while they sent for his father to bind her? Those few days of freedom from the fear of exposure had been such a relief, and it had all been lies. Lies that had broken her heart. She had been in tears more often than not during her time in the glamour forest, hating Darcy for betraying her, and hating herself for caring.

Soon, though, she could care about nothing but escaping from the forest before she starved, and that was Darcy's fault, too. If not for him, she would not have gone through the faerie ring. Then Darcy had magically appeared before her, made the deadly forest go away, and saved her life.

Now she was in his arms, exhausted, on the verge of tears, and feeling things she did not want to feel for a man she could not entirely trust, stranded in this new, terrifying Faerie. It had been a welcoming place for her as a child. Now it was filled with dangerous glamour traps which could kill her, and the mere presence of her feet on the ground was considered pollution. She had run to Faerie for safety and found it anything but safe. She frantically blinked back tears before Darcy could notice them.

And, of course, her only mortal companion would have to be a mage. All those years she had worked so hard to stay far from any mage apart from her father, and now she could not get away from them. Her opinion of mages had not improved for the experience, even if Darcy had saved her from the glamour trap.

Darcy said something under his breath that sounded like a curse.

"Is something the matter?" she asked.

"Apart from the obvious, no, simply a foolish thing I did in coming here. I had been planning to sit by the faerie ring and read, and I just realized I left a century-old spell book outside on a day that was beginning to look like rain."

Why did he have to choose that topic now when she was so anxious and exhausted? "It would make no difference to me if every spell book in existence was buried six fathoms under the ocean." She regretted her words as soon as she said them.

He paused, as if thinking carefully before responding. "I was under the impression you valued books."

"Books that I have even the slightest possibility of reading, yes. Books that are forbidden to me, even though the knowledge within them might be of great benefit to me, I cannot have a fondness for. I dislike the hoarding of knowledge. Sometimes I think the Collegium cares more about its own existence than anything else."

"I wish you were permitted to read them." His voice was low. "But the information in those books could be very dangerous in the wrong hands."

She could not seem to keep the words from pouring from her mouth. "Do you not realize how arrogant that is? But mages never lack for arrogance, no matter how amiable they seem. When I was exhausted after healing Lady Catherine, Colonel Fitzwilliam took it on himself to pour his magic into me. I am sure his motives were good, and I might even have appreciated it if he had asked me about it first. And he asked you to heal my burns. You, not me. It was my hand. How would you feel about someone performing unasked spells upon you when you were in a weakened state? But you and your cousin are mages, so you think nothing of forcing your magic on me, and you consider yourselves generous for having done so."

This time he was silent for longer, and she could feel the tension in his arm around her waist. "You were unwell, and we had been working together. But I acknowledge that we should have asked first. It was an unusual situation."

"But that is what mages always do. As soon as Lord Matlock was introduced to me, he tried some sort of spell on me. When I tried to run away, he cast another spell to hold me captive. Where was my choice there?"

"He should not have done that, and I told him so. But Richard and I would have protected you. There was no reason to be afraid."

"I had every reason to be afraid! Why should I have seen the two of you as my allies? You had schemed to summon Lord Matlock and kept it a secret from me. You are his family. None of the servants would have lifted a finger to protect me from Lady Catherine's brother and nephews, and my paltry untrained power was no match for three trained mages. I will grant that you, with your better knowledge of your uncle, are likely correct that he would not have harmed me further. Perhaps if the three of you had explained what you were about instead of leaving me helpless, I might not have felt that I had to flee. You mages are not even aware of how high-handed you are." She had said too much; she knew that, but she had spent such a long time dwelling on all this in the glamour forest. Oh, her cursed temper.

Darcy sucked in a long breath. "I could defend myself against some small parts of your charges, but there is no point. You have made your sentiments quite clear. May I suggest we put off any further discussion until we are safely back at Rosings?" His voice was cold.

She bowed her head. How could she have spoken so to him? He had come to Faerie to help her, and he had done nothing to deserve her ire apart from mentioning a spell book. She said quietly, "I do recognize you had no choice but to cast the spell of clear vision on me without my permission, and you likely saved my life by doing so."

"Thank you," he said stiffly, and then there was only icy silence.

Oh, why had she not held her tongue as she had for so long? He had tried to help her on more than one occasion, and even when she had not liked his methods of helping, his intentions had seemed good. But she was so hungry and so exhausted, and it was so hard being so close to him...

No. She would not start to cry. She would not.

Pepper slowed to a halt under the spreading branches of an apple tree. "Are we there?" asked Elizabeth hopefully.

The horse raised her head and looked pointedly up into the branches, sagging from the weight of ripe apples.

Darcy said softly, "This tree was not here. It just appeared."

Elizabeth swallowed back the desire to cry. "I was thinking that I was so tired and so hungry. Pepper must have heard my thoughts." She reached out and grasped the nearest apple.

Darcy caught her wrist. "Wait! Is that safe? What if someone is angry you took it?"

Elizabeth shook her head, her mouth watering. "Pepper would not have stopped here if that were the case."

"But we are not supposed to eat faerie food, or all mortal food will taste like ashes forever."

"That is an old wives' tale. I have eaten faerie food before."

He raised an eyebrow. "In that brief visit to Faerie that you told Richard about?"

Her cheeks grew warm. "Perhaps I might have left out a few things. He seemed a little too interested."

"Wise of you." He released her wrist.

She plucked two apples. "Would you like one?"

"In for a penny, in for a pound. Why not?"

She handed one to him and picked a third for herself. "I truly am very hungry," she explained.

"Should we take more in case you are still hungry afterwards?"

"It will be hard enough to hold these without falling off Pepper.

And I imagine Pepper can always create another apple tree if we need it." She patted the horse's neck. "You are very clever to produce a tree that bears apples in April. But I suppose nothing in Faerie follows the usual rules."

The apple was one of the most delicious things she had ever tasted. Elizabeth devoured the first one quickly, then spoke to Darcy. "There is one thing that is not an old wives' tale. You must always tell the fay the exact truth. They will know if you do not, and they will punish you with a fay trick. They will make your lie come true, but always in a manner that will be harmful to you."

"I will keep that in mind." He said nothing more until she had eaten her second apple and Pepper had started walking again. Then he added, "If I asked you how much time you spent here in the past, would you tell me the truth?"

Elizabeth hesitated. "That would depend on why you wanted to know, I suppose."

"It is simple curiosity about your life."

She wanted to be back on better terms with him, and there was no real reason to keep it a secret. "Like most people, I have forgotten a great deal of my early life, but I would guess it was many times. Bluebird enjoyed the human world where she could play tricks on people, but usually she brought me here. And I expect your uncle would be sadly disappointed by how very little I noticed of my surroundings at that age. I remember a sort of bower in the woods, a beautiful black-haired woman, and someone combing my hair, but not much more. Going to Faerie seemed much like going to visit a neighbor in Meryton. I did not realize how unusual it was until years later."

"We think the oddest things are normal when we are children," Darcy said.

"I have a question for you as well," said Elizabeth determinedly. "When did you realize I had magic?"

He looked reflective. "It was at a gathering at Lucas Lodge. I knew someone there had magic, but not who it was until Sir William Lucas suggested that I dance with you. Our eyes met, and I could feel the magic in you. But look – I see something." He pointed ahead of them.

Elizabeth squinted to make it out. There were three towers, made of something that looked more like silver filigree than stone. "That certainly looks like a laird's court."

The palace, for that was the only term Darcy could apply, truly was made of silver filigree. How could it possibly stand? The walls should not be able to hold a roof, and the towers ought to have collapsed of their own weight. It was disconcerting to see the laws of nature so casually violated.

No one met them at the door. Elizabeth looked at him, shrugged, and entered. Darcy followed close behind her, hoping uninvited guests were not slain on sight. It would seem in keeping with the barbaric glamour traps.

A tall silver throne sat at the far end of an impossibly long hall, with an equally tall, equally impossible being slouched in it. He was surrounded by fay folk. Darcy recognized dryads and sprites in his retinue, along with some diminutive figures he could not name. Drawing closer, he could see that everything about the laird was longer than he expected – longer legs, longer arms, and long, tapering fingers. His cheekbones were prominent and his chin narrow, and he was dressed in a tabard made from cloth of gold trimmed with sea green silk. His hair was spun gold and hung nearly to his shoulders, making him a picture of unearthly beauty sitting in a beam of impossible indoor sunlight. Cuffs of silver filigree covered his lower forearms. Darcy had never seen a Sidhe, the most powerful fay, but he had no doubt the being before him was one.

Elizabeth halted a short distance from the throne and lowered herself into a deep curtsey. Darcy opted for the most cautious course and made his court bow.

"What brings mortals to my hall?" The Sidhe's voice seemed to contain chiming bells.

Darcy's throat was tight, but he said, "We have come to seek your permission to return to our own world."

The fay lord stepped down from his throne and paced in front of them. Darcy was unaccustomed to having to look up to see someone's face, and he did not like it, especially given the fay's grim expression. There was something odd about his tilted, emerald green eyes, their pupils shaped in tall ovals not unlike a cat's eyes, under eyebrows shaped more like wings than arches. His skin was pale and translucent like fine porcelain. The sight of him sent a shiver down Darcy's spine.

"Why did you come here that you wish to leave so soon?"

Elizabeth seemed unperturbed by the astonishing sight. "I fled here to escape a powerful mage. Faerie was the one place I knew he could not follow me. I am told he is no longer pursuing me, so I may return home safely."

"The doors to Faerie are blocked to mortals."

She held out her stone. "When I was a child, I had a fay friend. She brought me to Faerie sometimes. She gave me this years ago in case I ever needed to return here. I did not know there would be glamour traps or that I would no longer be welcome. I should not have come here if I had."

The fay lord loomed over her. "Years ago there were no glamour traps. They were created after the war with mortals began." He whirled to face Darcy. "And you. Who are you?"

Absolute honesty. This would not be pleasant. "My name is Fitzwilliam Darcy, and I am a mage."

"The one she was fleeing?"

113

"No." In case that might seem less than honest, he added, "That was my uncle."

He turned to Elizabeth. "Are you a mage as well?"

"No. Mortal women are not permitted the use of magic."

"Not permitted? How barbaric. You, mage – why were you pursuing her?"

"I was worried about her. She had been missing for days."

The fay lord silently paced back and forth, back and forth. "Throwing yourself into Faerie because you were worried?" he asked scornfully.

He was going to have to say it. "I love her." He avoided looking in Elizabeth's direction.

"Ah, love and death, those human mysteries." With another one of his lightning quick twists, he turned to Elizabeth. "And you. Do you love him?"

Darcy interjected, "She does not." He would rather say it himself than hear Elizabeth saying it.

"Permit the lady to answer for herself!"

Elizabeth licked her lips, obviously uncomfortable. "My sentiments towards him are confusing. I cannot claim to love him, but I also cannot be certain I do not love him."

Darcy stared at her, repeating her words in his mind. They made no sense. But surely it was better than a straightforward denial, was it not?

The fay lord seemed pleased by this peculiar non-answer. "Have you ever murdered a tree?"

"Murdered? Do you mean cutting it down?" asked Elizabeth in bewilderment.

"Call it what you wish."

"I have never cut down or killed a tree. Once I asked my father to trim away a branch that was blocking my window, but the tree is still there."

Had he ever given an order to cut down a tree? Darcy frantically ran through his memory. No doubt his steward had done so on occasion, and could be considered to be acting in his name –

"I do not speak of that sort of tree, but the trees in a grove."

"I have never harmed a tree in a faerie grove." Elizabeth sounded more certain this time.

"And you?"

"I have never cut down any trees in a grove." Why was it so important? Were the trees sacred to the fay?

The fay lord demanded angrily, "Why have your fellow mortals broken our treaty?"

What treaty? How could he respond to this? "I beg pardon for my ignorance, Lord, but I do not know what treaty you refer to." Was that suitably humble?

"The only treaty! The Great Treaty between fay and mortals. We gave you your freedom, and you preserved our groves!" He practically spat out the words.

How was he to admit he had never heard of this treaty the fay held so dear?

Elizabeth, braver than he, asked, "Honored Lord, when was the Great Treaty made?"

He waved his hand as if shooing away nonsense. "Perhaps a thousand of your years ago, or a little more."

She took a deep breath. "Honored Lord, mortal life is fleeting and mortal memory is even shorter. A thousand years is more mortal generations than I can count. I am ashamed to admit that today's mortals do not know the Great Treaty ever existed. We do not know why the fay have been attacking us. Mortals do not even know you are at war with us."

"How can this be?" he cried. He stalked back to his throne and threw himself into it.

Elizabeth said quietly, "It must be the Enclosure Acts. Landowners have been cutting down wooded areas and enclosing them, but when they cut down a faerie grove, the faerie ring is destroyed."

It could not be. Or could it? Last spring one of the neighboring landowners had cleared a forested area that bordered on Rosings Park, and now fay attacks were common there. Surely the ring they had traveled through should serve the same purpose, and it was close by. But he knew nothing of how faerie rings worked or why they were important.

"Is there something we should do? Does he wish us to leave?" Darcy asked in a low voice.

"I think not," said Elizabeth slowly. "I believe we should wait to be dismissed."

A dryad-like creature draped in a diaphanous green silk drifted silently towards them, stopping just in front of Elizabeth, but not looking at them. An apple on a silver plate appeared in her hand.

Elizabeth stiffened, but she took the apple. "I tha... Eating this will give me great pleasure." Her voice shook.

The dryad made no acknowledgment before continuing her journey across the hall.

Elizabeth sidled closer to him, her face pale. "I should have warned you earlier. You must never thank them. It is a grave insult. And... And I do not believe our thoughts are fully private here."

How could their thoughts not be private? "I do not understand."

"Just a moment ago I was wishing I had eaten another apple. I was wishing it rather loudly, if such a thing is possible."

Good God, what might they have overheard from his thoughts? They could not hear them all, or there would be no need to ask questions. Perhaps they could only hear thoughts that expressed strong desire. If that was the case, the Sidhe lord should know all about his desire for Elizabeth's love. Even through his fear, he ached for her.

The Sidhe gestured to another dryad. She glided towards them with a gem-studded silver cup in her hands. She offered it to Elizabeth, who drank from it and returned it to her. The dryad held it out to Darcy. Society would hold it rude for a man to drink from the same glass as a lady, but here it seemed expected. He took a careful sip. It was a sweet, flowery wine that sparkled like champagne, and it made his head spin a little. He handed it back to the dryad, who offered it to Elizabeth again.

Elizabeth hesitated briefly before taking it and drinking from it again. She turned towards him and offered it directly to him, watching him closely. If she thought he should drink it, he probably should. He took it and drank again. Now his head definitely spun for a moment. Was there some drug in the wine? Was it safe? Elizabeth seemed untroubled by it.

The dryad took the goblet from him and walked away.

The Sidhe lord seemed to come to some sort of conclusion. He strode towards them once more. "Walk with me," he commanded.

Darcy and Elizabeth trailed after him through the impossibly long hall, half running to match the pace of his long legs. At the far end a wooden door suddenly appeared in what had been a filigree wall a moment before. It opened itself, revealing an enormous garden filled with climbing vines and exotic flowers with a hauntingly beautiful scent.

A silver filigree gazebo sat in the center of the garden. The lord stopped before it and spun to face them. "Our two worlds are bound together like twins residing in the same womb, and anything that interferes with that binding harms us both. Not all of us are happy with this war against humans. It is King Oberon's son who wishes it. Oberon is completely in his thrall."

"If there is a way to end the war, we would do anything in our power to promote it," Darcy said carefully.

"I am glad to hear it." The Sidhe held out his hand, now holding two tiny cakes. Was this some sort of ritual?

Elizabeth took one of the cakes and ate it. "I am honored."

Darcy followed her example. Like the wine, the cake tasted of flowers, and again, his head spun.

"We will speak further, but you must leave now," said the Sidhe. "Oberon's representative is nearing this place. There is a whitethorn tree in the grove from whence you came. Meet me there on Beltane at sunset. Both of you, and no one else. Do you understand?"

Darcy nodded. "We will be there."

"Into the gazebo," he ordered, pointing a long tapering finger.

The silver filigree looked too fragile to hold Elizabeth's weight, much less his own, but Darcy was beyond arguing. He followed Elizabeth, grateful the floor seemed to support him.

But only for a moment. The floor dissolved under him, and he struck cold earth with a bone jarring thud. They were in the faerie circle at Rosings and the spell book still sat outside it. Sharp knives seemed to be stabbing into the arm he had fallen on.

Beside him Elizabeth pulled herself to a sitting position and rubbed her hip.

"Are you hurt?" Darcy asked.

"I will have a bruise or two, nothing more. I must say these transitions seemed easier when I was younger, but perhaps I am simply less resilient. And you – are you injured?"

Darcy cautiously moved his arm. It hurt like the devil. "A bit sore. More stunned by how quickly everything happened."

"I had forgotten how abrupt the Sidhe are. One would think immortality would allow more time for civility, but it does the opposite for them, as if any wasted moment is lost forever. And they are accustomed to being in command, as you may have noticed."

"I noticed," he said dryly. His arm throbbed as he stood, but he was pleased that his legs seemed to be working. He held out his good hand to Elizabeth.

She looked up at him ruefully. "I thank you, but I believe I should rest here a few minutes longer before I try anything complicated like standing up. At the risk of sounding like my mother, my nerves are suffering."

"A few moments of rest sounds like an excellent idea." He collected the brandy flask he had left by the spell book before joining her again. "Normally I would hesitate to offer brandy to a young lady, but under these circumstances, perhaps it might soothe your nerves." He uncorked it and held it out to her.

She took the flask. "I am willing to try anything."

"I recommend small sips," he said as she raised it to her lips.

She coughed a little with her first sip but seemed more comfortable with the next. "I cannot understand why anyone would drink this for the flavor, but the sensation is not displeasing." She offered it back to him. "I imagine you could use some as well."

It was true, but they were no longer in Faerie, and he would not be able to offer it to her after he drank from it. "It is not necessary."

She raised an eyebrow. "Surely you are not worried about propriety after we shared a cup in Faerie, not to mention the way we rode together on my –" She stopped and pressed trembling lips together.

"What is it?" Darcy asked. She could not possibly be feeling the effects of the brandy this quickly.

She let out a breath. "I was about to say the way we rode together on my cat. Because that is what we did. We rode bareback on my cat." Her voice shook with nervous laughter.

He chuckled, relieved it was nothing more. "So we did. Or perhaps we rode your raven. But this is the last time I will refer to us riding double. It would be very difficult to explain here."

Her expression sobered. "I suppose so. And I suppose we had best relieve my friend's anxiety by returning to her."

# Chapter 5

Walking to the parsonage was agonizing. Each step jolted his injured arm, but even so, Darcy noticed Elizabeth's pallor increasing. It was hardly surprising, given her lack of sleep since her disappearance, but he was still concerned.

At the parsonage, Elizabeth was greeted with embraces and exclamations of relief by Mrs. Collins and a fashionably dressed man of middle years whom Elizabeth called uncle. They immediately began peppering her with questions which seemed only to confuse her.

Darcy managed to catch Mrs. Collins's eye. "Miss Elizabeth has not slept since leaving here."

"You poor thing!" exclaimed Mrs. Collins. "Come, I will take you up to bed this minute before you make yourself ill."   She hustled Elizabeth upstairs.

The unknown man said, "You must be Mr. Darcy. Pray permit me to introduce myself. I am Edward Gardiner, Lizzy's uncle."

Thankfully he had not held out his hand for a handshake. The pain of that would be unimaginable. Perhaps when Mrs. Collins returned, he could ask her privately for something to bind his arm for the trip to Rosings. "It is a pleasure to meet you, Mr. Gardiner."

"So you and Lizzy were in Faerie all this time," said Mr. Gardiner.

"I realize it must sound like a ridiculous story, but it happens to be true." Darcy tried to keep his temper in check. Naturally the man had doubts. Any sane man would doubt his story.

"That was not an accusation, young man. I believe you. In fact, I would have a great deal of trouble believing any other story."

"You believe me? Why?"

"Let me see. Lizzy disappears utterly. Two days later you also disappear. You return here the following day, and Lizzy is carrying a fresh apple in April. Faerie is the only explanation."

The following day? He must have been walking in the glamour woods for a very long time indeed. Richard would be frantic. "You seem to take that remarkably calmly."

"The idea of Faerie does not frighten me. For all that my mother appeared fully human, her father was fay, so you might say I imbibed Faerie with my mother's milk." Mr. Gardiner smiled self-deprecatingly at his little joke.

"You have fay blood? Does that mean Miss Elizabeth does as well?" Why had she never told him? It would have helped him understand a great deal.

"Some, yes. It shows differently in different people. You could see the fay in Lizzy's mother when she was younger, when she was much like Lizzy is now. My other sister, who is now Mrs. Phillips, seemed to have no fay in her at all. I am somewhere in between – human in essentially every way except for an inexplicable talent for magical healing."

It stung to be hearing this from her uncle. "Miss Elizabeth did not mention this to me."

"After a journey together through Faerie? I am surprised." He frowned suddenly. "Or perhaps I am not. It is possible she does not know. Mr. Bennet does not permit discussion of anything related to the fay at Longbourn."

"Yet he married a woman with fay blood."

"He did not always hate the fay. That came later. His wife was fascinated with Faerie, spending much of her time there, but something changed. She became a different person. Silly, shallow, and completely uninterested in anything about the fay. Bennet denied having done anything, but I have my own theories."

Darcy drew in a sharp breath. "You think he put a spell on her?"

"I am not a mage, and I do not understand these matters. It may be better that way for the sake of family harmony. She had just lost her firstborn child, a son who did not live, and he attributed the change in her to that."

At least a spell would explain how a ridiculous woman like Mrs. Bennet could have two such clever, well-bred daughters. But Mr. Gardiner must be correct that Elizabeth was unaware of her heritage. If she had known her mother was under a binding spell, she would not have the same affection for her father. "Mr. Bennet will not be pleased by the news that Miss Elizabeth visited Faerie, then. That is why you are telling me this, is it not?"

Mr. Gardiner's eyes twinkled. "I am not in the habit of revealing my family history to strangers."

This was too much for Darcy's exhausted brain and throbbing arm. "Miss Elizabeth's greatest fear is that a mage will put her under a binding spell. If she discovers her father put one on her mother, she will be furious at him. If she tells him about her journey to Faerie..." He sucked in a deep gulp of air. "He would not put a binding on her, would he?"

Mr. Gardiner pursed his lips. "I think not. Lizzy is not as wild as her mother was. But I cannot be absolutely certain."

"If Miss Elizabeth were ever to undergo a change in behavior, I hope you would contact me. I can discover if she is spellbound and, if necessary, have someone remove the spell."

"It relieves my mind to know the spell can be reversed. I have often wondered about that."

"Do you plan to tell her about her heritage now?" She would not be happy to discover Darcy had known it first.

Mr. Gardiner grimaced. "I think I must, though perhaps not the part about her mother."

"Good. She and I are to meet with a Sidhe lord on Beltane. Good God, I do not even know what day today is!"

"Not to worry, you have five days still. But a Sidhe lord! This is a story I must hear, but perhaps after you rest. Your eyes are glassy."

Darcy nodded, too tired to argue.

"As I mentioned, I do have some small skill in healing," Mr. Gardiner said conversationally. "If someone had, for example, a broken arm, I could speed the healing process and reduce the pain. A Collegium-trained healing mage would no doubt do better, but there is not one here."

"How did you know?" Darcy asked. "Never mind. I do not care how you know. I would be very appreciative of any assistance you can give." He did not have time for a broken arm, not with Beltane only five days off. He gingerly moved his arm out from his side.

Mr. Gardiner slid his chair closer and ran his hand along Darcy's forearm. Astonishingly, his touch did not hurt. "The bone is still in place. That is good." Holding Darcy's wrist in one hand, he laid the other over the throbbing spot in his arm and closed his eyes. After a moment he began to hum softly.

Darcy watched him, but his lips never moved. No spoken spell, the same as Elizabeth. But Elizabeth had been right. He would have hated it if her uncle had tried to heal his arm without asking him first. It did not matter that he needed the help. Elizabeth would be pleased to know he understood now.

The throbbing in his arm was diminishing as Mr. Gardiner worked his magic. Darcy leaned his head back and closed his eyes.

"Darcy, wake up! You can sleep after you tell me where the devil you have been." It was Richard's voice, and he did not sound pleased.

Darcy opened his eyes. Where was he? He must have fallen asleep in the chair. "I...what?"

Mrs. Collins said, "Apparently the pain was the only thing keeping him awake. Once Mr. Gardiner healed his arm, he went straight to sleep. It should hardly be a surprise; Lizzy lay down on her bed fully clothed and fell asleep midsentence."

Darcy attempted to pull his scattered thoughts together. "Richard, I have been in Faerie, as you must have guessed. It went well in that both of us are still alive, and poorly in that we discovered the fay are determined to make humans suffer for breaking a thousand-year-old agreement none of us remember having made."

"Good God! But how did you travel there?"

Darcy had thought ahead to this question. "I found a stone sitting in the faerie ring and recognized it as belonging to Miss Elizabeth. I picked it up to keep it safe for her and it sent me to Faerie. Perhaps it is a gateway of some sort." Now he had kept his word to Elizabeth and prevented anyone from suspecting Pepper was anything but an ordinary cat.

"Did you return the same way?" Richard demanded.

"No. We stepped inside a silver filigree gazebo."

"Not a faerie ring? How did you know to go there?"

"We did not know. A Sidhe lord ordered us to go into it, and he is not a man – pardon me, a fay – with whom you would care to argue."

Richard threw his hands in the air. "A Sidhe? Everyone knows the Sidhe are a myth."

"I beg to differ." Darcy yawned. "I understand your curiosity, but could the interrogation wait until I have slept?"

"Oh!" Elizabeth stopped in surprise. What was Mr. Darcy doing in the parsonage breakfast room so soon after sunrise? Her insides felt suddenly warm. He had been the first thought that came to her mind when she awoke, remembering the feeling of his arms around her as they rode Pepper and her decision to share a cup with him. Did he understand the significance of that? And why was his arm in a sling?

"Good morning, Miss Elizabeth," he said gravely. "I hope you slept well."

"Monstrously well. I cannot believe I slept through the day and all night!" She could feel the heat rising in her cheeks.

"As did I. Mrs. Collins offered me the use of her spare room when it became clear I was in no condition to return to Rosings Park."

She hesitated. "What happened to your arm?"

He grimaced. "A slight injury on our return from Faerie."

"A slight injury." She put her fingertip to her lips. "Would that mean a slightly sprained or a slightly broken arm?"

His lips twitched. "Slightly broken, but nothing to worry over. Your uncle helped me with it, and I am much more comfortable now."

How could Mr. Gardiner have helped him? Perhaps he had made the sling. "I am glad of it." She was far too aware of him, so instead of meeting his eyes, she studied the sheet of paper in front of him. It appeared to have hen scratches all over it. "What is that?"

Darcy sighed. "I thought to set down as much as I could recall of our conversation with the Sidhe lord while it was fresh in my mind, but my penmanship with my left hand leaves a great deal to be desired. Legibility, for one thing."

She could not help smiling. "Perhaps it would help if we pooled our recollections. I would be happy to do the writing."

"I will accept that offer since my efforts are an unpleasant sight." He pushed the paper and the inkwell in her direction.

The task allowed them to pass the time in relative harmony, though whenever she stole a glance at Darcy, she found him watching her with an intent look. Was she destined to blush every minute she was in his presence?

Mr. Gardiner joined them a short time later. He asked after their health, and then said, "Lizzy, I thought at first to leave yesterday as soon as I knew you were safe, but after speaking to Mr. Darcy, I decided it would be better to wait until I could talk to you. There is a matter your father has strongly discouraged me from discussing with you, but I believe it may be important for you to know about it now, if you have not already been told. Are you aware that my mother was half mortal, half fay?"

"Not Grandmama?" she asked sharply. She had only vague memories of a warm, white-haired, completely mortal woman.

"Yes."

It made no sense. "But that would mean my mother has fay blood, and so do I."

"Exactly so." Her uncle seemed to be waiting for something.

Elizabeth looked down at her hands. Hands with fay blood. "Well, I suppose that explains my fay friend. Why was I never told?" But something niggled at the back of her memory. Had she once known she was part fay?

"As you are no doubt aware, your father has a strong distaste for anything related to the fay. Most likely he wished you were entirely human. In truth, it is hardly a major matter that one of your eight great-grandparents was fay when the other seven were mortal, but I wanted you to be aware of it so you would take care in speaking to your father of your adventures in Faerie. He will not be pleased to learn of them."

Elizabeth bit her lip. "I learned long ago not to speak to him about the fay, though I do not know if I can disguise this. I wonder why my mother never said anything. Did she keep her fay blood a secret from him until they were married?" Was that why her father had such scorn for her mother?

"No, he was aware of it, and it seemed to amuse him when he was courting her. His dislike of fay did not develop until later."

So much of what she had believed about her family, even her sense that her magic came from her father, all that was turned upside down. And her father had hidden the truth from her. But she must not let her disturbance of mind show, especially not in front of Mr. Darcy. She had shown him enough of her weaknesses already, so she said lightly, "This last week has been full of one shock after another. I had so hoped for a few hours without a surprise, but it seems I was too optimistic. Perhaps I should limit my hopes to, say, no more than a quarter hour without a shock." There, she had responded calmly. She put her hands in her lap so her uncle could not see how they were trembling.

Mr. Gardiner looked relieved, but Mr. Darcy did not. His shoulders were tense and he was staring down at the table, his bottom lip caught in his teeth. Was he embarrassed by this news of her fay heritage? Did it horrify him that he had proposed to a woman who was not even fully human?

That made no sense. He had shown no disdain for fay folk. Then she recognized his look. It was the one he had worn in the days after his aunt's injury, when he was aware his uncle was coming and had not told her.

"What is it?" she asked sharply. "What are you keeping from me?"

He looked up, and the pain in his eyes told her she was not mistaken. Still, he said nothing.

She turned back to her uncle. "Mr. Darcy is a poor liar. Do you know what he is trying to conceal from me?"

Her uncle removed his spectacles. "It is a matter of conjecture, nothing more," he said slowly.

Darcy held up a hand to stop him. "Permit me to tell her. If she is going to hate the bearer of this news, better it be me than you." He took a deep breath. "Your uncle says your mother was once very different, witty and clever, proud of her fay heritage, and a frequent visitor to Faerie. Your father thought it was too much. One day she changed, never mentioned the fay again, and became the person she is today." He paused, his brow furled. "I am so very sorry."

For a minute she was perplexed, unable to understand why he was so distressed. Then her stomach lurched. "He put a binding spell on her?" It came out as a whisper.

He glanced at Mr. Gardiner. "There is no proof. Your father claims he did nothing."

Mr. Gardiner said, "It was around the time she had a son who died at birth, the year before Jane was born. Your father attributed the change in her to that. He was not the same either, but it was not as drastic a change. He just became more bitter and sardonic, especially towards your mother."

She shook her head slowly, not even knowing what she was denying. Her mother, whom she had always looked down on as unintelligent and silly, was spellbound. Her beloved, trusted father had done it, and nothing could ever be right again. Ever.

Darcy's warm hand settled on her wrist. "If you wish it, I will arrange for Richard to meet your mother. He will be able to tell you for certain, one way or another."

She nodded jerkily. "But why could I not tell? I was able to feel the spell on Miss de Bourgh."

"Would not any such spell simply have felt like part of her? After all, she was under it when you were born, and children do not question why their parents are the way they are."

"I suppose so." Blinking back tears, she pressed the back of her free hand against her mouth. "Now I pray you to speak of something else." Otherwise she might start sobbing then and there. A quarter hour without a shock had been too much to hope for.

After a brief silence, Darcy asked, "Mr. Gardiner, what are your plans for the day?"

"I plan to stay for breakfast and will head back to London after that."

"Would you perhaps consider staying a little longer? I must discuss with my cousin the question of our further meetings with the Sidhe lord, and I would appreciate your perspective, both as a non-mage and someone with some knowledge of the fay. I hope Miss Elizabeth will take part as well, if she is willing."

"Why, if you would like it, I would be most interested to take part in that discussion," said Mr. Gardiner. "I can delay my return without any difficulty."

It was too much. Elizabeth put her head in her hands. "Five minutes," she said plaintively. "Is five shock-free minutes really too much to ask?" At least this shock did not make her want to curl up in the corner and sob.

With a puzzled look, Darcy asked Mr. Gardiner quietly, "Did I say something I should not have?"

Elizabeth gave a humorless laugh. "This is my uncle, the one in trade, who lives in Cheapside on Gracechurch Street, for heaven's sake, and you just told him you want his opinion. You are not the Mr. Darcy I met in Meryton." And the more she came to know him, the more he confused her.

"Perhaps not," said Darcy, "but this Darcy has only recently come to realize the depth of his own ignorance on certain subjects and will accept wisdom wherever it can be found."

She swallowed hard. That was the Darcy she found altogether too attractive. "As I said, shocking. Would you be so kind as to ask the maid to bring me breakfast in my room? I feel the need for some quiet reflection."

"Of course." Mr. Gardiner cleared his throat and added

hesitantly, "Before you go, Mr. Darcy tells me you have a fear of being spellbound, but I think it is unlikely your father would attempt that with you. Your situation is different from your mother's."

Darcy touched her wrist again, sending a bit of his warmth into her. "I also asked Mr. Gardiner to inform me if he ever notices a change in you. I will make certain you are freed, whether it is tomorrow or in twenty years. You have my word of honor on it."

But even if she were freed, the very idea that her father would bind a woman, much less his own wife... It made her feel ill. "I thank you." Her voice seemed high-pitched even to her own ears. "It is unlikely to occur as, given these circumstances, it is improbable that I will return to Longbourn. I do not know where I will go, but it will not be there."

Her uncle's eyes were full of pity. "You always have a home with us on Gracechurch Street. Your aunt and I would be very pleased to have you."

"Thank you. Pray excuse me." She fled the room.

Darcy put down the pages he had just read aloud to the assembled group. "That was our conversation with the Sidhe lord as Miss Elizabeth and I recall it. The question is what we should do next." He looked at each of them in turn, careful not to let his gaze linger on Elizabeth. Her eyes were still red rimmed.

Richard tilted back his chair, balancing precariously on two of its legs. "You will meet him on Beltane, clearly."

"We must have something to offer him," Darcy said. "Some plan for how the groves could be protected, perhaps, but I am not empowered to make promises for any land but my own. He was very specific that it should be only the two of us, so even if I could convince someone from the government to take this seriously, I cannot bring them."

Mr. Gardiner stroked his chin. "Presumably he wishes to meet with you because he has more trust in a man he has met, but why did he insist on Lizzy's presence as well? You told him you were a mage, so it makes sense he would think you had the ability to make changes, but why would he think Lizzy could? If we can understand his reasoning, perhaps we can understand him better."

"Perhaps he sensed I had been influenced by fay, and that made me some sort of ally." Elizabeth's voice lacked its usual liveliness.

"Or perhaps that is how negotiations in Faerie are done, by both male and female fay," said Richard. "Devil take it, we know nothing of them!"

Darcy cleared his throat. "Miss Elizabeth handled the discussion with the Sidhe lord better than I did. She spoke fluently and seemed comfortable when I was tongue-tied and my discomfort must have been apparent. If they felt Miss Elizabeth's hunger, they must have known I was afraid."

Richard raised his eyebrows. "Afraid, cousin?"

Darcy met his eyes. "Yes. I would have been a fool to feel otherwise. I was stranded in a strange world where the horizon curves up instead of down and trees magically appear out of nowhere, and then I entered an impossibly huge hall built of silver filigree to be faced with an angry immortal with cat's eyes the color of emeralds, half a foot taller than me and a hundred times more powerful."

Elizabeth's brows drew together. "Hmm. You are correct about the horizon. It did not strike me at the time, perhaps because I had seen it before."

Mr. Gardiner asked, "Lizzy, were you afraid of the Sidhe?"

"A little, I suppose," she said slowly. "He was angry, and I did not know why, but I did not think he would harm me. He did not seem particularly odd to me."

Mr. Gardiner nodded. "He may want Lizzy's presence because he perceives her to be more accepting of him.”

Richard ran his finger along the arm of his chair. “Darcy,” he said slowly. “You may not like this, and I am certain Miss Bennet will not, but you ought to speak to my father. If there is any chance you will have to seek the cooperation either of Parliament or the Collegium, you will need his help.”

Darcy turned quickly to Elizabeth. “I could go alone. I see no reason for you to go to London to speak to him unless you wish to.”

The ghost of a smile crossed her face. “You will not be surprised to learn I would prefer to stay here.”

Elizabeth picked up a shift from the basket of torn clothes. She and Charlotte had made a dent in the pile of clothes to be mended and given to the poor, but it seemed a never-ending task. But it was far better than going to London to talk to Lord Matlock. She wondered how Darcy’s meeting was going.

Charlotte looked up at the sound of the front door. “Mr. Collins must be returning from Rosings already.” It was the first day he had been permitted to visit Lady Catherine, so they had expected him to be gone for hours.

She expected him to stop at the sitting room eventually to report on every detail of his visit, as was his habit. This time he appeared immediately, his face red with choler.

Charlotte jumped up immediately. “Why, husband, is something the matter?”

“Something the matter!” he spat out, pointing a shaking finger at Elizabeth. “That...that viper is the matter!”

Elizabeth’s stomach sank. “I am sorry if I have done anything to offend you.” But she knew what she had done, and there would be no avoiding paying the price this time.

"Witch!" he hissed. "I allowed you to stay against my better judgment after you disappeared for days, and this is how you repay me. Lady Catherine has told me of your sins and how you defiled her own person. You have deceived and dishonored me, and you will leave this house this very minute!"

Charlotte's mouth hung open.

Elizabeth had worried so much about being exposed by Mr. Darcy. How ironic that it should come at the hands of her foolish cousin instead! "Very well. I will pack my trunks."

"This very minute! Lady Catherine has decreed it so. Your clothes will be burned. Out!"

Elizabeth stared at him in shock.

Charlotte said soothingly, "Husband, if what you say is true and Lizzy must leave, should we not set an example of doing so with Christian charity? She can leave the house now, and I will pack her trunks and take them to the posting inn."

"She is fortunate I am allowing her to leave with her life!" Mr. Collins shouted. "She must leave this minute with nothing but the clothes she is wearing, or Lady Catherine will never see us again!" Fear showed in his eyes.

So that was the reason for this uncharacteristic behavior. She could well believe Lady Catherine would not be above such cruelty. "Charlotte, my money is in a reticule in the vanity drawer. Would you bring it to me?"

"Certainly." Charlotte took a step towards the door.

"Stop!" Mr. Collins ordered. "Her money will be sent to her father."

"But how is she to buy a place on the stage?" asked Charlotte anxiously.

"She ought to have thought about that before accepting the devil into her heart. Not another word from you, wife!"

Charlotte turned up her hands to indicate helplessness, but she cast a significant look towards the window.

Enough was enough. Elizabeth said icily, "Lady Catherine has magic and she knows it. So does Miss de Bourgh."

"You lie! Lady Catherine would never allow the taint of magic to touch her."

"She will not admit it, but you can ask Mr. Darcy, Colonel Fitzwilliam, or even Lord Matlock, and they will tell you the same. Lady Catherine is a hypocrite, and so, Cousin William, are you." She marched past him, snatched her bonnet from the vestibule before he could refuse her that as well, and left the parsonage, resisting the temptation to slam the door behind her.

Had he really cast her out with no means of getting home?

The door opened behind her and Mr. Collins flung Pepper onto the path. He did slam the door.

Elizabeth crouched down beside the cat. "Pepper, are you hurt?"

Pepper sat and began to primly wash her face. Was that blood by her mouth? She did not seem injured, so it must not be hers.

"Good Pepper! I hope you bit him hard," said Elizabeth vindictively.

The cat gave her look of great satisfaction.

How could Mr. Collins throw her out without the means to care for herself? If Colonel Fitzwilliam and Mr. Darcy were not there to help her, she would have no choice but to start for London on foot, hardly a safe proposition for a young woman alone. Walking in slippers never meant to be used out of doors, her feet would be bleeding long before she arrived. And Faerie could no longer be a refuge for her, not while there were glamour traps.

"We might as well start out for Rosings," she told Pepper. She had to do something. Walking through the grove would be easier on her slippers than the gravel on the road. If only she had her half-boots! But she would never see her half-boots again, the ones that had fit perfectly and kept her feet dry, nor her beloved blue dress, nor the shift of the finest linen Mrs. Gardiner had given her for Christmas. All those would be nothing more than ashes soon. Her breath caught on a sob. How utterly unfair this was! Lady Catherine was despicable, despicable. She had engineered this, no doubt in revenge for Elizabeth revealing her magic. Wicked, detestable woman!

What would Mr. Darcy say when he learned of this? She could picture him descending on Mr. Collins like an avenging angel. The thought almost made her laugh. Yes, far better to think about that than what she had lost. But Mr. Darcy had left for London that morning. What if Colonel Fitzwilliam had decided to go with him? Then she would have no recourse until they returned. Perhaps Charlotte would manage to help her somehow, to put money or food outside the window, but it would be a long, cold night without her pelisse. Oh, damn Mr. Collins!

She stopped short and, suddenly weak, leaned against a tree. Losing all her possessions was the least of her worries. Mr. Collins would insist on writing to Sir William Lucas with the news she had been exposed as a witch. Within days everyone in Meryton would know. She squeezed her eyes shut. Here she was again, facing the fate she had worried about if Mr. Darcy guessed her secret. And it had been so lovely, those few days at Rosings when she had felt no need to hide her magic! Now she would have to go away after all, to leave everything, and move to a refuge for wisewomen. No home, no family, no friends.

"Mrrow."

"Yes, at least I will still have you, Pepper," she said in a shaky voice. "That will be a comfort."

Her eyes must be red, but she did not care. It did not stop her from knocking on the door of Rosings House.

When the gaunt butler opened the door, she said, "I am here to see Colonel Fitzwilliam." If the butler thought it was inappropriate for a single lady to call on a gentleman, that was his problem. Elizabeth no longer cared.

He looked down his nose at her. "Lady Catherine has given instructions that you are not to be admitted under any circumstances."

Elizabeth gritted her teeth. "Then I will ask you to take a message to Colonel Fitzwilliam telling him I wish to speak to him."

"I cannot provide you any such services. Good day, Miss Bennet." He closed the door in her face.

Astounded, she glared at the door, her distress overpowered by fierce rage. Lady Catherine meant to make her helpless and destitute.

Elizabeth refused to oblige her, no matter what it took. She would find the colonel somehow. She could probably go in through the kitchen door since the staff were accustomed to her presence at Rosings, but she might be seen if she had to wander from room to room hunting for him. If she knew where he might be, it would be feasible.

"Pepper? Would you be willing to look in the windows to see where Colonel Fitzwilliam is?"

Normally Pepper would have considered such a request and perhaps waited to be bribed with a treat, but this time she simply walked behind a bush and emerged as a raven. She must realize how desperate a situation this was. The bird flew to the house, pausing on each windowsill for a minute or two, seeming to pick random windows each time.

Pepper flew out of sight to the other side of the house. Elizabeth chewed the side of her thumb, a habit she had left behind in childhood. What would she do if she could not find the colonel? Darcy had intended to return tomorrow morning, but he could easily change those plans. There was no need for him to return before Beltane. Two days away. Two nights when she would have no shelter and no way to protect herself. Her stomach churned.

Her nerves were nearly shattered by the time the white raven returned and perched on the same bush. "Where is he, Pepper? Will you show me where he is?"

The bird only tipped her head to one side.

Foreboding choked her. "He is not there, is he? That is why Lady Catherine thought she could do this to me." He must have gone to London with Mr. Darcy, leaving her helpless and alone. Was Lady Catherine watching her through the window and laughing?

At least she could discover whether Colonel Fitzwilliam had left or not. She set off for the stables. Apparently no one there had been instructed not to speak to her, as the stable master greeted her politely and asked how he could help her.

"I understand Mr. Darcy left for London this morning," she said.

"Aye, so he did, miss."

"Did Colonel Fitzwilliam accompany him?" She held her breath.

"No, miss. The colonel is out riding."

Her mind could hardly comprehend the words. "Does that mean he will return today?" Her voice shook.

"Aye, miss, he will be back before dinner, if not sooner."

By dinner the last stage to London would have left. But he would help her, would he not? She had hardly spoken to him since her return from Faerie, but he could not have changed that much.

"Is something the matter, miss?"

She burst into tears, his kindly words more than she could bear. Covering her face with her hands, she ordered herself to stop, but that only made her cry harder.

"Now then, miss, surely it cannot be that bad." The poor man clearly had no idea what to do.

"I... I am sorry. I need to speak to the colonel quite desperately."

He seemed relieved by this. "No need to worry, then, miss. He'll be back soon. You can wait for him at the house."

"No! Not the house. I will wait for him here, if I may."

His brow furrowed. "Here? In the stables?"

She swallowed hard, trying to keep the sobs back. "Is there a bench I can sit on where I will see him when he comes?"

His expression cleared. "Yes, right out here in the yard. You will be in the shade, and no one will bother you."

"Thank you," she said wearily. "That will be perfect."

She let her emotions grow numb along with her body. Although it was not as cold as winter, the April weather would have been easier to tolerate with her pelisse. Elizabeth was thoroughly chilled after half an hour or so.

At last Colonel Fitzwilliam trotted into the stable yard on a black horse, dismounted fluidly, and came straight to her, his riding crop still in his hand. "What is the matter, Miss Bennet?"

She tried to remember the speech she had carefully composed. "Forgive me, Colonel. I must return to London tonight, and I find myself without sufficient funds to purchase a ticket. I am hoping to impose upon you to loan me the fare, which I will repay once I reach my uncle's house." There. She had said it without starting to cry, although her voice had quavered a bit.

His brows drew together. "Miss Bennet, if you need to go to London tonight, I will take you there myself, but I must ask what has occurred to cause this urgent need? Has someone mistreated you?"

She tried to summon a shaky smile. "It is a complex story, and I do not wish to drag you into the middle of it."

He frowned. "In other words, yes, someone has mistreated you. Will you come to the house for a glass of wine? It may calm your nerves."

She should have known he would ask more questions. "Not the house," she said miserably. There was no point in hiding it. "Lady Catherine has decreed I am not to be admitted."

"What?" he cried. "That is ridiculous."

"Perhaps, but nonetheless true. That is why I waited for you here. The butler refused even to give you a message."

"That is intolerable." His expression was stormy. "I will resolve this, I promise you."

"Since I cannot remain here anyway, it does not matter." She raised her chin to disguise her trembling lips. "Mr. Collins has cast me out of his house with nothing but the clothes I am wearing. He plans to burn my other possessions. He would not even permit me to take what money I had, hence my request for a loan."

"The devil!" He jumped to his feet, his eyes burning with anger. "Why would he do such a thing?"

Elizabeth looked away, blinking hard. "He said it was on Lady Catherine's instructions, because I am a witch."

"Damn them!" He slammed his riding crop into the wall hard enough to crack the handle. Scowling, he snapped it in half, flung it on the ground, and strode across the stable yard. With his back to her, he laid one hand on the wall and appeared to study the ground.

Elizabeth bit her lip. She had known he would be angry, but she had not imagined the amiable colonel would react this strongly.

After a few minutes he returned. "Pray forgive my show of temper. I am trying to remind myself that I can postpone the pleasure of thrashing Mr. Collins until after I have arranged for your safety, but it is a struggle. And do not tell me I should not thrash him. When I think what might have happened to you, a woman, penniless and alone, had I not been here!" He sounded on the edge of fury.

Her eyes grew wet again. "That thought has already crossed my mind a number of times. I am beyond grateful for any assistance you can give me."

"I do not need your thanks for doing what any gentleman with an iota of decency would do!" he burst out.

She was too grateful for his assistance to worry about the

impropriety of it. "If I can only get to London, my uncle there will take me in."

"That is an option, but you would have to return the day after tomorrow. Perhaps we can take a room for you at the inn, with a maid to bear you company."

Elizabeth bit her lip. "If word reached them that I was a witch, a maid could not keep me safe, nor even a manservant," she said in a low voice.

"There must be a way. Let me think." He rubbed his hand over his forehead. "I have it. I know just the thing."

Richard greeted Darcy and Frederica in the imposing entrance hall of Rosings Park. "Welcome back, Darcy. Freddie, I had not expected to see you here."

His younger sister untied her bonnet. "I am in disgrace at home, and events here sounded more interesting than anything in London. I want to meet the famous Miss Bennet."

Richard raised a finger to his lips. "I strongly advise you against mentioning –"

"Is that you, Darcy?" Lady Catherine's shrill voice came from the drawing room.

Darcy made a wry face at Frederica. "I had hoped to avoid this," he said *sotto voce* before striding into the drawing room. "Yes, Aunt, I have only just returned from London. Lady Frederica has accompanied me." He bowed to Lady Catherine and her daughter.

"Frederica? Why is she here?" asked Lady Catherine querulously.

Darcy had preferred it when his aunt had been restricted to her rooms. "She wished to come, and I saw no reason to object. I am glad to see your health continues to improve."

"I have been in perfect health for days," snapped Lady Catherine.

Frederica said soothingly, "That is excellent news. I must write to my father tonight. He has been most concerned about you."

Lady Catherine ignored her. "Darcy, I do not see why you had to go running off to London on a fool's errand. I did not give you permission to leave."

As if he needed her permission! "I had vital information which had to be delivered to Lord Matlock in person. Now I must ask you to excuse me, as I need to find Miss Bennet."

Lady Catherine's face distorted with rage. Pointing a bony finger at him, she hissed, "Thou shalt not suffer a witch to live!" Her wits must still be wandering.

Richard strode in, his lips tight and his face white. What had been happening at Rosings while Darcy had been in London? "That will be quite enough, Aunt," Richard said firmly.

This time Lady Catherine shrieked the words. "Thou shalt not suffer a witch to live!"

Richard's hand snaked out and caught her wrist. "Sit down!" he commanded. "You must stop this. Miss Bennet is in London."

Confused, Darcy said, "Why did she go to London?" He winced as Frederica's foot connected with his ankle.

"It is a long story," Richard said through gritted teeth.

Lady Catherine declared, "You should have let me die before you allowed that witch to touch me!"

Richard snarled, "I wish I had taken her advice and let the surgeon cut off your arm!"

Darcy held up his hands. "Miss Bennet used no witchcraft on you, only magic, just as Richard or I would do." Out of the corner of his eye he saw Anne swooning, attended by Mrs. Jenkinson.

"A woman with magic is an abomination!"

Frederica stepped in front of Darcy. "You are a woman with

magic. So was your sister, Darcy's mother. So is your daughter Anne. So am I. None of us are abominations."

"How dare you? I have never been soiled by magic, nor has Anne!"

"That is not true." Richard swung to face Darcy. "She has been like this since you left. The servants let her out of her rooms yesterday and refused to put her back. Last night I had to throw her over my shoulder and carry her there myself, but somehow she got out again."

Lady Catherine cried, "He has abused me abominably. Laying his hands on me!"

"Richard," cried Frederica in shock. "How could you do such a thing!"

Richard glared at her. "Once you hear why I did it, you will berate me for not doing more."

Frederica crouched down by Lady Catherine's chair and placed her hand on her aunt's wrist. In a soothing, almost singsong voice, she said, "Pay no attention to Richard and Darcy. You know how foolish men can be, always angry about one thing or another. They do not understand what it means to be a lady or how hard we must strive every day. Perhaps I can explain it to them later when they are calmer."

Lady Catherine's head fell forward and she emitted a snore.

Frederica stood and brushed off her hands. "There. Now you can take her to her rooms. She will not awaken for half an hour or so. But you did not see me do that."

"See what?" asked Richard blandly. "Freddie, you may have saved her life. I was within an inch of strangling her."

"Within an inch?" asked Frederica. "It looked more like a hair's breadth to me."

Richard scooped up Lady Catherine in his arms. "I will take her upstairs and lock her in again. Maybe it will last a little longer this time."

Darcy waited impatiently until his cousin returned a few minutes later. "Why did Miss Bennet go back to London?" he demanded.

Richard put his finger to his lips for secrecy. "Come into the library and I will tell you there."

What was all this secrecy? After the wasted trip to London, Darcy was in no mood for games.

"May I join you?" asked Federica.

"If you do not mind the sight of Darcy losing his temper," Richard replied genially.

"My temper is already on edge," Darcy warned as Richard closed the library doors behind him.

"As is mine, I assure you. First, allow me to reassure you Miss Bennet is quite well and is ensconced safely at the Dower House." Richard opened a decanter and poured a generous glass of port. He offered it to Darcy. "Drink this."

"I do not want a drink. It is barely noon."

"You will need this if you want to hear the story." Richard was using his commanding officer voice, so he was not going to give in.

Annoyed, Darcy took small sip and set the glass aside. "Now what happened?"

"Lady Catherine happened. As soon as you left, she convinced the servants to let her out of her rooms. She would not listen to me, so I left her with her pet parson who had come to call. I decided it was a good day for a very long ride. I had been out for a few hours when one of the grooms came looking for me. The stable master had sent him to tell me there was a distressed young lady at the stables looking for me, crying her eyes out."

"Not Miss Elizabeth." Darcy was certain of that. She would never be found sobbing in a stable.

"It was indeed Miss Bennet, begging me to loan her money for the stagecoach to London. She did not want to tell me why, but I insisted. Mr. Collins, following our aunt's instructions, had named her a witch and cast her out of the house with nothing but the clothes on her back and without a penny to her name."

Icy rage poured through Darcy. He did not know how he had ended up on his feet, his fists clenched. "I will kill him."

"You will have to wait until he is well enough to walk and has recovered from losing a few teeth and assorted other injuries," Richard said with satisfaction. "But he is not the only culprit. When Miss Bennet came here looking for me, she was told Lady Catherine had given orders she was not to be admitted nor to leave messages. That is how she ended up at the stables."

Frederica's eyes were wide. "Are you certain Lady Catherine actually asked him to do that?"

Richard nodded emphatically. "She admitted it to me, although it appears that the detail of burning all her possessions was added by Mr. Collins in the hope of earning Lady Catherine's forgiveness for harboring Miss Bennet. Fortunately, Mrs. Collins managed to save a very few of her things by hiding them away, but if you have any spare clothing, Freddie, Miss Bennet might appreciate it. I took a few things of Anne's for her, but they are too short."

"She is at the Dower House, you say?" Darcy demanded

Richard nodded. "She wanted to go to London, but I convinced her this would be better, at least until Beltane. By the way, Darcy, I appropriated a few of the junior staff here and reassigned them to the Dower House. I told them you would dismiss them without a character if they breathed a word to Lady Catherine."

Darcy wished he could dismiss Lady Catherine without a character. He could not speak to her now, not when his fingers itched to go around her neck. He would never forgive her for this.

"But why?" asked Frederica. "Why would she do such a terrible thing? She has always been difficult, but this is so much worse."

Richard grimaced. "Our aunt is not fully in her right mind yet, and perhaps that accounts for some of it, but I believe the primary reason was to protect her secret. She knew Miss Bennet must have guessed she had her own magic, but since none of us had mentioned it, she thought we had not been told. If Miss Bennet was the only one who knew, she wanted to dispose of her and discredit her. It seems not to have occurred to her that I would take Miss Bennet's side against her."

Darcy's feet started moving towards the door. He had to reach Elizabeth.

"Where are you going?" asked Richard sharply. "Do not do anything rash."

Frederica chuckled. "One of the Fighting Fitzwilliams telling Darcy not to be rash. Impossible."

"I will have you know I was remarkably restrained, Freddie," said Richard. "I broke my riding crop in half when she told me, but I did not thrash Mr. Collins until after I had arranged a safe place for her."

"I am going to the Dower House," said Darcy icily.

"I will come with you," said Richard. "Freddie, you might want to stay there with Miss Bennet."

"I have never met her, but I am quite certain I will prefer her company to Lady Catherine's," declared Frederica.

Richard said, "Darcy, one more thing. Miss Bennet has been very concerned about your reaction to the news. If you can at least appear calm, that will help her."

"Welcome," Elizabeth said stiffly. "Lady Frederica, it is a pleasure to make your acquaintance."

Richard laughed. "You need not worry about Freddie, Miss Bennet. She is in disgrace with our father, and I promise you there is no one more in agreement with you on binding spells than she is."

"That is why I am in disgrace," Frederica said candidly. "I had not known about the binding spell on Cousin Anne until Darcy mentioned it, and my reaction was a bit unseemly."

"Explosive is the word I might have used," said Darcy. He had to appear calm for Elizabeth's sake.

"Well, yes. Mama thought it would be wise to send me away to calm down, but I do not know how she thinks that will happen when I have to see poor Cousin Anne's sufferings every day."

"Mother must have had an ulterior motive," said Richard resignedly. "She always does."

Elizabeth canted her head and looked at Darcy questioningly. "Permit me to guess. Colonel Fitzwilliam told you to appear calm."

Darcy sucked in a sharp breath. "I beg of you not to tease me on this matter. I am sorry I was not here when you were in need."

"I am just as glad you were not here to see what I looked like yesterday." But she said it in the kindly manner.

Frederica stepped close to Elizabeth and held a hand at the level of the tops of their heads. "Good. We are much of a height, and I imagine my clothes will fit you well enough."

Elizabeth's cheeks colored. "I am not accustomed to asking for the assistance of strangers, and I wish I could say that it is unnecessary, but sadly, it would be a help. I do not need much, just a few things until I can obtain new ones."

"I have too many dresses, anyway. You may ask anyone." Frederica's gaze traveled down to Elizabeth's feet. "Shoes. Are you in need of shoes?"

Elizabeth looked away suddenly, blinking rapidly.

Richard said softly, "There were none among the things Mrs. Collins sent."

"What? You had to walk to Rosings in those?" Frederica sounded outraged. "Richard, I hope you hit that man very, very hard."

146

Elizabeth said quickly, "Mr. Darcy, did you meet with any success in your conversations with Lord Matlock?"

He hated to give her more bad news. "Lord Matlock was very interested in trying to preserve the faerie groves. He took me to Whitehall to meet with Mr. Pitt to discuss what the government could do, but that was less successful. At first Pitt said he could not help since it is impossible to legislate how landowners could use their land. Then he discouraged us from even raising the issue because it would only lead to greater destruction of faerie groves."

"But why?" cried Elizabeth.

"Because most landowners consider the fay a nuisance. Now they have become an active danger as well. Why protect the rings and hope for the best when you could destroy the rings and remove both the danger and the nuisance?" Darcy rubbed his forehead. "I am sorry. I did my best."

Richard frowned. "There must be a reason why the fay come to our world. We need to find out what it is."

If only he had an answer! But Darcy had been wracking his brain for reasons why contact with fay should be protected. His uncle wanted it so he could indulge his researcher's curiosity. Darcy did not even have that much of a reason, only a sense that the fay were a natural part of England. But foremost in his mind was Elizabeth. Faerie was part of her.

Elizabeth said, "Thousands of people across England leave bread and milk out for the fay every day, and each one tells stories of gardens and crops that would not grow when someone failed to do so. It might be superstition, or we might be risking crop failures across England if the groves are destroyed."

Darcy said slowly, "The last two harvests have not been good. The fay attacks also started two years ago."

Frederica rubbed her fingers together thoughtfully. "I wonder if harvests are worse where groves have been destroyed."

"Was anything decided?" Elizabeth asked.

"Nothing will be done at least until we know more," said Darcy. "They suggested I should explain to the Sidhe that this is their own fault, and their war risks destroying all the groves. I told them I would rather walk into King George's presence and speak treason than threaten the Sidhe lord."

"I agree," said Elizabeth. "If we have nothing positive to offer, I think we are better off trying to learn more about the situation."

"I also spoke to Lord Matlock about the spell on Cousin Anne," said Darcy. "He will not remove it. He also said there would be no point in trying to get someone else to do so, since he had designed it so no one else could break it."

"That was when I became explosive," said Frederica.

"She truly did." Darcy was glad of the opportunity to change the subject. "Richard, I had not realized your sister is also a Fighting Fitzwilliam, although she uses words instead of fists or swords. I would not want to cross her!"

"Fighting Fitzwilliams?" asked Elizabeth.

Richard grinned. "The *ton* nickname for the three Fitzwilliam brothers. We are known for, ah, having a bit of a temper when it comes to questions of our honor."

"A bit of a temper!" Frederica mocked. "The three of you have fought more duels than the rest of the *ton* put together."

Richard wagged his finger at her. "You should not complain, Freddie. That is why you never have to fight off impudent young men. They know better than to try anything with our sister."

Frederica put her hands on her hips. "I do not have to fight them off because I stop them myself," she said in a dulcet voice. "There is a reason why I spent months perfecting a spell to make someone fall asleep immediately."

Her brother's eyes narrowed. "Names, Freddie. I want names," he said fiercely.

Frederica turned to Elizabeth. "You see?"

"I do. I saw a little of it yesterday as well." Elizabeth's eyes were dancing. "I cannot say I objected at the time."

"Names, Freddie. Now." Richard's hands were clenched into fists.

"So you can challenge them to a duel and make sure everyone in London knows they tried to kiss me? How, precisely, will that be helpful in protecting my reputation?"

"Names," Richard rumbled. "This is your last chance."

"Names?" said Freddie airily. "Let me see. Humpty Dumpty, Peter Piper, Jack the Giant Killer –"

Darcy spoke over her. "Miss Elizabeth, would you care to join me in the dining room until these two manage to settle their differences?"

Richard glared daggers at him, grabbed Frederica's elbow and pulled her out of the drawing room and slammed the doors shut behind them.

"Oh, my," said Elizabeth faintly. "I had no idea the good colonel could be so...."

"Belligerent?" Darcy offered. "As you can see, it runs in the family."

"I think I like Lady Frederica, especially if she fought with Lord Matlock."

"She did. She called him a hypocrite, liar, and a great many names I had no idea any lady knew, and when he told her to behave herself, she threw a glass of wine in his face and told him he was a sorcerer's spawn and she hoped someone would put him under a binding spell someday. That was when Lady Matlock announced Frederica would be coming here with me today."

Elizabeth pressed her hand to her chest. "Good heavens! What did he do to her?"

"He roared and grumbled for a time and threatened to cut off his sons' allowances for teaching her inappropriate words. His bark is worse than his bite."

"I remain unconvinced of that, but you should be proud of me for overcoming my prejudices. Who was the first person I asked for help when Mr. Collins named me a witch? A mage," she teased.

"I am glad you were able to trust Richard that far." It was not fair to feel bitter that it was Richard she trusted. He had not been there, but it was hard not to believe she preferred his cousin. "Are you finding it comfortable here?"

"It is quite comfortable, I thank you."

"We can send over more servants from the main house if you wish." It was all he had to offer.

Elizabeth shook her head. "There is no need. You would hardly know the house has been empty."

Somehow Darcy managed to keep a façade of calm as the discussion continued, but he knew he would not be able to maintain it forever. The day after tomorrow was Beltane, and neither of them needed any extra stress before that. But afterwards, he was going to tell Elizabeth he wanted the right to protect her.

His sleep was haunted by the image of Elizabeth, alone and helpless.

# Chapter 6

The following afternoon, Richard examined the Dower House drawing room from the armchair in which he was sprawled. "Pleasant place, this. I should visit you more frequently. There is a delightful absence of Lady Catherine here."

A footman stepped into the room and bowed. "There is a caller for Mr. Darcy. I regret that we have not yet located a salver for calling cards. I hope you will forgive the impropriety." He handed a card to Mr. Darcy.

"Naturally. One can hardly expect a household to be fully set up on such short notice." Darcy's eyebrows rose as he read the card. "Show him in."

The footman left and reappeared a minute later. "Viscount Eversleigh for Mr. Darcy."

"Eversleigh!" cried Darcy. "I had been wishing you were here. What brings you to Rosings?"

"Lord Matlock told me about your recent encounter in Faerie, and I wished to know more about it. You had already left London, so I had to follow you. The butler at the main house directed me here, saying Lady Catherine was indisposed. I hope she was not the one screaming, 'Thou shalt not suffer a witch to live.'"

"Not again," groaned Richard. "I was so enjoying the respite."

"Miss Bennet," said Darcy, "May I present Viscount Eversleigh? He is a distant cousin on the Darcy side and a rising star in the

Collegium. Miss Bennet is the one who led me into Faerie."

Elizabeth curtsied. "I am also the witch thou shalt not suffer to live, so you might wish to deny my acquaintance should you speak to Lady Catherine."

"It is a pleasure, Miss Bennet. Lady Frederica, Colonel Fitzwilliam, I am glad to see you again. Darcy, why were you wishing to see me?"

"I would like your opinion on whether a particular spell can be broken. You are ten times the spellmaster I am," said Darcy, "but first I should ask what your position is on forbidding women the use of magic."

"It is a barbaric rule," said Eversleigh promptly.

"How odd," said Elizabeth slowly. "The Sidhe lord also called it barbaric."

Eversleigh bowed to Elizabeth. "I suspect most Sidhe would say precisely the same. Miss Bennet, you have nothing to fear from me."

"I am glad to hear it," said Darcy. "The spell to be removed is a binding spell."

"I will be happy to help if I can," said Eversleigh. "But first I would like to hear more about the situation in Faerie. Matlock seemed to think you might be out of your depth, not that he could offer anything better. I have some small knowledge of Faerie, and given the gravity of the situation, I thought perhaps I should put myself at your disposal."

"Odd," drawled the colonel. "I do not recollect hearing about your interest in Faerie before."

Eversleigh looked amused. "Of course not. It is no secret that I harbor political ambitions. Being a mage is already a strike against me, and a connection with the fay would be a killing blow. However, war with the fay would be even worse. I would not have mentioned it were the situation less grave."

"What sort of knowledge do you have?" asked Darcy.

Eversleigh flicked open his enameled snuff box and took a pinch.

"Perhaps this is something you and I can discuss in private. Although I have the greatest faith in the discretion of both Lady Frederica and Colonel Fitzwilliam, I do not wish to put them in the situation of having to keep a secret from their father."

Frederica said, "If you are willing to trust me, I would be pleased to be part of your discussion. It would not be the first thing I have kept from my father."

"Having been in this from the beginning," said the colonel, "I would feel it rather odd to be excluded at this stage. I will, however, bow to your wishes, Eversleigh."

"Then perhaps we can all discuss it." Eversleigh stopped to straighten his already perfectly aligned cuffs. "I hope you will forgive my hesitancy. I have never discussed this matter with mortals before."

Darcy eyed him suspiciously. "That sounds as if you have more than a slight knowledge of Faerie."

Eversleigh bowed to him. "You are quite correct. To put it bluntly, something I am generally at great pains to avoid, I am half mortal, half fay."

The colonel's eyebrows shot up. "You have kept that a very close secret."

"That was my intention," said Eversleigh dryly. "My mother took me on several occasions to Faerie to visit a gentleman of the Sidhe who – how shall I say it? – bore more than a slight resemblance to me. Those visits stopped when I went off to school, but I retained a certain curiosity about Faerie. In due course I went off on my Grand Tour and returned with stories of all the usual attractions. Those stories came from reading books. I had actually spent those two years in Faerie."

Richard chuckled, shaking his head. "And my father, so desperate to gain even the least knowledge of Faerie, knew nothing of this, despite working closely with you?"

With a cool smile, Eversleigh said, "I have never had an interest in becoming the subject of academic research. My goal, apart from pure curiosity, was to position myself should there ever be the need for an emissary between Faerie and the mortal world."

Frederica nodded. "And now the time has come when the Sidhe are so desperate for an emissary that they are willing to accept any mortal who crosses their path."

"Precisely, Lady Frederica. As it happens, I am not likely to be well received by those who disagree with their king, as my fay connections are strongly tied to him. However, as a mortal, and therefore on the opposite side of the war, I must naturally support whichever side is working for peace."

Darcy said, "A convincing argument, I would think. Miss Bennet and I are to meet with the Sidhe lord tomorrow at sunset, and while he insisted no one else should accompany us, any insight you can give us into the politics of Faerie would be greatly appreciated. I know nothing of even the basic laws of nature there."

Elizabeth smiled. "Mr. Darcy is kindly trying to avoid saying that I am somewhat useless as well. I do have some knowledge of Faerie, but I am not aware of what I know. If he had asked me the proper address for a Sidhe lord, I could not have told him, but faced with one, I knew what to say."

Darcy looked at her soberly. "You have a great advantage over me in that you are comfortable with the fay. They do not strike you as frightening, foreign, and incomprehensible."

Elizabeth considered this. "I suppose that is true. I am no more troubled by them than I am troubled by cows or dogs."

"Rrowr." Pepper jumped up onto Elizabeth's lap and began to wash her face.

"Or cats," said Elizabeth with a laugh, stroking Pepper's back.

Eversleigh raised his quizzing glass to inspect the cat. "Odd. I have never seen a white phouka before."

Elizabeth shared a surprised look with Darcy. "How can you tell she is not just a cat?"

The viscount furrowed his forehead. "The same way I can tell she is not a cow or a dog, I suppose."

Elizabeth laughed. "That is fair enough, I suppose, but you have just given away my secret. The colonel and Lady Frederica were not aware Pepper is fay."

Wide-eyed, Frederica asked, "Is she truly a phouka? Does she change shapes?"

Elizabeth nodded. "She can change into a white raven in our world, but in Faerie she became a horse."

Richard chuckled. "Do you suppose my father would be more horrified or pleased to discover that it was a fay cat that attacked him?"

"Pleased," said Frederica without hesitation. "It is the closest he has ever managed to come to one of the fay."

"You spent a long time talking to Miss Bennet after dinner." Darcy tried not to sound jealous, but watching Elizabeth and Eversleigh's heads leaning together as they conversed had been enough to spoil his digestion.

"An interesting girl." Eversleigh accepted the glass of port.

Darcy could not help himself. "She is not unprotected."

Eversleigh turned a surprised gaze on him. "I am not planning to seduce her, if that is your concern. I simply wished to know more about her."

Richard shot Darcy a warning look. "We feel rather responsible for her. If she had not tried to heal Lady Catherine at our request, no one would be calling her witch, and her cousin would not have thrown her out of his house."

"I confess that is where I am mystified," said Eversleigh. "I understand she does not wish to return to her father's house, but she has an uncle who would take her in. Instead she is staying here with Lady Frederica whom she has just met. You are an acquaintance of a few weeks standing, and Darcy only slightly more. It is an odd situation in which to find a gently bred young lady."

"I agree. It is not an ideal situation, but with the Sidhe lord insisting on her involvement, it seemed simplest to keep her here," said Richard. "After Beltane, I expect she will go to her uncle."

"Unless he continues to insist on her involvement," said Darcy flatly. Was it wrong for him to hope for that?

"I could give you better advice if I knew which Sidhe this is," said Eversleigh. "Miss Bennet spent ten minutes telling me every detail she could remember about him, but I can think of three or four Sidhe who would match that description."

"Perhaps he will give his name when we meet." Darcy was looking forward to this meeting even less after hearing Eversleigh's views on the convoluted relationships of the Sidhe.

"It would be a poor idea to ask his name if he does not offer it. I will make some suggestions to Miss Bennet about identifying signs to look for."

Was Eversleigh manufacturing opportunities to speak to Elizabeth? "Perhaps I can help you with that."

Eversleigh set down his glass of port. "Darcy, I assure you I have no designs on Miss Bennet. In fact, I feel rather protective of her. Are you concerned that I will be giving her expectations?"

"Possibly," said Richard.

Darcy said, "No. She does not think in those terms."

"I am glad to hear it, but I will make a point of indicating to her that I am not on the marriage market. Will that satisfy you?"

It would have to, but Darcy intended to keep a close watch on him in any case.

"You have made quite a conquest," Lady Frederica told Elizabeth.

How had she guessed about Darcy's interest in her? "I do not know what you mean."

"The elusive Viscount Eversleigh. He is always careful to avoid the appearance of interest in any single young lady, yet he spoke to you for nearly half an hour," said Lady Frederica coolly.

Eversleigh? Elizabeth gave a disbelieving laugh. "Only to ask me questions, I assure you! His manner was not in the least bit flirtatious. I doubt he even noticed what I looked like."

Lady Frederica's fingertip traced the gilded carving in the arm of her chair. "You do not know how unusual that behavior is for him."

"Doubtless you are well acquainted with his habits in the *ton*, but this is different. Most likely he simply enjoyed being able to speak about Faerie with a mortal woman."

"Yes, he would like that." Frederica's voice was flat.

This was ridiculous. Clearly Lady Frederica had an interest in Eversleigh herself. Elizabeth said, "Even if he had an interest in me, which I doubt, I am well aware that a viscount could never offer me an honorable connection. If he were to flirt with me, I would assume his intentions were dishonorable and pay no attention."

"Wise of you." But Frederica did not sound mollified.

The next day was Beltane. Elizabeth awoke with a frisson of excitement. Tonight she would see the Sidhe lord again.

Lady Frederica had already finished breakfast when Elizabeth arrived. "Oh, good, you are awake. I thought we might go into the village this morning to see the maypole dancing."

Elizabeth's pleasure in the day faded. She had always loved May Day celebrations. "I had best remain here, but I hope you will go and tell me all about it later."

Lady Frederica's brow furrowed. "Do you wish to rest in preparation for your meeting?"

"No." A little distraction would be welcome, but not this. "I am known in the village, and I have treated a few of them when they were ill. Now I have been named a witch, and their clergyman has thrown me out of his house. I do not wish to put the villagers in an uncomfortable position with my presence." She had to learn not to let this hurt; it was a price she would be paying for the rest of her life.

"That is horrid!" declared Lady Frederica. "How could they accept your help and then reject you for the very help you gave?"

Elizabeth helped herself to a roll and jam on the sideboard. It gave her a moment to get her expression under control. "It is always that way. Many of the common people suspect that wisewomen use a little magic, but they are happier being able to pretend it is not true. Some wisewomen employ smoke, rabbit's feet, and the like to give their patients the comfort of thinking they were healed by charms, not by magic."

"Do you do that?"

Elizabeth managed to smile. "Until quite recently, I was the quiet apprentice in the background and did nothing. Sometimes I have one of the family rub lavender oil on the patient's temples to draw out the evil humors. Lavender oil does nothing of the sort, but it exerts a calming influence and distracts attention from what I am truly doing."

"How interesting. I wish I could watch you someday."

"There is little to see since I cannot use spells, only wild magic. May I ask how you managed to learn so many spells? Do your father and brothers ignore the rules against teaching women magic?"

"Oh, no, they will not violate Collegium rules, even if they find them ridiculous. My youngest brother will sometimes leave spell books open where I would be likely to come across them. He always says it is an accident, but Jasper enjoys mischief like that. I have a circle of lady friends who have managed to learn a spell or two from observing their husbands and fathers. We pool our knowledge and teach each other. All very discreetly, of course."

"How fortunate you are to have friends with magic! Wisewomen are usually lonely." Elizabeth would have loved to have a confidante with magic.

"And none of your sisters have magic? That is unusual."

Elizabeth shrugged. "Perhaps they do but are unaware of it, or I suppose they might be hiding it as I did. My eldest sister knows enough about my activities to guess, although she never said anything, but my younger sisters must have been surprised to hear I am a witch."

"I wish you would not use that word! It is so ugly and has been used so cruelly."

"I do not like it either. I never used it before, but I cannot pretend that other people are not calling me that. But I am enjoying the freedom to use my magic now. I always had to check carefully before using it, and it was easier to do things without magic than to hide it. Being exposed has been freeing. I light candles with my fingers and ask a breeze to blow away smoke from the fireplace. I have even been experimenting with new skills. Shall I show you my favorite?"

"Pray do."

"I need a stain. There – do you see that yellowed spot on the damask chair?"

"Yes."

Elizabeth licked her forefinger, wrapped it in her handkerchief, and rubbed her covered fingertip over the stain.

"Good heavens! It is gone!"

"Not gone. It has moved to my handkerchief." Elizabeth held out the square of fabric to show a yellow stain on it. "As you can see by the number of spots, I have been hunting down stains to practice on." She was quite proud of her accomplishment. If only she had known how to do it before the ill-fated Meryton Assembly, she would have worried less about Darcy discovering her magic.

"That would be an extremely useful bit of magic. How did you figure it out?"

"The same as always. I wanted to remove a stain from my dress, and I let the magic show me how to do it."

"Do you think you could teach me how?"

"Why not? It will help to pass the day."

After breakfast at Rosings, Eversleigh asked Darcy and Richard, "What is the spell you wished to ask me about?"

Darcy flushed. "I should not have said anything. While I would like your help in removing the spell, Matlock is the one who placed it, and he does not want it removed. He is your colleague and friend, so I cannot ask you to go against his will."

"Remove one of Matlock's spells against his wishes? No. I am not prepared to do that, and I am surprised you would consider it, Darcy. I trust his judgment."

"I would have said the same until I discovered he had cast a binding spell on his niece."

"A binding spell? Ridiculous! Matlock opposes them, and he knows better than to cast a spell on a family member. There must be some misunderstanding here."

"No misunderstanding," said Richard. "He admitted it in front of both of us. He did it."

Eversleigh stared at them in disbelief and began to pace the floor. Finally he said, "If what you say is true, the spell should be removed. I am almost more shocked that he would break the rules against using magic on a relative than the binding spell itself. One of my duties on the Council of Mages is to deal with improperly set spells, usually ones set on a family member. Matlock often sends those cases to me. He knows the rules."

"Still, he seems to think he did the right thing in this case. He even warned me against trying to remove the spell myself. He said it was unbreakable."

"Unbreakable, is it? We will see about that." Eversleigh seemed offended by the idea of a spell he could not break. "I will not try to remove it behind his back, but I will do this much. I will check the spell to confirm it is of his making and to judge if I would be able to break it. If it is his, I will speak to him about it. He will see reason."

Darcy was not as certain about that. Lord Matlock could be quite obdurate when he set his mind on something.

Darcy managed to persuade Anne to join them in the drawing room, but he could not convince her companion, Mrs. Jenkinson, that there was no need to follow her. Mrs. Jenkinson reported most of Anne's activities to Lady Catherine, so their efforts would not remain secret long.

Anne seemed perfectly willing to listen to Eversleigh, whom she had met at dinner the previous evening.

"Darcy has told me you are frequently subject to fainting spells and that doctors have been unable to find a reason," said Eversleigh. "I have some expertise in the matter. Would you consent to allow me to see if I can find the source? It would only involve touching your wrist and possibly your neck where I can feel your pulse."

"If you wish, I have no objection," said Anne.

Mrs. Jenkinson said, "Miss de Bourgh, I cannot permit this without Lady Catherine's knowledge. We must wait until she is recovered."

"I do not want to wait. I hate swooning."

"Lady Catherine must make that decision," Mrs. Jenkinson insisted.

Darcy said, "I am Anne's guardian, not Lady Catherine, and I give my permission. Mrs. Jenkinson, you may leave."

"I cannot leave poor Miss de Bourgh alone with three gentlemen!"

"The doors are open. She does not need a chaperone. Now go."

"Lady Catherine will hear of this!" Mrs. Jenkinson gathered her shawl and shuffled away.

"I'm sure she will," Richard muttered.

Anne actually smiled. "Thank you, Darcy. She never listens to me." She held her hand out to Eversleigh.

Eversleigh carefully wrapped his fingers around her wrist. "I will be using magic."

Anne swooned, of course. Darcy gently laid her back on the fainting couch.

Eversleigh moved his hand to her neck and began murmuring the Latin words of a spell. After a few lines, his speech began to slow. With a puzzled look, he held out his free hand towards Richard.

Richard jumped up and put his hands around Eversleigh's wrist. If a mage as powerful as Eversleigh needed help, he must be using an enormous amount of magic. Darcy stepped out of the room and asked a footman to bring food immediately. They would be ravenous when this was over.

With Richard supplying power, the words of the spell were flowing easily again. When Eversleigh's chant finally stopped, he removed his hand from Anne's neck.

"What happened?" asked Darcy. "I thought you were only assessing the spell."

"That is what I thought, too," said Eversleigh grimly. "I suspect I know why Matlock refuses to remove the spell. I do not believe he has the ability to do so."

Richard whistled. "Are you certain? Poor Anne!"

"I cannot be certain. The standard binding spell incorporates a method for removal. It appears he excised that portion of the spell and wrapped the remainder in a strong defensive spell. I had to penetrate the defensive spell to see the actual binding spell, and I would not have made it through the defenses without Fitzwilliam's timely assistance. The actual spell would be extremely difficult to remove. Matlock is unmatched at creating spells, but I do not boast when I say I am better at removing spells than he is."

"It truly is unbreakable, then?" asked Darcy.

The footman brought in a tray of food, and Eversleigh took a piece of bread and cheese before he had even set the tray down. He bit into the bread, and when he had swallowed it, he said, "I might be able to break it, given sufficient time and several sessions. Then again, I might not. I was able to remove part of the defensive spell so it would be easier next time. The spell itself is a masterpiece. No one but Matlock could manage a two-layered spell without creating a hopeless tangle. But I will have words with him when I see him next."

"A cruel masterpiece," said Darcy. "If, after speaking to him, you are willing to try to remove it, I would support that."

"It will have to wait until we know the outcome of your meeting tonight," Eversleigh said. "But it is possible Miss de Bourgh may feel some slight relief from the weakening of the defensive spell. Usually a binding spell does not cause as much impairment as she has, which inclines me to think the defensive spell has an effect as well."

Darcy remembered the look on Anne's face when he asked her whether her thoughts drifted away. "Let us hope so."

"What do you think?" Darcy gestured to the table laden with a wide selection of cold meats, pastries, bread, cheese, and fruit. The servants had arranged it under the whitethorn with three chairs, believing it to be a picnic for the three ladies.

"Excellent," said Eversleigh. "Given how much the Sidhe value food from the mortal world, you could serve breadcrumbs and he would happily eat those, but this does him honor." He peered into one of the jugs. "Good. You have milk. That is better than wine for them."

"Elizabeth's suggestion," Darcy said. "But if the Sidhe crave mortal food so much, why do they not simply take it?"

Eversleigh smiled. "It must be freely given, or it will not nourish them. In the old days, food was left out as tribute for them. Now it is in short supply."

Elizabeth shaded her eyes and gazed into the grove. "I wonder if he will even come. Perhaps he has thought better of it."

Eversleigh said, "He will come. If he offers you food from his hand, be aware that eating it will create a bond between you. Refusing it would be an insult, though."

"He has already bonded us," said Elizabeth calmly.

Darcy stared at her in shock. "He did?"

"When he gave us the faerie cakes before we left his keep." She sounded completely undisturbed by it.

Darcy rounded on Eversleigh. "What is this bond?"

"Nothing to worry about. It creates a certain amount of shared loyalty and trust, but it is not a strong bond. It is a good sign that he offered it to you. It means he will not betray you."

He had taken on a bond without knowing it? It was a sickening sensation. "What else creates bonds?" He did not want to make that mistake again.

"Food is the weakest bond. Sharing a cup is somewhat stronger," said Eversleigh. "Mingling your blood in a spell will augment your magic and form a strong loyalty tie. Beyond that is only claiming blood right, and you need not worry about that."

Sharing a cup. The dryad had given them wine from the same cup. "What if two mortals in Faerie share a cup?"

Eversleigh looked thoughtful. "I do not know if it would work for two mortals."

"It does." Elizabeth sounded certain.

"Does it? Interesting," said Eversleigh. "I wonder if food binding would work between mortals in Faerie. That is hardly relevant to tonight, though, and it is time for us to go and leave you to your meeting."

Frederica gave Elizabeth a quick hug. "Good luck."

After the others left, Darcy sat with Elizabeth by the whitethorn, Pepper in his lap, remembering how the dryad had offered the cup first to Elizabeth and then to him. When the dryad had returned the cup to Elizabeth, she had hesitated before taking it, then drank from it and offered it directly to him. She must have understood what she was doing, and she did it anyway. Why? And what did the bond mean? They had not quarreled since then, and he had been more aware of what she might be feeling. He had thought it was only from knowing her better. Before that day, it had seemed impossible that he and Elizabeth could work together in harmony as they were now. Something had definitely changed, and Elizabeth had been willing to make that change.

The sun neared the horizon. Darcy drummed his fingers on the table, but Elizabeth seemed quite at ease. Was she truly relaxed, or was she merely pretending?

"I wonder how the fay celebrate Beltane," Elizabeth said idly.

"The stories speak of dancing and music, but there must be more. Do you suppose they have maypoles?"

They had spent so much time planning for this meeting, and now he could think of nothing but why Elizabeth had accepted the bond with him. If only he could ask her! But instead he had to make appropriate conversation. "I cannot say. When all this is over – and no, I do not know what I mean by that – I hope to journey to Oxford and search through the Collegium library for references to the fay. It will be interesting to see how much truth there is in the old books."

"I have just been contemplating all the possible definitions of sunset. Is it when the sun first touches the horizon or when it disappears completely? Perhaps it is somewhere in between."

"An interesting philosophical –"

Out of nowhere the Sidhe lord appeared in front of them, accompanied by a Sidhe lady dressed in diaphanous silks that fluttered around her legs. Instinctively Darcy averted his eyes as he rose to bow. Like the lord, she wore wrist cuffs of silver filigree.

"I am pleased to see you followed my instructions." The Sidhe's voice chimed like a bell. "If you are carrying a firearm, be aware that it will not function in my presence."

As if a pistol could somehow protect him against the Sidhe! "I am unarmed." Darcy stepped away from his chair. "Honored lady." Since there were only three chairs, he would stand. A bit awkward but –

The lady waved her hand and a fourth chair appeared, a match to the other three. She gracefully sat in it. "You honor us with your preparations."

To think Darcy had once been proud of his prowess as one of the most powerful mages in England! Compared to the Sidhe, he was no more than a child playing with toys.

Elizabeth said, "We are honored by your presence. We hope you may enjoy these small tokens of our appreciation. May I offer you a plate?"

The two Sidhe did not hesitate to heap their plates high. Their manners were elegant as they ate steadily, making no conversation. Darcy and Elizabeth preserved the silence as they nibbled at their cake for the sake of politeness. Darcy refilled the milk glasses twice and wondered if he should have asked for a second pitcher.

Finally the Sidhe finished their food.

"Will you be able to stop the destruction of the groves?" The Sidhe lord wasted no further time on niceties.

"By ourselves, no," said Darcy. "I have spoken to the Master of the Collegium of Mages, our most important mage, and he also wishes to stop the destruction. Unfortunately, according to a government minister, it could be detrimental to our cause if we instruct people to leave the groves alone."

The Sidhe scowled. "They will not listen to you?"

"Honored lord," said Elizabeth. "First, permit me to say that Mr. Darcy and I do not agree with the position I am about to explain. Because of the recent attacks on humans, the government fears people will see the faerie rings as a danger rather than something to protect, and some might believe they can prevent the attacks by destroying all the rings."

Darcy braced himself for a thunderous explosion, but instead the Sidhe lord exchanged a perplexed glance with the lady.

The lady tittered. "How remarkably foolish of them."

"Why?" asked Darcy urgently. "We have lost the memory of why the groves are important. Forgive our ignorance. What would happen if all the groves were destroyed?"

The Sidhe lord gave him a look of pure disgust, but the lady took pity on him. "Why, when a grove is destroyed, the lesser fay, the ones who can only use that particular ring, wither and die. The Sidhe can use any ring, so it matters less to us. When it is only an occasional grove lost, the lesser fay at nearby rings attempt to take on extra duties around the lost ring. If they did not..." She shrugged delicately.

Darcy leaned forward. "What would happen? What are these duties you mention? This is what we must know if we are to convince our government the rings must be saved."

"Why, many crops would fail and fewer babies would be born, both humans and animals. Your mages would lose their power, since it emanates from the faerie rings."

Elizabeth paled. "No crops would grow?"

"They would struggle. Seeds would still sprout but would grow poorly. The land would become barren."

His mouth dry, Darcy said, "That changes the question. There should be no difficulty protecting the groves if we can convince the government of this."

Elizabeth said slowly, "I can see why it is in our best interest to protect the groves, but how does it benefit the Sidhe?"

The lady's laugh chimed harmoniously. "Why, our vitality comes from you, from having those with human blood among us and by mingling our blood with yours."

Darcy's mind was racing. "Honored lord, I will report what I have learned to the mages and to the minister. Lord Matlock, the Master of the Collegium, will wish to meet with you to confirm my reports, if that would be possible."

"No. Only the two of you." His expression glacial, the Sidhe added, "Meeting with your leader would make it appear as if I am betraying my king. No one will question my desire to spend time with a beautiful young mortal who stumbled into my hall in Faerie."

Elizabeth blushed. Darcy ignored a rising tide of jealousy.

Darcy said carefully, "We did speak to another mortal who wishes to stop the war. He asked us to give you this." Darcy reached under the table and produced the basket Eversleigh had provided, filled with fine sweetmeats he had brought from London for this purpose. Uncertain which of the Sidhe to present it to, he set it on the table between them.

The lord pulled the fine linen cloth from the top of the basket, revealing a letter. He read it with a frown before handing it to the lady. Her eyebrows rose as she perused it.

"Do you know what this says?" demanded the lord.

"Viscount Eversleigh told me it says that he wished you to know he supported your endeavor, and that he has a great deal to lose in the event of open war. He will not reveal what he knows to the king and hopes he can be of service to you." Had he forgotten anything?

Elizabeth added, "He cannot reveal who you are since we do not know your name."

The lady inclined her head. "You have shown us honor. I am called Aislinn."

The lord said nothing.

Darcy tried a different tack. "If we can protect the groves, will that be enough to stop the attacks?"

"No. We must also remove Oberon from the influence of his mortal-hating son. It will not be simple; he is very attached to the boy. But that is not a task for you."

The lady said something in a musical language incomprensible to Darcy, but she seemed to be asking her companion a question.

The lord's eyes narrowed, and he answered her at some length.

Elizabeth made a soft choking sound and interrupted the lady's reply – and spoke in the same language. Darcy stared at her, his breath hitching. Why should he be so surprised she had kept one more secret from him, and why did it have to hurt?

Elizabeth turned to him apologetically. "I was just telling the honored lord and Lady Aislinn that in fairness they ought to know I understand their speech."

Darcy said stiffly, "I had not been aware you spoke the language of the fay."

"I had not been aware of it myself, and I find it quite disturbing," she said with an edge of sharpness.

The lord placed two elongated fingers under Elizabeth's chin and studied her face. How much could he see in the dying light?

In his chiming voice, he said, "Someone has tampered with your memories."

Elizabeth stiffened. "Who did it?"

"That I cannot tell you, but it seems to affect only your oldest memories."

"My father," she whispered bitterly.

"Unlikely," Darcy said. "I know of no human mage who has the power to change memories. That would be far more difficult than a binding spell. Could it have been a fay?"

The lord lifted his chin. "There are those among us who have that ability. It is a tricky business, mortal memory."

If only Darcy could see Elizabeth's face! But she must be devastated, given her fear of binding spells altering her mind. The least he could do was to take the conversational burden from her. "What is the next step for us, then?"

The lady said, "I would like to introduce the young lady to our queen. She has no love for either this war or Oberon's son, and she has greatly missed having mortal visitors. She might benefit from hearing a mortal perspective on the war."

"Might I accompany her on this visit to provide her with a mortal companion in Faerie?" He did not like the idea of Elizabeth alone in Faerie, especially after the lord had called her beautiful.

The lady's silvery laugh sent a shiver down his spine. "My dear boy, if I were to take a handsome mortal man into Titania's presence, any hope of serious discussion would be at an end. Our queen is fond of handsome mortals."

Elizabeth asked hesitantly, "Might I take a female companion?"

"If she has fay blood, or, as you mortals call it, magic, and if she comes as a friend to Faerie, I would have no objection. Do you have someone in mind?"

"Mr. Darcy's cousin. She is visiting here."

"Bring her to the faerie ring early tomorrow morning. I will sense your presence there."

The lord looked searchingly at Darcy. "Tell your friend that Cathael appreciates his assurances."

"I shall, honored lord."

Pepper stood, stretched, arched her back and made a trilling sound.

Sounding amused, Lady Aislinn said, "As if I could stop you, phouka." And with that, both Sidhe disappeared, along with the basket.

"Cathael? Not whom I would have expected, but I suppose it makes sense. He is young enough, only a century or two, to take risks like involving mortals in his struggle to stop the war. He is not particularly influential among the Sidhe. Aislinn is less of a surprise. She gets on well with everyone and dislikes conflict," said Eversleigh. "It is a good sign that they offered you their names."

"I wish you would tell us something of the etiquette of the Faerie court," complained Frederica, who had been practically bursting with excitement since learning she would accompany Elizabeth to Faerie.

Eversleigh said, "It is better if I do not instruct you on what to expect. That way you will seem to be innocent outsiders."

"What if we inadvertently offend the queen?" Frederica asked.

"She is not the sort of lady to take offense at an honest mistake, I assure you."

The next morning it became clear that Frederica would have no difficulty passing as an innocent outsider. From her gasp when Lady Aislinn appeared in the faerie ring to her wide-eyed examination of their surroundings in Faerie, she could not be mistaken for anything but a new visitor.

But it seemed altogether too familiar and comfortable to Elizabeth. This part of Faerie was more park-like than the countryside she had been in with Darcy, and this time she was not frightened, exhausted and half-starved after being lost in the glamour trap. It felt natural to have sprites dashing by on their way to some destination. Even the flowery scent of the air was familiar.

They trailed behind Lady Aislinn, passing through a tunnel of saplings covered with flowering vines until they reached a spacious bower. The branches of living trees wound sinuously to form a loose latticework roof from which viburnum blossoms hung and scented the air with their rich fragrance. The floor was soft, springy moss. At the far end sat a dark-haired Sidhe lady surrounded by dryads and sprites.

Heedless of the breach of manners, Elizabeth caught at Lady Aislinn's sleeve. "I have been here before," she said quietly. "When I was young. I know her." More of those thrice-cursed tampered memories she could not quite catch, like a squirrel who ran out of sight whenever she came close to it.

"The queen? That is unexpected. But she has seen you, so we must proceed." Lady Aislinn propelled her forward until they neared Titania. The Faerie queen was smaller than she seemed in Elizabeth's vague memory, but every bit as hauntingly beautiful.

Lady Aislinn made a deep curtsy. "Great lady, my most respectful greetings, and may the moon's blessings shower on you eternally."

Titania's eyes slowly turned to focus on her visitors. "Greetings to you, Lady Aislinn. Whom have you brought me today?"

"These are two young mortals who stumbled into Faerie. I thought you might find them amusing. This one speaks some of our language, although she does not know where she learned it. Perhaps her memory is lost in the mists of Faerie."

"Mortals? How delightful! I have so missed having mortals among us." The queen beckoned them towards the bank of flowers where she reclined. "Come forward."

Honesty. She must be honest. As if by second nature, Elizabeth sank to her knees and then sat back on her heels. "Great lady, forgive me. I think I have seen you before, but my memories are not clear," she said humbly.

The queen of Faerie leaned forward. Searching eyes seemed to tingle through Elizabeth as Titania gracefully trailed her fingertips down Elizabeth's cheek. "Are you not my little Libbet, child?"

Libbet. Her childhood nickname, spoken in a golden tone, resonated deeply. "I... I am Libbet, great lady, but I cannot remember," she said hesitantly.

"Bluebird!" called Titania. "Bluebird, my love, come to me."

A dryad appeared from the trees, tall and willowy now, but unquestionably Elizabeth's childhood friend. "I am here, lady."

"Bluebird, is this not our little Libbet come back to us?"

"Libbet!" cried Bluebird. "Oak and ash, you have come at last!"

At last?

Titania patted the ground beside her. "I am so happy you have returned! Come sit by me and tell me your story."

Elizabeth obeyed. It felt natural, even familiar, as Titania's sprites began to play with her hair and stroke her dress, their touch like delicate butterfly wings dancing over her.

"Who is your friend?" asked the queen.

Elizabeth glanced at Frederica. "Her name is Lady Frederica Fitzwilliam, and she is the daughter of a powerful mage. She speaks only English, I fear."

Titania's gaze drifted over Frederica, her head tipped to one side as she tapped her fingertips against the corner of her mouth thoughtfully. In English she announced, "Your name does not suit you. We will call you Meadowsweet for your hair of white gold – nay, you shall be Marigold Meadowsweet, for you are both strong and delicate."

Frederica inclined her head. "I will be honored to be Marigold Meadowsweet. You have named me aptly. It indeed suits me much better," she said, blithely discarding one of the proudest surnames in England.

Titania clapped her hands. "Bring wine and faerie cakes for our guests. Libbet, what brings you back to Faerie?"

"Bluebird had given me a talisman to allow me to use the faerie rings. I was frightened by a man, so I fled here, and Lady Aislinn brought me to you." Elizabeth's scalp tingled as the sprites pulled out her hairpins and teased her hair loose. This was familiar, too, the sensation of being treated like a doll come to life.

"What man dared frighten my Libbet?"

"He was a powerful mage, lady. He had discovered my use of magic. In the mortal world, women are forbidden to use magic."

Titania drew back. "Still?" she asked in blank disbelief. "How barbaric. It is good you are here now."

Did the faerie queen think she would stay there forever? Perhaps it was better not to discuss that.

A sprite pressed a delicate flute of sparkling wine into Elizabeth's hand. The flowery scent was achingly familiar, and it tasted of apple blossoms and elderflowers in the moonlight. As the first sip slid down her throat, Elizabeth remembered.

She remembered sitting by Titania just like this, being primped and coddled until something else caught the queen's attention, and being put aside to play with Bluebird until the queen's fancy returned to her. She remembered spending long days in Faerie and loving it better than Longbourn – and she remembered the day Oberon had taken her away.

174

She had trusted him, and he had gone into her mind, shrouded her memories in mist, and told her not to return. But why had he done it? Why had she been in Faerie at all? The answers remained elusive as the sprites spread her hair over her shoulders, weaving strands of flowers through it.

"Marigold Meadowsweet must be made ready as well," commanded the queen. "We dance with my lord the King tonight."

Tonight? They were expected back at Rosings tonight. And whatever Lady Aislinn had hoped they would communicate to Titania, it had not yet happened.

Elizabeth whispered to Frederica, "Your mother might not recognize you. I certainly would not have."

Frederica fluttered the colorful gauzy silks the sprites had somehow attached to her dress, matching the flowers and ribbons winding through her loose hair. "True, but she would approve, saying it is only right to dress in a manner which makes my hosts comfortable, although this is perhaps not what she had in mind when she said that! And my father – he would not mind what I wore if only he could have this opportunity. He will be green with envy when he hears."

What would Elizabeth's own mother think if she saw her daughter in Faerie? Would it bring back her own memories or simply make her swoon as Anne de Bourgh did at the mention of magic?

A flourish of hunting horns made the fay fall silent. Titania floated regally to the center of the glade. Elizabeth and Frederica joined the queen's sprites and dryads behind her. No one seemed to find the presence of two mortal women in her train odd.

On the other side of the glade, a tall Sidhe – tall even for a Sidhe – strode in, dressed in black and silver. Oberon. Even now his presence sent a shiver of fear down Elizabeth's spine. Why had he betrayed her trust?

Behind him followed a group of retainers, mostly elves, but with a few Sidhe and a mortal man in a red coat. Was that a uniform? Yes, even a King's soldier!

Lady Aislinn brushed against her. "The one just behind the king on the left, the young fellow dressed all in black, is Oberon's son, of whom we have spoken."

He looked young, but it was difficult to tell when none of the Sidhe seemed to age beyond a certain point. His resemblance to his father was striking, and he reminded her of someone else, too, but she could not remember another Sidhe with that look. The curl of his lip – did that mean he scorned this gathering, or was it simply his usual expression? She would trust him no more than she trusted his father.

Titania spread her arms. "Come, the moon is rising. Let us dance!"

Everyone was taking hands and forming small circles. Elizabeth tried to step away, but Lady Aislinn caught her hand. "You must dance, or you insult our king and queen."

"But I do not know the dance." But she had thought she did not know the Faerie queen, either.

"You will learn as we go. Come."

Elizabeth cast a look of amused desperation at Frederica, who took her other hand. "Very well. If I make a fool of myself, at least there is no one else here who knows me."

That had to be the exact moment she saw a familiar face.

It could not be. George Wickham stood across the circle from her, red coat and all. What could he possibly be doing in Faerie? She looked away quickly. Perhaps he would not recognize her. With her hair loose and draped in flowers, she did not look like Miss Elizabeth Bennet of Longbourn.

The musicians struck up a tune with fiddles, flutes, drums, and an instrument she could not identify. Elizabeth tried to watch Lady Aislinn's steps, and the pattern quickly became clear – step to the side, hop, put her left foot behind her right and step twice, hop. She could manage this, even if she lacked the grace of the sprites and dryads.

But could she manage George Wickham?

How could he be here? Wickham had told her he had trained as a mage, but nothing about fay connections. She now knew the truth about Wickham and his history of lies and deception, but he would not be aware of that. He would still consider her to be his friend. This was not the time to confront him about his lies.

The music sped up and so did the dancers. They moved faster and faster until it took every bit of her concentration to keep from falling over her own feet. It was a relief when the music finally stopped with a clash of cymbals.

Gasping for breath, Elizabeth leaned towards Lady Frederica. "I have a problem."

"What is it?"

But it was already too late. Wickham's smooth voice – how had she ever thought it pleasing? – said, "Miss Elizabeth, this is a most unexpected pleasure. You have been keeping secrets from me."

She turned slowly to face him. "I might say the same of you, sir." She smiled to make it seem like teasing flirtation.

"To think of the many times I mentioned the fay to you, and you never showed any sign of interest! I am impressed."

Trust Wickham to be impressed by what would seem to be lying by omission. "How do you come to be in Faerie, Mr. Wickham?"

His smile was self-deprecating. "I am half fay, as you must have guessed, and Prince Aelfric is my liege lord. But you would have already known that. My prince has also been playing his cards close to his chest."

What on earth did he mean by that? "The prince's liege man and wearing the uniform of King George's militia?"

His smile displayed his perfect, even teeth. "The prince has been very helpful to me in certain matters pertaining to someone we both dislike. I joined the militia on his orders. The ladies of Faerie are as fond of a red coat as any Englishwoman."

"I thought you decided to join after an accidental meeting with Mr. Denny."

"I put myself in his way. It gave me an easy excuse to be in Meryton so I could become acquainted with your family."

Startled, she said, "My family? Why would you have any interest in us?"

He cocked an eyebrow. "Not I, but my prince. And his interest is self-evident."

"Not to me." The knowledge was a sour taste in her mouth. Not only had he lied to her, but he had used her to meet her family. How could she even pretend to flirt with him?

"Is that so? I find that difficult to believe."

"I assure you it is the truth."

His expression grew puzzled. "You truly do not know, do you?"

She had been so intent on his words that she had totally missed the approach of the prince until Lady Frederica touched her arm in warning.

"Wickham, introduce me to your friend." The prince's chiming voice was deep and smoky.

Wickham hesitated. "My lord, I am not altogether certain that is a wise idea under these circumstances."

The prince narrowed his eyes. "I told you to introduce me to the mortal."

"Very well," said Wickham with a light but uneasy laugh. "My lord, permit me to present to you Miss Elizabeth Bennet of Longbourn. Miss Elizabeth, I find myself in the highly unusual position of introducing you to your own brother, Prince Aelfric."

This was too much. Elizabeth had seen enough of Wickham's trickery and games. "I do not know what you hope to accomplish by this," she said frostily. "I have no brother, nor have I any connection to a prince of Faerie."

Wickham wore an oddly uncomfortable expression. "Your mother's first child was a boy."

"Yes, and he died the day he was born. You and I spoke of this before. I even showed you his grave at the bottom of the orchard."

The prince said haughtily, "I do not know who is buried in that grave. I was abandoned in a faerie ring, and I would have died of exposure had it not been for the mere chance of a dryad who happened to pass that way and found me."

This story must be some odd form of fay mischief. "I do not know what you hope to gain from this, my lord. If I might state the obvious, my parents are mortals, and you, sir, are not."

"Your mother, who is also mine, is mostly mortal. My father is King Oberon." His voice was ice cold.

Elizabeth glared at him. "My parents were married at the time my brother was born."

The prince's long face took on an expression of puzzlement. "Why does that matter?"

Wickham said quickly, "My lord, by the laws and customs of England, a woman's husband is considered the father of all her children, even if he has not been in her presence for more than a year. By fay custom, the father is the one..."

"The father is he who begot the child upon the mother," said the prince without a hint of embarrassment. "How could it be otherwise?"

"Very well, I understand your meaning, but I still say it is ridiculous and this is some sort of trickery." Elizabeth barely managed to remain civil.

The prince looked down his nose at her. "I tell you it is the truth, and Sidhe do not lie."

With a fawning smile, Wickham said, "Miss Elizabeth, you and I are both accustomed to mortals who bend the truth easily, sometimes for no better reason than their own amusement. The Sidhe can be mischievous and cunning, but not untruthful."

It was true, at least according to her untrustworthy memories. The Sidhe always told the truth. Elizabeth rubbed her arms. She had to calm herself. "I cannot know if you are who you say you are. Clearly you believe it, as does Mr. Wickham, but I remember seeing my mother cry over my brother's grave. She would sneak out of the house at night and be found there in the morning, shivering, with her nightdress damp with dew. That is not the behavior of a woman who abandoned her child."

The prince stared at her in silence.

Frederica said slowly, "Is it possible your mother truly believed her son had died and was buried in that grave?"

Prince Aelfric's expression became shuttered. "You believe someone else left me in the ring and lied to my mother? Her husband, perhaps?"

"It seems a possibility, my lord," said Frederica.

"And who are you?"

Frederica ducked her chin and looked up at him through her eyelashes. "You may call me Marigold Meadowsweet."

"Marigold Meadowsweet, Wickham, leave us," the prince commanded.

Frederica swept a curtsy that encompassed both Elizabeth and the prince. "Libbet, should you need me, you have only to call." Then she left, accompanied by Wickham, leaving Elizabeth alone with the glowering prince who hated humans and might be her brother.

This was not what was supposed to happen during this visit. She should be safely back in the Dower House at Rosings, having had a brief conversation with Titania. How had everything spiraled so far out of control?

"Why does she call you Libbet?" he demanded.

"That is what Titania has always called me." It could do no harm to remind him she was under the queen's protection.

"Titania does love her human followers." He said it with the scorn of a faerie prince for a mere mortal. "Tell me about your mother." Not his mother, nor our mother, but her mother.

"My mother is…" Should she tell him their mother was a silly, ignorant country gentlewoman, or could she even say that? "I cannot truthfully tell you anything about her beyond her appearance and that she likes raspberries and dislikes currants, but I do not think that is what you are asking. I learned recently that everything I thought I knew of her may be wrong, and she is not now the woman she was before your birth."

"That sounds remarkably like an excuse. I do not like excuses, Libbet."

She stiffened, as much at his menacing tone as at his use of her name without any of the usual formalities of Miss and her last name. That familiarity was the risk of using her fay name, since the fay had little use for rules of that sort. "I will answer your questions, but pray give me a moment to collect my thoughts. This has been a great shock." To say the very least. How could it be true?

"A moment, then," he said grudgingly.

Something about his tone reminded her of Mr. Darcy. Not the man she had come to know recently, but the proud gentleman whom she had first met in Meryton. Why did the comparison seem so amusing when all else was nightmarish?

"Very well," she said slowly. "I recently learned from my uncle – my mother's brother – that once she was clever, witty, and loved all things fay – quite unlike the woman she is now. She changed abruptly after the death of her son, by which I mean what she believed to be his death, if that is the case –"

"I understand what you mean," the prince said coldly.

"The next time my uncle saw her, she was different – silly, nervous, and completely uninterested in magic and the fay."

His lip curled. "Is that common to mortal women after childbirth?"

"No, of course not. But it is characteristic of a woman who has been bespelled by a mage to bind her magic so that she cannot use it." Did the fay even have binding spells?

"Is that what you think happened? What mage would dare to lay such a spell?"

"I do not know for certain, and I am basing this only on my uncle's word –"

"The truth, Libbet," he snapped.

He was right; she had not been telling her own truth. "I believe that is what happened, and that my father set a spell on her," she said in a rush. "I have been trying to understand why he would bespell her, but now I wonder if perhaps it had something to do with... you." She did not want to admit that this unpleasant, haughty Sidhe might be her brother, but the pieces fit together. If her mother had given birth to a fay child, her father would have reason to hate the fay and to keep her mother from them by any means.

Lady Aislinn interposed herself between them. "Libbet, Titania wishes you to dance."

The prince grasped Elizabeth's wrist in an iron grip. "I am not finished with her yet." It was a warning.

"My lord, she belongs to the queen, not to you."

Belonged? Elizabeth belonged to no one, but it seemed unwise to say so. "My lord, perhaps we could speak further after the dancing –"

"No. We will speak now."

Lady Aislinn grasped Elizabeth's other wrist, as if she were a rope in a tug-of-war. "My lord, you have no right –"

"I claim blood right."

Lady Aislinn froze in consternation, but her voice remained dulcet. "My lord, you cannot. She is a stranger among us and does not know our ways. You have just met her."

He shot her a look of disgust. "Not that sort of blood right. She is kin to me. We share a mother."

"You do?" This time Lady Aislinn's astonishment could not be contained as she stared at Elizabeth.

Elizabeth licked her dry lips. "I... I did not know, but it seems it may be true, if what the prince has told me is correct..." She gazed pleadingly at Lady Aislinn.

Carefully Lady Aislinn removed her fingers from Elizabeth's wrist. "Then I cede to your blood right, my lord, but I urge you not to make an enemy of the queen. This girl has great value to her – as I understand her mother did before her." She turned and walked away.

"Your mother was one of Titania's followers?" the prince demanded.

"It is the first I have heard of it, but as I said before, despite living with her for twenty years, I clearly know nothing about my mother. Our mother." With luck, the prince would not be able to tell how close she was to hysterical laughter – or to outright fury.

"But why would your father punish your mother for bearing me? Giving birth to a Sidhe should be a matter for rejoicing."

Was he serious? Forcing herself to speak evenly and slowly, she said, "Because it meant his newlywed wife had been unfaithful to him."

A line formed between his brows. "How was she unfaithful to him?" Then his expression cleared and he laughed. "Oh, yes, I had forgotten the foolish mortal custom that men and women should have only one lover."

That was beyond enough. "You may call it foolish, but that

custom is what prevents young people from unexpectedly meeting unknown brothers and sisters and discovering they knew nothing of their parents!"

"Yet that same custom apparently causes men to abandon helpless infants like so much rubbish."

Trembling now with rage, she said, "And what should he have done? Raised you as if you were a mortal when everyone would be able to see you were not? He at least tried to return you to your own people."

"He could have told your mother the truth and had her bring me here safely!"

"Yes, he was unjust to you in that. But is it just for you to declare war on all mortals because of what one man did to you?"

"That is not the reason. Mortals are not..." He stopped, no doubt deciding he ought not insult mortals to his mortal sister.

"Well, this mortal is finished with this conversation. I do not care what sort of right you think our shared blood gives you. No mortal gentleman would ever behave so rudely to a lady!" She hurried past him into the glade.

Where was Frederica? The light of the moon was bright, but it cast many shadows, and the differing shapes of the various fay races made it impossible to pick out one mortal in the mass of swirling dancers.

It was Frederica who found her. "What happened, Lizzy? Did he say something? I saw you practically running from him."

Elizabeth said blankly, "I want to go home." It was all she could do not to burst into tears.

"Home to the Dower House or to your parents' house?" asked Frederica, ever practical.

"I do not know." Half a sob escaped her. "I want to apologize to Mr. Darcy." Where had that come from?

"Darcy? What has he to do with this?"

"Nothing. Nothing at all." Elizabeth swallowed a sob.

"I think we had best find Lady Aislinn." She took Elizabeth's arm and steered her past the dancers.

But Lady Aislinn, when they found her, shook her head. "Had I known you were Prince Aelfric's sister, I would never have brought you here, nor would Cathael have agreed to it. The prince is not our friend. That, with the matter of Titania's prior claim on you, makes this matter too deep for me." She sounded displeased.

"But I did not know he was my brother," Elizabeth said despairingly. "I do not want him to be my brother. I hope I never see him again. I beg you, can you not simply send me home?"

Lady Aislinn's expression softened. "I am sorry, child. I do not envy your position. We are both pawns in this game. I can do nothing but help you to tell Titania about your brother, and then it is best for you to think no further of me."

Was Lady Aislinn truly abandoning her in Faerie?

Frederica frowned. "Will the queen send us back if we ask her to?"

"Of course. We do not hold mortals here against their will. Come, the dance is ending."

She led them to Titania. "My queen, Prince Aelfric claims your Libbet is his sister."

Titania showed no sign of surprise. "Did you not know, Libbet? Did your mother not tell you of him?"

"My mother…" Tears stung the corners of Elizabeth's eyes. "My mother is bespelled." She could hold back no longer. Surrounded by scores of celebrating fay, she burst into tears.

"My poor dear child!" cried Titania, holding Elizabeth close. "We will return to my bower. No one can hurt you there. You must tell me everything."

Elizabeth might not remember Titania well in her head, but her body recalled the sensation of being held by the faerie queen. And so she told her everything, from removing the elfshot from Lady Catherine's arm to Mr. Gardiner's revelations to her encounter with Prince Aelfric, leaving out only the parts about Lord Cathael.

Titania made soothing sounds and instructed a dryad to play sweet harp music. "Now you must go to sleep, my dear child. I have a special place for you here with the softest moss, and you will have only sweet dreams."

"But I must return to Rosings." It was the one thing she still knew for certain.

"It will not harm you to spend the night in Faerie, child. Now lie down here, and my dryads will sing you a lullaby."

As if a lullaby could cure her problems! "I thank you, but I could not possibly fall asleep."

An amused smile crossed Titania's flawless features. "There are some things that are easier in Faerie." She waved a graceful hand, and Elizabeth slept.

# Chapter 7

"Where are they?" asked Richard explosively. "They should have returned hours ago."

Eversleigh looked up from his book. "There is no reason to think they have come to any harm. Presumably something has delayed them, and they will be spending the night in Faerie."

"Freddie does not simply decide to stay away overnight. She must know we would be concerned. Something is wrong." Richard flung himself down in a chair, making it creak ominously.

"I agree," Darcy said, struggling to keep his voice level. "I am concerned for them. Who could they turn to for assistance if a problem arose?" They would be helpless, and he could not stop it.

Eversleigh closed his book and set it aside. "Lady Aislinn is reliable, and they are with her. If nothing else, she would protect them because she knows I am involved with them, and she wants me to keep her role in this matter secret. There really is nothing to worry about."

Darcy scowled. "Having spent a day and a night in a glamour trap designed to kill me, I am less certain that Faerie is a welcoming place." The last time Elizabeth failed to return from Faerie, she would have died had he not come for her.

Richard nodded. "I should never have agreed to let Freddie go without someone to protect her."

"How do you think you could have stopped her? You would have had to tie her up." Darcy was in no mood to hear Richard blaming himself.

"I still believe they are perfectly safe, but if they do not return in the morning, I will go to Faerie myself to look for them. Simply to ease your minds, I might add," said Eversleigh.

"I would like to accompany you if I may." Darcy could not bear sitting around and waiting any longer, even if it meant returning to Faerie. The last trip had been nightmarish enough.

"A good idea," said Eversleigh. "Perhaps you will see a different side of Faerie than you did last time."

A hand shook Elizabeth's shoulder, rousing her from a deep sleep. "Libbet, love, wake up!"

Elizabeth rubbed her eyes. What was Bluebird doing here? The previous day came rushing back. Titania's bower, that was where she was. Sprites tripped around the raised bank where Titania still slept. "What is it?"

"Prince Aelfric wishes to speak to you immediately," said Bluebird. "He waits beyond the bower."

Elizabeth pushed herself up on her elbows. Who would have thought moss could make such a comfortable bed? "Perhaps I do not wish to speak to him." Horrid man. Or horrid fay, in this case.

Bluebird hesitated. "I would not advise starting a conflict over a minor matter. If he were to claim his blood right, Titania would be placed in an unfortunate conflict with Oberon."

"And I suppose the prince is more important to Oberon than I am to Titania." Elizabeth made a face. "Very well, I will speak to him." She stood up, wobbling on the springy moss. She must look a sight after sleeping in her dress, but she had no intention of wearing the scanty robes the fay favored. She tried to smooth her wrinkled skirt but it made no difference.

"I can do that for you." Bluebird ran her hand down the skirt, and wherever she touched, the wrinkles disappeared.

As the dryad continued her magical pressing of the dress, Elizabeth said, "Oh, Bluebird, it is so good to see you again. I have missed you. I hope we will never have to be parted for so long again."

"Indeed not!" said Bluebird with a warm smile. "It has been far too long."

A thought crossed Elizabeth's mind. "Why did you bring Pepper to me?"

Bluebird seemed unsurprised by this complete change of subject, but she would be accustomed to the Sidhe, who darted from topic to topic constantly. "She wanted to leave Faerie, and Titania asked her to look after you."

Titania had been behind it? "Why did she want to leave Faerie?"

"White phoukas are considered unlucky. Female phoukas are rare and even worse luck because they do not have a human form. A female white phouka does not have an easy life here. She is much happier away from other fay." Bluebird began working on the back of Elizabeth's dress.

Poor Pepper. "If female phoukas are rare, how are more phoukas born?"

Bluebird laughed as she turned her attention to Elizabeth's hair. "Oak and ash, child! Phoukas do not breed. When a brownie and a gnome have children, some are brownies, some are gnomes, and some are phoukas. Do you not remember?"

"These things are much less complicated in the mortal world, where all creatures look like their parents. When I was here as a child, I never thought to question such things."

"Oberon should never have sent you away. The poor queen missed her Libbet so, and she could not visit you as I did." Bluebird stepped back and admired her work. "There. Now you look lovely."

189

Elizabeth sighed. This was one time when she would have been happy to have her preparations take longer. "I suppose I should not keep Prince Aelfric waiting. Where is he?"

Bluebird guided her to the prince, who wore a doublet and hose that would have fit in perfectly at Queen Elizabeth's court. "Good morning, my lord," she said.

The prince did not even bother to nod. "I need you to take me to your father."

"Oh, you do? Permit me to tell you how this conversation should go if you wish my cooperation. You would say 'Good morning, sister; I hope you slept well.' When I replied that I had, you might say, 'I feel the need to speak to your father, but I do not know how to find him. It would be a considerable kindness if you would consider accompanying me.'"

He stared at her blankly. "That is a waste of time. How do mortals manage to accomplish anything when they have to use all those ridiculous words?"

"I shall not waste your time, then. I am certain Mr. Wickham is perfectly capable of guiding you to my father. Good day, my lord."

"Wait!" He grimaced and spoke slowly through gritted teeth, as if each word pained him. "Would you be so kind as to take me to your father?"

His request still left a good deal to be desired in terms of proper address, but it had been a great concession on his part, and she felt an urge to oblige him. Of course she did – she remembered vaguely that fay kinship held magical bonds of obligation. Her throat tightened. Prince Aelfric was the last person in the world she wanted to feel compelled to obey.

Or perhaps she was doing it on her own behalf this time. After last night, she had a few things to say to her father as well. She had thought to have more time before she had to face him, but perhaps it was best to get it over with. "I will, but I would prefer not to be seen by the rest of my family."

"Then be invisible."

She sighed. "I am not fay. My skills are insufficient for me to maintain invisibility while I am moving."

The prince wrinkled his nose. "I will make you invisible."

"I than –" she caught herself just in time. "I would appreciate that. Bluebird, will you tell Lady – Marigold Meadowsweet where I have gone and that I shall return soon?" She certainly had no desire for a long conversation with her father.

"I will, but the queen spoke with her through much of the night, so she might not awaken for some time."

What had Titania found to talk to Frederica about for hours? Whatever it was, Lord Matlock would be even more envious now.

"Why do you smile?" the prince asked suspiciously.

"Marigold's father will be annoyed that she had that opportunity. Annoying him amuses me." She waited for his reaction but he made none. Of course, the fay were always amused by playing tricks on mortals.

"We can use this circle," he said.

"This one goes to Longbourn?"

"It goes wherever I tell it to go." He sounded insulted she would think otherwise.

"So for lesser fay, a circle only goes to one place, but Sidhe can go anywhere?"

"Your education is sadly lacking if you did not already know that." He stepped into the ring and waited for her.

"Yours is equally lacking about mortals if you believe they know they should not cut down faerie groves. You could save yourself a war by explaining it." The familiar disorienting sensation was followed by the even more familiar earthy scent of the woods near Longbourn.

"They know. They are trying to harm us."

She felt the tingling of magic being applied to her. He must have made her invisible. "You are wrong. You know more about the fay than I do, but I know more about mortals than you do."

He frowned ferociously, reminding her once more of Mr. Darcy, but said only, "Which way must we go?"

"This way." She gestured down the path from the ring and set forth. When the path widened as they emerged into a pasture, permitting them to walk side-by-side, Elizabeth said, "You told me you wanted to see my father. What of my mother?"

He shook his head. "Not if she is under a spell. I will wait until she is herself again. You will have the spell removed."

Stung, she said, "I have every intention of doing so, although not at your behest. I was already seeking a way to do so when I was interrupted by having to go to Faerie to tell Titania the truth about your foolish war. And then so much has happened that I have not had an opportunity to do even that much."

He curled his lip. "Your truth being that mortals are ignorant of the groves."

"More than that. We know people are falling ill and dying, and that it is because of the fay, but we do not know why they are hurting people. You, my lord, are fighting an enemy who barely knows your army is there, much less the reason for your war."

He frowned. "I find that difficult to believe."

"You ought to be able to tell I am not lying."

He showed his teeth. "That particular skill only works in Faerie."

"If I tell you again in Faerie, will you believe me then?"

"I will believe that you believe it. Are you always this argumentative?"

She gave him a patently false smile. "Only to those who deserve it. Look, there is Longbourn across the field. That is where you were born."

He studied it, his expression shuttered.

How absurd this situation suddenly seemed! Not only was she magically at Longbourn without having traveled from Rosings, but she was here with a man who was clearly not human, one of a sort almost never seen in the mortal world. Her own sentiments on seeing Longbourn were decidedly mixed, the usual pleasure at viewing her home after time away mingled with the knowledge that so much of her life there had been based on falsehoods.

Better not to think too much of that, not when she had her father to face. She set off across the last field at a brisk pace, not looking to see if the prince followed her.

She stopped at the garden gate. "He will most likely be in his library, but if he is not alone, I prefer not to reveal myself to him."

"As you wish." He sounded less confident now.

"You are certain no one can see us?" Oh, how she wanted to run away! Anything but to face her father.

"Yes, but they could hear us, so we must be quiet."

"We will be less likely to be heard if we go in through the back." She squared her shoulders. It was time to finish this.

Fortunately there were no servants to notice the opening and closing of the door, and then it was just a matter of tiptoeing through the empty dining room to reach the library. She nodded to Aelfric and gestured to her body, and the cloak of illusion slipped away from her. Should she knock on the library door? No, someone might notice. She opened the door and stepped inside.

Her father looked up and his face lit with pleasure. "Lizzy! I did not hear you arrive. I am glad you are back. Is Jane with you?"

"Jane is still in London. This is a private visit just to speak to you." In the familiar warmth of the library, the scene of so many happy memories, it was hard to maintain her anger with her father. "Or rather I brought someone who wishes to speak with you."

"Who is it?" Mr. Bennet's eyes widened as the prince dropped the illusion that hid him.

"Father, this is Prince Aelfric of the Sidhe." A rude introduction, but it avoided the possibility of her father refusing to acknowledge him.

Mr. Bennet's mouth settled into a straight line. "Fay folk are not welcome in my house, regardless of rank. I must ask you to leave."

Prince Aelfric moved forward faster than any mortal could and stabbed his long forefinger on Mr. Bennet's desk. "The last time you ejected me from this house, I was an infant, and I had no recourse. This time I will not leave until my questions have been answered."

"You!" hissed Mr. Bennet. "Ask your questions, then, and be gone!"

The Prince raised his chin. "Who left me in the faerie ring?"

Mr. Bennet crossed his arms. "I did."

"Did my mother know?"

Mr. Bennet's eyes slid to Elizabeth. "No."

"Did you tell her I was dead?"

A long hesitation this time. "Yes."

The prince's eyes narrowed. "Did you cast a spell on her to prevent her from going to Faerie?"

Elizabeth held her breath as she waited for his answer. When he finally spoke, Mr. Bennet sounded defeated. "Yes."

Prince Aelfric's eyes flashed. "That is all." He spun on his heel.

"Wait! I have a question for you as well," called Mr. Bennet.

"I owe you no answers."

"Then you need not answer. But here is the question. Beautiful young mortal women seek out Faerie, where they are admired and treated as pets. What happens to them a few years later, when the bloom begins to fade from their cheeks, lines appear on their forehead, and their flesh begins to sag? Have you ever seen a mortal woman like that in Faerie? Or are they cast away like old rubbish?"

"Since there are no longer mortal women in Faerie, I cannot say."

He cloaked himself once more in illusion and left the room, leaving Elizabeth alone with her father.

Mr. Bennet removed his spectacles and rubbed the bridge of his nose. "I suppose you know who that creature is."

Elizabeth could hardly speak for the nausea roiling her stomach. "I found out when I met him last night."

"I am sorry you had to discover it. I had hoped none of you would ever know about your mother's infidelity."

He thought she would blame her mother? Now she wanted to cry. "Do you know what my greatest fear has always been?"

He sighed. "No, but I assume you are about to tell me."

"I am terrified of being put under a binding spell and having my mind no longer be my own. You placed my mother under just such a spell. Now I must leave before anyone discovers my presence here." She could not bear being in the same room with him any longer.

His bitter smile told her he knew she wanted to leave. "Very well. If you see your so-called prince, tell him he is fortunate I left him in a faerie ring. Any other man would simply have strangled him in his cradle."

Elizabeth shrugged. She would tell him if she saw him. He was most likely back in Faerie by now, and she would have to skulk back to the ring to avoid being seen.

At the end of the garden, Elizabeth paused to look back at Longbourn. Familiar, beloved Longbourn where she and Jane had pretended to be princesses and pirates, the forbidden chestnut tree she had climbed, her bedroom window, the panes glinting in the sunlight, behind which she had shared so many confidences with Jane. Would she ever see it again? If she did, it would only be for a brief visit. It could never again be her home.

She gritted her teeth, trying to hold back tears. Her father's role could no longer be denied. In some deep part of her, Elizabeth had nursed a hope that somehow he might have had an explanation for his behavior. Now she no longer had even that tiny consolation.

She trudged back to the faerie ring, not bothering to try to avoid the brambles on each side of the trail. At first she thought Aelfric must have left because she did not see his tall form in the glade, but as she pushed past the last bushes, she saw him crouching by an old oak, his long fingers scratching under the ears of a tabby cat with white paws.

"Gus!" she exclaimed, hurrying to the cat's side. "I am so glad to see you." Her voice caught.

"He came looking for you," said Aelfric. "He followed your scent."

She scooped Gus up in her arms and hugged him, a tear or two leaking into his thick fur. "He is a cat, not a phouka."

"That is obvious." He sounded insulted.

"Oh, Gus, I wish I could take you with me. Pepper misses you, too. But you would hate the long carriage ride so much," she whispered to the cat.

"You could take him through Faerie." Aelfric's hearing was apparently acute.

She blinked hard to keep the tears back. "I thought only mortals with magic could travel to Faerie."

"He is a cat," said Aelfric, as if that explained everything.

Had they not already been through this discussion? "Yes, I know."

"All cats have magic. Phoukas can only take the shape of animals with magic – horses, cats, dogs, ravens, and foxes."

"Then I want to take him." No one would miss him at Longbourn. "It was kind of you to wait for me. I did not expect it."

He reached out a long, slender finger, and rubbed the fur under Gus's chin. "I did not know if you had your talisman stone to allow you to use the ring."

She could not bear it if Aelfric was kind to her right now. "I do, but it was thoughtful of you to consider it."

He scowled. "I do not abandon people."

That had to have been one of the shortest truces on record.

Just as Eversleigh was about to step into the faerie ring at Rosings, Darcy asked suspiciously, "Where will it take us?"

"To Oberon's court. We will start our search there."

"Because your father is an adherent of his?"

The corners of Eversleigh's mouth turned up impishly. "No. Because Oberon is my father." And the ground dropped out from under them.

This time the landing was gentle. They stood at the entrance to a long colonnade in the now familiar flower-scented air.

"Your father?" Darcy asked. "Are you serious?"

"Quite. Oberon is one of the few Sidhe who still regularly seek out mortal lovers. There are probably dozens of his children scattered around England. Well, perhaps not dozens, but quite a few."

"Oberon's son." Darcy shook his head. "This is already different than my last visit. When I was here before, a gnome told me I should not pollute the ground of Faerie with my human footsteps, so I had to ride to the lord's estate. Is it acceptable for me to walk here?"

Eversleigh grinned. "My friend, you have been the subject of a fay prank. The gnome could have sent you anywhere in Faerie using the rings. You may walk wherever you please."

That long, precarious, blissfully torturous ride with Elizabeth in his arms had been a prank?

His stupefaction must have shown, for Eversleigh added, "The lesser fay love to play jokes on mortals, and they are very good at it. Come;

we do not have far to go."

"But Pepper must have known it was a prank, and she still took part in it."

"Did you think your phouka friend does not also enjoy pranks?"

They set off down the colonnade. After a short distance it intersected a wide path leading to a living arch of trees. Eversleigh strode through it without hesitation, so Darcy did as well.

"I must pay my respects to Oberon before proceeding. It would be a slight if I did not," said Eversleigh apologetically.

"I can wait outside while you do so." It was not mere politeness. Meeting Lord Cathael had been terrifying enough. Darcy had no desire to be face-to-face with the Sidhe king who wished to wage war on all mortals.

"Sorry, my friend. You cannot escape that easily. I cannot have it said that I brought a mortal here without Oberon's knowledge. Besides, it will do him good to be reminded that not all mortals are monsters." Eversleigh clapped his arm. "Don't worry. Faerie royalty requires far less ceremony than their mortal cousins do."

Darcy was beginning to regret not waiting at Rosings while Eversleigh searched for Elizabeth and Frederica. "Very well."

"One moment." A flower appeared in Eversleigh's extended hand and he offered it to Darcy. "Wear this in your lapel. It will permit you to understand the language of the Sidhe. No need to gape at me – fay spells are very simple. I wished for a flower to allow you to speak this language, and it appeared. Had I wished for a flower to kill you with slow poison, that would have appeared."

Darcy gingerly tucked the small white flower into his lapel. Elizabeth had wished for an apple, and it had appeared. "I will be cautious from whom I accept gifts."

"A good idea, although it would be considered poor form to give you a harmful gift."

The trees in the colonnade began to be more frequent until their trunks were close enough together to become a wall of sorts. When they came to a door guarded by two elves armored in heavy leather holding crossed halberds to block entry, Eversleigh nodded to each of them in turn without breaking step. They uncrossed the halberds and stood them upright. One reached behind him to open the door.

For a moment Darcy thought the door had led them outside again. Unlike Lord Cathael's hall of silver filigree, the walls of this room were alive. Branches heavy with leaves grew out of the walls made of tree trunks. Vines and ivy grew upward covering much of the bark. By some magic, the branches arched up at equal intervals, joining together in the center like the peak of a fine pavilion. Beyond them something twinkled.

A Sidhe scribe sat to one side, working at a burlwood desk covered with ancient parchments. A map hung from the wall in front of him.

Eversleigh swept a full court bow to the scribe, so Darcy did the same.

The scribe carefully set his quill in an inkstand before rising to hold out his hands to Eversleigh. "Evlan, my boy. You have returned." He grasped wrists with Eversleigh.

My boy? Surely this simple Sidhe dressed in a nondescript tunic could not be Oberon!

"It is a pleasure to see you once again," said Eversleigh.

"Your brother misses you," the king said.

"I have missed him as well. I have brought a friend with me today, a mage known among mortals as Darcy. He has been meeting with our mortal leaders in the hope of persuading them to protect the sacred groves."

Silver eyes turned to assess Darcy. "Why?"

Darcy's mouth went dry. What had Cathael said? "Because our two worlds are bound together like twins in the same womb, and anything that interferes with that binding harms both of our worlds. We mortals have been too busy in our short lives and have forgotten our ancient responsibilities. It is time for us to remember them." The magic flower must be granting him eloquence as well as a new language.

"Your efforts do you honor." Oberon stepped forward in that unnaturally quick fay movement and laid two tapering inhuman fingers on the side of Darcy's neck just above his cravat. His cold fingertips tingled with magic. "I grant you the freedom of Faerie, Darcy." He said the name with an odd accent, as if it had three syllables.

"You honor me," said Darcy, his newfound eloquence abandoning him.

Oberon turned back to Eversleigh. "You will see your brother?"

"I will." Eversleigh bowed again.

Oberon shuffled back to his desk. Apparently they were dismissed.

Darcy let out a long breath as he followed Eversleigh past the halberd-bearing elves and further down the long colonnade.

"Well done," said Eversleigh. "It is a great honor to be named by the king."

"What do you mean?"

"He gave you a fay name. Most mortals who come to Faerie are renamed here, just as I am Evlan here and Eversleigh in our world. To all fay you will be Diarcey. It is a traditional fay name that means dark. Not a very imaginative choice in your case, I grant you, but easy to recall."

"I thought he was simply mispronouncing my name." A fay name? He was not certain he liked that idea.

They reached a set of open doors tall enough for giants to pass through. "Here is the King's Hall, grown over many centuries by the finest fay architects. It is an impressive sight, and it is not a bad place to begin our search."

They entered a towering hall reminiscent of a cathedral, but instead of being built of stone, it appeared to have been grown of living wood. Branches coiled themselves into decorative spirals and statues, and vines formed latticework windows. A sculpted fountain tossed glistening drops of water in the air, and an empty throne, also made of living wood, dominated the hall. Beside it two Sidhe fenced with glittering swords. Darcy would have found it breathtaking had he not been so worried about Elizabeth.

A young-looking Sidhe with a welcoming smile strode towards them. "Evlan! I thought I felt your arrival."

Eversleigh gripped the newcomer's wrists. "Aelfric. Well met."

"It has been months! It is good to see you. How long can you stay?"

The two fencers had noticed them now and came to join them, giving Eversleigh the same two-handed greeting.

Eversleigh slung an arm around the shoulders of the one he called Aelfric, an impressive trick given the Sidhe's greater height. "This is just a brief visit over a matter of business, but I plan to return for a longer stay at the equinox."

Some of the animation fell from his companion's face. "Business with our father?"

"No, I am looking for two young mortal women who came to Faerie yesterday. They failed to return last night as they had planned. Their friends are very concerned. I assume they were simply delayed, but I offered to check on their well-being."

One fencer asked, "Is one of them the delectable Marigold Meadowsweet? I hope you have not come to take her away. I would welcome her for a much longer stay. There have been so few mortals to choose from of late."

The other fencer added, "I liked the looks of her little friend Libbet, even if she did not stay long enough to dance."

Aelfric's face contorted. "Libbet is off limits."

The Sidhe raised his eyebrows. "My apologies, prince. I did not realize you had a proprietary interest." He sounded amused.

Fine lines appeared between Eversleigh's brows. "Are these ladies recent arrivals? If not, my friend and I must continue our search elsewhere."

"I have never seen them before," said the first fencer.

Aelfric swiveled and narrowed his eyes at Darcy. "Is he your friend?" he asked ominously.

Eversleigh cuffed him lightly on the side of the head. "Obviously I have been away too long, since your manners are slipping. You might even like him given half a chance. At times he can be almost as proud and aloof as you are. Aelfric, this is my friend Diarcey. Diarcey, my half-brother Aelfric, also known as the bane of my existence."

Darcy bowed. "Prince Aelfric." Eversleigh might as well have thrown cold water in his face. It might be good-natured teasing, but it was far too close to Elizabeth's accusations.

"Now, about those ladies –" Eversleigh began.

"What are their mortal names?" Prince Aelfric interrupted.

Eversleigh raised an eyebrow, apparently surprised by this question. "Lady Frederica Fitzwilliam and Miss Elizabeth Bennet."

"Libbet is called Bennet in that world. Your friend Diarcey – what is she to him?"

Elizabeth was safe! But could this odd prince possibly be enamored of her after only a day? If Darcy had not already taken a dislike to him, this would be enough to do it. "She is a friend, and she has done me a service. Lady Frederica is my cousin."

"Is Libbet's father your friend as well?" the prince demanded.

Since he had to respond with the truth, it was just as well it was to someone who would never encounter Mr. Bennet. "I have met Mr. Bennet, but he is not a friend."

"Why not?"

Did everyone receive this sort of interrogation? Carefully Darcy said, "I am under the impression he cares more for his own comfort than for what is best for his daughters and his wife."

The prince smiled, so apparently this had been an acceptable answer. "Indeed."

Eversleigh asked, "Would it be possible to speak to the ladies?"

"They are with the queen's retinue. I took Libbet back to Titania's bower earlier, so they are most likely still there."

Something was definitely odd. Darcy asked, "Might I inquire as to your interest in Miss... in Libbet, Prince?"

"She is my sister. Evlan, I will accompany you to Titania's bower, if you do not object."

Eversleigh's jaw dropped. "Your sister? How can that be?"

"We share a mother."

"Well, well." Eversleigh shook his head and laughed. "That does explain a few things."

"It does? You can tell me on the way to the bower."

Stunned, Darcy trailed after them. Could it be true? No, of course not. The mere idea was ridiculous. He needed to focus on important things. Elizabeth was safe, and that was all that mattered. If everyone in Faerie was as moon mad as this young Sidhe, that was not his affair.

Elizabeth would have liked some time alone after her visit to her father, but being alone was impossible in Titania's bower. Instead she sat beside the queen again as the sprites played with her hair. It was going to take hours to get all the tiny braids and tangles out when she got home.

"Lady, Prince Evlan humbly requests the honor of a few minutes of your time," a dryad said to Titania. "With a great deal of praise for your timeless beauty and infinite generosity, naturally."

"Certainly!" exclaimed Titania. "He has the nicest manners. That brother of his could benefit from studying his ways. You need not worry about this prince, Libbet. He is quite charming."

Elizabeth could make out a shape approaching them along the path. An odd prince of Faerie, since he appeared to be dressed in the latest London style, but as long as his behavior was better than Prince Aelfric's, she did not care what he wore.

He stepped out of the shadows, fell to both knees gracefully in the pool of sunshine before Titania and then sat back on his heels. "Gracious queen, a thousand blessings upon you for your generosity in admitting your most humble slave to your glorious presence."

Prince Evlan? The man before Titania was unmistakably Viscount Eversleigh.

Titania languidly held out her hand to him. "Prince, it has been too long since you graced the halls of Faerie."

He kissed her hand and rose to his feet. "The loss has been mine. Whenever I am away, I tell myself you cannot possibly be as lovely as I remember, yet when I return, you are always even lovelier."

"You see," said Titania to Elizabeth. "He is completely different from his brother. Your brother. That makes you *shurinn*, you and Prince Evlan."

*Shurinn*? The word caught at a hidden memory. People who were both kin to the same person, but not to each other. Yes, that was it, and there was a special bond between them. She remembered the concept, but she had never expected to have a *shurinn*, nor a Sidhe brother.

Eversleigh – no; Prince Evlan – said, "So I have just learned. Libbet, my dear, it is a pleasure to see you again and to acknowledge you as *shurinn*. I see you have another of my friends from the mortal world here." He turned to Frederica, who had chosen to dress in the same diaphanous and revealing silks as Titania's dryads. His eyes raked down her to her feet and then back up again. "The exquisite Marigold Meadowsweet. Faerie suits you, dear girl."

"Just as I have been telling her," said Titania with a hint of a pout. "I would like to keep her, but she stubbornly insists on returning to your mortal world."

He bowed. "My journey hither involved this very question. The friends of these young ladies had expected them to return last night and were deeply concerned when they did not. I offered to come on their behalf to check on the welfare of the young ladies."

"What foolishness!" the queen cried. "What harm could befall them here?"

Apparently Titania did not view glamour traps as dangerous.

"Mortals can be very foolish, but they do mean well," Eversleigh said.

Elizabeth said quickly, "We had indeed meant to return last night, but a surprise delayed us, and then this morning Prince Aelfric asked me to accompany him on an errand. We intend to return later today."

Frederica said slowly, "I planned to return because I did not want anyone to worry, but if you will be able to reassure them of my well-being, I would not mind staying here a few days longer, if the queen will permit it."

"Certainly you must stay, my little Marigold," said Titania. "It has been so dull here without mortals!"

Eversleigh bowed to Frederica. "As you wish. It would be a terrible shame to force you back into mortal clothing so quickly, my dear Marigold."

Color burned in Frederica's cheeks. "I would by no means suspend any pleasure of yours, Prince Evlan."

He sighed dramatically. "I suppose you are safe in saying so, since your father knows at least a dozen ways to end my life. And you, Libbet?

Do you wish to remain?"

Elizabeth opened her mouth to say she was more than ready to return – but was it true? There was no reason for her to remain at Rosings now that Beltane was past, and she would lack even Frederica's company and chaperonage. Had she never met Prince Aelfric, she would have been happy to remain for a time in Faerie where no one called her a witch, she did not have to depend on charity, and she had no responsibilities. But she had met Aelfric, and he had torn her heart apart. "I suppose if you tell Mr. Darcy of our plans, I need not hurry back."

"You can tell him yourself if you like. I left him just outside the grotto."

Darcy was here? A rush of relief filled her. When had that happened, that she stopped dreading his presence? "Can you take me to him?"

"Certainly. But might I suggest that Marigold Meadowsweet remain here? I do not think Darcy would appreciate your present attire as much as I do."

"Libbet is welcome to him," said Frederica, seeming unperturbed by his blatant flirtation. "I prefer to continue my education in all things Faerie."

Eversleigh made an extravagant bow. "I shall hope for the opportunity to take part in your further education."

"I must show Evlan my foals while he is here," Prince Aelfric told Darcy. "Since there are so few Sidhe steeds left, I am experimenting with breeding them to your thoroughbreds in the hope of offspring that retain the Sidhe characteristics."

Since this conversation was an improvement over the open hostility the prince had shown until now, Darcy asked politely, "Have you had good results?"

"Not yet. The colts are fast, but their legs are too spindly. Look, here comes Libbet."

Darcy caught his breath at the sight of Elizabeth. She was dressed in a combination of mortal and fay styles, her hair loose around her shoulders and entwined with flowers. His fingers itched to bury themselves in her tousled curls and the rest of his body seemed to think she would look even better with that hair spread across a pillow. His pillow, to be precise, after passionate love-making.

Elizabeth curtsied. "Prince Aelfric, we meet again. Mr. Darcy, I give you good day." A tabby cat twined around her feet.

Darcy bowed. "Miss Elizabeth, I am glad to see you are safe."

Prince Aelfric stiffened, but Elizabeth put her hand on his arm. "I pray you to call me Libbet. The fay prefer us to use the names they have given us when we are in their lands."

"Libbet, then." Darcy could almost hear the swish of his governess's rod descending in response to his poor manners. Still, to show he had learned his lesson in this case, he added, "I am Diarcey here. I am glad Prince Evlan found you."

"I am sorry to have caused concern. We had intended to return last night, but the situation was more complex than I had anticipated. I see you have already met Prince Aelfric, who holds a great distinction: I quarrel with him even more frequently than I do with you." The warmth in her arch tone took the sting from the words.

Darcy could not help smiling back. "I believe you found some of our quarrels enjoyable. I know you sometimes take great pleasure in expressing positions that are not your own."

Eversleigh clapped Prince Aelfric on the shoulder. "No need to scowl. Quarreling is what brothers and sisters do."

The lines in Prince Aelfric's face smoothed out. "Is it? I have never had dealings with a sister before."

"Most assuredly," said Eversleigh. "I am an expert on the subject, having three mortal sisters. I never have a moment's peace from quarreling."

"So it is a form of affection?"

"Often it is," said Eversleigh. "Before I forget, Diarcey, your cousin, Marigold Meadowsweet, has expressed a preference to remain here for several days. Libbet has agreed to stay with her."

Darcy glanced at Elizabeth, whose expression suggested she just swallowed a pincushion full of needles. Was it in response to the prospect of remaining in Faerie or that quarreling with Prince Aelfric might mean affection? "If that is what you wish, I see no difficulty with it." No difficulty except that he wanted Elizabeth to be with him every moment, not off in Faerie with Frederica.

The cat at Elizabeth's feet meowed. She bent and picked him up. "It appears Augustus wants an introduction. I brought him here from Longbourn today. I plan to take him to Rosings."

"He is yours as well? Is he a phouka, or does he have other powers?"

Elizabeth's expression lightened with amusement. "Gus's special powers include catching mice and the occasional barn sparrow. Apart from being Pepper's particular friend, he is but an ordinary cat." A sad look filled her eyes. "I had best return to the queen," she said stiffly, in a voice quite unlike her own.

Darcy frowned. Something was wrong. "Might I speak to you privately for a moment first?"

Elizabeth hesitated and shrugged. "If you wish." She put the cat down and walked a few feet away.

He followed her. In a low voice, he said, "Is something the matter?"

Elizabeth looked down. "I spoke to my father this morning," she said in a low voice. "It is all true."

"I am sorry." The words seemed such a weak way of saying it when he longed to take her into his arms and comfort her. "He did not deny it?"

She shook her head.

"I wish it could have been otherwise." What else could he say to comfort her? Telling her he loved her would only distress her more. "Is it your preference to remain here, or would you rather leave?"

"Here or at Rosings, it makes little difference."

"Is there somewhere else you wish to go, or something you would like to do?"

She met his gaze then, her eyes shiny. "I would like to turn the clock back a week, before I knew my father put a binding spell on my mother, that I have fay blood, and that my memories had been tampered with. I most especially do not wish to have a brother," she said fiercely. "Particularly not that brother. And I do not wish to have a father who abandoned my brother." She stopped and took a gasping breath.

He had never felt so wretchedly helpless. "He truly is your brother? I am sorry. Is there anything I can do to help?"

She closed her eyes and shook her head. "No, but I thank – I mean, it is kind of you to ask." Before he could reply, she hurried away and disappeared down the path.

Elizabeth was in pain, and he could do nothing for her. Even worse, he had been lusting after her when she was suffering. Quelling a totally improper urge to run after her, he returned to Eversleigh and Elizabeth's new brother. How could she have a Sidhe brother? It made no sense. He would have to ask Eversleigh later.

Eversleigh gave him a probing look, so Darcy changed the subject. "I am relieved you found her. How do I return to the mortal world?"

"There is no rush, is there?" asked Eversleigh. "Aelfric wants me to look at his colts, and your opinion could be useful. I imagine you know the northern breeds better than I do." A careful truth on his part;

Eversleigh probably knew nothing of the northern breeds, so Darcy would perforce know more. But he clearly felt it was important for Darcy to come with them, even though the idea did not seem to please Prince Aelfric.

"I would be happy to be of assistance," said Darcy.

"Excellent." Eversleigh took Darcy's arm, stepped forward, and the ground disappeared from under them.

"I see what you mean." Eversleigh ran his hand down the colt's foreleg. "He has the length of a Sidhe horse without the strength. Are they all like this?"

"All three that have been born so far." Prince Aelfric leaned over his brother's shoulder.

"Perhaps thoroughbreds were not the best choice. I wonder what would happen if you bred one of these colts to a Sidhe horse."

"They may not be fertile," said the prince. "Sidhe horses do not reproduce for centuries. We need the fertility of mortal steeds."

"Have you any ideas, Diarcey?"

Darcy suspected Eversleigh knew perfectly well that horse breeding was not one of his skills. "If I understand, you are looking for a tall horse, one with strong bones and powerful muscles."

"Exactly," said the prince eagerly.

"I am not an expert, but I wonder if a Bakewell Black might serve. They are strong boned and tall. My cousin swears by Bakewell Blacks. He says they make the best cavalry horses because of their strength and stamina. They have not the speed of a thoroughbred, but they are still graceful and attractive." Richard would laugh to hear Darcy parroting his words. His cousin could talk for long, boring hours about the virtues of Bakewell Blacks. "He says they can take a sword blow to the leg and keep going."

The prince straightened. "That sounds ideal."

Eversleigh dusted off his hands. "An excellent thought, Diarcey. Could you obtain a few mares for Aelfric?"

"If I cannot, my cousin certainly can. He knows the breeders."

"Evlan took me to Tattersall's last time." Aelfric pronounced the strange name carefully. "Would they have them there?"

"No, Tattersall's caters only to the racehorse market," said Eversleigh. "Diarcey, do you suppose Aelfric could meet the Bakewell Blacks breeder?"

Why was Eversleigh so determined to have Darcy help the Prince? "I cannot see why not, though they are in Derbyshire, which is several days journey from London."

Eversleigh and Aelfric looked at each other and laughed. "As long as there are faerie groves in Derbyshire, it is only minutes away. It may take you some time to accustom yourself to how we travel, now that you have the freedom of Faerie."

"Does that have some particular meaning? I thought it meant that I was welcome here."

"It does mean that, but also that you can use the rings to travel by yourself."

Could it possibly be true? "That is a very generous gift."

Eversleigh shrugged. "You are doing a great service in protecting the groves, and the king rewarded you for it."

"But how do I use the rings? Is there a spell?"

Eversleigh shook his head. "Fay spells are much simpler than what you are accustomed to. Simply step into a ring, visualize where you want to go, and you will be there."

"That is all?" It sounded impossible.

"That is all." Eversleigh snapped his fingers. "I know! Fitzwilliam is at Rosings, too. We should go and speak to your cousin about the

Bakewell Blacks." He hesitated. "That is, if you are willing to talk to another mortal, Aelfric."

The Sidhe flushed. "If you say he is not despicable, I will believe you."

Eversleigh winked at Darcy. "All mortals are despicable until proven otherwise, according to Aelfric."

Richard Fitzwilliam jumped to his feet when Darcy, Eversleigh, and a disguised Prince Aelfric entered the drawing room. "Did you find them? Are they well? Where are they?"

"As I expected, they are not only perfectly well, but ensconced in the Faerie queen's bower," Eversleigh said. "They are free to leave any time they please."

"But why did they not – Good God!" Richard went pale.

Aelfric had dropped the glamour that made him appear human.

"We have a guest who came here particularly to meet you. Aelfric, may I present Colonel Fitzwilliam of His Majesty's Army? He is Marigold Meadowsweet's brother. Fitzwilliam, this is my half-brother Aelfric."

Richard's eyes darted back and forth between them. "Marigold Meadow – what?"

Eversleigh grinned. "Lady Frederica has taken to Faerie like the proverbial fish to water. She is now known as Marigold Meadowsweet, dresses in fay silks, and sits by the queen's knee. She and Miss Elizabeth plan to remain there for a few days."

"My father is going to kill me," breathed Richard, his eyes on Aelfric. "He would die for this opportunity. "

"He will have to kill me as well once he discovers I have seen your sister in fay attire," said Eversleigh dryly. "But that can wait. Aelfric wants to learn about Bakewell Blacks, and Darcy said you are an expert on the subject."

Richard's eyes lit up. "Bakewell Blacks? Why, they are unmatched as cavalry horses. Have you ever seen one? No? Mine is in the stables if you would like to meet one."

"I would be most grateful for the opportunity!" said Aelfric.

Once Richard had led the enthusiastic Aelfric off to the stables, Eversleigh sank onto a sofa and folded his hands behind his head. "Something is not right," he told the ceiling.

"Something to do with Elizabeth and Frederica?" Darcy asked.

"No, with Aelfric. He is avoiding telling me something. I may have to return to Faerie to find out what it is. At least I have managed to convince him that there are a few mortals who are not monsters. Thank you for your cooperation with that."

"I did wonder why you wanted me to be with him."

"He has a strong bias against mortals. His mother abandoned him, so he distrusts all mortals. It never concerned me before, but now Lord Cathael says Aelfric is supporting the war on mortals, so something must be done."

Startled, Darcy said, "He is that prince? I assumed it was someone, well, older."

"You have met the only two acknowledged princes of Faerie. There were others in the past, but they have long since died of old age. No doubt Oberon has other mortal sons, but none have found their way to Faerie, and the birth of a Sidhe is a great rarity these days."

"Aelfric is his heir?" That sounded ominous. "How much longer will Oberon live?"

"Aelfric is not heir to the throne. He is acknowledged, but the throne does not pass from father to son. Titania will choose the new king when Oberon dies, but it will be an experienced Sidhe, not Aelfric. Oberon was young when William the Conqueror landed at Hastings, but he is likely to live only a century or two more. Unless he is killed, of course. An iron bullet can kill even the Sidhe. That is why they do not ride among mortals anymore. Our worlds were closer before the days of firearms."

"So the old tales of the Sidhe are true?"

"Many of them are. But this is why the idea of war against humans is so odd. Most Sidhe will not enter the mortal world because of the danger. How do you fight a war without soldiers?"

"I would think invisibility would be a great advantage." The idea of fighting an invisible foe was terrifying. "But if true war is impossible, why do they want one?"

"That is indeed the question. I only wish I had an answer."

"Here, now I can show you," Richard told Aelfric on their return. He took a chess set from the sideboard and began setting the pieces in random lines on the tea table. "Now, the white is our position, and the black are the French and Spanish. We were on the high ground here, and we had placed stakes at the bottom of the hill."

Aelfric moved two of the black pieces. "Could they not have come up around you like this?"

Eversleigh murmured in Darcy's ear, "Toy soldiers."

"I heard that," said Richard indignantly. "Aelfric had a question about cavalry charges."

"What did you think of the horse?" asked Eversleigh.

"Colonel Fitzwilliam is going to introduce me to the man who bred his horse," said Aelfric with enthusiasm. "If I can get two mares, I will be very pleased."

Anne de Bourgh's voice came from the doorway. "Pardon me. I did not realize you had company."

"Just one of my friends who came by to speak to Fitzwilliam about horses," said Eversleigh smoothly. "May I present... Mr. Alfred to you? Alfred, this is Miss de Bourgh of Rosings Park, cousin to both Darcy and Fitzwilliam."

Aelfric's Sidhe face had smoothed into human lines as he stood and bowed.

Anne held out her hand languidly. "Welcome to Rosings, Mr. Alfred. For a moment you looked somehow..." The familiar pained expression crossed her face. "Do you enjoy chess?"

Aelfric, clearly at a loss for the proper response, bowed over her hand, but he did not release it afterwards. Instead he gazed uncertainly into her eyes. "Are you well?"

Richard said with false heartiness, "Young Alfred has been enjoying a bit too much port. Pay no attention to him."

Aelfric laid his hand on the side of her face. "What has been done to you?" he asked gently. "Shall I fix it?"

Darcy sidled closer, preparing to catch Anne in her inevitable swoon. "Miss de Bourgh's health is delicate," he said pointedly.

Anne merely looked into Aelfric's eyes, seemingly mesmerized, and nodded.

The young Sidhe held her gaze for perhaps half a minute before removing his hand and tossing something in the fire. A rope, or could it be a snake? Where had that come from?

"There; it is done. Now you must have a long sleep to let your body recover." Aelfric guided her to the fainting couch and supported her as she sat down.

Her eyelids were already drooping. She made no resistance to lying back on the couch. Richard darted over and placed a pillow beneath her head.

Aelfric said softly, "Sleep now. Sleep and heal."

Anne's eyes closed, and her chest began to rise and fall evenly.

Richard laid his hand on Anne's neck and almost instantly snatched it away. "She is burning up with magic. He must have removed the spell." He chuckled. "Father's unbreakable spell. He will be furious."

Aelfric, his sudden gentleness vanished as quickly as it had come, glared at Eversleigh. "Why did you not help her? She was in pain!"

"I tried," said Eversleigh mildly. "I was unable to break the spell. Why do you say she was in pain?"

"You could not tell?" Aelfric's shock was obvious.

"Apparently not. How did you know?"

But it must be true, for the pinched look Anne had borne for as long as Darcy could remember had vanished. She looked much younger now.

"Can you not smell the pain?"

Eversleigh shook his head. "That is beyond my abilities."

"Elizabeth knew." Darcy was suddenly sure of it.

"Naturally Libbet would know," Aelfric said disdainfully.

Darcy asked, "How long will she sleep?"

Aelfric studied her. "For a mortal, I cannot say. A fay would sleep half a day."

When she awakened, she would have all that magic burning in her. What if she tried to kill someone again? Could Darcy and Richard contain her? Would she listen to them?

Mrs. Jenkinson, Anne's companion, peeked into the room. "Oh! Miss de Bourgh! You ought to have called me when she fainted." She took a vinaigrette from around her neck and opened it under Anne's nose.

Darcy moved her hand away. "She is not fainting, merely asleep. You could assist by bringing a blanket to cover her."

She looked as if she wished to argue, but Darcy had been giving the orders at Rosings since Lady Catherine's illness. With a frightened glance at Anne, she scuttled off.

"That is going to be a problem," said Richard. "We cannot leave Anne to awaken without a guide in magic, but Mrs. Jenkinson will not permit a man to remain by her all night. We need Frederica and Miss Elizabeth."

Eversleigh straightened his cuffs. "Under the circumstances, I believe they would agree to return. But – no, there is still the question of tonight, so there is no choice. I will fetch them." He looked troubled.

"What were you about to say?"

Eversleigh grimaced. "That I could not go to Faerie until tomorrow. Traveling through the rings is not without cost for mortals. Using them is always tiring, and it is hard to think clearly afterwards, but using them to travel between worlds more than twice in one day causes increasing confusion. I will not be able to use the rings for a week or two afterwards, but this cannot wait until tomorrow."

# Part Three

# Dark Magic

# Chapter 8

"Anne is stirring." Frederica's voice was quiet, but it carried through the silent room.

Darcy closed his book without marking the page. He had not been able to keep his attention on it anyway, not with everything that had been happening.

Frederica chafed her cousin's hand. "Anne, can you hear me?"

"Of course. I am not deaf," said Anne sharply. "Where is he?"

"Whom do you mean?"

"That strange man, the one who said he would fix me."

Elizabeth said, "He is a Sidhe, not a man, and he has returned to Faerie."

Frederica asked hesitantly, "How do you feel?"

Anne's brow furled. "Odd. As if I have been trapped in treacle and am suddenly free. What happened?"

"You have been under a spell, a binding spell. We could not explain that to you because part of the spell made you swoon whenever anyone mentioned magic. We had been trying to find a way to break the spell for some time. Yesterday our Sidhe friend was able to remove it. You have been asleep since then."

"A spell." Anne's voice went flat. "I suppose my father set it up before he died."

Frederica cast a concerned glance at Darcy. "No," she said slowly. "We believe he had nothing to do with it."

"You think he would not stoop so low? I assure you he would."

Frederica bit her lip. "That might be true, but my father was the one who cast a spell on you."

"Lord Matlock?" Anne gave a harsh laugh. "And he is the one who is supposed to protect us from sorcerers."

"You do not remember him casting a spell?"

Anne shook her head. "I remember he came for the funeral. I was still weak. When I stopped being able to think clearly, I assumed it was God's punishment for killing my father."

Eversleigh said quickly, "Miss de Bourgh, children who lose a parent often feel as if they are responsible for their – why are all of you looking at me like that?"

Elizabeth finally broke the silence that followed. "I cannot claim much knowledge of the episode, but my understanding is that Miss de Bourgh did cause her father's death, though I have not heard any evidence that it was done deliberately."

"Oh, it was deliberate, I assure you," said Anne coldly. "I had to feign illness for a week to keep him from draining my magic long enough that I could recover it to kill him."

Eversleigh said in a strained voice, "Miss de Bourgh, only a sorcerer would drain a child of magic. Are you attempting to tell us your father was a sorcerer?"

"Did you not know?" Anne stared at them. "He had been stealing my magic for as long as I could remember. He needed it to fuel his spells to force others to do his bidding."

Darcy was stunned. Could it be true? But his own father had known Sir Lewis well. Could he and Lord Matlock both have missed the evidence? Past sorcerers had managed to hide their endeavors for years. All Darcy could remember of Sir Lewis was him standing with his hand on Anne's shoulder, always on her shoulder, and Anne being perpetually exhausted and eating enough for three children. Good God, it really was true.

Anne shuddered. "I need to release some of my magic. All these years with it bottled inside me – I thought it would drive me mad."

Frederica's face might be ashen, but she still remembered her manners. "Would it help to cast a spell?"

Anne's eyes were sad. "I do not know any spells, only how to unmake things. It would be rude to unmake any bits of you when you have been helping me, and mother was very cross the time I unmade part of the house. And yes, that was supposed to be a jest."

"I could teach you how to light a candle with magic. All you have to do is to concentrate on the wick and imagine it growing hotter and hotter, say '*Ardescas,*' and it will be done." Frederica fetched a small candelabra from a sideboard and set it before Anne.

"Just that?" asked Anne dubiously. "I thought there was more than that to spells."

"That is all you need for this one. That is why it is good for beginners."

Anne squinted and stared at the candle. "*Ardescas.*" The wick began to emit smoke and burst into flames.

So did the draperies and the rug.

Eversleigh and Frederica began frantically chanting spells to douse the fire, but no sooner would one area of flames go out than another would start. Elizabeth, coughing, tried to say something to Anne, gesturing to the door.

Darcy frantically called to the lake, holding the water near the high ceiling, and released it. Icy water cascaded down.

The flames sizzled and died. Darcy told the knee-deep water to quench any last bits of fire it had missed and return to the lake.

Frederica coughed and spluttered while Eversleigh wrestled to open the windows.

Richard shook drops from his hair like a water dog. "Very impressive, Darcy," he drawled. "I am certain all the maids would be delighted to learn that little trick."

Exhausted and oddly embarrassed, Darcy called the last of the water, the droplets soaking everyone's clothes, gathered them into a small pool at his feet, and sent it away.

Elizabeth touched her now dry skirt in astonishment. "How did you do that?"

"My affinity for water," he said awkwardly. "It listens to me."

"Apparently it listens quite well!"

"Well," said Eversleigh in a tone perfectly suited for an assembly at Almack's, "I suggest we adjourn the magic lessons and regroup in the garden. I can see Miss de Bourgh is still brimful of magic, and pent-up magic will be safer outside."

Frederica touched a lank strand of hair that had been a ringlet before the deluge of lake water. "First I must... Oh, never mind. This is more important."

Darcy grabbed pastries in both hands on his way out. He was grateful to Eversleigh for taking charge of the situation. Eversleigh had not experienced the same shock he had, of realizing his aunt's husband had been a sorcerer, or the disconcerting discovery that his cousin Anne was not at all the woman he thought her to be.

Ahead of him Anne said to Eversleigh, "I did not intend to burn anything but the candle wick, but I have always hated the decorating scheme in that room. Perhaps the fire knew that."

"I would be surprised by that, but I must say, Miss de Bourgh, though I have only known you a very short time, I am certain you have many surprises in store."

Darcy said, "It takes very little intention for an elemental mage to set a large fire, even using a spell. I have to be very careful of my focus when lighting a candle to keep the fire contained to the candle. Most likely she will need to do so as well." Someone would need to train her to control her elemental magic before she did some real damage, and unfortunately he was the only elemental mage in this part of England. Another unwanted responsibility.

"But she used a spell, not elemental magic," said Frederica.

"It does not matter," said Darcy. "Elemental magic is instinctive. She was thinking about creating a flame, so her elemental magic created flames. Elemental mages set fires while they are still in their cradles. Spells have to be taught."

Elizabeth looked puzzled. "Is it a completely different kind of magic, then?"

Richard answered while Darcy was still trying to think of a response that would not frighten her. "It is a different beast altogether. Some scholars think it must be a remnant of a Sidhe power because elemental mages have a death curse, just as the Sidhe do."

Elizabeth drew back. "He can make people die?" She sounded horrified.

"Only if they kill me first," Darcy said quickly. "It is a curse that takes effect on my death rather than a curse to cause death. It was used more in the past than it is now."

"Oh." Elizabeth's face cleared. "I am learning a great deal! My magic works so differently. I neither use spells nor the elements. I do not think about fire at all when I make it." She held up her hand and rubbed her thumb against the tips of her first two fingers. A blue flame rose out of her thumb. "I light the candle with this. Do not worry; it does not burn." She ran her free hand through the flame to demonstrate, then quenched it by blowing on it.

"Nicely done. That is wild magic," said Eversleigh. "Rubbing your fingers together simulates how a fire is made, so there is no need to think of fire."

"How did you learn that?" asked Frederica.

Elizabeth said, "I wish I could tell you. It simply came to me one day when I wanted to light a candle and was too tired to go downstairs to the fire to do so."

Eversleigh smiled warmly at her. "Definitely wild magic. It starts with your intent, and then the magic leads you."

"I wish it were so simple for me!" exclaimed Frederica. "Will you show me that again?"

When Elizabeth complied, Frederica attempted to imitate her, her face screwing up in concentration. "Bother! I cannot do it."

"Wild magic is hard when you have used spells all your life," said Eversleigh.

They had reached a little wilderness between the formal gardens and the orchard, stopping by the banks of the stream. Frederica asked Anne, "Do you wish to try again? The spell for this is '*Crescas.*' Say it as you touch the plant, send your magic down into its roots and its leaves, and encourage it to grow. This should be safer than creating fire."

Anne knelt beside the new growth of plants pushing their way up into the spring air. She pointed to a furled fern. "A plant like that?"

"Certainly."

"*Crescas.*" Anne held the stem between her thumb and forefinger and frowned in concentration. "Nothing is happening."

"Do not give up. Almost everyone with magic can make plants grow, even if just a little. It is a matter of finding the knack for it. It is intensive magic, so do not expect dramatic results."

Darcy suspected that was why Freddie had picked this particular task. If Anne needed to burn massive amounts of magical energy, growing a plant or two should be enough to exhaust her. Then they could decide what to do next.

The fern slowly began to unfurl and extended itself inch by inch. Leaves began to form on the fronds. Darcy encouraged the water in the stream to soak into the bank, since the rapid growth must be draining the soil of every bit of moisture it contained. Soon the fern stood a foot tall, towering over its neighbors in its full glory.

"Impressive," remarked Eversleigh. "I doubt any of us could have taken it that far except perhaps Darcy, and even he would have had to make an enormous effort."

Anne stared at the fern. "I need more." She ran off towards the orchard, her skirts kilted up in her hands. Frederica followed at her heels.

Eversleigh raised his eyebrows expressively at Darcy. They followed the path to the orchard at a more sedate pace.

In the orchard, Frederica remonstrated with Anne, whose hands were wrapped around the trunk of a recently planted sapling. "You will exhaust yourself. It is not wise."

"I want to exhaust myself!" Anne closed her eyes and leaned toward the sapling, twigs brushing against her forehead. The leaf buds swelled and burst forth in greenery. Then, incredibly, the tree grew taller inch by inch. The trunk thickened between Anne's hands, even as she grew pale, her arms trembling. Frederica wrung her hands.

Elizabeth appeared followed by two footmen, one with a tray of food and the other with a pitcher of lemonade. She stopped short when she spotted Anne, her mouth open.

Anne's head now leaned against a trunk too wide to wrap her hands around. The growth appeared to have stopped. Slowly Anne slid down to her knees. She seemed to be barely breathing, but she whispered, "That is better."

Darcy could not believe it. Lord Matlock had believed Darcy would be able to manage Anne's outbursts of magic if he married her. Based on this performance, that task would be as far beyond his abilities as flying to the moon.

Elizabeth motioned the footman forward to offer the food to Anne, who grasped a roll in one hand and a piece of sausage in the other and did her best to devour them simultaneously.

Eversleigh sidled over to Darcy. "I am rather glad I did not know the powder keg we were sitting on when I weakened that defensive spell," he said quietly.

"I would not have believed it possible."

"I can tell you one thing," said Eversleigh. "If her father was indeed studying sorcery and he had that magnitude of magical power to call upon, I think we are all very fortunate he died when he did."

"Amen," said Richard.

Frederica raised her head, her arm around Anne's shoulders. "I fear she has fainted. She will need assistance returning to the house."

Richard stepped forward. "I will carry her."

"Not you, Fitzwilliam," said Eversleigh. "You are a source, and if you touch her right now –"

"She will drain every ounce of magic out of me, even unconscious. You are correct. It is going to take some time for me to grow accustomed to this new Anne," said Richard.

"I will take her," said Eversleigh. "No, not you either, Darcy. Your arm is injured. It might be improper, but to be honest, my carrying your cousin to the house is probably the least shocking thing that has happened today."

"Take her to the Dower House," said Frederica. "We do not need Lady Catherine hearing about this."

"What are you going to do about Sir Lewis?" asked Frederica from her place beside Anne's unconscious body on the fainting couch.

"Damned if I know," grumbled Richard. "I am not looking forward to telling my father."

Darcy said, "Surely we should at least investigate his study before troubling Lord Matlock."

"First things first," Eversleigh said crisply. "Neither of you is going to do anything unless I ask you to do it. I do not want to deal with questions later about why blood relatives were allowed to lead this investigation – and that goes for Lord Matlock as well. By default, that means this is my investigation, and you are following my instructions."

"You will hear no objection from me," said Richard. "I am happy to cede this responsibility."

"I was going to suggest the same thing," said Darcy. "Especially since you are on the Council of Mages."

"There is that," said Eversleigh dryly. "This would have fallen to me in any case, since of the other three mages on the Council, one is in Ireland, one is 83 years old and can barely remember his own name, and one is crippled by gout. It is merely good fortune I am already here."

Elizabeth asked, "Pardon me, but if there are questions later, how are we to account for your being here already? I assume you would prefer not to bring Faerie into it."

"A good point." Eversleigh's gaze drifted thoughtfully over each of them in turn. "Gentlemen, perhaps you would join me in spreading the rumor that I am dangling after Lady Frederica. Naturally I followed her here." He bowed to Frederica. "Unless you object, Lady Frederica?"

Richard chuckled. "No one will have any trouble believing that. There is always some fellow or another dangling after Freddie."

"Is that so?" Eversleigh raised his quizzing glass and examined Frederica. "I suppose there would be."

Frederica's cheeks were red, but whether from embarrassment or anger was impossible to tell. "If it is convenient for your lordship, I can have no objection. But I would prefer to hear your plans for stopping the sorcery here."

Eversleigh glanced in the mirror and made a microscopic adjustment to his cravat. "Darcy is correct. The three of us must examine Sir Lewis's study. I tend to believe Miss de Bourgh's assertion that he was a sorcerer, since she would have no reason to lie, but let us prove it before going any further."

Richard heaved a sigh. "You are right, I suppose. At least we will be done faster with three of us working."

Darcy shook his head. "It may take longer than a day. The room has been locked up since Sir Lewis's death, and I am likely the only person who has entered it since."

"That was an unfortunate choice under the circumstances, but I suppose you could not have known." Eversleigh's voice was tinged with disapproval.

"No, I could not have known," retorted Darcy. "I was looking for books that might have information on Faerie. The room was covered with dust. You will be able to see where I was and what I touched."

"You saw no evidence of sorcery?"

"I was not looking for it. There was some odd equipment that looked alchemical, and some of his books were in Italian, but I thought nothing of it at the time." There was no need to say more. Every mage knew most books on sorcery were written in that language.

Richard stretched. "Fortunately, we do not need to do a complete search. All we need is confirmation that he was engaged in sorcery, and then it will be my infelicitous task to ride to London and break the news to my father. Even if it is your investigation, Eversleigh, he cannot be left out of it."

"You could send an express," said Darcy.

Richard shook his head somberly. "My father is not a young man, and this will devastate him. Telling him in person, with my mother there to support him, is safer."

Frederica said, "I agree completely, Richard. He will blame himself for failing to see it."

Something else to look forward to.

The corridor to Sir Lewis's library was still dust covered, the footprints from Darcy's previous visit visible. At least now he understood why the servants had been afraid to clean it.

He unlocked the door and held it open for Eversleigh and Richard to precede him. Darcy almost bumped into Richard who stood frozen in place a few feet beyond the door.

"It is true," said Richard.

"What?" asked Darcy.

"Can you not feel it?" Richard's face was ashen.

"Feel what?"

Richard moved his hands through the air. "Evil. Death. Corruption. I have never felt sorcery, but I know this is it."

Eversleigh turned to him. "Can you generally sense the magic of a mage who is not present?"

"No, but this is... It is like a stench. It is simply there."

"Your father will be interested to know that sources can sense long departed sorcery."

"If it is sorcery. We still have to prove that," said Darcy. "Eversleigh, I do not suppose you can read Italian."

The viscount gave a dry smile. "Indeed I can. I like living on the edge of danger." Many mages would deny even the appearance of knowledge of the language. "I will look through his books. One of you should go through his desk while the other checks his experiments."

Richard shuddered. "You take the desk, Darcy. I do not want to touch anything he touched. This is worse than the aftermath of a battle. At least death in battle is clean." He gingerly approached the laboratory table, his hands tightly clasped behind his back.

Darcy opened the top drawer of the desk. Quills, a knife for mending pens, paper, a bottle of ink – nothing surprising. To be safe, he felt along the back of the drawer for signs of a hidden compartment, but it seemed solid.

The next drawer held leather-bound notebooks. Darcy lifted out the topmost and opened it. The ink had faded, but the crabbed handwriting was still legible. The first page seemed to be a list of ingredients for an experiment, followed by the annotation 'Useless. Waste of time.' The next page showed a recipe that seemed to have been more successful, since it was followed by a list of names and quantities – one dram, two drams. The names all sounded like commoners. Had Sir Lewis been experimenting on the servants and the tenants? Bile rose in Darcy's throat.

A book slammed shut with a bang. Richard said tautly, "Eversleigh, whatever you were doing, stop it."

"I was merely reading the book," said Eversleigh mildly.

"Well, don't read it!" Richard sounded on the edge of an explosion.

Darcy asked, "What were you reading?"

Eversleigh looked apologetic. "It was a spell. It is indeed a book of sorcery, but I was only reading through the spell, not performing it, as if I would ever do such a thing."

Richard was standing on his toes, his hands clenched. "Then skip the spells!"

"Certainly," Eversleigh said calmly. "Fitzwilliam, it seems to me we have enough evidence already to say that your father will need to see this, so perhaps you would do best to ride for London now. You are one of the strongest men I know, but clearly you would be better off out of this place."

Richard looked at Darcy who nodded. "Very well. I cannot be of much use here in any case."

"But if we ever need a sorcery-sniffing hound, you will be very useful."

Richard grimaced. "I would be happy never to smell sorcery again. I imagine I will return in the morning. Any messages, Darcy?"

Darcy shook his head. "Safe travels."

After Richard left, Eversleigh said, "I have sometimes envied sources for their peaceful abilities, but I am grateful not to be one today. I cannot imagine what it took to distress him so much."

"You were right to encourage him to leave. I have never seen him react that way." But the more Darcy saw in the notebooks, the more he sympathized with Richard. "How damning are the books?"

"Very damning indeed. Apart from a few on alchemy, all the ones I have looked at are sorcery texts." Eversleigh heaved down another large volume from the shelves.

Darcy turned reluctantly back to the notebooks.

Elizabeth jumped to her feet. "Mr. Darcy wishes to see me? At this hour? Did you tell him Lady Frederica and Miss de Bourgh have already retired?" She would have been abed herself if her body had not still hummed with nervous energy from the stressful day, or so she tried to convince herself. Or perhaps the rushing noise of the wind outside was responsible for her agitation. But those were just excuses. It was thoughts of Darcy that had kept her awake. Now he was here, and her body felt suddenly alive, her skin tingling with anticipation.

"I explained that, miss, but he insisted you were the one he wishes to speak to. Do you want me to stay with you while he is here?" The maid's heavy eyelids were at odds with her offer.

"I will ring for you if I need you." Elizabeth spoke with more assurance than she felt. She had been alone with Darcy on several occasions, both before and after his proposal, and he had never made any attempt to take advantage of the situation, but now she wondered how much she could trust herself. She had not been able to stop thinking about him since their brief conversation outside Titania's bower when she had experienced that unaccountable urge to throw herself into his arms. He must know it, or why would he wish to see her alone in the middle of a windstorm? Or perhaps something had gone amiss at Rosings.

She tidied her hair, although at this point nothing would make it look freshly styled, and made her way downstairs to the sitting room. The maid had not yet taken the time to clean it fully, since she would have had no reason to expect guests before morning.

Darcy stood by the fireplace, his elbow resting on the mantel and his hand across his eyes. His hair looked as if the gardeners had taken a rake to it, and his usually tidy cravat was wrinkled, the earlier complex folds now retied into a simple schoolboy knot.

Her heart sank. Something must be very wrong. "Mr. Darcy, what is amiss?"

He started at her words and collected himself enough to bow. "My apologies for calling at this hour. I was walking the grounds and saw the light in your window. I hoped talking to you might clear my head."

How did he know which window was hers? He had not been upstairs in the Dower House since she had moved there. And why did his head need clearing? He did not appear to be foxed, but he might well be less than sober. "It is late to be walking the grounds."

His mouth twisted. "Going to sleep was not an appealing option."

He was not going to make this easy for her. "How did your examination of Sir Lewis's library go? Did you find proof of sorcery?"

His shoulders sagged. "We found an abundance of proof. I spent hours reading his journals. Sorcery is a viler thing than I ever realized. I feel unclean, as if nothing can ever wash away what I saw. That any man could do such things, much less a man I knew…" He turned haunted eyes to her.

The poor man! He was clearly suffering. But what comfort could she offer? "It takes great courage to confront the stuff of nightmares. The old stories of sorcerers – they are terrifying."

"It is not courage. Richard is the bravest man I know, and he could not even bear to be in the room. He said the stench of sorcery made him ill."

"How long did you stay there?"

He shrugged. "I left perhaps half an hour ago. Eversleigh is still there. I did not even stop for dinner because the mere thought of food turned my stomach." He wiped the back of his hand against his mouth.

"I am so sorry." If only she could relieve his pain!

"I am the one who should be sorry for imposing on you with my tale of woe."

"Pray do not be sorry. If speaking of it can provide any comfort..."

"Talking to you was not my only reason for coming here." He took a few quick steps across the room to look out the window. "When elemental mages feel something strongly, the elements respond. If I do not keep my emotions in check, there can be floods, fires, whirlwinds. I have learned how to control my moods to prevent such things. Tonight I could not do so. You heard the wind." He clenched his hands. "For reasons I cannot explain, the elements do not respond to me as strongly when I am with you, so I came here before I flooded the village or burnt down Rosings."

Elizabeth stared at him. "You think that I somehow interfere with your magic?"

"I do not know what it is. I only know that certain people seem to lessen my effect on the elements. Or perhaps I should say certain creatures, since your cat has the same effect. When Pepper is on my lap, the elements might as well not exist." His agitation seemed to be increasing rather than decreasing.

"No wonder you are fond of her." Could this be why he had sought out Elizabeth's company so often? "I assume proximity must help, then." She crossed the room to sit next to where he stood, trying to pretend she would not rather be closer still.

His mouth twisted. "Proximity helps to subdue the elements, but in your case, it is also dangerous."

"Dangerous? I do not understand."

He stepped jerkily until he was directly in front of her, his face drawn. "Elizabeth," he said hoarsely. "I know you do not want me. I know you despise mages and would never consider... But I beg of you, do not send me away." He grasped her hands. "For the love of God, let me hold you, so that I can remember there is some good in the world, and that I am not all alone against the darkness." His voice throbbed with raw need, but it was the need for comfort, not the desire of a man for a woman.

How could she refuse him what he so desperately needed, especially when she wanted it so badly herself?

He drew her to him before she had time to think further. Her cheek rested against his chest, the superfine wool of his coat providing softness over the muscle beneath it. Her hands clutched his shoulders, and there was nothing soft about them. But it was his hands splayed against her back she felt most of all, tempting her as he held her close.

The weight of his head rested on top of hers in a way that felt all too natural. She could hear the steady thudding of his heart. His clean scent of shaving soap and spice was overlaid by dust and ink. Sensation surrounded her – the warmth of his arms around her, his somehow delicate touch on her back, and the astonishing intimacy of pressing herself against him so closely that she could feel his chest rise and fall with each breath, creating an ache deep within her. If only she had not been wearing her shawl, she might have felt the warmth of his long fingers through the thin fabric of her dress. The mere thought raised the tide of longing.

How mortifying it was! He wanted comfort, and all she could feel was wantonness. What a triumph for him, could he know that the proposals which she had proudly spurned less than a fortnight ago would now have been gladly and gratefully received! He was as generous, she doubted not, as the most generous of his sex. But while he was mortal, there must be a triumph, even now, when any connection between them was impossible. So much had changed since that evening when she had so bitterly and foolishly refused his proposal.

Now his heartbeat sped up, so perhaps he was not altogether indifferent to her charms. Not that it mattered now.

He released her then, leaving her even more bereft. "I apologize, Miss Elizabeth. You are generous, but I should not be imperiling your reputation for my own selfish needs."

"My reputation?" She sank down onto the sofa, hoping he would not realize that it was because her legs were having trouble supporting her. "The only reputation I have is an unsavory one."

He stiffened visibly. "Because of our journey to Faerie?"

She half smiled at the thought of riding bareback in his arms. "Compared to everything else I have done, that was nothing. Everyone knows now that I am a woman with magic. Society may grudgingly accept a magical woman who consents to a binding spell, but a woman who refuses one? Never. At present I am in a fragile artificial world where those around me are willing to accept magic in a woman, at least to some degree, but this is not reality. The minute I step off the grounds of Rosings, there will be children throwing stones at me."

The color drained from his face. "But that has never happened to you before."

"No, because I have always kept my abilities a secret. Now Lady Catherine is shouting to the rooftops that I am a witch. Mr. Collins has no doubt already written to Sir William Lucas with the shocking news, and all Meryton will know it in a day. And if that were not enough, I was gone for several nights, returned in your company, and then accepted an offer of protection from Colonel Fitzwilliam."

"What?" He sounded half strangled. "If he dared –"

She held up her hand. "The colonel did nothing improper, but that does not matter. When a young woman accepts an offer of housing and support from a gentleman, it does not matter how pure his intentions are. I assure you the rest of the world will see it as improper. Before all this happened, I would never have dreamed of accepting his invitation to stay at this house, but it does not matter anymore."

"Of course it matters!" He raked his hand through his hair. "It is not too late. We can give out that Anne was the one who invited you, and then it is perfectly proper. Frederica has been here the entire time, so you have been chaperoned."

"You might not wish to make that fact public. I spent most of the afternoon trying to convince Lady Frederica to return to London immediately. She does still have a reputation, but it will be harmed, not just from exposure to me, but by the taint of sorcery that will cling to all of us, no matter how many years ago the sorcery took place. It would be wiser for her to leave immediately and pretend she was never here. I wish you would speak to her about it, because she will not listen to me."

"She has been with Anne, and that will protect her reputation."

"My dear Mr. Darcy, Miss de Bourgh will have even less reputation than I do. Even if she somehow manages to keep her magic secret, she is still the daughter of a sorcerer. She will never be welcome in polite company."

Now it was Darcy's turn to sink down in the chair. He covered his face with his hands. "Sir Lewis is still harming people, even today." His muffled voice was despairing

So much for having offered him comfort. She went to the sideboard, poured two glasses of wine, and brought him one. "It looks as if this might not go amiss."

He did not meet her eyes. "I thank you. I only wish I could help ease your pain."

"Mr. Darcy, do I sound as if I am in pain?" she asked sharply. She was, of course, but it was not about her reputation.

"No. You sound remarkably calm about your life falling apart."

"That is because I am calm. A little sad, perhaps, for the future I once hoped to have, but I never really believed in that future. The price of remaining in society, of someday marrying and having a family, was living a lie. I am relieved it is over, and I no longer have to pretend to be someone I am not. For the first time in my life, I feel free of fear. I can perform small everyday magics without worrying about being seen. And Miss de Bourgh is free, too. I cannot see her being a fine society lady, and she is already considering plans for what she wishes to do next." She took a sip of the wine, its tartness bringing her back to the present.

"It is admirable of you to try to make the best of your situation, but I am not ready to admit it is hopeless. We could set up a new identity for you, perhaps a recent arrival from India. We can arrange for references. My uncle can claim to have known your father as a child and that he was appointed your guardian after your parents died. You would be completely respectable."

Elizabeth sighed. "You do not believe me. I do not need a new identity. There are places I can go, enclaves of wisewomen where it is safe to be a woman with magic. Or perhaps I will remain with Miss de Bourgh. She dismissed her companion this afternoon, so she will need a new one, and I am interested in the plans she is making. She wants to make Rosings a haven where women can learn magic."

"What of Eversleigh?" he asked harshly.

Taken aback by his anger, Elizabeth said, "I imagine he would help me if I asked, but I do not intend to do so. I do not see why you are so troubled that I am not fighting the inevitable."

"Because it is not inevitable, and it is my fault you are in this position! If I had never asked you to treat Lady Catherine, none of this would have happened. You would still be visiting Mrs. Collins and looking forward to returning to Longbourn."

"Your fault? I could have refused to treat her or simply not used magic, and the result would have been the same as if you had not asked me. But Miss de Bourgh would still be swooning and unable to finish a sentence, Lady Catherine would be dead, and we would have no hope of stopping the fay attacks. All in all, I think it is not an unreasonable exchange."

"Well said, but I also remember you telling me in Faerie that you did not want a brother, nor a mother under a binding spell, nor a father who would bespell your mother."

She sighed, trying to keep her emotions in check. "I do not want those things, but I would rather know the truth than a pretty lie. Well, apart from the Sidhe brother. He is still a bitter pill to swallow. I could do without the knowledge that my father abandoned a helpless infant in addition to binding my mother. Still, Eversleigh keeps saying it is good for Aelfric to have met me, so at least someone benefits." She somehow managed to make the last sentence sound droll.

"I would have been happy not to know Sir Lewis was a sorcerer." Darcy's voice was flat.

There was nothing she could say to that. It was terrifying to realize there had been a sorcerer in their midst, and no one had discovered him. If Anne de Bourgh had not killed him...She shuddered to think what might have happened.

The wind rattled the window panes.

Darcy abruptly moved to sit beside Elizabeth on the sofa, his shoulders slumping. "My apologies. The wind is picking up again."

How could she bear to watch this proud man brought so low? She placed her hand gently over his. "Does that help?"

He nodded silently. After a moment he said explosively, "I cannot believe this is happening. I never lose control like this."

"Never? That is a very high standard."

"It is a necessary standard," he snapped.

She hated to see him criticize himself so harshly. "You have had a difficult time as well, learning about Miss de Bourgh's binding spell and that your uncle had been the one to place it, not to mention that she had murdered her father whom we now know was a sorcerer. Your family has been turned upside down as much as mine, and that does not count being thrown into Faerie twice, nearly dying in a glamour trap, and watching Miss de Bourgh perform impossible feats of magic. And that was before you had to face Sir Lewis's sorcery tonight." Not to mention having a heartfelt, if ill-expressed, proposal of marriage thrown back in his face. "It would be more astonishing if your control were not slipping."

Somehow she had to help him. Without conscious thought, she found herself laying the fingers of one hand against his cheek. It was rougher than she had expected, but he would not have shaved before the dinner he had not eaten. The poor man deserved so much better, and she ached because she could not give it to him.

He stiffened and turned his head to face her, his eyes dark with pain. She could not have looked away to save her life. Tension hung in the air between them.

Then his lips sought hers, the gentle pressure making her lips part instinctively. This was what she had needed, this all too human touch from this particular man. She made a little choking noise in her throat as an ache rose deep inside her. As if it had been an invitation, his kiss became hungrier, with a desperate need.

She arched towards him, instinctively seeking more of him. More of his lips, the tantalizing, spicy taste of him, and more of the flutters of pleasure expanding from her deepest parts. She leaned into the hand cradling the back of her neck as he nibbled her lip. The sensual onslaught only intensified as he deepened the kiss as if responding to the need building within her. The last of her remaining ability to think fled as he explored her mouth, and she became a creature of pure sensation and need. She needed his touch and his closeness more than she needed air to breathe.

Her hands seemed to develop a life of their own, winding around his neck, seeking even more contact. He groaned and pulled her closer, but it could never be close enough, even as she felt the warmth of his body through his clothes. She gave a whimper of protest as he dragged his mouth away from hers, only to begin a new onslaught as his lips fluttered along her cheek, nibbled her earlobe, and found the exquisitely sensitive spot where her neck met her jaw.

Oh, who could have known her neck could provide such overpowering, burning pleasure? She tipped her head to the side, exposing more of her flesh to his forays.

Her clothes suddenly seemed to constrain her, chafing tender skin as his tongue skimmed her collarbone. When he discovered the notch at the base of her neck, something inside her seemed to melt. The cascading intensity of her need began to overpower her. Surely he would go lower, to that skin bared by her neckline that was longing for his touch! But he did not, and she thought she might expire from the loss until he reclaimed her lips, this time with a devouring certainty. She met him with her own demands even as she accepted his claim. As his hand finally began to explore the curves of her body, a swell of desire swept through her, leaving her trembling and straining against him.

A loud crash broke through the sensual spell trapping Elizabeth. She pulled back from him just as a second crash was followed by the sound of shattering glass. Something slammed shut with a resounding bang. It seemed to be coming from above them.

Good heavens, how had she ended up on Darcy's lap?

The third crash made the walls shake. Elizabeth scrambled off Darcy's lap and raced up the stairs, Darcy close behind her.

The wild racket was coming from Miss de Bourgh's room. Elizabeth threw open the door. Inside a whirlwind had knocked over furniture, pulled paintings off the wall, and scattered bits of debris everywhere. A window hung open, dangling from a single hinge.

Darcy's hand on her shoulder tugged her back. "Do not go in. It is not safe for you." He strode past her into the room, ignoring the whirlwind tearing at his clothes, and pulled back the bed curtains to reveal a sleeping form.

How could Miss de Bourgh possibly sleep through this racket?

"Good heavens!" Frederica stood behind her in nothing but a nightgown, staring at the wreckage.

Pounding footsteps on the stairs signaled the arrival of a footman and the maid, now wide awake and gaping at the sight. A blur of white fur passed by them, racing into the room. Pepper leapt onto the bed and sprawled herself across Miss de Bourgh's sleeping body.

There was sudden silence as the whirlwind vanished. The whistling of the wind outside disappeared.

Darcy tipped his head back, as if consulting heaven. "It was not me," he said incredulously. "It was her."

"She created the windstorm while she slept?" Elizabeth asked in astonishment.

He nodded. "Your cat is worth her weight in gold. She stopped it."

"Pepper did? Then she deserves all the fish she can eat tomorrow."

Pepper purred loudly enough to be heard from the door.

Darcy came back out to the landing, rubbing his forehead. "Since my father died, I have been the only strong elemental mage in England. It never occurred to me that the windstorm could be caused by someone else. I should have seen it coming. My uncle said Anne had elemental magic."

"What should we do, sir?" The footman's voice trembled.

Darcy glanced back into the bedroom. "It will be safe as long as Pepper stays with her, but we should be prepared in case she leaves. We will need five basins of water, one under the bed and the others around it. The banked coals should be removed from the fireplace and replaced with paper, and metal pots with paper placed around the bed as well."

"Water under the bed and paper in the fireplace?" The maid clearly thought he had lost his mind.

"She is stirring the elements when she dreams, and whatever items are closest to her will be affected. If she calls water in her sleep, the water under the bed will spill, but the lake will not flood. If she calls fire, the paper in the fireplace will burn rather than the house. Placing things with little value around the bed will help if she casts unmaking – better that she unmake some crockery than the walls. I have no idea what to do about calling wind. I rarely had difficulties with that." He shook his head in disbelief. "Someone will have to stay awake to watch over her in case the precautions are not enough."

Frederica, her eyes wide, said, "I hate to think what she could have done if she had not exhausted her magic earlier."

"I will start teaching her elemental control tomorrow." Darcy ran his hands over his face. "This is like revisiting my childhood."

"You did this sort of thing?" said Frederica, sounding horrified.

"Every night. Usually I created floods in my sleep rather than windstorms, though."

The maid asked, "Should we wake her if it starts again?"

"No. That could be dangerous. There is no telling what she might do if she is startled awake. Fortunately, it appears she can sleep through almost anything." He looked at Elizabeth. "It was not me. Or at least it was mostly not me. Most likely I added to the disturbance. I cannot believe it."

Frederica smothered a yawn. "What are you doing here anyway, Darcy?"

Elizabeth said quickly, "He stopped by to tell me what they had found in Sir Lewis's study, and I am very glad he did. His timing was impeccable." At least the shadows on the dark landing would hide her blushes.

"Darcy, I think you should stay here tonight, or whatever is left of it," said Frederica. "You are the only one who understands this."

Darcy turned to the maid. "Is there a bed that can be prepared for me? A sofa or a cot in the servants' quarters will do."

"Yes, sir." The maid hurried off.

Heat tingled through Elizabeth. She knew Darcy would not attempt anything further with her, but simply knowing he would be in the same house while she was sleeping made her senses more alive. He might not do anything, but she suspected he would be thinking about it. She certainly would be.

How could she even be thinking about what had passed between them when the room in front of her looked as if it had been ransacked by hobgoblins? Her body was not listening to her mind; it only wanted to feel Darcy's hands on her again, to touch him, to experience the sensual awakening of his kiss. Where was the mortification she ought to be feeling? She had to find a way to keep this desire under control. Heavens, she sounded like Darcy when he explained how his moods affected the elements, but one could not help having moods. Perhaps one could not help feeling this aching need, either.

She rubbed her arms, trying to create new sensation to replace her memory of Darcy's touch, but it did not work.

"Elizabeth, are you unwell?" asked Frederica. "You look as if you are in another world."

"I am perfectly well," said Elizabeth firmly. But she did feel as if she were in a new world, one which did not have the sense of familiarity that Faerie did. "I was thinking about poor Miss de Bourgh. She must feel so lost."

Lost. She was the one who was lost, adrift on an unknown sea. Anchors had always held her in place, but now they had vanished one by one. Her father, her mother, and even her uncle had all become unknown to her. Her home was no longer safe. Charlotte had been cut off from her. She had letters from Jane, but how could she even begin to tell her sister what her life had become? Even her memories were untrustworthy. She had a brother who was not a brother. The only time she had felt anchored and safe was when she had been in Darcy's arms, and that was the one place she should not be.

"You are not well," said Frederica decisively. "Come to your room. You can sit down, and we can talk about it."

Elizabeth realized she was crying. "Not my room!" Somehow that was very important.

"My room, then," said Frederica. "Darcy can handle matters here."

She allowed Frederica to put an arm around her and steer her into her bedroom.

Frederica pulled out a chair from in front of the vanity. "Sit here. I will bring you a handkerchief."

Elizabeth took a deep breath, but she could not calm herself. Hot tears kept running down her cheeks as she choked back sobs. She accepted a handkerchief Frederica thrust into her hand and pressed it over her eyes.

Frederica said soothingly, "It must have been a shock to see that Cousin Anne could do so much damage in her sleep, but Darcy will find a way to make it safe for her. He always does manage to solve these things. In the morning it will look better."

She cried even harder. The disaster in Miss de Bourgh's room was the least of her worries. She could not tell Frederica what she and Darcy had been doing before that. A sob tore through her. As if that were her only worry! Somehow she managed to regain just enough composure to speak. "I met you five days ago. Five days! It seems like a year. Less than a fortnight ago everything was normal in my life, until your father came and I fled to Faerie. Now it never seems to stop. What disaster will happen tomorrow?" And now she finally knew what she wanted, and she could not have it. She dissolved into sobs again.

"It is shocking, is it not? I remember being so excited to hear you tell me about what Faerie was like, and how thrilled I was to have the opportunity to go there. And then to have Titania want to speak to me and ask me to stay! It should have been everything I wanted. But now all this with Cousin Anne and Sir Lewis – the world is becoming a frightening place. But we will muddle through somehow." Frederica paused in reflection. "This is not so bad. Oliver Cromwell was the last sorcerer in England, and he nearly destroyed the country. He was a nobody, and yet he took over England with his power. A hundred thousand dead, including the king, and so many people enslaved by him. Bloody Mary the Sorceress had hundreds killed and nearly put us under Spanish rule. It seems Sir Lewis did not even do enough damage for it to be noticed. He could not do more without causing trouble in the Collegium. That is progress, is it not?"

"That might be little comfort to those people who suffered under Sir Lewis, but you are right. It is not the same as Cromwell or Bloody Mary, or even Henry VII stealing the throne with sorcery. We should be grateful Sir Lewis did no more."

"I think you have managed admirably through one shock after another," said Frederica.

"I have done my best." Elizabeth wiped her eyes. Speaking of history was calming, but a glance in the mirror over the vanity showed her eyes were red and swollen. She did not want Darcy to see her like this. Perhaps she could talk to Frederica until she looked more like herself.

The landing was empty when Elizabeth left Frederica's room.

Now she needed an excuse to go downstairs. Even if nothing else was possible, she wanted to be in his presence, if only for a few minutes. That was why she had not wanted to go to her bedroom earlier. She would have been expected to retire, and she could not have seen him.

She felt her way downstairs through the dark, one hand gripping the railing. Light still spilled from the drawing room. Would he be there?

He was sitting in an upholstered chair, staring thoughtfully into the remnants of the fire. He jumped to his feet when Elizabeth entered.

"Pardon me for disturbing you," she said, her voice almost steady. "I left my candle here earlier." She took the chamberstick with its lighted candle from a side table.

"Your presence could never disturb me." His voice was low and intimate.

The heat of desire began to grip her once again. "I will say goodnight, then."

He stepped closer to her and brushed her cheek with his knuckles. "About what happened earlier –"

She had to be strong. "Nothing has changed. There is no future for us, despite a moment of weakness."

He was silent for a moment. "What if I am not willing to accept that?"

There was a tiny comfort in knowing he still wanted her. "Are you willing to explain to your sister why, despite being under suspicion of misusing your powers, you decided to take up with a woman who was beneath you to start out with and is now an active scandal, even knowing it would destroy your sister's chance of being accepted in society and making a good marriage? The Collegium's suspicions would not be allayed by discovering you had married a witch, and you would be in greater danger. It does not matter what either of us want."

"I still say there are ways of dealing with the scandal." There was a plea in his voice.

"Perhaps there are, but it would mean living a lie for the rest of my life. That is too high a price."

His fingers lifted her chin, and then she tasted the yearning, delicious heat of his lips again. He teased her mouth open with his tongue, but not in the hungry, demanding manner of his earlier kisses. This was slower, more intimate, and made her long for more.

Too soon he pulled his lips away and rested his forehead against hers. "If you deny this, you are living a different kind of lie."

She wanted to give in so badly. Instead she retreated into the simplest excuse. "It is late."

One side of his mouth turned up as he straightened. "So it is. We can speak more tomorrow."

Elizabeth already felt the lack of his touch. "Good night, then."

"Sleep well." He lowered his voice. "And Elizabeth? Lock your door."

Oddly, that helped her regain her composure. "Am I supposed to believe you are one of those very rare mages who cannot perform an unlocking spell?" she asked archly.

His eyes flared. "Go to bed, Elizabeth – while you still can."

# Chapter 9

Darcy spent a troubled night in an uncomfortable bed in the Dower House. Or perhaps the bed only felt uncomfortable after Elizabeth's refusal to consider a future with him. How could she kiss him so passionately and then turn away from him? By morning he was filled with a simmering anger and judged it best to return to the main house before he saw Elizabeth and said something he would regret.

By the time he had changed into clean clothes and shaved, it was well after he usually breakfasted. He found Eversleigh still in the breakfast room, shadows under his eyes.

"How late were you up last night?" Darcy asked him.

"Too late, and my dreams were not pleasant. Textbooks of sorcery make for poor bedtime reading."

"I can imagine. I had a late-night adventure of a different sort." Darcy poured himself another cup of coffee as he told Eversleigh about Anne's disturbance of the elements. "I will need to spend some time training her in how to control elemental magic. Or at least I will try. I have never taught elemental magic before, and I do not know how well Anne will respond to teaching."

Eversleigh pursed his lips. "Indeed. She does not strike me as someone who enjoys taking direction."

They said little more as Darcy picked at his food, his stomach too tied in knots to feel any hunger. He pushed his plate away. "I suppose we should discuss our findings of last night." It was the last thing in the world he wanted to do.

Eversleigh grimaced. "Let us at least do so in the comfort of the drawing room."

They had no sooner arrived there when the sound of hoof beats made Eversleigh twitch aside a curtain and peer out the window. "It appears we have visitors. Colonel Fitzwilliam and Lord Matlock, if I am not mistaken."

Darcy frowned. "They must have set off at dawn to arrive so early."

"I am not surprised Lord Matlock would want to investigate immediately. We must do our best to keep him from overworking himself."

When Lord Matlock entered the drawing room, his ashen face looked a decade older. Richard trailed after him carrying a wooden box.

Eversleigh guided Lord Matlock to a sofa. "Rest, sir. They will bring tea and refreshments shortly."

"I must see his work room first," Lord Matlock said wearily.

"No, sir, you must sit and rest for a few minutes. Darcy and I can tell you of our discoveries last night, so it will not be wasted time."

Lord Matlock shook his head. "I will see it first."

Suddenly Richard loomed over his father. "You will sit down," he ordered. "Mother charged me with keeping you from overwork."

The older man almost smiled as he lowered himself to sit. "And you are more frightened of her wrath than of mine."

"Of course. Any sane man would be."

Lord Matlock sighed. "Eversleigh, I have business with you in any case."

"I am, as always, at your service. As it happens, I have some business with you as well," said Eversleigh.

Lord Matlock waved to Richard who handed him the polished wooden box about the size of a chess set. He set it on his lap and rested his palms on it briefly before holding it out to Eversleigh. "This is yours now."

Eversleigh, his brows furled, took the box and opened it. His throat bobbed as he swallowed. "My lord, this is your chain of office." His voice was low.

"No, it is your chain of office now," said Lord Matlock testily. "I wrote my letter of resignation last night, appointing you the Acting Master of the Collegium until next winter's meeting."

"But –"

"Stop it. I failed to see that my own brother-in-law was a sorcerer. I cannot lead the Collegium with the inevitable questions that will be asked. It must be you or Debenham, and Debenham is in Ireland. Do not waste my energy with arguments."

Richard said gently, "He is right, you know."

Slowly Eversleigh closed the lid of the box. "I will do my best to live up to your trust. I only wish the circumstances could be different."

Lord Matlock said gruffly, "You said you had business with me. What is it?"

Eversleigh's cheeks colored. "It is more a matter of a confession I must make. Lady Frederica and Colonel Fitzwilliam are now aware of this matter, and I do not wish to put them in a position where they must choose between keeping a secret from you or betraying my confidence." He took a deep breath. "I am half fay."

The older man's jaw dropped. "Good God. You never told me."

"I have preferred not to reveal this particular blot on my escutcheon, as it were. As we have more contact with Faerie, it will become difficult to disguise. Darcy, might I ask you to do the honors of explaining my situation? It is difficult to say it myself without sounding infernally conceited."

Darcy nodded. "He is a prince of Faerie. Oberon begot him on his mother after her marriage. Eversleigh is well known in the Faerie court."

"I think..." Lord Matlock seemed to look off in the distance. "I think I would like some port, even if it is still breakfast time."

"Right away, sir." Richard strode to the sideboard.

"There is nothing like a good glass of port when life becomes too interesting." Lord Matlock's shoulders sagged in an uncharacteristic look of defeat.

He had only begun to sip his port when the butler entered and bowed. "Colonel Fitzwilliam, there is a gentleman come to call on you, but he has no calling cards. He says he is Lord Eversleigh's brother."

Richard chuckled. "No calling cards indeed! Do bring him in."

Lord Matlock narrowed his eyes. "You have no brother, Eversleigh."

"No mortal brother. This is my Sidhe brother."

Lord Matlock's face lit up. "A Sidhe? Here?"

Aelfric strode in, the illusion of humanity already dissolving to reveal his true features. With Sidhe abruptness, he asked Richard eagerly, "Are you ready to visit the breeder?"

Richard slapped his forehead. "I had forgotten about that! So much has happened."

Aelfric looked crestfallen. "Perhaps another time," he muttered.

"Aelfric, a moment," said Eversleigh with quiet command. "We have been dealing with a crisis which has distracted us from other plans, but I believe today would still be a good day for the colonel to take you to the breeder."

Richard shook his head. "I must remain here while my father does his investigation."

"Your father will not be investigating anything." Eversleigh put one hand atop the box containing his new chain of office. "The investigation is in my hands. I will be asking your father to place bindings on the books of sorcery since no one can do it better than he. However, I cannot imagine you wish to spend any more time in Sir Lewis's study."

"No, but –"

"Your presence here will only create more worries," said Eversleigh pointedly. "Take Aelfric to meet your breeder. But first, brother, might I impose on you to spend a few minutes with my friend, Lord Matlock? He has a great interest in Faerie. Lord Matlock, may I present Prince Aelfric? He is the youngest son of the king of Faerie, and I will warn you not to raise the subject of horses or he will never speak of anything else."

Some message seemed to pass between Eversleigh and Aelfric, for the Sidhe seemed suddenly to relax and put on public manners. "Of course."

Lord Matlock struggled to his feet and bowed. "Your Highness, it is a pleasure."

Eversleigh waved Aelfric to a chair. "You and Lord Matlock have some acquaintances in common. He is father to Colonel Fitzwilliam and Lady Frederica, whom you know as Marigold Meadowsweet, and he also knows Miss Bennet. She is a half-sister of Aelfric's. It is a pity English has no term for the person who is my half-brother's half-sister, don't you think?"

"I had not realized Miss Bennet had fay kin," said Lord Matlock, sounding displeased.

"Neither did she until a few days ago. She was quite astonished," said Eversleigh lightly. "Do you have any questions for Aelfric? The Sidhe are more direct and abrupt than we are, so he will appreciate equal directness."

Lord Matlock shifted in his seat. "Er... Are there many of the Sidhe?"

Aelfric said, "I believe there are nearly two hundred. And sixty Sidhe horses."

"So few! In the stories it always seemed as if there were

thousands."

"There have never been thousands, but our numbers were greater long ago, when my father was a young man. Until my birth, it had been some fifty years since the last Sidhe was born."

"The reason for the decrease," interjected Eversleigh wryly, "which Lord Matlock is too polite to ask but is no doubt desperate to know, is the reduced contact between our two worlds. Sidhe are born of a union between a Sidhe and a mortal. Most such couplings lead to a mortal mage, but occasionally a Sidhe is born."

"A mortal mage? But not a mortal without magic?"

"Of course not," said Aelfric, sounding surprised by this lack of knowledge. "Your magic is a sign of fay blood. Those with no fay blood will never have magic. A half Sidhe will always have magic."

Eversleigh smothered a smile. "Yes, I am afraid all the pure Norman bloodlines of our mages have been polluted."

"That would be great shock to many in the Collegium," said Lord Matlock faintly.

"Still, Sidhe magic is rather different from ours," said Eversleigh. "Aelfric, would you be so kind as to display some Sidhe magic for Lord Matlock? He was surprised to learn that apples could be created rather than grown."

Aelfric looked at his brother dubiously, but he obediently put out his hand. A shiny red apple appeared on it. He set it on the tea table and methodically produced a pear, a peach, three strawberries, and a cluster of grapes to accompany it.

Lord Matlock reached out a finger and touched one of the strawberries. "And you can eat these?"

Eversleigh leaned forward and popped one of the grapes in his mouth. "They are perfectly edible. They taste delicious and will quench your hunger, but they will not nourish you. If you ate nothing else, you would eventually starve to death. Nourishing food must be grown from the earth."

"Still, the possibilities... Can you do this as well, Eversleigh?"

"Create fruit? Alas, no, that is a Sidhe skill."

"Can you create anything you want, Prince Aelfric?" Lord Matlock asked.

"No. Nothing that comes from inside the earth, such as metal or jewels. Only things that grow or are made of things that grow. Except silver filigree. We can make that as long as we carry silver." He touched his filigree wrist cuffs. "Now may I go to the breeder?"

Eversleigh laughed. "Yes, you may go to your precious horses, pest! If Colonel Fitzwilliam is agreeable, of course."

Richard tore his eyes from the impossible fruit and shook his head in disbelief. "Certainly."

"Then let's go!"

"You may have the bills sent to me," said Eversleigh dryly. "No Faerie gold that will turn into leaves overnight. Fitzwilliam, if you would be so kind, do attempt to keep Aelfric from bankrupting me."

Aelfric's eyes lit up. "Two mares. May I get two mares? Or perhaps three?"

"Three mares and not a single one more. Besides, you will have to take them through the rings, so you do not want an entire herd."

Aelfric's expression suggested that he did indeed want an entire herd, but he said nothing more as he and Richard departed.

"My apologies for Aelfric's abrupt behavior," said Eversleigh. "His youth is showing."

"How old is he?" asked Lord Matlock, still staring at the fruit the Sidhe had created.

"They do not celebrate birthdays in Faerie, but I would guess he is in his early twenties. The Sidhe grow to manhood quickly, in perhaps ten years, and then they remain at the same apparent age until they enter their decline, which is also rapid. Their behavior changes, they begin to age, and are dead within a few years. Usually they retire from society when the changes begin."

"There are so few of them! And the other types of fay?"

"They are plentiful – the gnomes, dryads, brownies, redcaps, phoukas, sprites, and elves."

"Do they breed with mortals as well?"

"Usually not."

Lord Matlock wore a calculating look. "I suppose you know the fay spell for shape-changing as well."

Eversleigh laughed. "I have never bothered to learn it, and it would do you no good if I had. It does not work on mortals, even those who are half fay like me."

Lord Matlock scowled. "I could try." He picked up a strawberry and examined it carefully, sniffed it, and took a tiny nibble. "Astonishing."

Darcy said, "Perhaps it is clearer now why I was unwilling to threaten the Sidhe. Their power dwarfs ours."

Matlock popped the rest of the strawberry in his mouth. "It would seem so. I would like to learn more about it." His expression sobered. "But while I appreciate the distraction, we have some unpleasant work to do."

"Less than you might think," said Eversleigh. "Darcy and I have already gone through most of his study. I would like your opinions on Sir Lewis's experiments, but apart from that, all that remains is to place magical seals on everything and remove it to the Collegium vaults."

"You work quickly." Lord Matlock sipped his port with a frown. "Where is Frederica? I thought she was here."

"She is staying at the Dower House with Miss Bennet and Miss de Bourgh."

Lord Matlock scowled. "How convenient. That way they can spend hours telling each other how evil I am. And do not look at me like that, Eversleigh. I know full well I should not have been the one to bind my niece, that I should have sought out someone else, someone unrelated to her. I did not trust what the Collegium might decide to do about a girl who could kill with a thought. How did you manage to break the spell?"

"I did not. Aelfric was the one who freed her."

"I suppose it would be child's play for him." Lord Matlock looked displeased by the concept. "But no matter. I am more worried about the conflict in the Collegium. I have no doubt you will handle it well, Eversleigh, but I am concerned for Darcy."

"For me?" Darcy said, startled. "Why?"

"Now that I have given up my position, I can no longer protect you." Lord Matlock sounded defeated.

"Protect me from what?" Foreboding filled Darcy.

Eversleigh was the one who responded. "The inquiry into whether you had abused your power was a very near thing. Lord Matlock's support of you tipped the balance in your favor."

Darcy's hands clenched into fists. "That again? I thought it was put to rest."

"It should be, and I wish it were," said Eversleigh. "There are those who are still whispering, though, and your proximity to this discovery of sorcery will not help. I will do what I can on your behalf."

Darcy forced the words out. "I did not do it."

"I know," said Eversleigh matter-of-factly. "I always supposed you had not, and now I know it without a doubt."

Darcy's mouth twisted. "Perhaps I have been lying to you."

"I do not blame you for being angry. I can be certain because I asked you about it when we were in Faerie, and I would have known if you were lying. It is not a defense I can put before the Collegium, but I know it."

It was a relief to be believed. "What must I do?"

"Nothing at present. If someone raises the question again, you may need to take a stand. Otherwise my only suggestion is to try to find the mysterious water mage who is determined to harm your reputation."

"I have tried, I assure you!" There had to be an answer to the mystery, but he was damned if he could find it. Of course, he was also damned if he could not.

Miss de Bourgh and Frederica were already breakfasting when Elizabeth came downstairs. She had taken extra time with her appearance, but it made no difference. Darcy was not here to see it. She refused to let herself be disappointed. "Did the rest of the night go smoothly?" she asked.

"We were just discussing that," said Anne. "I had forgotten all about my night troubles, but it is nothing to worry about. Before I was under the binding spell, the maids were instructed to keep breakables out of my room, but I never caused fires or floods. I unmade a few bedsheets, but that was all. Darcy worries too much."

"It was a fairly frightening sight, and the windstorm extended far beyond the house," said Frederica pointedly.

"Well, I will consider that. Perhaps draining some magic just before bed would help. But in the meantime, I must speak to my mother. Although the Dower House is pleasant, Rosings Park belongs to me. I will not live in the same place as her, but I should be the one in possession of the main house, and she should have nothing but the Dower House."

Lady Frederica touched her napkin to the corners of her mouth. "She is likely to be unhappy if you tell her that."

"I have been unhappy for years because of her. It is her turn now, and I intend to tell her so today."

Elizabeth looked down at the untasted food on her plate. "Perhaps it would be wise to speak to Mr. Darcy and Colonel Fitzwilliam first. They could provide support if Lady Catherine becomes distraught." She was more concerned about outright violence from Lady Catherine, but it seemed unwise to say so.

"I do not need them to claim my heritage. I am strong enough to face my mother. I would appreciate it if both of you would be witnesses, though."

"I would be happy to, as long as you plan nothing beyond speaking to her," said Lady Frederica carefully.

"You need not worry that I plan to attack her as I did my father. Even if she deserves it, it will take me days to recover all the power I used yesterday." Miss de Bourgh sounded completely untroubled by this talk of killing her parents.

Frederica pushed her plate away. "Are you certain Lady Catherine is well enough? She may not be fully in her right mind yet."

"There is nothing wrong with her mind," said Miss de Bourgh. "She has always insisted that I eat dinner with her, even while she has been locked in her rooms, and she sends a servant for me if I do not appear. Last night she did nothing. Someone must have told her the binding spell has been removed. The servants are her spies, you know. I will allow her to take a few of them with her, but I will hire all new servants for Rosings, ones who will be loyal to me, not her."

"It might be wiser for me to stay here," Elizabeth said carefully. "My name alone seems to provoke Lady Catherine into a rage, and after her attempt to ruin me, I may have difficulty keeping my temper if she provokes me."

"All the better," said Miss de Bourgh. "She would not be so angry if she were not also afraid of you."

It seemed Miss de Bourgh did not plan to waste any time.

The walk to the main house took no more than ten minutes, but they seemed very long minutes. Elizabeth did not know what she dreaded most: seeing Lady Catherine for the first time since she had been ejected from the parsonage, Lady Catherine's inevitable fury about being displaced, or Mr. Darcy's reaction when he discovered her presence. Would he think she was seeking him out? Was he angry with her about the previous night or shocked by her shameless behavior? She already knew Lady Catherine despised her, but that did not matter to her. She now cared about Mr. Darcy's good opinion.

Inside Rosings she could hear Lord Eversleigh's voice in the drawing room. Was Mr. Darcy with him? She was destined not to know since Miss de Bourgh led them straight past it in a determined manner. The route to Lady Catherine's rooms was all too familiar to Elizabeth after the days she had spent tending to her ladyship, the service for which Lady Catherine had punished her so severely. Perhaps Lady Catherine deserved whatever Miss de Bourgh was about to say to her.

She was surprised to see Mr. Darcy's valet sitting outside Lady Catherine's rooms. Apparently Mr. Darcy did not trust the servants at Rosings either, and preferred someone he could trust to keep the door locked. The valet did not hesitate to let them in but warned them to beware of flying crockery.

Lady Catherine greeted them with a beaming smile. On this occasion she was apparently prepared to overlook the presence of the witch who should not be suffered to live. Miss de Bourgh must be right about her ability to understand what was happening.

"My dearest Anne!" cried Lady Catherine. "How I have missed you!"

"Stop it, I pray you," said Miss de Bourgh coldly. "You are no doubt aware the binding spell has been removed, and I am myself again. I am taking my position as mistress of Rosings Park. I expect you to move to the Dower House immediately."

Lady Catherine clasped her hands to her chest. "You cannot mean it! I have devoted my life to you. No one could have cared for your every need as I did."

Miss de Bourgh wrinkled her nose as if smelling an unpleasant odor. "You have kept me under a spell which took away my free will and my ability to think. You are an unnatural mother, and I want nothing more to do with you."

"I had no choice! Was I to allow you to attack me as you did your father?"

Miss de Bourgh's upper lip curled. "As I attacked Sir Lewis for sorcery and his mistreatment of me. Goodbye, Mother." She turned to leave.

"Wait!" shrieked Lady Catherine. "If I cannot have Rosings, neither can you. You have no right to it. You are nothing but one of Sir Lewis's by-blows by some loose woman. Look at you – small and scrawny. You look nothing like me."

Pausing in midstride, Miss de Bourgh looked back at Lady Catherine with an odd smile. "I am delighted to hear it. Nothing could make me happier than knowing you are no relation to me."

"I shall not permit it!" Lady Catherine yanked at the drawer in her bedside table and scrabbled with the contents. She pulled out a paper, held it close to her face, and began to mumble.

Miss de Bourgh made a gesture, and the paper crumbled to dust in Lady Catherine's hands.

"No!" Lady Catherine cried in despair.

"Surely you did not think I would allow you to use that," said Anne coldly. "I expect you to be at the Dower House tonight." She left the room, followed closely by Elizabeth and Frederica.

Elizabeth closed the door behind them just as some unfortunate piece of crockery slammed into it. It was oddly satisfying to know it was Lady Catherine's turn to be cast from her home. She exchanged glances with Frederica as they hurried after Anne. For such a small person, she moved very quickly.

Anne stormed into the drawing room, heedless of interrupting the men's discussion. Without any preliminaries, she said, "Darcy, you are my guardian. I told Lady Catherine to move to the Dower House. Now she claims I am not her daughter, but a by-blow of Sir Lewis's. Can she use that to stop me from inheriting?"

Darcy stared at her in shock, so stunned by her words that he barely noticed Elizabeth and Frederica standing behind her. "I believe not. Sir Lewis acknowledged you as his daughter by Lady Catherine, and that is all that matters legally. In any case, I have no reason to think what she said is true. She may simply have been lashing out."

"She is making it up," said Lord Matlock with annoyance. "I recall when she was carrying you."

Anne flung herself down in a chair. "Or pretending to. I do not care if it is true or not as long as I keep Rosings."

Viscount Eversleigh cleared his throat. "If you wish, I might be able to tell you whether she is your mother."

"What do you mean?"

"I could check your magic. If you have Fitzwilliam magic like your uncle, then logically she must be your mother. If you do not..." He shrugged. "We know no more than we do now. The type of magic is not always inherited. Colonel Fitzwilliam does not have Fitzwilliam magic, but his heritage is written in his face."

Anne considered. "Would you need to take my magic as my father did?"

"No. This would be more akin to dipping my hand into a stream of water to test its temperature. I take nothing and leave nothing behind."

She gave a single sharp nod. "Then I would like to know."

Eversleigh reached out to touch her wrist for no more than a few seconds. "You have nothing of Fitzwilliam power. Your magic is elemental and wild. I do not know what kind of magic Sir Lewis had."

"I would be perfectly happy if neither of them were my parents." Anne stroked her wrist where Eversleigh had touched her.

"I think it very possible that is the case," said Eversleigh calmly, as if questioning her legitimacy were normal drawing room conversation.

Lord Matlock stiffened. "Do not be ridiculous."

Anne ignored him, fixing her gaze on Eversleigh. "Why do you say that?"

"I have thought so since I saw you use your magic. No mortals have magic that strong, even if they have a fay parent. Your wild magic is more like Sidhe power than mortal magic."

"But I am not a Sidhe."

"No, but on those rare occasions when a Sidhe man begets a child on a Sidhe woman, the child is always mortal. I believe you may be one of those children. If Sir Lewis wanted a helpless child with strong magic, he could do no better."

Anne eyed him dubiously. "You think this simply because my magic is strong?"

Eversleigh's teeth flashed as he smiled. "Not just that. Your temperament has a good deal in common with the Sidhe."

Darcy stared at him. He was right. This new Anne had the same mercurial shifts in mood as the Sidhe, and her attention darted from one thing to another as theirs did. He had thought it came from spending so many years under a binding spell, but it was also much like Sidhe directness.

"Was there such a child seven-and-twenty years ago?" Anne's voice was low.

"I do not know, and I cannot ask. It is one of the very few topics the Sidhe will not discuss."

Anne tapped her foot as she considered this. "I would like to meet a Sidhe for longer than the brief moment I saw your brother when he removed my spell."

"No doubt Aelfric would be happy to speak to you again, or if you prefer, I can take you to Faerie."

Anne shook her head decisively. "If what you say is true, Faerie sent me away once. I do not need it now. But I would be happy to meet with your brother."

Lady Frederica asked, "Cousin Anne, forgive me, but what was that piece of paper you unmade, the one Lady Catherine was holding?"

"That? It was her favorite obedience spell. I was expecting her to try to cast it on me now that the binding spell is gone. That was why I asked you to come with me, since I thought she would not dare to use it in front of you. It seems I was wrong. Why are all of you staring at me?"

After a silence, Eversleigh spoke. "Do you claim, then, that Lady Catherine has employed an obedience spell?"

"Yes, did I not just say as much?"

"On whom has she cast it?" Eversleigh sounded oddly distant.

"Mostly servants whom she felt were not sufficiently deferential. She cast it on the new parson, Mr. Collins, to stop him from arguing with her. She tried to cast it on Darcy many times, but it did not work. That made her furious."

Lord Matlock said hoarsely, "You saw this happen?"

"How could I? Thanks to your spell, I fainted every time she began to speak Latin. The results were unmistakable, though. Have you never wondered why the servants are so slavishly devoted to her?"

Eversleigh said, "The spell was written on paper?"

Anne nodded. "Yes, in her bedside table. No one else is allowed to touch that table under any circumstances. When she pulled it out today, I unmade the paper. Why are you so concerned about this? Do you think I should not have destroyed it and simply let her cast the spell?"

Eversleigh shook his head slowly, but it was Frederica who answered. "Obedience spells are sorcery of the worst sort. We are upset to learn Lady Catherine employed them."

Anne's eyebrows rose. "I assumed all ladies used them, but I have had no contact with other households. It appears there is much I do not know."

Eversleigh frowned. "It also appears I must ask you some further questions. What other spells does Lady Catherine use?"

"I do not know. Perhaps it was only the one spell, or there may be more. I can only tell you what results I have seen."

"That would be helpful."

"It makes the servants obey her instantly, even if they are ill or exhausted, and they will not say a word against her to anyone, no matter how unreasonable she is. Mr. Collins stopped arguing with her and instead began praising her constantly. One time a neighboring landowner came to her with some complaint about her land management, and suddenly he no longer cared about the problem and apologized for troubling her. As far as I know, she has never sought out people to cast spells on as my father did, but only used them to make people around her behave as she chose."

"Have you seen her use magic for other things? Does she light candles with magic, or cast illusions, or create a breeze?"

Anne tipped her head to one side thoughtfully. "I do not think so, but I would have swooned at any sign of magic, so I am not the best witness."

"Does she read books on magic?"

Anne laughed scornfully. "She never reads books."

Elizabeth gasped. She laid her hand on Eversleigh's arm and pointed towards Lord Matlock with the other. The earl's face was ashen, his eyes were closed, and he clutched his hand to his chest.

Eversleigh and Frederica were by his side in an instant, and Darcy not far behind. Eversleigh said, "Lie down on the sofa and breathe slowly, sir, as the doctor told you. Slowly. I know it hurts."

"Not important," muttered Lord Matlock, wheezing as he spoke. "Deal with Catherine. Tell my wife. Tell her. I am sorry."

"You will tell her yourself," said Eversleigh. "You have survived these before."

"Not...like this."

Frederica sank to her knees beside her father. "You must not die," she said shakily. "Mama will be very cross with me if I allow you to die, and you know what Mama is like when she is cross." Her voice caught at the end.

"I will try...not to subject you to that, child."

Frederica covered his hand with her own and pressed her forehead against it.

That was a bad sign. Darcy had not been too worried until now, since his uncle had suffered these spells before, but he had not heard Lord Matlock call Frederica 'child' since, well, since she had been a child. He turned to Elizabeth. "Can you do anything to help him?" he asked desperately.

Elizabeth opened and closed her mouth before saying, "I do not know. Possibly. But cannot Lord Eversleigh heal him?"

"Eversleigh lacks healing magic. I beg you to do what you can."

She hesitated. "Only if Lord Matlock wishes me to try, and I cannot imagine he does."

"Healed Catherine, did you not?" Lord Matlock coughed. "I wish you had not."

Elizabeth took a small step backwards, her cheeks flushed. "I will leave you, then."

Lord Matlock lifted his hand a few inches. "No, I will accept...your help. Just that..." He stopped to catch his breath.

"Do not try to talk, sir." Eversleigh placed a small chair beside the sofa and gestured to Elizabeth to take it.

"I can say it for him," said Darcy. "He would rather Lady

Catherine had died than for her to be alive as a sorceress." He had been thinking the same thing.

Lord Matlock bobbed his head in agreement.

"Mr. Darcy, could you try to call Pepper while I begin here? I may need her help." Elizabeth sat and took Lord Matlock's hand in both of hers. "Your Lordship, your daughter told me you sometimes feel great pressure in your chest. Is that what is happening now?"

He nodded again.

"You will feel magic moving up your arm, and it may make you somewhat sleepy. That is to be expected." Then she deliberately lightened her tone. "This is one for the annals of great hubris, is it not? The hedge witch who tried to heal the Master of the Collegium?"

Darcy winced at her words as he struggled to open the latch on the window. Did no one ever oil the cursed things? It gave way finally and he pushed the window open. He stuck his head out as far as he could. "Pepper! Elizabeth needs you!" Nothing. Only silence. He counted out a minute and tried again. "Pepper, I beg you to come."

Behind him, Elizabeth said, "My lord, I pray you, do not try to follow my magic with yours. You are making it more difficult."

Lord Matlock's lips twitched. "Simply...curious." He closed his eyes.

"Thank you. I will be happy to answer your questions later." Her expression suggested she was not certain there would be a later.

If only there were something he could do! For lack of anything better, he stuck his head out the window again. "Pepper, I will give you every fish in the lake if you help us!" Still nothing.

At least Lord Matlock was still breathing. Elizabeth's head was bowed in concentration. Eversleigh stood behind her, his eyes shut and his hands on her shoulders. Even through his fear and grief about his uncle, jealousy burned in Darcy's stomach. Was Eversleigh the true reason she had pushed him away?

"Caw?" Pepper sat on the windowsill in raven form.

Not even Pepper's appearance could lift the heaviness in Darcy's chest. Mechanically he said, "Elizabeth – Miss Elizabeth, that is – is trying to help Lord Matlock. He is having a heart paroxysm. She asked me to call you." At least he could still be useful to her in this small way.

Lord Matlock turned his head in their direction. "What is that?"

Darcy said quickly, "There is no need to worry. Pepper is a phouka. Usually she takes the form of a cat."

As if on cue, Pepper flew down to the floor and transformed.

"Is that the cat who attacked me?" Lord Matlock sounded sleepy.

"Yes, but only because she thought you intended harm to Miss Elizabeth. She will not hurt you now."

Pepper padded to the sofa, jumped up on Lord Matlock's chest and began to knead, pushing her paws into him rhythmically and purring.

"Is she doing that for a reason?" asked Lord Matlock.

"I do not know, but Pepper usually has a reason for what she does."

"Her eyes do not match." Lord Matlock did not show the excitement at meeting a phouka that Darcy would have expected. Another bad sign.

"No, they do not."

"But I do feel a little better. I can breathe. Perhaps she is doing something."

"I have great faith in Pepper," said Darcy.

Elizabeth began to hum, but she did not open her eyes. It made quite a tableau, Lord Matlock on the sofa with Pepper on his chest, Frederica kneeling by his shoulder, Elizabeth sitting beside him holding his hand, and Eversleigh standing behind Elizabeth.

Lord Matlock blinked. "The pressure is gone." He sounded surprised. He took a deep breath and released it. "Definitely better." He started to pull himself up to a sitting position.

Without opening his eyes, Eversleigh reached out, put a hand on Lord Matlock's shoulder, and pushed him back down. "Stay there," he ordered.

"Papa, you must not stress yourself. We are all here to help you, and you need do nothing but rest."

Elizabeth released his hand. Her voice seemed to come from far away as she asked, "How do you feel? Does it still hurt?"

Pepper jumped off Lord Matlock's chest.

"Not at all. The pain and pressure have disappeared." Lord Matlock sat up and swung his legs off the sofa. "Definitely better. I thank you, Miss Bennet." He sounded drowsy.

Elizabeth frowned. "I was not able to fix everything. I patched the broken area of your heart, but I could not heal it. It is a temporary measure."

"You made me well enough to deal with Catherine, and that is the important thing." He heaved himself to his feet.

"Papa, you must rest!" Frederica cried. "Elizabeth, should he not rest?"

Elizabeth turned her palms upwards. "I cannot say. Wild magic is different from normal healing. Lord Eversleigh may know more."

"I rarely use wild magic," said Eversleigh. "I have been determined to prove I could succeed as a mage using only mortal magic, but in this case it does not matter. Lord Matlock, you might as well rest because I cannot allow you to have any part of this matter of Lady Catherine. No part at all, do you hear me? Lady Frederica, I would be obliged if you would send an express to Lady Matlock informing her of what has happened and that I will be sending Lord Matlock back to London by carriage as soon as I am certain he is well enough."

"No need," grumbled Lord Matlock. "She is already on her way. She wished to come with me, but Richard and I rode ahead."

"All the better," said Eversleigh. "You can go back to London together."

"I should stay. Even if I do not see Catherine, I can still be of use to you here," said Lord Matlock.

Eversleigh paused. "Until we have a clearer idea of what spells Lady Catherine can use, it is safer to send everyone far away from her. Everyone except Darcy. Although I would prefer not to have any of Lady Catherine's kin here, I would ask you to stay simply because you are apparently immune to her spells, and I have no reason to assume I am. Miss Bennet, I will need your assistance in setting wards of power this afternoon, but after that, you should go as well."

Darcy did not like Eversleigh's appropriation of Elizabeth. "I will stay here if you wish, but I must remind you Miss Bennet is not obliged to follow your orders."

Elizabeth gave Eversleigh a teasing look before turning to Darcy and saying lightly, "In fact, according to fay protocol, I do have to honor his requests, but I still prefer to be asked. In this case, I am willing to do what I can, but I know nothing about setting wards. Surely Mr. Darcy or Lord Matlock or even Lady Frederica would be of more use to you."

"Can't do it," grunted Lord Matlock with some annoyance. "Wards of power are blood magic. Using the blood of one of Catherine's relatives creates a weakness she could exploit. Eversleigh, does your blood count as fay blood?"

"Alas, no. I am a mere mortal," said Eversleigh.

"Pity. It would be more interesting that way," said Lord Matlock. "Is it true that spells mingling fay and mortal blood are more powerful?"

"It increases the power greatly when both are mixed. I was once the mortal component of such, and it is quite remarkable, even by the standards of Sidhe magic. One of the great wonders of Faerie is the giant oak – and it truly is giant – at the end of the void where Caerdic of blessed memory and his mortal brother Alber spilled their heart's blood together to break Faerie in twain."

"Heart's blood?" asked Elizabeth. "Is that different?"

Eversleigh straightened his lapels. "Quite different," he said. "It happened only in ancient times, and it is not something you will ever see. This spell will not mingle our blood, but it will require giving four drops of your blood to the wards, and you must give it willingly. Blood magic is tricky business, and using blood given under duress can lead to unpredictable results."

"You would be perfectly safe," added Lord Matlock. "The worst thing that can happen is that the spell will not work."

"But I only know wild magic," said Elizabeth.

"That does not matter." Eversleigh smiled suddenly. "I can teach you what you need to know as we go along. Discovering sorcery qualifies as an emergency which authorizes me to teach anyone at hand, including women. And while I might pride myself on using formal spells whenever possible, I do have wild magic in my blood, as you just saw while you were healing Lord Matlock. "

Lord Matlock frowned. "You were involved in that, too?"

Eversleigh nodded. "I worked with Miss Bennet, following her lead and taking some of the effort on myself. I wanted to protect her strength so she could make the wards. Since we are *shurinn*, I can work in tandem with her."

"What are you talking about?" Darcy could barely hold his anger in check.

"It is complicated," said Elizabeth quickly. "Just a fay matter. Because we are both connected to Aelfric, Viscount Eversleigh and I can entwine our magic. I can explain it later if you like."

Darcy nodded tersely, not trusting his voice. He was not a fool. Magic was not the only thing Eversleigh wanted to entwine with Elizabeth. How dare he use her connection to the fay prince to accomplish it? To think he had the gall to tell Darcy he wanted to protect her!

Frederica blurted out, "May I watch you set the wards?"

Eversleigh bowed to her. "It would be most ungentlemanly of me to forbid a lady to be in a particular room." He paused, as if deliberating. "I am notoriously careless with spell books. I often leave them open in my room rather than locking them with spells. It is a failing of mine."

Lord Matlock said ominously, "Eversleigh, if you are trying to tempt my daughter into your bedroom –"

"Don't be ridiculous," said Frederica. "He is merely commenting on his natural untidiness."

Eversleigh was perhaps the tidiest and most organized person Darcy had ever met.

"Darcy, while Miss Elizabeth and I are preparing the wards, could I ask you to write letters for Collingswood, Winston and Elliott telling them I require their immediate assistance here on a matter of sorcery?"

"Certainly." But he was glad Frederica would be with them. He did not trust Eversleigh alone with Elizabeth.

# Chapter 10

"It worked!" exclaimed Eversleigh. "Well done, Miss Elizabeth."

Elizabeth rocked back on her heels, admiring the unearthly glow of the four chess pawns they had used for the wards. "So that is how wards are made. I have always wondered."

"Common wards are easier. It is simpler to keep out malicious fay than to keep out magic – or to keep it locked in, as we have done here."

Elizabeth touched her forefinger to the glowing head of the nearest pawn. The two walls, inner and outer, flared to visibility. Eversleigh's wall was made of moving words, while hers was a fisherman's net covered with vines and darting fireflies. "Our walls look very different. Will that be a problem?"

"It should not be." He tilted his head to admire their work. "Mine is a very traditional mage's barrier. Yours is pure wild magic. I understand the net, but what are the vines?"

"Deadly nightshade. It sucks magic out of redcap bites, so I think of it as blocking magic."

"And the fireflies?"

Elizabeth gave a rueful smile as she reached for one of the pastries Eversleigh had ordered earlier. "I do not know. The magic put them there."

"How could the magic put them there?" demanded Lady Frederica.

Eversleigh turned to her. "Wild magic is full of surprises, unlike traditional spells which have been channeled and tamed. I knew exactly what my wall would look like, and it will always look that way with that spell. If Miss Bennet made another wall tomorrow, it might be an impassable jungle of vines instead."

Frederica frowned. "Why bother with spells if wild magic can do the same things?"

Eversleigh smiled at her. "Properly constructed spells strengthen the magic and make it more predictable. Most mages do not have magic strong enough to use wild magic, so they need spells. Miss Bennet's magic is strong, despite what I was told by Colonel Fitzwilliam, which leads me to believe she had not used it to its full extent before these last weeks. Magic, like muscles, requires exercise to be strong."

"Of course I did not practice my magic!" exclaimed Elizabeth. "I tried to use it as little as possible. I never used to get so hungry after using my magic, either."

"The more of your magic you use, the hungrier you become," said Eversleigh. "Lady Frederica, you have the potential to use wild magic. Darcy's elemental magic is wild, but he can use spells, too."

Something about Frederica's smile reminded Elizabeth of a satisfied tiger, and she said, "Lady Frederica, I hope you can wait until tomorrow before asking me for more lessons in using wild magic. Between healing your father and these wards, I doubt I have any magic left."

Eversleigh laughed at Frederica's crestfallen look.

Lady Matlock said regally, "Lord Eversleigh, I understand that under the circumstances you wish my husband to leave Rosings Park. I could not agree more. We will leave tomorrow morning once he has had a good night's sleep." She made no reference to Eversleigh's earlier plan that they should leave immediately. Only Lady Matlock could make disagreement with a fixed plan sound so much like agreement.

Eversleigh bowed to her. "Your ladyship shows great wisdom. Now that the wards of power are set, I can see no harm in a slight delay."

Naturally, Lady Matlock was not done. "Miss Bennet, it is lovely to meet you at last, and I understand we are now in your debt for saving my husband as well as Lady Catherine. I hope you will be so generous as to return to London with us and stay at Matlock House. My nerves could not possibly survive the strain of worry over my husband's heart if I did not know you were at hand to assist him should his symptoms recur." She sounded not the slightest bit nervous.

Elizabeth looked taken aback. "I had planned to return to Faerie, although I could visit my uncle in London instead. My mother will be visiting him soon. Given the recent damage to my reputation, it might be wiser for me to stay there. I would not wish Lady Frederica's name to be associated with mine at present."

"Nonsense," said Lady Matlock kindly. "Staying with us will help to rebuild your reputation. Given that you have suffered this exposure in the course of helping our family, it is the least we can do. You can easily call on your uncle and mother from Matlock House."

Elizabeth was shaking her head when Eversleigh said quietly, "I think it is a good idea, *shurinn*."

She looked as if she wished to argue further, but she said, "Very well, your ladyship, I will accept your kind invitation. I will first need to inform Titania of this change of plans, since she is expecting my return to Faerie soon."

Why did she agree with whatever Eversleigh suggested? She had only met him a few days ago, and already she submitted to him. Something was not right, and Darcy did not like it at all. And she had been avoiding looking in his direction all day. He did not like that, either.

Lord Matlock said sharply, "Titania, as in the queen of Faerie?"

Elizabeth hesitated and glanced at Eversleigh before responding. "Yes. My last trip to Faerie led to some interesting discoveries, but when we found out about Sir Lewis's sorcery, that pushed everything else aside."

Richard appeared in the doorway. "Ah, here you are. Our mission was successful. Three Bakewell Black mares are now in the stables in Faerie, Aelfric is happy, and the breeder is so pleased to have your custom, Eversleigh, that he has promised me a colt from his next breeding. I could grow to enjoy spending your money. Oh, hello, Mother. I did not see you there. I hope your journey was easy." He went straight to the sideboard and poured a glass of port.

"It was, thank you, Richard," said Lady Matlock. "Unfortunately, nothing else has gone according to plan. Your father nearly died from a heart paroxysm, but Miss Bennet was able to heal him. And your aunt has been practicing sorcery."

"Lady Catherine?" he exclaimed in disbelief. "Lady Catherine, who would rather die than admit she has even a drop of magic in her veins?"

"Yes, that Lady Catherine," said Anne, who had been silent since Lady Matlock's arrival. "I would like to raise a question that has not been resolved."

"What is it?" Lord Matlock asked with a frown.

"The punishment for sorcery is immediate execution. There are no exceptions. Yet you hesitate to do so. Is it because of me? Are you afraid of what I might do, given my history?" Now she looked straight at Lord Matlock.

His eyes widened. "No. That thought had not crossed my mind. Should it have?"

Anne eyed him considering. "No."

"What do you think should be done with her?" asked Lord Matlock with unusual gentleness.

Anne balled her fists at her side. "The punishment for sorcery is death. It is what she deserves."

"That is harsh!" exclaimed Lord Matlock. "She raised you."

"No, that is not harsh. Harsh is putting a binding spell on a helpless child and leaving her that way for half a lifetime." Anne raised her chin. "Lady Catherine committed a crime. She knew the punishment."

Lord Matlock merely looked at her, his expression puzzled.

Why did he not respond? Could he be having another heart paroxysm? Quickly Darcy said, "It can be difficult to contemplate killing a woman we have known all our lives. That is why the decision must be made by mages who have no connection to Lady Catherine."

Anne pursed her lips. "That is acceptable, I suppose," she said grudgingly.

"Gentlemen, I must speak to you privately." Lord Matlock's expression was grim. "In the library, if you will be so kind."

"Certainly." Darcy bowed to the ladies before following his uncle.

Eversleigh sat down in a leather armchair by the library desk. "What is the matter?" he asked Lord Matlock.

"There is a new problem," said Lord Matlock, his expression foreboding. "It appears your Miss Bennet did more than patch my heart. I am suddenly unable to account for my decision to bind Anne, something I have never doubted before. I allowed Miss Bennet to use her magic on me, and now I find myself in agreement with her position."

Darcy was so shocked he could barely speak. "Are you suggesting that Miss Bennet is a sorceress?" He would never believe it. Not Elizabeth, who fought so hard against binding spells.

"Yes. I suppose I am," Lord Matlock said slowly.

"No," said Eversleigh. "I was with her all the way while she was healing you. She did nothing to your mind."

"How can you be certain? Why else would I be feeling this?

Nothing else has changed."

"I do not –" Eversleigh broke off suddenly, a look of horror twisting his face. "One other thing has changed," he said harshly. "We stopped Lady Catherine's sorcery from leaving her room. It may be blocking the spells she has already cast."

"What?" roared Lord Matlock. "You think she cast a spell on me? Ridiculous!" He stopped short and sat down heavily behind the desk, all his anger suddenly draining away. "Good God. She wanted Anne bound, and I refused. That she would dare to put a spell on me!"

For once, Darcy knew the answer. "Lady Catherine has never lacked the audacity to tell any of us what to do. If anyone would dare to put a spell on you, she would be the one."

"But how could I have failed to notice it? I, of all people, should have known I was bespelled." Lord Matlock put his elbows on the desk and covered his face with his hands. "Leave me, all of you."

Richard made a shooing motion, indicating he would remain with his father. Darcy silently wished him luck.

"Miss Bennet wishes to speak to you," Colonel Fitzwilliam told his father a short time later.

Lord Matlock rose slowly. "Miss Bennet, I fear I am not good company at present."

"I understand. I merely wished to check on your health before I return to the Dower House."

He spread his arms. "I am quite well, as you see. Thanks to you." His voice was heavy.

"I am glad. I also wanted to say that, while I cannot apologize for the conclusion I reached about you at our first meeting, I am relieved and happy to know it was based on false assumptions."

"Very prettily said, Miss Bennet. I wish I could forgive myself as easily."

Elizabeth cocked her head to the side. "Mr. Darcy also has an odd tendency to blame himself for things completely beyond his control. I would suspect it to be a Fitzwilliam family trait, but the good colonel seems free of the curse."

Colonel Fitzwilliam chuckled. "Very perceptive, Miss Bennet. Sir, did you not wish to ask Miss Bennet about her healing techniques?"

"Not now, Richard," the earl said wearily.

The colonel laid his hands on the desk and leaned over it until his face was a foot from his father's. "Yes, now," he said firmly.

"I can return another time," said Elizabeth hastily.

Colonel Fitzwilliam turned back to her with a winning smile. "Miss Bennet, I throw myself on your mercy. You are my best hope for distracting my father out of his gloom. Once you start speaking of wild magic, he will be unable to restrain his curiosity."

Elizabeth tapped her chin with her fingertip. "Now this is a dilemma. Naturally I would wish to oblige you, Colonel, but your father does outrank you."

"I am glad someone realizes that," grumbled the earl.

"Miss Bennet, must I threaten to tell my mother? I assure you she will take my side."

"Colonel, your mother has been nothing but kind to me, yet to hear you talk, one would think her a veritable Gorgon!"

A smile twitched the colonel's lips. "Exactly so!"

Elizabeth ostentatiously looked heavenwards, but from the corner of her eyes she could see Lord Matlock did look better for watching their banter. "Very well. Purely out of respect for the gentle creature who is your mother, I will torment his lordship with my inarticulate description of the indescribable. I hope that will satisfy you."

"Very much so." He offered her a chair.

She sat and folded her hands in her lap, trying to disguise her sudden anxiety. Was she truly going to explain her magic to the Master of the Collegium? "I hardly know where to begin. I will tell you what I can, but I beg you to understand that it might be completely different for someone else. There is a reason we call it wild magic. What would you like to know?"

"How do you do it? How do you reach inside a person's body?"

She had never tried to put it into words before. "I start by feeling for the life force. It is like a tingling sensation under the skin. When I feel it, the force tugs at my hands, and I let it pull me inside. Wild magic tends to be metaphorical, so it transforms the complexity of the body into something I can understand. In your case, I found myself in a flat-bottomed rowboat skimming along the surface of a rocky river."

"How did you know I was trying to sense what you were doing?"

She laughed. "That was simple. Suddenly you were standing behind me, looking over my shoulder and tipping the boat. Wild magic can be very literal."

"Hmm. What did you do next?"

"After a time, I reached a pier and tied up the boat. I walked through a narrow valley until I came to a small clearing where I found a cabbage and an embroidery basket."

"A cabbage! How...unique. Do continue."

"It is not as odd as it sounds," Elizabeth said. "I once saw a pig's heart, and it had big veins branching off all over it, just as a cabbage leaf has veins. It looked like a brown misshapen cabbage. This cabbage was green, naturally, but one of the leaves had a small area that was wizened and gray. Since the wild magic had given me an embroidery basket to work with, I began to embroider new veins across that area."

The colonel's face was filled with mirth. "You embroidered a cabbage?"

With mock dignity, Elizabeth replied, "No, sir, I embroidered a cabbage leaf. There is a difference. Once I had mended the gray spot, I returned to the river. It was flowing the other direction, and I took the boat back."

Lord Matlock tapped his fingers together thoughtfully. "This sounds like one of those strange, nonsensical dreams that wakes you in the middle of the night."

"Strange and nonsensical perhaps, but not a dream. Wild magic is real." Elizabeth held up her forefinger, displaying several pinpricks in the fingertip. "I am not fond of embroidery, and I rarely trouble myself to practice. I pricked my finger embroidering the cabbage leaf."

Lord Matlock leaned forward to examine her finger. "Astonishing. Was it an ordinary needle?"

"No, it was made of silver. Wild magic dislikes iron, so anything metal is usually silver."

"Ordinary thread? What color was it?"

Elizabeth's eyebrows shot up. "Green, of course. Green silk. Nothing but the finest for your lordship's cabbage."

An unladylike snort came from where Frederica stood in the doorway. Darcy, standing next to his cousin, looked unamused, not at all like the man who had kissed her so passionately the previous night.

Elizabeth's heart sank. "Now I will leave you to the tender mercy of your family. If you have more questions later, I will be happy to answer them."

"What are the words to the shape-changing spell?" Lord Matlock asked.

She wrinkled her nose at him. "Oh, no. Besides, the spell would be of no use to you. Mortals cannot change shapes."

"Bah," he grumbled. "It was worth a try."

After leaving Lord Matlock, Elizabeth found Viscount Eversleigh leafing through a book in the drawing room.

"How is Lord Matlock?" Eversleigh asked her.

"Calmer, I think. We talked about wild magic, and that seemed to distract him." Elizabeth hesitated a moment. "Why did you tell me to go to Matlock House instead of my uncle's home? Was it to please Lady Matlock?"

"Not at all, *shurinn*. It was for your safety. If Lady Catherine proves to be a more powerful sorceress than we currently believe, we may not be able to contain her immediately. She blames you for her troubles, so I want you under the care of one of our strongest mages."

"Would I not be even safer from her in Faerie?" And she felt oddly at home in Titania's bower.

"You would be safer from Lady Catherine, but there is also the danger to your reputation. Assuming Lady Catherine's sorcery was limited to a few spells she had written down, I suspect the mages examining her will be reluctant to recommend execution for her. The other option would be to have her declared insane and confine her for the rest of her life. If you are clearly under the protection of Lord Matlock, it will appear that you did nothing wrong other than to land in the path of a madwoman."

"A lost reputation is not that easy to restore." No matter how much she might wish for it. The loss of her good name had cost her any hope of a future with Mr. Darcy.

"Restoring it completely is likely impossible, I admit. Scandal tends to cling even when proven untrue. Still, it is possible to make you socially acceptable again, and if a few old biddies still whisper about you behind their hands, so be it."

She bit her lip. "It is more than that. To remain respectable, I would have to go back to pretending I have no magic and living in constant fear of exposure. I have enjoyed these days of freedom when I have not had to hide who I am. I do not want to give it up."

"I cannot blame you for that." His voice was flat. "I feel the same way about hiding my fay connections. There is always a distance, even with my closest friends, because I am lying about who I am. These few days here have been a taste of freedom. I know it cannot last, and it will be that much harder when I return to keeping my secret, but I cannot regret it."

"Why do you do it, then? Is it only for the sake of your ambitions?"

He gave a bitter laugh. "No, I have ambitions because I have nothing else. I keep my secret because I have three sisters who do not deserve to have their reputations ruined simply because my mother could not resist Oberon's wooing."

Her sisters. A lump formed in her throat. They were why she could not follow her dream of being a woman with magic. She could choose to destroy her own good name in society, even if it cost her Darcy, but she would drag down Jane, Mary, Kitty, and Lydia with her. Allowing Lady Matlock to present her in society would protect them. She said slowly, "I have no choice, do I?'

"No. But at least now we will both have the comfort of not being completely alone with our secrets. When I look across a crowded ballroom and see one of you, I will remember that there are a few select people who know me for who I am."

If her reputation was miraculously restored, she might be able to marry Darcy, and she would not have to lie to him. She still did not think it could be done. Everyone in Meryton had already heard the news, thanks to Mr. Collins, but she would not give up Darcy without at least trying. "I still do not believe my reputation can be fully restored, but I will do my best."

He inclined his head. "I thank you, both on my own behalf and that of your sisters. It would be a pity to lose my *shurinn* now that I have found you."

"You are worrying about your other *shurinn* Bennet sisters," she teased.

"Naturally," he said with a smile. "I used to think myself bedeviled by having three sisters. How will I survive with eight?"

Frederica opened her bedroom door reluctantly. She had been expecting her mother to corner her sooner or later. Lady Matlock had an unnatural ability to know when something was troubling her.

Lady Matlock did not trouble to disguise her intentions. "Distressing as it is to have learned that Sir Lewis and Lady Catherine were practicing sorcery – I never did like that man – I gather there is something else disturbing you."

There were several somethings, in fact, and only some of them were safe to tell her mother. She sighed. "Everything is in such a muddle, Mama, and I see no escape from it, either for the fay or for my friends – or, for that matter, for myself. You say there is always a solution, but I defy you to find one this time."

Lady Matlock seemed unperturbed. "Perhaps you should tell me about these problems, my dear."

"Very well, but do not say I did not warn you. Cousin Anne will be ruined once word gets out that not only is she a sorcerer's daughter, but she refuses to hide her magic after having been forced to do so for so long. We can attempt to save Elizabeth from ruin, but there is no guarantee it is possible. If I wish to protect my own reputation, I must abandon Cousin Anne and perhaps Elizabeth, and without her to take me to Faerie, I am exiled from it and unable to help the fay with their problems. Moreover, this has made me realize I am in an untenable position in searching for a husband. Am I to lie to my husband my entire life about my magic? There are very few men like Papa who will accept a wife with magic, and even they would not marry a known witch."

"Language, my dear," Lady Matlock chided gently. "Those are serious problems, indeed. But what is this about the fay? Is it the difficulty with the groves?"

Frederica shook her head. "That is but part of it. I had a long talk with their queen. Even if the groves survive, the Sidhe will continue to diminish until only a few are left. The number is already far less than it was in the past, and almost no Sidhe are being born."

Lady Matlock raised her eyebrows. "What has caused this change?"

"We have. The Sidhe were once able to travel freely through our world, safe in the knowledge they could heal from any wound inflicted by a mortal. That was before we had guns. Once rifles and pistols became common, Sidhe began to die. Now they rarely leave Faerie, and only in hiding."

"Ah. They must travel in our world in order to have children?"

"Not precisely." Frederica hesitated. "Pray forgive the unseemly topic, but they must have mortal men and women to have children. Two Sidhe cannot produce a Sidhe child. Only a Sidhe and a mortal can. Once it was an honor to be wooed by a Sidhe, and poets and artists sought out Sidhe ladies in Faerie, but very few Sidhe will take the risk to find a mortal lover now."

Lady Matlock raised a delicate eyebrow. "You are not speaking of marriage, then?"

Frederica shook her head. "They are not Christian. They have something akin to marriage among themselves, but fidelity is not expected."

"Why are you so concerned with saving them, even at the cost of leading mortal men and women into sin?"

Frederica chewed her lip. "I like their queen. She is beautiful, but it is not that. She is not selfless. Still, there is something about her. It is like watching an exquisite butterfly flit from flower to flower, and suddenly I want to write a poem about it. Like the butterfly, she is something beyond my comprehension, yet her presence makes me feel somehow more alive. She told me that the Sidhe bring inspiration to artists, musicians, and even scientists, and I believe it. Without them we would be less than we are."

Lady Matlock's lips tightened. "I hope you will not prove susceptible to the blandishments of Sidhe gentlemen."

"Oh, no, Mama. I do not want a Sidhe lover. But I do wish I could spend more time with the fay."

"I wonder if anyone has ever tried to bring Christianity to them."

"I cannot say." Frederica doubted the Sidhe would have any patience for missionaries, but if the possibility warmed her mother to the idea... But no. "We will never know for certain, since nothing will change. Their world and ours will continue to drift apart. People who are afraid of things they cannot understand will cut down the groves. The Sidhe will slowly die out, and so will we when our crops fail, our magic no longer works, and we are unable to conceive enough children because there are no lesser fay bringing fertility to our world."

"Surely there must be some better option than that melancholy prospect." Lady Matlock tapped her fingers together as if considering the matter.

Frederica stared at her hands. "I have been unable to find one." Would the crops start failing in her lifetime, or would it be that of her children?"

"Nonsense. There is always something one can do." Her mother looked thoughtful. "I believe I should host a grand soirée."

# Chapter 11

"Mama, you cannot possibly think a soirée will distract me from any of this!" wailed Frederica.

"I am glad you recognize I cannot possibly think that," said Lady Matlock with some asperity. "This is a matter of fashion."

"Ordering a closet full of new dresses will not make me happier, either." Frederica jumped to her feet. "Pray forget I said anything."

"Temper, my dear. Fashion goes far beyond clothing. The fay are out of fashion. Women performing magic is out of fashion. If you do not like it, you must be prepared to change the fashion."

Frederica asked cautiously, "What do you mean?"

"We must make the Sidhe all the rage, so that no society hostess would dream of holding an event without a Sidhe or two in attendance. We must also establish that no young lady can be considered truly accomplished unless she can perform some feat of magic to delight an audience. I have not yet seen how we can tie the two together, but it will no doubt come to me."

If anyone could accomplish this, it was her mother. "The Sidhe think it is barbaric that our women are not permitted to practice magic."

Lady Matlock beamed. "There it is! Well done. Now I believe I must speak to your Faerie queen."

Speaking to Viscount Eversleigh came first, however. He seemed quite pleased with the idea of the soiree, although Elizabeth was more dubious. When Lady Matlock asked him if he had any suggestions, he raised his quizzing glass to look at her and said, "Lady Matlock, should there ever come a day on which I dare to offer you a suggestion on how to plan a successful entertainment, I pray you to be so kind as to send me to Bedlam, as it would be a sign I had completely lost my mind."

It was no wonder he was so popular with ladies. Elizabeth hid a smile despite her disquiet with their idea. Mortals had been frightened of the fay for too long to be easily convinced to accept them.

"Lord Eversleigh, will you be able to conduct me to Faerie to speak to Queen Titania?" asked Lady Matlock.

"Sadly, if you wish to go today, I cannot assist you. I have overused the rings, and it will be several days before I can use them again. Miss Bennet is perfectly capable of taking you there."

"I am?" asked Elizabeth.

"Certainly. Have Lady Matlock enter the ring before you, and when you enter, you must visualize the entrance to Titania's bower. Your talisman will do the rest."

"You are Marigold Meadowsweet's mother?" asked Titania.

"I am."

"You are fortunate, then. I have no children, so I must borrow other women's daughters. It might be different if more mortal men visited Faerie."

Lady Matlock showed no response to this risqué statement. "That is something I hope to change. I asked to see you to discuss an idea for increasing contact between mortals and fay. Long ago, mortals honored the Sidhe, and it is time to restore that as the natural order."

Titania leaned forward. "You have my interest."

After disappearing for most of the morning, Richard strode into the library where Darcy, Eversleigh, and Lord Matlock were discussing plans for dismantling Sir Lewis's study. He tossed a sheet of paper onto the table in front of Eversleigh.

Eversleigh picked it up and examined it. "What is this?"

Richard scowled. "There are certain people I do not like being near. For lack of a better word, they make me queasy, the way I feel when I eat jellied eels. I always assumed I just did not like them. Sometimes it was someone who had made me angry, but mostly they had done nothing to me. Darcy knows about this."

"Richard has spoken to me of it many times," said Darcy. But why was he bringing it up now?

"When I was fifteen, I had a fight with my father. The next time I came back from school, I had that feeling about him, and I assumed it was because of the fight. It never went away, though, not until yesterday. I used to have that feeling about Cousin Anne as well, but not now. The Rosings servants, too. All gone now." Richard pointed at the paper. "That is a list of every person I can remember who has given me that jellied eels feeling."

Eversleigh ran his finger down the list. "There are several mages listed here."

"It used to be a joke," said Richard with some bitterness. "I went into the Army because Collegium meetings made me feel sick. That was what the fight with my father was about. He wanted me to study magery and become the next Master of the Collegium."

Lord Matlock wiped his forehead, his expression grim. "That disagreement was not long before Sir Lewis's death."

"Which was when Lady Catherine placed the spell on you. I am not saying everyone on that list is under a spell. Perhaps none of them are. As I said, sometimes it happens when I am angry. Recently it started happening with a young girl who had disappointed me, but she is certainly not under a spell. I thought you should know." Richard dropped into a chair.

Lord Matlock grabbed the paper from Eversleigh. "Good God. You cannot possibly be angry with all of these people. Mages. Ladies of the *ton*. Even tradesmen." He looked up at Richard. "Not a single officer."

Richard turned his hands upwards. "I cannot explain it. It is simply what I feel. And I do not like it."

Eversleigh peered at the paper over Lord Matlock's shoulder. "How many of them have had contact with Lady Catherine?"

"None that I know of, apart from the servants and Mr. Collins," said Richard. "She did not go out in society."

"Some of them knew Sir Lewis," said Lord Matlock. "Perhaps you react to the residue of a spell."

"Then why does it not happen with you now?" Richard's frustration was obvious.

Darcy came to look at the list. "Some of these he has mentioned to me. The servants here in particular."

"How many of these people make you angry?"

Richard grimaced. "Very few. Unless I have a good reason, I tend to stay far away from people who make me feel that way."

Eversleigh tapped his fingers on the table. "If these people – if *any* of these people are under a spell, you know what that means."

"Another sorcerer," grunted Lord Matlock. "One we do not know about."

"Or more than one," said Eversleigh. "But none of this is proof."

"I know!" Richard said, his voice raised. "I do not like it. I like things that are certain, things I can see in front of me. I do not like feelings. I do not like making accusations based on whether someone makes my stomach turn. But I hate sorcery worse than any of it."

"You were right to bring this to me," said Eversleigh. "It is not proof, but ever since Miss de Bourgh told us her father was a sorcerer, I have been wondering if he was the only one. If we missed him, we could have missed another. I am inclined now to think it is probable."

"What do we do?" asked Darcy.

"Fitzwilliam, are you willing to be deployed as a spell-sniffing hound?" asked Eversleigh.

"No. But I will do it anyway," grumbled Richard.

"Your first task is to remain here until the three mages arrive to examine Lady Catherine. If any of them make you feel queasy, I need to know that," said Eversleigh.

"Collingswood, Winston, and Elliott? You cannot possibly suspect any of them," said Lord Matlock.

"If I were to list the mages whom I believed least likely to be under a sorcerer's spell, you would have been at the top of the list, my lord," said Eversleigh with a touch of acid in his voice. "I intend to suspect everyone."

Frederica collapsed onto the drawing room sofa across from Eversleigh. Elizabeth followed her more sedately.

"What happened in your meeting with Titania?" asked Eversleigh. "You look exhausted."

"It went well, once we moved past the disastrous beginning," said Frederica. "Titania told Mama that she had not known ladies of her advanced age could still be elegant even though their faces were lined."

"Oh, dear," said Eversleigh. "She probably meant it as a compliment."

"Lady Matlock could not have been more gracious, although I doubt she felt that way," added Elizabeth. "She said Frederica had told her there were no older mortal women in Faerie. 'It is a shame,' she said, 'since what we lose in beauty is made up in becoming more interesting. Young people can be very dull.' Titania seemed to consider it."

Frederica nodded. "Then they talked for hours about bringing the fay into fashion. Titania was quite taken with the idea of attending a soirée, though perhaps that was only because Mama mentioned that there would be handsome young men to wait upon her. But Titania said it could not be in London because the fay are uncomfortable with so much iron about, so instead it will be a moonlight revel somewhere near London, perhaps here if Anne is willing to permit it. Mama plans to string lanterns like Vauxhall Gardens. It will start as an ordinary gathering and then become increasingly in the fay style."

"There is to be complete secrecy about the presence of the fay. We are only to tell guests it will be beyond anything they can imagine, and that anyone who misses the revel will forever regret it. If pressed, we are to hint at the possible presence of members of the Russian royal family," said Elizabeth archly.

"I am to call on my dressmaker and convince her to lend her talents to making us a version of the dryads' clothing which will be decent for young ladies to wear," said Frederica with a sly glance at Eversleigh.

Elizabeth laughed. "I would say it is an impossible task."

Eversleigh teased, "Shall I tell your mother I liked seeing you in the original version?"

Frederica's cheeks reddened. "If you dare to tell her, I will – Oh, Mama, I had not seen you there."

"If you dare tell me what?" Lady Matlock looked at Eversleigh.

Eversleigh bowed to her. "Merely that when I called upon Titania some days ago, I had the pleasure of seeing Lady Frederica dressed as a dryad."

"Eversleigh!" yelped Frederica.

"You did dare me," he pointed out.

Lady Matlock eyed him and said, "St. George's, Hanover Square?"

"Naturally," said Eversleigh.

"In two months, perhaps, to allow time for the revel," added Lady Matlock.

Eversleigh straightened his cuffs. "Perhaps Lady Frederica would prefer to choose the date."

"I prefer never!" Frederica jumped to her feet and ran from the room.

Eversleigh stretched his hand out towards her, but she was already gone.

Elizabeth knocked on Frederica's closed door. "It is I, Elizabeth. May I enter?"

"Are you here to plead his case?"

"No. I came to see if you wanted anything. I thought you might prefer me to your mother or Viscount Eversleigh."

"You may enter." Frederica sounded resigned.

Elizabeth opened the door and slipped inside.

Frederica lay crosswise on her bed, her legs dangling off the edge, staring up at the bed canopy. "I suppose you think I am foolish for refusing such an excellent match."

"I have only known Viscount Eversleigh a few days, and I know you only a little better. I fail to see how my opinion of a match between you would be of any use."

"I thought I knew him, but that was before I discovered he was keeping half his life a secret, and now this. How dare he assume my consent?"

"Now that is something we agree on, and your mother does as well. When she discovered he had not yet made you an offer, she told him he was cork-brained."

Frederica propped herself up on her elbows. "Did she truly? I would have liked to see that."

"I thought her a little cork-brained as well for jumping straight from a situation of compromise to planning the wedding. Only a few of us are aware of what happened, and if we all hold our tongues, there would be no compromise."

"Stupid men and their stupid sense of honor! It was a complete accident he saw me that day. There is no reason he should feel bound to marry me." Frederica's voice wavered.

"Is it possible that is not his only reason? He flirts with you and seems to enjoy your company."

"He barely noticed me before that day in Faerie. If he is paying me attention now, it is because of his sense of honor."

"Well, he certainly liked what he saw that day. I do not need fay abilities to tell that!" And he had not appeared indifferent to her afterwards, but clearly Lady Frederica was not interested in hearing that. "He did not handle himself well today, though."

"No, he did not! He always knows the right thing to say, so why did he behave so foolishly? Every gentleman knows how to make a proposal. All he had to do was to ask me to be his wife and make him the happiest man in the world. But no, this is the one time he chooses to be different!"

Elizabeth was half tempted to tell her that Darcy had made an even worse disaster of his proposal, but it was better to keep Frederica unaware of that event. But it was worth considering. Mr. Collins had cared nothing for her, but his proposal could have been written for a book of etiquette. She had always felt Mr. Darcy's disapproval, but after the first set down he delivered at the Meryton assembly, he had not insulted her nor criticized her family to her face. He knew better than to do that, but when he offered her his hand, he could hardly have done worse. She could not attribute it to a lack of caring; Darcy would never have deigned to offer for her unless he was half mad with desire. "I wonder if gentlemen under the influence of an ardent attraction may have more difficulty with the proper proposal. Those who feel less can stay with their script, but is it possible that strong feelings interfere with a man's choices?"

"You are trying to convince me to accept him after all! I pray you to stop at once."

"No, I am only attempting to make sense of his out-of-character behavior. I think you would be wise to find out more about his fay connections before considering him. Or it may be fay behavior. Perhaps this is how they propose marriage."

Frederica said, "I do not know, but I have no desire to marry a man who would prefer a different woman."

"You think Eversleigh prefers another woman?" asked Elizabeth in surprise.

"I know it."

Elizabeth knew when there was no point in arguing.

Eversleigh jumped to his feet when Elizabeth reentered the sitting room. "What did she say? May I speak to her?"

Elizabeth curtsied despite his lack of formality. "Lady Frederica is resting, and she does not wish for company at present."

"Is she angry?"

Lady Matlock said, "Of course she is angry. Otherwise she would be here herself."

Elizabeth deemed it best not to respond to that. "Lady Frederica asked me to inform you that you are under no obligation to offer for her because there was no compromising situation. She dressed in the appropriate attire for one of Titania's court, as is only good manners. You were given permission to enter. Within that setting, neither of you behaved inappropriately, and there is no reason to consider marriage as a remedy."

"Surely she does not think that is the only reason I want to marry her!"

Elizabeth gave him a long serious look. "I would not be certain of that. Unfortunately, she is unwilling to discuss the matter at present."

"Perhaps I could write her a letter." He slanted his eyes towards Lady Matlock. "If her mother is kind enough to give me permission."

"No letters, I am afraid," said Elizabeth. "She has already said as much."

Eversleigh made a wan attempt at a smile. "Am I so predictable, then?"

"I would not dream of attempting to answer that," said Elizabeth demurely.

Lady Matlock dusted off her hands, although she had been doing nothing with them. "Well, she will have to speak to me sooner or later, and perhaps this can be resolved then. After all, if she does not wish to marry, all she needs to do is to say so. We will not insist on a marriage that is against her will."

"Of course not." Eversleigh seemed to be trying to put a brave face on it.

"In the meantime, we have a revel to plan. Lord Eversleigh, might I impose upon you to locate three handsome young men, either mages or poets, to act as Titania's court at the revel?"

"I can manage that."

"Frederica and Elizabeth will also be her attendants. Titania hopes to convince Oberon to join her."

"Most likely Aelfric will attend as well if I ask him," said Eversleigh.

Elizabeth's shoulders tightened. "Might he not offend some guests?" He certainly offended her often enough.

"I will speak to him about the importance of temperance. It may be difficult to believe, but he is generally a pleasant fellow, and he has the advantage that we can present him as royalty."

"That brings up the delicate question of your own status, Lord Eversleigh," said Lady Matlock. "Do you intend to reveal any of your own connections with Faerie?"

Eversleigh looked thoughtful. "I would prefer not to bring my parentage into question, but if I am there, Oberon, Titania, and Aelfric will not pretend they do not know me and will not lie for my sake."

"Yet it would be best to have your presence in case of misunderstandings. Would your Sidhe friends be willing to tell a partial truth – that you are descended from Oberon, and Aelfric has always considered you his brother?"

"Clever," Eversleigh acknowledged. "That might work."

"Good. Now we must return to London without any further delay, but we will be in contact."

Darcy bowed over Elizabeth's hand as she prepared to depart from Rosings with the Matlocks. He dared not draw attention to her by kissing it, but he tried to show her with his gaze how much he cared.

She looked at him longer than propriety required, with both warmth and sadness, he thought. She said, "Goodbye, Mr. Darcy. I hope we will meet again soon."

"You may depend upon it, Miss Bennet." Now he was certain she could see the burning desire in his eyes as he released her fingers.

It was all he could hope for.

When Eversleigh took her hand, he leaned forward and said something too quiet for Darcy to hear, but it made Elizabeth laugh and say, "I have no doubt of it! But be careful, *shurinn*."

Eversleigh bowed to her. "*Shurinn*, I hope you will do the same, as we discussed."

Blood rushing through his ears, Darcy did not hear what, if anything, Richard said to her. How dare Eversleigh behave so familiarly with his Elizabeth? They had been introduced for the first time only a week ago. Anyone seeing it would think there was an understanding between them. It could not be an accident. Eversleigh was usually so careful to avoid that sort of thing.

He watched the carriage start off, taking Elizabeth away from him, leaving him bereft. Why was he remaining here to help the man who was winning her away from him? He should be going with her, but instead he trudged back to the breakfast room.

Eversleigh poured himself a third cup of coffee. "It will be dull here without the young ladies. Collingswood, Winston and Elliott are good fellows, but not as pleasant to look upon."

"Definitely not," said Richard.

Darcy asked abruptly, "That thing you and Elizabeth call each other – *sharin* – what does that mean?"

"*Shurinn*," Eversleigh corrected. "It means that we are kin through Aelfric."

"Not true kin, though. More like a stepbrother, if anything." Darcy had no intention of allowing Eversleigh to presume on his very slight connection to Elizabeth.

"To a mortal, yes. Among the Sidhe, half brothers and sisters are the rule rather than the exception, and *shurinn* is considered a blood tie."

"Ridiculous," said Richard. "You can call it what you like, but you and Miss Elizabeth are not related."

"It may seem illogical, but nature works differently in Faerie. It is a true bond we are born with. Lord, this is difficult to explain to a mortal!" Eversleigh rubbed his hands over his face. "When two Sidhe, or a Sidhe and a mortal, are close kin, they share a magical connection, and it comes with obligations and bindings. If I concentrate, I can sense certain things about Aelfric – where he is, what he might be feeling, if he is in pain – even when he is not present. The bond also forces me to protect him. If I allowed him to be hurt when I could prevent it, I would feel physical pain."

"So you have a magical bond with your brother. Fine. But Miss Elizabeth is not related to you." Richard crossed his arms.

Eversleigh took a sip of his coffee, looked at the cup dispassionately, and pushed it aside. "There are three kinds of fay blood kinship. What you think of as relatives, close kin who share blood, like Aelfric and me, are called *tiarinn*. *Shurinn* are kin through a blood relation. Elizabeth was carried in the same womb that carried my brother, and that makes us kin. Titania is *shurinn* to me by her blood tie to Oberon. *Shurinn* is not as intense a bond as *tiarinn*, but it is still strong. I had never experienced it with a mortal before meeting Elizabeth. It is a strange sensation."

"How can that be?" asked Darcy. "Would not all the Sidhe be *shurinn* since their bloodlines are intertwined?"

"No. Only close blood ties matter, within two steps of relation. Father, mother, brother, sister, child – each of those is one step. Aelfric is one step from both Elizabeth and me. If Elizabeth had a child, Aelfric would be *tiarinn* to the child, but the child would not be *shurinn* to me because that would be three steps. The fay recognize the concept of aunt and uncle, since that is two steps, but not the concept of cousin, because that is three steps."

"You and Elizabeth are related despite having no shared blood, while Aelfric and his own cousin would not be?" Richard asked in disbelief.

"Essentially, yes. Still kin, but without the bonds of obligation or magic. The shared food ties between a Sidhe and his mortal followers are stronger."

"This makes no sense!" exclaimed Richard.

"It does not matter if it makes sense," said Eversleigh irritably. "It is not a choice, but something we are born with. Perhaps it is the same inexplicable instinct that makes mortal mothers protect their newborn babies with their lives."

Darcy shook his head. "Elizabeth does not seem to feel that connection to Aelfric. She seems to have taken him in intense dislike, and certainly does not feel protective of him."

Eversleigh sighed. "Ah, that is the other side of Sidhe kinship. Sometimes kin do not like each other, but because there is forced mental closeness, the bond can turn oppressive and lead to even greater conflict. Aelfric and Elizabeth met badly. I hope they will not always have a troubled relationship, but it is possible they will. Even if they do, should Elizabeth see someone trying to hurt Aelfric, she would stop them at all cost. And if Aelfric asks her to do something, she will do it unless she feels it is immoral." He gave a slight smile. "She will also resent having no choice."

Darcy could easily believe that part. "Are you also *shurinn* to Elizabeth's sisters, then? You may not find that a comfortable bond. Her younger sisters would be very pleased to be able to give orders to a viscount."

Eversleigh groaned. "I will try to avoid meeting them. The closeness of *shurinn* is often not as comfortable as it is between Miss Elizabeth and me. We each treat the bond with care."

Darcy could not help himself. "Do the Sidhe forbid incest?"

"Between *tiarinn*, yes, but not between *shurinn*." Eversleigh picked up his abandoned coffee cup and drained half of it.

Darcy stood and strode to the window. He could not even bear to look at Eversleigh. So that was why Elizabeth had said nothing was possible between them. She might be attracted to him, but what did he have to offer compared to a viscount with whom she had a magical bond?

"Wait," said Richard. "Did you not say there were three kinds of Sidhe kinship?"

Eversleigh nodded, for all the world as if he had not just shattered Darcy's world. "The third kind, *eliarinn*, is rare. You may safely forget about that one."

Darcy wished he could forget the entire conversation, but he expected it would haunt him forever.

# Part Four

# London

# Chapter 12

"Did you sleep well?" Frederica asked Elizabeth the next morning in the breakfast room at Matlock House.

"Tolerably well, I thank you." But she had dreamed of being in Darcy's arms. She had barely seen him at Rosings after Lord Matlock's heart paroxysm. He had always been off with Anne de Bourgh or meeting with the other mages. He did not come to the Dower House again. She had seen him only for a minute when he came to bid his aunt and uncle farewell, and she had been able to speak only a few sentences to him. Her chest had ached all the way to London.

"Good. You will need to be well-rested. Mama is planning to take us to the modiste today to discuss our costumes for the revel. The designs are likely to take hours, and Mama also wants to order a dress for you."

Elizabeth's shoulders stiffened. "That is kind of her, but I am not in need of a new dress." In truth, she was greatly in need of new garments after losing what she had in Kent, but Lady Matlock's modiste would be far more expensive than the seamstress in Meryton.

"I would not recommend fighting her on it, or she will claim to be heartbroken that you will not allow her to buy you a dress after saving her husband's life. When it comes to my mother, it is better to save your stamina for important battles. Besides, she intends for us to attend a few soirees while you are here, so a new dress will be useful."

"I suppose there is no point in saying I have no particular desire to attend a soiree."

"No point at all. She is determined to make certain the *ton* knows that you are here under our protection. She has already prepared the ground by writing to a friend with a propensity to gossip, telling her in strictest confidence that Lady Catherine has run mad and thrown wild accusations at a poor girl who tried to help her with some herbal simples."

"Is there truly any point to this? You can defend against Lady Catherine's accusations, but soon enough everyone will know that I have been to Faerie."

"Hence the herbal simples. Mama plans to claim they were faerie potions."

"Is this what a sheep feels when confronted by a particularly persistent sheepdog?" asked Elizabeth. "Well, I have no fixed plans for the next few days until my mother arrives in London. Then I will need to visit her and start dropping hints about binding spells."

"Will you tell her about Aelfric?"

"Not immediately. I think it would be better to lead up to that gradually."

Frederica fiddled with her fork. "If I were a mother who believed my child was dead, I would want to know immediately that he was alive."

"I wish it were that simple, but in this case, telling her Aelfric is alive also means informing her that her husband has lied to her all these years about it. What a tangled web we weave, indeed!"

"Perhaps the quote should be 'Lord, what fools these mortals be!' Do you wish to go alone to visit your mother, or would you like me to come with you?"

Elizabeth considered. She was not eager to expose Lady Frederica to her mother, but her presence might provoke better behavior. "If you have nothing else to do, I would be happy to have your company."

A tall, tousle-headed young man smothered a yawn as he entered the breakfast room. "G'morning, Freddie. Sorry, I did not know you had company."

Frederica rolled her eyes. "Miss Bennet, may I present my youngest brother, Jasper Fitzwilliam? Jasper, this is Miss Bennet of Hertfordshire. She was at Rosings with me."

"A pleasure, Miss..."

"Bennet," said Frederica wearily.

"My apologies, Miss Bennet. I'm not good at remembering names, or much of anything else, for that matter." He had an engaging grin.

"I am glad to make your acquaintance, Mr. Jasper. You may not know my name, but you have doubtless heard your father complaining about me," she said wryly.

"Oh, I never listen to his complaining. He does plenty of it about me." Jasper tossed two slices of toast onto his plate and speared several pieces of cold meat. "I'm the Fitzwilliam family failure." He did not sound in the least perturbed about it.

"Jasper," Frederica warned.

"Oh, Freddie, you know it's true, and I'd rather admit it openly than slouch about trying to keep it a secret. And don't tell me that it would be different if I would just think for a minute before I opened my mouth, because I can't do it." He cut his meat into large chunks and stuffed one into his mouth.

"I am not going to throw stones," said Elizabeth soothingly. "You should hear what my father says about me these days."

Frederica said, "Mother has invited Miss Bennet to stay here at least through midsummer."

Jasper swallowed his food. "I hope you enjoy it. You won't see much of me. I generally don't eat with the family. Can't stand sitting still for two hours. The food gets cold, too. I don't care for cold fish. Do you like fish?"

Elizabeth cocked her head and turned to Frederica. "Your brother is a Sidhe in a mortal body!"

Frederica shook her head. "He cannot use his magic."

"That is not what I mean. He acts just like one. Mr. Jasper, someday I will have to introduce you to my Sidhe half-brother. You would get on splendidly together."

"You have a Sidhe brother? Oh, you must be the one who went to Faerie! You are so fortunate. I wish I could go to Faerie. I love the fay. There is a gnome in the garden at our country estate and I used to leave out biscuits and milk for him. He would grumble whenever I talked to him, but I think he liked me. It is too bad there are no fay in London."

Frederica choked on a sip of coffee. "You can see the fay?"

"Of course. Can't you?"

She set down her coffee cup with care. "I could not before I went to Faerie with Elizabeth. Now I can see them again. Why did you never tell our father?"

"Tell him what?"

"That you can see the fay!"

Jasper looked bewildered. "He never asked. You went to Faerie, too? You have all the luck!"

Elizabeth smiled. "Mr. Jasper, if you would like, I would be happy to take you on a visit to Faerie."

His eyes lit up. "Would you? Oh, that would be marvelous!" His face fell. "It might not be a good idea, though. I always say the wrong thing, and someone will be offended."

Elizabeth laughed. "Definitely Sidhe! You would be welcomed there. The Sidhe men think it is a great virtue to blurt out whatever happens to be in their minds. Do you like horses?"

He beamed. "I love horses."

"Then I definitely must introduce you to my Sidhe brother."

It was after calling hours when Phipps announced Viscount Eversleigh.

Finally! Elizabeth had been wondering and worrying about what might be happening at Rosings Park for the last three days. Perhaps now they would get some answers.

"Lord Eversleigh, it is a pleasure, as always," said Lady Matlock. "Do sit down. I hope your journey back from Rosings Park was an easy one."

"It was uneventful, thank you, which was a great relief after my overly eventful stay there. I hope you are all in good health?"

Bother. They would have to sit through a quarter hour of social niceties before she could ask about Lady Catherine's fate.

"Very well, I thank you. The weather has been a bit dreary, but we have entertained ourselves with plans for the revel. I am happy to report Lady Jersey has agreed to join me in hosting it," said Lady Matlock.

"That is excellent news. I trust she will be handling the royal invitation, then?"

"Yes, although I will, of course, send the Prince Regent a card."

"You are inviting Prinny?" Frederica blurted out.

"Do not worry; it is unlikely he will bestir himself for an event that is not in town," said Lady Matlock. "He must be invited, though. It would be most improper to have visiting royalty and fail to invite our own."

As if it were not difficult enough to deal with the constant mentions of this and that aristocrat, now they were bandying about royalty! At least this was better than discussing the weather.

Eversleigh said, "I have news from Titania. She says Oberon does not wish to attend the revel, but as a gesture of good faith, he will halt the attacks on mortals until then."

"That is excellent news," said Elizabeth. But it still did not tell her what had happened to Lady Catherine. Was she to be executed? Had it already been done?

Eversleigh ostentatiously placed his hand over his ear and directed a mock reproachful look at Elizabeth. "Lady Matlock, could I ever hope for forgiveness from you if I rudely proceed to a matter of business? I fear Miss Bennet may deafen me with her silent questions otherwise."

Elizabeth's cheeks grew hot under Lady Matlock's quizzical gaze. "You must forgive me, Viscount Eversleigh. I fear I have been thinking too loudly."

Lady Matlock turned back to Eversleigh. "Doubtless there is some explanation for that odd interchange."

"Forgive me, your ladyship," said Eversleigh. "Among the fay, it is possible to communicate a thought simply by directing it at a certain person and putting a degree of force behind it, or, as Miss Bennet so aptly puts it, thinking it loudly. She shows a particular aptitude for it. Because of our bond through Prince Aelfric, I am susceptible to her thoughts, with the result that I am aware my life may be in danger if I do not quickly assure Miss Bennet that Lady Catherine is alive and as well as any strong-willed lady who is forced to submit to being blindfolded and having her hands tied." He inclined his head towards Elizabeth.

Lady Matlock did not appear amused. "You are able to have conversations which exclude the rest of us completely?"

"Not conversations as such," said Elizabeth hurriedly. "Only very general concepts. If I were thinking hard about being hungry, Viscount Eversleigh might be aware of that, but not what I was planning for my next meal."

Eversleigh nodded. "In this case, I perceived Miss Bennet as pounding at the door of my mind with both fists because she was desperate to know something. I was able to guess what that something was, but she could not have told me that. It is much like our mortal ability to tell when someone is angry with us, but not necessarily why they are angry or what they wish us to do about it." He nodded to Frederica, even though she had said nothing.

Frederica met his gaze without flinching. "It is quite possible that I might become angry if you do not tell us what has happened at Rosings Park. I assume you have already informed my father."

"I did, but I thought you might like to hear directly from me rather than secondhand, hence my presence here."

"That will be enough from both of you," said Lady Matlock disapprovingly. "Lord Eversleigh, might I hope that you could be prevailed upon to relieve our ill-bred curiosity about the recent events?"

Eversleigh shifted uncomfortably in his chair. Frederica looked as if she would have run from the room if she had not been even more eager to hear the news.

"I would be honored to do so." Eversleigh's words were polite, but his voice had gone flat. "The three mages who were to examine Lady Catherine arrived shortly after you left Rosings Park. We searched Lady Catherine's rooms thoroughly, but the only incriminating item found was another spell written in Sir Lewis's hand which she had hidden inside her pillowcase. She apparently took the precaution of removing it from her bedside table but was unwilling to destroy it. It appears to be a spell to insert a particular thought or belief in someone's mind."

Frederica's indrawn breath was audible, and even Lady Matlock paled.

"From questioning her, they believe she has no knowledge of how to develop sorcerous spells on her own. The mages have determined that the sorcery of Sir Lewis and Lady Catherine should not be made public to prevent a general panic about sorcerers living among us. Certain influential members of the Collegium and the government will be told. No doubt rumors will spread, but they hope to limit that." It sounded as if Eversleigh did not agree.

"What will happen to Lady Catherine?" asked Elizabeth.

"Since she has not actively pursued sorcery, they feel execution is inappropriate, not to mention difficult to explain. They cannot prove she does not know any other spells, so she will need to be kept away from people. Initially she will be sent to a remote hunting lodge where she will be guarded and warded at all times, but eventually they wish to find an isolated island where she would have less opportunity for contact with innocent people."

Lady Matlock raised her delicate eyebrows. "She will be very unhappy about that."

"She shows no remorse over what she did, only regret that she was caught. This sentence is extremely lenient. They are not only allowing her to live, but also to keep her vision. Blinding her would be the best precaution, since she cannot cast spells if she cannot see."

"Has Miss de Bourgh expressed an opinion about it?" asked Elizabeth.

"Miss de Bourgh continues to believe execution is the appropriate option, but she has agreed to accept the judgment. The blood wards we set are still working, so those people Lady Catherine had bespelled are free from her influence. The servants – well, they appear to be taking it calmly. The only difficult case has been Miss Bennet's cousin, Mr. Collins."

Elizabeth's mouth went dry. "What has happened to him?"

Eversleigh straightened his cuffs. "When the spell stopped affecting him, he became furious at himself for submitting to Lady Catherine's demands and angry at his wife for doing the same. Knowing of your concern for Mrs. Collins, I spoke to them both and told them the truth." He paused. "I cannot say it went well. Mr. Darcy brought Mrs. Collins back to London with him, but I think she would prefer to tell you the rest of the story herself."

Elizabeth's hands flew to cover her mouth. "Where is she?"

"At Darcy House. If you would like, I can take you there on my way home. It is but a short walk."

"I would be most obliged."

Eversleigh steered Elizabeth into Grosvenor Square. "Sit on the bench, *shurinn*, and tell me what is troubling you."

"Do not *shurinn* me! I am in no need of assistance. I just want to see Mrs. Collins."

"Perhaps you do not need assistance, but I suspect you will help your friend more if you are calmer when you reach her."

Elizabeth huffed, but sat down without her usual grace. "Does it not become dull, always being wiser than everyone else?"

He hooted with laughter. "Shall we ask Lady Frederica if I am always wise? I defy you to outdo my ability to say the wrong thing in her case."

Elizabeth's lips twitched. "You were indeed impressively unwise."

"She does not seem to have forgiven me."

"She still believes you proposed only as a matter of honor."

Eversleigh's lips formed a straight line. "Well, I will simply have to persist until she realizes that is not true."

"A little wooing might not go amiss."

Eversleigh groaned. "The one skill I have never learned. But you are distracting me from the question of what is distressing you."

She could not tell him it was the prospect of seeing Mr. Darcy made her stomach churn, but she could explain the rest. "Mrs. Collins's suffering is my fault. Had I refrained from showing my magic when healing Lady Catherine, none of this would have happened. Charlotte would still be contentedly married. I would still trust my father, and I would still have my family and my reputation. I would not know of my mother's infidelity or my father's use of binding spells. I am well punished, but Charlotte does not deserve to suffer for my error."

Eversleigh folded his hands over his knee. "You have suffered for it, but Miss de Bourgh has her life back because of it, and the servants at Rosings are no longer slaves. Mrs. Collins's marriage has been damaged, but that would have happened eventually at Lady Catherine's death when the spell died with her. You simply moved the date forward. You are now caught between your parents, it is true, but we have a chance to stop the war with Faerie before more people die. And that is without considering the most important benefit of your choice."

"What is that?" she asked guardedly.

His teeth glinted as he smiled. "Aelfric now has three Bakewell Black mares to breed with Sidhe horses. That alone should be worth the rest."

The gurgle of laughter escaped her tight throat. "Someday you must explain Aelfric's obsession with horses to me. He tells everyone else about it, but he just scowls at me."

"He does have a very nice smile when he remembers to use it."

"I will never understand him. The day Aelfric removed the spell on Miss de Bourgh, he came back to Titania's bower looking for me. He wanted me to tell him more about my mother crying over his supposed grave. Do you know how very little there is to add to the description of someone crying over a grave? She knelt. Occasionally she would lie on it. And she cried. Her eyes became red, and her face was blotchy. But he kept asking for more. I would have made up some details, but he would have known I was lying. In the end I just kept repeating the story, and that seemed to satisfy him."

Eversleigh shook his head with a smile. "Aelfric has yet to learn wisdom about certain things. I hope you will not hate him for what he represents. The sins of your parents are not his fault. But what am I saying? This is not the time to worry about Aelfric."

"Still, I am feeling a little better. Where is Darcy House?"

"Less than two streets away. Come."

"Miss Bennet to see Mrs. Collins," Eversleigh told the butler at Darcy House. He bowed to Elizabeth. "Until we meet again."

Elizabeth barely managed a distracted curtsy because she caught sight of a familiar figure that made her heart pound.

As the butler closed the door, Mr. Darcy's deep voice said, "Hobbes, I will escort Miss Bennet upstairs." He did not look happy.

"Thank you," said Elizabeth. "Lord Eversleigh tells me Mrs. Collins is here." Why was she stating the obvious?

"I offered her a place to stay, since she has a long-standing acquaintance with me and had only just met Eversleigh." He gestured to the staircase.

"That was generous of you." She started up the stairs, conscious of his presence behind her.

"Mrs. Collins is also welcome in the public rooms here, but she has expressed a preference for some time alone." He sounded defensive.

"I have no doubt of your hospitality." Once she would have, but not now.

He rapped on a carved wooden door. At Charlotte's invitation to enter, he held it open for Elizabeth.

Elizabeth flew to embrace her friend. "Oh, Charlotte! I am so sorry!"

Charlotte clung to her wordlessly for a moment as the door closed behind her, leaving the two of them alone. Elizabeth stepped back to look at Charlotte, leaving one arm around her.

Her friend looked weary and grim. "Thank you for coming, Lizzy, especially after how badly Mr. Collins treated you. I was not sure if you could ever forgive me."

"Do not be foolish! I never blamed you for what he did. I know you would have helped me if you could. And now I cannot even hold Mr. Collins responsible for it since he had no choice but to obey Lady Catherine." At least that was what she wanted to believe. In truth, she did not think she could ever forgive him for sending her away as he did.

"I am glad. I have worried about it, but I was afraid of what Mr. Collins would do if he caught me trying to contact you," said Charlotte. "Now that no longer matters." Her eyes grew shiny.

"What happened? Viscount Eversleigh said only that Mr. Collins had changed after the spell on him was gone."

Charlotte lifted her hands in a gesture of helplessness. "He came in from working in his garden, tossed his gardening gloves on the floor, and announced that he hated gardening and it should be my responsibility. He had always been happy to spend time in the garden before, but I told him I would do it if he wished. At dinner he was silent until I said something about hoping Lady Catherine's health had improved. He shouted that Lady Catherine was a fool, and he was tired of being her lapdog. I know you never liked him, Lizzy, but he was not an ill-tempered man. This man was a stranger. When he was not back to himself two days later, I asked Mr. Darcy for help." She buried her face in her hands and sank down onto a wooden chair.

"Oh, Charlotte, how terrible for you! I am so sorry."

"Viscount Eversleigh came to the parsonage and talked to Mr. Collins, but whatever he said seemed to make no difference."

"What did Mr. Collins do?"

"The next day he rode off to Canterbury without telling me where he was going and did not return that night. When he came home the next day, he said he wanted to annul our marriage."

Elizabeth gasped. "Can he do that?"

"The church allows marriages that are compelled by sorcery to be annulled." Charlotte's voice broke.

"But that would leave you with nothing!"

Charlotte brushed away tears. "That does not matter as much as the things he said, about how he would never have married someone like me if he were in his right mind – oh, Lizzy, it was so horrible. When he proposed to me, I knew it was too good to be true. What man would want poor, plain Charlotte Lucas? But I wanted my own home so much that I let myself believe it."

"He does not deserve you. Oh, Charlotte!"

Charlotte swallowed hard. "He was always annoying and foolish, and I am much better off without the man he has proven to be."

"What will you do? Will you return to Meryton?"

"I cannot. Meryton was bad enough when I was merely a poor spinster. It would be worse as a rejected wife. I do not even know if my father would take me back."

"What will you do, then?"

Charlotte lifted her chin. "I will swallow my pride and accept charity. Mr. Darcy has offered me a cottage on his estate with a maid and a small income. He claims to feel an obligation to provide for me since my life was ruined by his aunt's actions." Charlotte's hands stole over her stomach. "I will have a home of my own without needing to tend to a foolish husband, and I will have someone else to care for soon. I do not need Mr. Collins."

"A child? I am so glad you will have someone to love. You will be a wonderful mother. Mr. Darcy is doing the right thing in helping you."

"He is a much better man than Mr. Collins, but that does not take much. Are you and he..." Charlotte tapered off her question delicately.

"Not after Lady Catherine ruined my good name. The Matlocks are trying to repair my reputation, and it may change over time, but for now, no." She shrugged, hoping to appear untroubled.

"That horrible, selfish old woman has caused so much pain. It is not right."

And it was hard to see how Lady Catherine's sorcery could be kept secret if Mr. Collins was trying to gain an annulment based on it.

Darcy pretended to read a book as he waited for Elizabeth to emerge from Mrs. Collins's room. He suspected she might try to leave without seeing him, and he had no intention of allowing that to happen. It had been three days since he had said goodbye to her at Rosings. After those weeks when he had seen her every day, often many times a day, these three days had felt like an eternity.

An eternity of missing her and an eternity of doubt. One minute he would remember her passionate kisses and her gentle touch on his cheek, and he could not understand how she could deny him. The next minute he would hear Eversleigh's voice describing his magical bond with Elizabeth, and he wanted to rend his own flesh with his fingernails. Until he knew what – and whom – Elizabeth wanted, he would drive himself mad with questions.

He heard her footsteps on the stairs and hurried to meet her. "Miss Elizabeth, may I have the honor of escorting you back to Matlock House?"

"I would like that," she said quietly, but he could not judge her mood. She took her bonnet from the butler and tied it on.

Darcy held the door open and followed her down the steps. She waited at the bottom, and he took that as an invitation to offer his arm. She tucked her hand in his elbow without hesitation. At least she was not afraid to touch him.

As they began to walk, she said, "I must thank you for intervening on behalf of Mrs. Collins and for your generosity to her."

Her gratitude made Darcy uncomfortable. "It was the least I

could do. Lady Catherine's behavior harmed many people, but perhaps none more than her, and certainly no one could be more blameless." It was not what he wanted to speak to her about, but he was grateful they were speaking at all.

"You could have done nothing, and no one would have been the wiser, so I thank you."

"I knew you would want her to be protected."

She hesitated. "You are very kind."

He had to say something. "I hope you have found Matlock House comfortable."

The corners of her lips turned up in that delightful expression that told him he was about to be teased. "Comfortable at Matlock House? Are you certain you remember who I am – Lizzy Bennet who walked through three miles of muddy fields, who is terrified of Collegium mages, and who had never dealt with an aristocrat before these last weeks? The chairs at Matlock House are comfortable. So are the rooms and the beds. I am not comfortable, merely out of place."

"I was surprised you agreed to go there."

"As well you might be! I decided to take your advice and at least attempt to rescue my reputation. I have not even used my...things that I use." She wiggled her fingers.

Of course. She would not wish to speak of magic on a public street. "I thought you were determined to keep using those things."

"I was." She gave him an arch smile. "But I am not without the ability to change my mind or to listen to advice."

"Are you following Eversleigh's advice or mine?"

She huffed. "Perhaps, just perhaps, I am clever enough to think that when two gentlemen I respect offer the same opinion, it might be worth listening to."

"I see." But his opinion alone was not enough.

She did not reply for some time. "How is Miss de Bourgh?" she asked with forced cheer.

He had upset her. "She is well. I am glad to report that an adult woman can learn control of the elements far faster than a young boy. She has made good progress, although it still gets windy at night now that Pepper has left. Eversleigh has asked Aelfric to visit her every few days to help her with any problems that may arise."

"Aelfric?" She sounded dubious.

"It seems the Sidhe have elemental magic, although they do not struggle to control it as I do." A passerby gave him an odd look. "It is easier in...the place where Aelfric lives. I felt no pressure from the elements there."

"Has Miss de Bourgh met him again, then? Dare I hope it was not a disaster?"

"She seems to like him, and she listens to his advice more than she does to mine."

"I am glad I was not there to see that! You might not have resented it, but I would have done so on your behalf."

"Oh, I resented it." That made her smile. "I did not mind resigning my teaching duties to him."

"I would imagine not!"

Since they seemed more in accord on the subject, he continued, "He may be able to help her where I could not. Her strongest abilities, unmaking and air, are my weakest ones. I have never unmade anything by accident, for which I am profoundly grateful."

"That would be an uncomfortable skill."

"Indeed. Aelfric has promised to bring her some fay-made bedding he claims is resistant to unmaking. It will make life easier for the maids."

Elizabeth giggled. "I suppose it is impossible for her to disguise her abilities from her staff."

"Quite impossible."

She asked in a more serious tone, "Will that be a problem for her?"

"I think not. I brought in a curate from a neighboring parish to talk to the staff, since they would not talk to me, and it appears they were well aware of Lady Catherine's abilities and Sir Lewis's experiments. Once they learned Anne was responsible for Sir Lewis's demise, she became a heroine to them. Elemental abilities are substantial improvement over..." He glanced from side to side before saying quietly, "Sorcery."

"I should say so!" she exclaimed. "But if they knew what was happening, why did they say nothing?"

"They thought we would not believe them. Although I do not like to admit it, they may have been correct. We were so convinced we had made England safe from sorcerers, and Sir Lewis's behavior was nothing like Oliver Cromwell's. It has been a lesson for us."

"A frightening one."

At least they were talking, but it did not answer his most important question. "I asked Eversleigh to explain fay kinship to me."

She looked up at him through her lashes. "Are you thoroughly confused yet?"

"I am confused about your bond."

"So am I! When I was a child in Faerie, I knew about kinship bonds, but I did not think I had any apart from my bond to Titania because I was one of her mortals. I did not know Oberon was my *shurinn,* but I trusted him very easily, even when I should not have. I have vague memories of playing with a Sidhe child who must have been Aelfric. I remember feeling unusually close to him, but I did not realize those were kinship bonds. It is a new experience for me now. I have never had a brother, and suddenly acquiring two of them, both with kinship bonds, is very strange. But it has been useful in making me feel at ease with Eversleigh."

He could not help himself. "Do you plan to marry him?"

Elizabeth halted in place. She carefully extricated her hand from his arm and said coldly, "Mr. Darcy, if you think I could behave as I did that night while planning to marry Eversleigh or any other man, I have nothing further to say to you." Her voice shook on the last words. She hurried away from him without looking back.

He stared after her in dismay. What had he done? Should he go after her and try to explain?

She hesitated when she reached the corner, looking back and forth between the street straight ahead and the one to the right.

He caught up with her in a few strides. Stopping behind her, he said quietly, "Matlock House is to the right."

She did not acknowledge him, but turned and blindly darted out into the street, right in front of a high perch curricle drawn by a pair of matched bays at a fast trot.

His heart in his throat, Darcy grabbed her arms and pulled her back. The wheel boss bumped against his thigh. Good God, that had been too close! But she was safe, her back pressed against him.

Once the pounding of his heart had slowed, he asked, "Are you hurt?"

She paused before answering. "Pray release me."

His hands dropped to his sides. At least this time she looked before crossing the street.

His chest ached as he followed her. Even if she would not speak to him, he was not going to let her walk unprotected and alone in London. He stayed a pace or two behind her until she was forced to stop by a delivery cart blocking her way. He had to try again. "Elizabeth." No, that was too familiar. "Miss Elizabeth. Miss Bennet."

She did not turn to look at him. "If you are composing a list of what I am called, you have forgotten Lizzy, Eliza, and Libbet."

At least she was responding! "I once told your cat that I am a very stupid mortal, and it is still true."

She seemed to relax a little. "I will not argue with you on that, sir."

"It is confusing to me. I know you dislike many things about me, yet you seem so comfortable with Eversleigh. You have a magic bond with him. He understands your life in Faerie in a way I cannot. He is a viscount. And I would be very surprised if he has not thought about marrying you."

She gave a gurgle of laughter and finally looked at him. "Oh, yes, he thinks about marrying me. Whenever he is particularly frustrated with Lady Frederica, he thinks, 'It would be so much easier if I simply married Libbet.'" She caught Eversleigh's grumbling tone perfectly. "That does not mean he wants to marry me. And there are two very good reasons why I would never marry him."

He took a deep breath. "Why is that?"

"First, he is Master of the Collegium, and second, I could never match his sartorial elegance. I feel perpetually rumpled and disheveled when I am with him. He needs a wife who will look as effortlessly elegant and stylish as he does."

Relief washed over him. Of course Elizabeth would never marry the Master of the Collegium. He should have realized that on his own. "You never look rumpled to me."

She cast a glance down at the splashes of street muck on her skirt from the horses' hooves. "If that is true, you are indeed a very stupid mortal." But she said it with laughter in her voice.

He made a slight bow. "At your service."

"It is not true that I dislike many things about you. I did once, but I know you better now. I am still not happy you are part of the Collegium, but I have been so surrounded by mages of late that I am becoming inured to it."

Surely there had to be something he could offer in return. "I plan to speak to Bingley about your sister."

"That is good of you. Do you know I am afraid to write to Jane?"

"Because you spoke to me about Bingley?"

She shook her head. "Because I cannot tell her about anything. She knows that I went to Faerie the first time, but how do I explain to her what I have been doing since without mentioning the second trip, sorcery, Aelfric, Eversleigh, either of my parents, or Mr. and Mrs. Collins? Mr. Bingley is but an afterthought on that list. The last letter I wrote to Jane was about the weather and Pepper's adventures catching mice because I could hardly say that I was waiting to hear whether Lady Catherine would be executed, after learning how to make blood wards from a peer of the realm who is also a prince of Faerie, and healing Lord Matlock who was under a sorcerous spell. I certainly cannot explain why Lady Matlock insisted I stay at Matlock House when she had never met me before that day."

"That is a dilemma. Should I be encouraged my name was absent from the list of forbidden topics?"

She blushed. "It seemed impolite to mention you to your face."

He took a deep breath. "If you did tell your sister about me, what would you say?"

She was silent for some time, but it was not the silence of anger. When she finally spoke, her voice was soft enough that he had to lean towards her to hear over the street noise. "I would tell her I think very highly of you and wish you could play a different role in my life, but I do not know if it will be possible. I am doing what I can to make myself marriageable again, but a great deal will depend on what happens at the revel. If society chooses to frown on the Sidhe and women with magic, Lady Frederica and I will both be pariahs. But if it goes well....We will see." She looked up at him with a question in her eyes.

It was all he could do not to take her in his arms. "I thank you. That is all I can ask. But I do not promise to accept society's judgment if I

321

disagree with it."

Her smile was sad. "It never crossed my mind that you would."

They had reached Matlock House. "Thank you for answering my questions."

"Would you like to come inside?"

He shook his head. "They will be dressing for dinner soon, and I do not wish to leave Mrs. Collins alone for long. But I will tell my aunt that I would be happy for an invitation to dine soon."

"I would like that." She offered him her hand. He raised it to his lips and kept it there as long as he dared. If only he had the right to do more!

"Viscount Eversleigh to see you, sir." Darcy's butler held out a silver salver.

"Eversleigh? Send him in." It was a timely distraction from counting the hours until he could see Elizabeth when he dined at Matlock House tonight. It could not come soon enough.

Eversleigh strode in, his eyes shadowed. "Darcy, thank you for seeing me."

"It is my pleasure. Some port?"

"That would be most welcome."

Darcy poured two glasses and brought one to Eversleigh. "Have you heard anything further regarding the plans for Lady Catherine?" That seemed the most likely reason for his visit.

"Not yet. There is to be a meeting of senior mages about it tomorrow, which will be a pleasant change from working on Lady Matlock's charge to me of finding a few handsome young mages and poets to take part in her Midsummer Night's Revel."

"Have you had any success?"

"I have, which is somewhat surprising since I could not tell them anything about the role they are to play. Even FitzClarence has agreed. Titania will be pleased to have a swain with royal blood." Eversleigh loosened his cravat.

Something about that niggled in the back of Darcy's mind. Eversleigh always kept his appearance immaculate. He did not do things like loosening his cravat.

"Is something wrong?" asked Darcy abruptly.

Eversleigh set down his glass. "Unfortunately, yes. The three gentlemen on your Board of Inquiry called on me earlier to inform me that they were reopening your case, and to delicately warn me that if I tried to interfere, they would put up their own candidate for Master."

Not again! Bile rose in Darcy's throat. "But they declared me innocent of the charges."

"With some pressure from Lord Matlock. Now they see their opportunity."

"What did you say to them?"

Eversleigh's lip curled. "I told them you did not do it, but I could not stop them from wasting their time if they chose. And that if they had a better candidate for Master, they should put him forward in any case. It was an empty threat; none of them hold much sway in the Collegium. Troublemakers, every one of them."

Darcy had not eaten since breakfast, but his stomach felt full of lead. "What would you advise me to do?"

"Nothing at present. They plan to ask you to come to a hearing again, and I suggest you decline the invitation. They will twist everything you say. Put anything you want them to know in a letter and give me a copy for the archives. I do not know why they have such malice towards you, Darcy. You may not be gregarious, but you have done nothing to earn this sort of hatred."

If only the port could wash away the bitter taste in his mouth.

"Do you recall the case of George Wickham? He was expelled for using his magic to cheat at cards."

"Vaguely. It was an easy decision, as I recall."

"He did not even try to defend himself. He knew he had been caught. I was the one who brought the charges against him. He was very popular among a certain circle of malcontents in the Collegium. Oddly enough, three of them offered to be on the Board of Inquiry for me."

"Revenge, then? Does Wickham have elemental magic? Could he be behind some of this?"

"He has no skill with water. I have thought about that often. The only skill he ever bothered to practice was illusion, but I have checked and there were no illusions involved in the droughts I am charged with causing." He had wanted so badly to prove Wickham was behind his problems, but there was not a scrap of evidence.

"I cannot blame you for being bitter. I wish there were more I could do. I thought perhaps of adding other members to the panel, but the Collegium charter does not permit it. If they do find against you, your best chance will be to put the matter to a vote of the entire Collegium."

"Where I have very few friends."

"Lord Matlock, though, has many friends among the members, and his powers of persuasion will help you."

"If it were just a matter of expulsion from the Collegium, as it was for Wickham, I would not care. But since my powers are elemental, I would face binding as well," said Darcy bitterly.

"I know. I have not forgotten that for a moment. I hope it will not come to that, but do remember that you have the freedom of Faerie, and the Collegium cannot pursue you there."

"You could."

"Grant me some credit, Darcy. I would take expulsion from the Collegium myself before I would put a binding spell on an innocent man. Or guilty one, for that matter. Placing binding spells should be a crime like any other sorcery."

"Yet you supported my uncle, even when you thought he had chosen to cast one."

Eversleigh grimaced. "It is hard to give up years of friendship on discovery of one poor decision made many years before. I am glad we can now acquit him of casting the spell of his free will. Still, if he had not spent years campaigning against binding spells, I might not have been able to forgive him at the time."

"I did not mean to raise a painful subject." Darcy had enough pain of his own. "I will remember your advice. Faerie might provide a temporary refuge, but I cannot see myself spending the remainder of my life there."

"I hope it will not come to that."

So did Darcy. "How long do I have?"

"Until they ask for your testimony, there is no need for concern. Afterwards I hope they will follow the usual protocol of informing the Collegium before taking action, but I cannot guarantee they will not attempt to act on their own. I suggest you take precautions against being caught unawares. Either Lord Matlock or I will be checking on you regularly, and we will remove a spell if one has been cast."

Darcy would still have lost control over himself and his body. Nothing would be the same again. He understood all too well why Elizabeth had feared being spellbound even when she knew it would be removed. "You were not able to remove the binding on Anne de Bourgh."

Eversleigh turned his hands palm up. "That spell was of Lord Matlock's devising, and he is the best spellmaster we have. These men are far less skilled." He smiled suddenly, a tense smile. "I am also not above asking Aelfric for help. You saw what quick work he made of the spell on Miss de Bourgh."

Darcy stared into his untouched port. "Do you know how long it took me to learn to control my elemental powers? When I was a boy, anything I tried to drink turned into a whirlpool in my glass. Water jumped out of buckets when I walked past, and there were buckets of water everywhere because I also accidentally set things ablaze. My mother would not pour tea when I was in the room. When I had nightmares, the lake outside my window would overflow its banks. I prayed every night for God to take this curse for me. My father worked with me daily to teach me control, but I did not want to watch every thought I had or every step I took. I wanted to run and play like other children, but they would not be allowed to play with me because if I became angry, a sinkhole might open under them. When I finally learned the control I needed, I was sent off to school where everyone said I was too serious. When other boys were cruel to me, I could have made the contents of their chamberpots fly up in their faces or their ink spill, but I did not because that would be the wrong use of my powers. I know I have not made the wells of men I dislike run dry because I take great care to keep that from happening, always checking to make certain I am not affecting the flow of water deep in the earth. I always envied men like you who could learn to use their powers when I had to learn not to use mine, which is very much like learning not to breathe."

"I had no idea."

But the words would not stop now that he had let them loose. "Do you know why elemental mages are so rare? Most of them die as children. They drown in their own beds while asleep or are burned alive by fires they started but could not put out. I had servants watching me every minute, day and night. I was never alone. I learned illusion to hide myself from those prying eyes. And now these workaday mages who have never done anything more than set locks or build wards are sitting in judgment on me, and I can do nothing about it. Sometimes I think Miss Bennet is right, and the Collegium is rotten to the core. I wonder how many other petty sorcerers like Sir Lewis de Bourgh may be hiding their sins by participating in the Collegium."

"I have been wondering that as well." Eversleigh frowned. "Darcy, I hate to ask you this, but is there any possibility you might have acted on the water while you were asleep?"

Darcy wanted to hit him. "No," he said savagely. "My power works on the water nearest me. A clever servant came up with a solution. There are always five basins of water in my bedroom, one on each side of the bed and one beneath it. Now the worst I can do in my sleep is to soak the floors."

Eversleigh seemed to relax slightly. "I am sorry. It sounds like a curse."

Uncomfortable, Darcy said, "Sometimes it is easier and not so burdensome. It does not weigh on me as much when I am with other mages. Some more than others – both you and George Wickham somehow relieve the pressure."

"Anyone else? Perhaps there is a pattern. Your cousins and uncle?"

"No more than any other mage. Miss Elizabeth's presence makes it easier, and the pressure goes away completely when her cat is on my lap."

"The phouka?" Eversleigh leaned forward.

"The very one."

Eversleigh's eyes narrowed. "I have an idea. May I try an experiment?"

"If you wish, but I have tried everything."

He stripped off his gloves. "Give me your hand." When Darcy obeyed, Eversleigh put his fingers on the inside of his wrist. "Does that make any difference?"

The awareness of water all around him faded. He could still sense its presence, but it took effort. "Yes," he said hesitantly. "What spell are you using?"

"No spell. I am doing nothing apart from being myself, which is to say being half-fay." He released Darcy's wrist and produced a snuff box from his pocket and a ring from his finger. He placed them both on the little table beside Darcy. "Try holding each of them, one at a time."

Darcy picked up the enamel snuff box and sent his senses for water. Was it a tiny bit better than usual? No, that was just wishful thinking. "No difference."

"Try the ring."

The incised gold band was still warm from Eversleigh's hand. Startled, Darcy said, "Yes. That helps." Could there truly be a source of relief?

"It is of fay manufacture, a gift from my father. The snuff box is just a snuff box. Perhaps the reason you are more comfortable around mages is because they all have traces of fay blood. I have more than that, and I wonder if Wickham may as well. The phouka is pure fay, as is the ring."

Darcy said slowly, "Elizabeth had some inert elfshot. Touching that helped, too."

"Perhaps the fay influence neutralizes some of your elemental sensitivity." Eversleigh pocketed the snuff box. "Keep the ring until I can find you something else from Faerie. I have some items at home that would serve."

Darcy stared down at the ring in his hand. Such a small thing to make such an enormous difference. He might be able to sleep now without all those basins of water. If only he had known this years ago! But even this could not protect him from the machinations of his fellow mages. "Thank you," he said abruptly. "I never thought of that. When Elizabeth told me her cat was fay, I thought it might have done magic on me, but it never occurred to me it could be the cat itself."

"I am glad it can help. I am sorry to have brought bad news along with it. I will do my best to protect you, and I only wish it could be more."

"I know."

Eversleigh snapped his fingers. "I almost forgot. There is one other thing I wished to ask you. I have somewhat reluctantly agreed to take Lord Matlock to Faerie tomorrow. Would you be willing to join us? I would feel better with two of us to curb his over-enthusiasm, and he does tend to listen to you better than to me."

"Certainly. It should be interesting."

After Eversleigh departed, Darcy spun the ring in his hand. He needed to think. If the mages decided against him, one thing was certain. He would not accept the punishment for something he had not done, even if that meant giving up the life he led and going into hiding.

Perhaps there was another option now. Leaving England had never been a possibility before. The sea was too dangerous for him, and the risk he might accidentally swamp a boat full of innocent people had kept him on *terra firma*. But if he could use something like the ring to keep his powers in check, perhaps it would be possible. The Collegium had no power outside of England. He could leave until he was able to clear his name. He did not know how he would do that, but do it he would.

But if he left England, he would leave alone. He could not ask Elizabeth to share his disgrace. The Board of Inquiry threatened more than his good name and safety. It was the end of his hopes for a future with Elizabeth.

Since walking her back to Matlock House, he had been in an elated dream of a future together. Now it was gone. He had to stay away from her, just as he had thought to start wooing her in earnest. It was too late.

Elizabeth had taken particular care with her appearance, even borrowing Frederica's maid to do her hair. Tonight Darcy would be dining with them, and she wanted to look her best. She might not have much opportunity to speak to him, but she could look at him and know he was in the same room.

The butler brought Lady Matlock an envelope.

She took it, opened the seal and frowned as she read it. "It is from Darcy. He will not be joining us for dinner tonight after all. He has received word the Collegium investigation into him has been reopened, and the Board of Inquiry is very hostile to him. He thinks it would be wiser to keep some distance from Lord Matlock during this time."

All of Elizabeth's pleasure turned to ashes. A lump in her throat kept her from speaking, even as Frederica denounced the stupidity and evil of the Board of Inquiry.

She did not want either Lady Matlock or Frederica to know that her future had just been destroyed. Darcy was keeping his distance from her, not from Lord Matlock. It no longer mattered if she became respectable, not when any shade in her past could bring Darcy down. Even if he were acquitted again, the suspicion would linger even longer this time. He could not afford to marry a witch with fay connections. The dream had ended.

She could not bear it. "My head has started to ache. I think I will lie down for a few minutes."

Lady Matlock said, "A good idea. There is still time to rest before dinner."

There was plenty of time. Elizabeth had nothing but long, empty months and years ahead. Plenty of time.

She made it halfway up the stairs before the first sob tore through her.

Darcy gazed down the corridor to Oberon's chambers. They had left Lord Matlock there half an hour ago. Did conversations with the Sidhe not tend to be much briefer than that? "I hope it is going well."

"There is no reason why it would not," said Eversleigh. "Lord Matlock has always been half in love with the mere idea of Faerie. Oberon will be able to tell his motives are good."

"Yet you seem concerned."

Eversleigh straightened his cuffs. "Not about that. Something is odd, though. When I brought you to meet Oberon, he spoke little to me and dismissed us quickly, although it had been months since my last visit. Today he sent us away so he could speak to Lord Matlock alone. I would have expected him to keep me there. Perhaps he has his reasons, though."

"Or it could be mere coincidence."

"I suppose so." But Eversleigh's expression remained troubled. "Ah, Lord Matlock is finally coming. He looks pleased with himself."

"Smug," Darcy muttered. "He looks smug."

Eversleigh laughed. "That, too."

When Lord Matlock reached them, he announced, "That went very well. Very well, indeed."

Under his breath, Darcy said, "Modest, too."

By the quiver of Eversleigh's lips, he knew it had been heard.

Eversleigh bowed. "What happened, if I may ask?"

"He deserves his epithet. Cunning Oberon, indeed! He asked me a great many questions designed to reveal any prejudice against Faerie. Finally I told him the only thing I held against Faerie was not being allowed to visit years ago."

"I imagine he liked that," said Eversleigh.

"Then I asked him some questions about obscure Faerie lore. I would kill for some of the books in his library, but he says they are not for mortals." Lord Matlock held his hand out as if to admire it. "He gave me a ring."

Eversleigh reached out to touch the silver band. "I should warn you that ring is bespelled."

"I know it is," said Lord Matlock with pride. "He put a blood spell on it so I could communicate with him if there should be a crisis. He has one for contacting me as well. He said my spell work was most satisfactory for a mortal."

Definitely smug. At least he was not dancing with glee from having the Faerie king's blood spell on his hand. "I assume he must have a reason to wish to communicate with you."

Lord Matlock waved his hand. "It is nothing. A little plan we came up with to deal with the faerie ring problem. I cannot reveal the details." He was clearly enjoying the mystery.

"I wish you good fortune," said Eversleigh mildly, but there was something bleak in his eyes. "Do you still wish to see the Great Spell before we return?"

"I would not miss it! Our Great Spell tree was lost to the sea centuries ago."

"It is but a short walk. The King's Hall was built here to honor it." Eversleigh led them down a stone path into the forest.

After a few minutes, the dense wood opened into a clearing. An enormous oak towered over the center. Its size was unnatural, at least twice as tall as the other trees in the forest. Standing under its branches was like walking into a great cathedral.

"Nearly two thousand years old," breathed Lord Matlock. "Magnificent."

"This is where the Sidhe Caerdic and his mortal brother Alber, may their names live in blessed memory, spilled their heart's blood to split Faerie asunder," said Eversleigh.

"Can their presence still be felt?" asked Lord Matlock.

"Yes. They will be there as long as the tree stands. They are vague and have forgotten who they were after all these centuries, but you can still converse with them if you wish."

"What would I have to do?" Lord Matlock's excitement was palpable.

"Go to the tree and place your palms against the bark. You will understand what to do from there," Eversleigh said.

"Have you done it?" asked Lord Matlock.

"Oh, yes. It is traditional for a child coming of age to ask their blessing. I did it when I returned here after university. Go ahead, if you wish."

Lord Matlock hesitated. "The Great Spell," he murmured. He walked forward and rested his hands on the tree.

Darcy asked quietly, "Do they give advice?"

"Not now," said Eversleigh. "Oberon says his grandfather could converse with them for the first century or two. Now it is but a sense of their spirits that remains."

Darcy gazed up into the branches. The giant tree made him feel very small. "Why did they want to split Faerie?"

"The same reason as the lost Great Spell in the mortal world, the one that broke England from Europe and drowned an invading army led by sorcerers. In Roman times, many fay were practicing dark magic. The Sidhe here are the descendants of those who had spent their lives fighting the evil fay. This spell was created to divide Faerie with the dark magicians on the other side. It also gave the Sidhe the ability to determine if someone is lying, which exposes most sorcery."

"Were there other Great Spells?"

"The legends speak of one thousands of years ago, but nothing of it remains. During the Black Death, two mortal mages attempted a Great Spell to halt the illness, but it failed. Most likely it was because they were both mortal instead of having a Sidhe and a mortal, but I suppose they were desperate enough to try anything."

"Then it is thanks to the Great Spells that England and English

Faerie are mostly free of sorcery. What happened to the other half of Faerie?"

"No one knows. The Great Spell also blocked anyone of our part of Faerie from traveling to the other side. Given that parts of Europe are strongholds of sorcery, I suspect the dark magicians in the other half of Faerie are still up to their old tricks."

Lord Matlock dropped his hands and made his way back to Eversleigh and Darcy. "Astonishing," he said reverently.

"Were you able to understand them?" asked Eversleigh.

"Yes. I tried to ask about the construction of a Great Spell, but they could not remember. Then I explained that we were fighting sorcery in the mortal world and asked for their blessing."

"Apparently they gave it." Eversleigh pointed behind Lord Matlock, where small white flowers had blossomed in his footprints.

Lord Matlock's eyes widened. "How..."

Eversleigh clapped a hand on his arm. "You cannot expect magic to follow its usual rules this close to a Great Spell. Accept their blessing and be glad of it. We need all the help we can get."

"This is it." Elizabeth gestured to her uncle's house.

Frederica's gaze moved up and down the façade of the townhouse. "It looks very pleasant."

"How kind of you," said Elizabeth wryly, wondering if Frederica had ever been inside a tradesman's house.

"You look worried," said Frederica.

"A little." She did not know how her mother would react to her, but suspected it would not be pleasant. Still, Elizabeth could not leave London with this undone, and she could not bear remaining at Matlock House any longer than necessary.

The manservant admitted them, and Elizabeth introduced Frederica to Mr. Gardiner in the front hall of the house on Gracechurch Street.

"It is an honor, Lady Frederica. Lizzy, you are welcome, although my conscience is not completely clear in this matter," her uncle said quietly. "I feel as if I am working behind your father's back."

"But only in the best interest of your own sister," said Elizabeth.

"That is true." Mr. Gardiner sighed. "I have been talking with her about the time before her marriage, trying to help her recall how different she was then. She seems to enjoy the recollections, but as usual, she cannot stay on any topic long."

"Did you tell her I was coming?"

"Only that you had written to say you might be in London for a few days and would call if you could."

"Good. Is she in the drawing room?"

"Yes. Come, let us begin." He preceded her along the corridor to the drawing room. "Look who is here! Our Lizzy has come to call, and she has brought a friend."

"Oh, my poor nerves," cried Mrs. Bennet shrilly. "I do not know how you dare show your face here after shaming us in front of the neighborhood with your horrid magic. Why, I had to come here because I could no longer stand it in Meryton. Oh, you do not know how I suffer!"

Not a promising beginning. "I am sorry it has been difficult for you. Lady Frederica, may I present Mrs. Bennet, Mrs. Gardiner, and my sisters, Miss Bennet and Miss Mary Bennet? Mama, aunt, permit me to introduce Lady Frederica Fitzwilliam. Lady Frederica's father is the Earl of Matlock."

Mrs. Bennet's mouth opened but no words came out. Her awe at being in the presence of an earl's daughter was apparently more powerful than her nerves.

Frederica paid all the proper courtesies to Mrs. Gardiner and

Elizabeth's sisters. Turning her attention to Elizabeth's mother, she said, "I hope you will not let this nonsense about Elizabeth's magic upset you. The ban on women using magic is nothing but old superstition. Why, my father, the earl, has said that Elizabeth did excellent work in healing Lady Catherine, and he was Master of the Collegium of Mages for many years. If he did not object, why should anyone?"

Since Mrs. Bennet remained dumbfounded, Mrs. Gardiner replied, "I am happy to hear Lord Matlock holds such enlightened ideas. It is unfortunate that most people still think it a sin for a woman to have magic."

Frederica shook her head sadly. "How foolish is that, when there are as many women with magic as men? Are we to ostracize every mage's daughter in England? Why, since Mrs. Bennet has fay blood and Mr. Bennet is a mage, I imagine all their children have some degree of magic, as does Mrs. Bennet herself."

Mary, her face a mottled red, said stoutly, "I fear you may be misinformed, Lady Frederica. We have no fay blood."

Frederica put on a creditable mask of confusion. "But I thought... Mr. Gardiner, did you not tell Elizabeth this?"

"Yes," said Mr. Gardiner dryly, apparently not fooled by Frederica's act. "We do have fay blood, but Mr. Bennet prefers it not to be spoken of."

In the silence that followed, Mary said flatly, "Papa says Faerie is not a real place."

Elizabeth took a deep breath. "He would like it not to be real, but he does know better. Do you remember Faerie at all, Mama, sitting on the soft moss by Titania's side with the sprites combing out your hair and decorating it with flowers, and the faerie wine that tastes of apple blossoms and elderflowers in the moonlight?"

Mrs. Bennet wore a look of bewilderment. "I had a dream like that once, but Mr. Bennet said it was not real."

Lady Frederica said calmly, "I assure you Faerie is quite real. I traveled there with Elizabeth, and I heard Titania speak of you."

"Then why can I not remember it?" Mrs. Bennet began tugging at her handkerchief.

Carefully Elizabeth said, "Do not let it worry you, Mama. You cannot remember Faerie or your magic because you are under a binding spell."

"A spell?" asked Mrs. Bennet querulously. "How could I be under a spell? Your father would have noticed it."

This was the moment. "I am sorry to say that my father is the one who cast the spell. He admitted it to me."

"How can you tell such a lie, Lizzy?" burst out Mary. "Or is Lady Frederica again going to tell us that she heard it as well?"

It took more than Mary's spite to ruffle Frederica. "No, I was not there, but Prince Aelfric, Oberon's son, was and I can ask him about it if you like. The Sidhe never lie."

Jane put a gentle hand on Elizabeth's arm. "Perhaps you misunderstood what he said. I cannot imagine our father casting a spell on anyone, least of all our mother."

Elizabeth hated to disillusion her tender-hearted sister. "I did not want to believe it, either, or that our mother has been under a spell since before any of us were born."

"Lord, why must you say these things, Lizzy?" wailed Mrs. Bennet.

Frederica laid her hand on Mrs. Bennet's arm. "I pray you, do not allow it to upset you. It is not a sin to be under a spell, and you are far from the only one. It takes great courage and strength to accept these things, but I know you have those."

"I have no courage! Oh, my nerves!" Mrs. Bennet dabbed at her eyes with her handkerchief.

"Forgive me for distressing you," said Frederica. "I should not make assumptions. I feel as if I already know you because Elizabeth has talked about you so much. Not all to me, of course. Mostly it was to Prince Aelfric, but I heard it, too, since I was there. I forget that you do not know me at all."

Mrs. Bennet fanned herself frantically. "You are, oh, you are too, too kind, your ladyship."

"Lizzy," said Mrs. Gardiner in a voice that was a little too even. "Who is Prince Aelfric and why have you spoken to him so much about your mother?"

Frederica clapped her hand to her mouth.

Elizabeth glared at her. How could Frederica have done this to her? It had to have been deliberate. "Prince Aelfric of the Sidhe is King Oberon's son. He has taken a special interest in me," she said slowly. But what was the point in dragging the matter out now? "He was found as a newborn twenty-three years ago in the faerie ring near Longbourn." She held her breath.

"Nonsense," said Mrs. Bennet. "No one would abandon a newborn at Longbourn. We take care of our people."

"He was a Sidhe baby, born to a mortal mother, the first Sidhe baby in fifty years." Elizabeth's mouth was dry. "That is why he is so very curious about my mother."

All the color was gone from Mrs. Bennet's face. "But he died," she whispered.

A chair scraped the floor as Mr. Gardiner stood suddenly and went to Mrs. Bennet's side.

"You were told he had died," Elizabeth corrected. "He is very much alive." She glanced around the room. Jane appeared perplexed, while Mary's face was still red.

Mrs. Bennet burst into noisy sobs. Mr. Gardiner put his arm around her, glaring at Elizabeth.

Elizabeth contemplated killing Frederica.

Jane leaned towards Elizabeth. "What is all this, Lizzy?" she asked reproachfully.

It was hard to hear over Mrs. Bennet's wails. Elizabeth said, "I will tell you out in the corridor. Mary, do you wish to join us?"

Mary stomped after them. Perhaps that had not been a good idea.

In the corridor Elizabeth took a deep breath. "I am truly sorry. I would not have chosen to tell you this way. As you may have guessed, Mama's first child, the boy we were told had died, is still alive, and is one of the fay. Our father left him in a faerie ring and told Mama he had died. He used a binding spell to stop her from questioning it. Uncle Gardiner says our mother was very different before the spell, much less silly and nervous."

"We have a brother? Could it be true?" whispered Jane.

Mary interposed, "Can he break the entail?"

Hysterical laughter tried to bubble up in Elizabeth's throat. "He is our brother, but he is not human. I cannot imagine the courts even being willing to consider it." After all, what would a prince of Faerie want with Longbourn?

"How can he be fay when both of our parents are human?" demanded Mary.

"Because his father is Sidhe."

Stunned silence met her words.

Jane clasped her hands in front of her mouth. "Oh, poor Mama. Poor, poor Papa. He would not have known what to do."

"He put a spell on his own wife so that we have never known the woman she truly is. I saw a binding spell removed recently and the lady involved was utterly changed." Elizabeth's voice shook on the last words.

"He could not have meant to change Mama." Jane could never bear to think ill of anyone. "Our brother – goodness, how strange that sounds! What is he like?"

"He is –" Elizabeth broke off. It would be unfair to prejudice her sisters against Aelfric. "A friend who has known him all his life says Aelfric has a good heart. Aelfric and I did not start off well, mostly owing to a misunderstanding, and he has improved with further acquaintance." Not improved much, but it was still true.

"I do not want a fay brother," said Mary in a low voice. "I do not want fay blood or magic or a different mother."

Given how hard it had been for Elizabeth to accept those things, it must be overwhelming to pious Mary. "I was devastated when I first found out about him only a few days ago. I still am, for that matter."

"Why did you hide your magic from us?" said Mary abruptly.

"Why?" asked Elizabeth with a hint of incredulity. "Because I did not wish to be an outcast."

Jane said soothingly, "Mary, I am sure Elizabeth intended to protect us."

Mary made a gesture with her hand as if brushing the argument away. "That is not what I mean. Why did you not tell your own sisters?"

"I –" Elizabeth stopped short. Why was Mary asking questions with obvious answers rather than sermonizing? "The same reason. Lydia or Kitty would never remain quiet about such good gossip. I expected you would disapprove and might mention it in confession. Telling you would have been dangerous and would have accomplished nothing."

Mary looked away, blinking behind her spectacles. "That is not true. If you had told me, I would have known that I was not alone, that it was not because of my personal failings. I tried so hard to be obedient, to pray, to read every book of sermons I could find, all in the hope that if I were only virtuous enough, the stain of magic would leave me."

Dumbstruck, Elizabeth could only gaze at her sister. At last she said, "I had no idea. Magic has nothing to do with virtue. It is something you are born with, like the color of your eyes. I hid it, but I was not ashamed of it. I wish I had known what you were thinking."

"Then why is magic forbidden to women?"

"The mages would prefer women not to have magic, but that is a prejudice on their part. The fay think it is barbaric that mortal women are not allowed to use magic. I had thought no ladies practiced magic, but I have learned that is not true. They learn as much as they can of magic, but very discreetly."

"Lydia knows how to use her magic." Mary sounded angry.

Jane gasped.

"Lydia has magic? I had no idea." Elizabeth said.

"Why do you think Kitty follows her around and all the officers pay so much attention to her? She uses it to dazzle people." Her words dripped scorn. "Surely that is not something to aspire to."

"No." One shock after another. At Longbourn, Elizabeth had an outlet for her magic with the wisewoman; what might she have ended up using her magic for had she not? "Lady Frederica told me once that it was surprising none of my sisters had magic, but I paid no attention. I should have listened to her."

"Did you assume you were the only one of us to be so gifted, then?"

"Gifted? It sounds more like it was a curse for you. Our father knew I had magic, and I suppose I thought he would have said something to me if any of the rest of you did."

Mary scowled. "He probably did not notice. He never sees anything he does not wish to see."

"No, he does not," said Elizabeth sharply. "It is probably better for me not to speak of him at present, though. I am still very angry about the spell he put on our mother. Have you thought of what you might wish to use your magic for? It can be a force for good."

"I do not even know what it can be used for! Not to impress other people, that is certain."

"I do not know all the possibilities either. I learned to use my magic by trial and error, and I have only recently discovered how little I know. Would you mind if I asked Lady Frederica to join us? She can answer your questions about magic better than I can, and she would be very happy to do so. She wishes to see more women practicing magic."

Mary hesitated. "Would she not think me foolish?"

Elizabeth had never before felt a desire to protect Mary. "Not foolish at all, only untutored, and that is no fault of yours."

"Then I would like to speak to her."

It seemed Mary was yet another person Elizabeth had misjudged. She ought to be used to this by now.

"Lizzy!" Mr. Gardiner's voice came from the drawing room. "Come in here. Your mother has a question for you."

"Oh, dear," said Elizabeth under her breath, but she obeyed. Standing before her mother, she asked, "What would you like to know?"

Mrs. Bennet blew her nose. "If he is alive, why did he never come to see me?" she asked plaintively.

Elizabeth studied the toes of her slippers. "He knew he had been abandoned in the faerie ring, but not who had done it. Until he met me, he assumed you must have agreed to it, so he thought you wanted nothing to do with him. Once I told him that you believed he had died, he wanted to see you very much."

"But he still has not come!"

Elizabeth grimaced. "He is angry that you were put under a binding spell. Furious, in fact. He wants to meet the mother who bore him, not the results of the spell."

"You must take that spell off, then! This minute! Oh, my nerves!"

Elizabeth took a step back at her mother's ferocity. "I do not have the ability to remove spells of that nature, nor does Lady Frederica."

From behind her, Frederica said, "Eversleigh could do it, and he is here in London."

"Then take me to him!" cried Mrs. Bennet. "I cannot bear this."

Elizabeth held up her palms. "Mama, I cannot go to Viscount Eversleigh's house uninvited and demand that he remove a spell!"

"I can," said Frederica quietly. "I will take you there if you wish, Mrs. Bennet."

"Oh, you are so very kind! I thank you again and again. But a viscount? Will he be angry?"

"Not at all," Frederica soothed. "He will be happy to help you. Your son is a friend of his."

"He knows my...my son?" Miss Bennet's voice broke.

"He does," said Elizabeth.

"I want to go this very moment!"

Elizabeth sighed.

# Chapter 13

"I will be happy to do my best to help you," Eversleigh told Mrs. Bennet. He had received his unexpected guests with his usual grace. "Pray make yourself at home. I must ask Miss Elizabeth a question first."

Elizabeth hoped it was not about her father's spells. "Of course, my lord."

He took her into an anteroom. "I actually have two questions. Does your mother know Aelfric is my half-brother?"

"I told her only that you were his friend. I hope that was the right thing to do."

"Very wise. She does not know, then, that she and I are *shurinn*?"

"Oh, dear. That had not occurred to me," said Elizabeth. "Will that be a problem with removing the spell?"

"No. *Shurinn* can perform magic on each other since we do not share blood. It may feel more natural to her because of it. She will likely learn about me from Aelfric, which brings up my second question. Is Pepper nearby?"

She had not expected that. "I have not seen her today, but she usually is."

"Do you think she would be willing to carry a message for me to Aelfric?"

Elizabeth could not help smiling. "My lord, she is a cat, so there is no telling what she is willing to do. I will be happy to ask her. Is there a window I can open, preferably one not on the street?"

"Certainly." He opened a window into the garden. "Will this do?"

"Admirably." Elizabeth leaned out the window and called, "Pepper! Can you hear me, Pepper, my love? I have a question for you." She turned back to Eversleigh. "Now we wait."

Eversleigh nodded. "Thank you. I imagine you would prefer it if I did not invite Aelfric at this stage, but I must. It would be a violation of our blood bond for me to fail to do so."

"Blood right again? I wish I could say I understand completely, but I do believe you. As long as you remove the spell, I will be happy."

"It should not be a problem. I cannot keep it a secret, though. I will have to write to your father to inform him I have removed the spell. Since he should not have placed it himself, I can use that as a reason and tell him that if he wishes to restore it, he must follow proper procedures and find another mage to do it. If he does that, there will be little I can do."

"I hope he would not, but I cannot say. Look, there is Pepper."

The white raven managed to fly in through the window despite it being no more than half her wingspan. She perched on a chair back and regarded Elizabeth quizzically.

Elizabeth gently stroked the top of the raven's head. "Pepper, you are very prompt. Viscount Eversleigh would like to know if you would be so very kind as to bear a message for him. He is about to remove the binding spell from my mother."

Pepper cawed.

"Yes, it is about time someone did," said Eversleigh with amusement. "It would help me greatly if you would bear a message to Prince Aelfric that I am doing it and guide him here. Aelfric would not be able to manage London on his own. This is a very great favor I ask."

Pepper tilted her head to one side as if considering the matter.

Recognizing the signs, Elizabeth said quickly, "Lord Eversleigh, does your cook make ginger biscuits?"

"She makes excellent ginger biscuits, and I shall ask her to make an entire batch for Pepper – and what is more, I shall not give Miss Elizabeth even one of them."

Pepper spread her wings, pecked at Eversleigh's perfectly arranged hair, and flew out the window.

Eversleigh shook his head. "Phouka humor."

Eversleigh kept his fingers on Mrs. Bennet's wrist. "Tsk, tsk. We must review our training for mages, I see. There are three spells layered atop one other. The first is a binding spell, the second limits speech about certain topics, and the third is an attempt to remove the first spell. Naturally, that only entangled the first two spells together. The first spell should have been removed before the second was placed."

"Can you still remove it?" asked Mr. Gardiner, since Mrs. Bennet stood in too much awe of a genuine viscount to speak a word.

"I can. It will simply take longer, and I must remove one spell at a time. Miss Elizabeth and Lady Frederica, might I ask you to close your eyes? It will be simpler if there are no stray bits of magic about."

"I must be thinking too loudly again," whispered Elizabeth to Frederica.

"Indeed you are. Mrs. Bennet, shall I begin?" At her nod, he spoke in sonorous Latin, making it sound almost like poetry. "There, the second and third spells are gone. Mrs. Bennet, how do you feel?"

"Odd," she said calmly. "I do not know why I was so distressed before."

"That was most likely from the entangled spells. Now let me see about the original spell." The Latin began again.

When he ceased speaking, Mrs. Bennet asked, "That is all?"

"That is all," Eversleigh agreed. "You may feel as if your thoughts are tumbling over each other because there is nothing holding them back. After a binding spell is removed, there is often a period of euphoria at first, followed by intense anger. That is normal."

Instead of brushing off his words as Elizabeth expected, Mrs. Bennet nodded. "I thank you for the warning, as well as for removing the spells. I feel as if my wits have been addled for years. Lizzy, come let me look at you. How odd it is to have a grown daughter and to feel as if I do not know her."

Her mother's voice had never sounded so calm, and even the lines on her face seemed softer. Tears pooled in Elizabeth's eyes. "I look forward to knowing you better."

The butler's aggrieved voice came from outside the room. "Sir, you cannot simply push your way inside! You must permit me to announce you."

"That will be Aelfric," said Elizabeth dryly.

Mrs. Bennet – the new, seemingly younger Mrs. Bennet – jumped to her feet. "He is here? Now?"

Aelfric burst in the double doorway of the drawing room. His breeches and boots were passable, if old-fashioned, but his coat had the silver lacings and large turned back cuffs that had been stylish twenty years earlier.

"Oh, dear," drawled Eversleigh. "Wrong decade, brother." He waved his hand and Aelfric's clothes melted into an outfit similar to his own. Not that it made him fit in any better, since now his disguised features had dissolved to reveal his tip-tilted cat's eyes and flying eyebrows.

Aelfric's eye raked the room, going past Elizabeth and Frederica, and paused briefly on Mr. Gardiner before freezing on his mother.

Mrs. Bennet stepped forward and held a tremulous hand to his cheek. "Are you my boy? You must be, with such a look of your father."

She shook her head. "If only I had known you were alive!"

"You...you did not hate me for being Sidhe?" Aelfric asked.

"Good heavens, no! I had never dreamed of such an honor, and I was grieved you would have to live in Faerie where I could only visit, but I was so proud of you! I could not wait to present you to Oberon. And then when I was told you were dead..." She turned her face away and covered it with her hand.

Eversleigh stood behind Mrs. Bennet and mimed embracing someone. Aelfric took the hint and hesitantly held out his arms to his mother. A moment later she was sobbing into his chest. A tear ran down Aelfric's cheek.

Elizabeth bit her lip hard. Had her mother ever held her like that?

Eversleigh materialized next to Frederica. "Shall we adjourn to the library? I believe we are somewhat *de trop*."

Yes, that was it. Her mother and her brother were weeping together, and she was *de trop*. Lydia had always been their mother's favorite child and Elizabeth her least favorite. Aelfric might have usurped Lydia's position, but Elizabeth's was unchanged.

Elizabeth turned to follow Eversleigh, Frederica, and Mr. Gardiner from the room, but before she could go out the door, Aelfric's arm snaked out and caught her, tugging her to join the embrace. She allowed herself to be seduced into it, the feeling of her mother's arm around her as strange as Aelfric's. They were both strangers to her.

She gently disentangled herself. "I have been with her all my life," she said to Aelfric. "You have not." And because for once it was not Aelfric's fault – he had even tried to be kind – she stood on tiptoe and kissed his cheek.

"I will never forget what you have done," he said, a Sidhe way of thanking her without saying those dreaded words.

She slipped out of the room. A footman directed her to the library where the others were waiting.

"Was there a problem, Lizzy?" asked Mr. Gardiner. "Lord Eversleigh has assured me your mother is safe alone with Prince Aelfric."

That was the one thing which had not worried her. "Aelfric will not hurt her." She walked past the chair by Frederica that clearly had been left vacant for her, perching instead on a windowseat between two tall bookcases. That way the others would see nothing but her profile.

She listened abstractedly as Eversleigh answered Mr. Gardiner's questions about Aelfric, but none of it seemed real.

Eversleigh approached her and held out a glass of wine. She took it with quiet thanks.

He said softly, "You have been thinking loudly again, or perhaps feeling loudly would be a better description."

She took a sip of wine to cover her discomfiture. "My apologies. I will try to be quieter."

"Perhaps instead you could tell me what the matter is. Are you sad over the years your mother spent under the spell?

Elizabeth gave a bitter laugh. "I suppose I should be, but I am not. No, I am being a selfish soul, grieving over the mother I knew and will never have again."

Eversleigh looked pensive and then nodded. "Because she is so different now?"

"You saw her at her best. My mother was silly and nervous. She regularly embarrassed me in front of our neighbors. She had no idea of proper manners, and she encouraged my younger sisters to be ridiculous flirts. We had little in common, and she never liked me, but she was the only mother I have ever known. Now she is gone, and I am the one who killed her." Her voice broke.

He pulled up a small chair and sat beside her. "It must seem as if she died. I am sorry for your loss, and even sorrier that you never had the chance to know the mother you should have had. The woman you remember – she was not real, just a distorted reflection in a cracked mirror, but that must be little comfort at present."

"No," said Elizabeth bleakly. "But as I said, we were never close. It will be harder for my sisters."

Mr. Gardiner had approached silently. "It will be difficult for all of you. It is a shock even for me, and I knew all along she was not herself."

Elizabeth dabbed her eyes. "I never thought past having the spell removed. I am glad for her that it is, and I hope she will have slightly warmer feelings towards me after bringing her Aelfric, if nothing else."

"That speech savors strongly of bitterness, Lizzy," said Mr. Gardiner. "I always wondered why your mother kept saying you were her least favorite child since you are the one most like her original self. I thought you must be a reminder of all she had lost."

"No doubt." Elizabeth strove for a nonchalance she did not feel.

The butler entered carrying a silver salver to Eversleigh, distracting the uncomfortable attention on Elizabeth.

Eversleigh looked at the calling card. "Show him in."

The butler disappeared. On his return, he announced, "Mr. Darcy."

Elizabeth's head snapped around. Yes, it was him, with Pepper in raven form riding on his shoulder. But it did not matter. After the sleepless nights and long hours without him, not knowing if she would ever see him again, he was here.

"Darcy, this is an unexpected pleasure," said Eversleigh. "We are in the midst of a certain amount of upheaval, but you are already aware of some of it."

Darcy frowned. "I do not know what is happening, but Pepper seemed to feel I needed to be here. She appeared on my windowsill, pecking and scratching at the glass until I let her in. She insisted I follow her if I did not want my ear ripped off. This is where she led me."

Pepper cawed.

"Really?" Eversleigh asked the raven in surprise.

Pepper responded with more cawing.

"If you say so, I will believe you," said Eversleigh dubiously.

Darcy asked, "You speak the language of ravens as well as cats, Eversleigh?"

"No, it is only the language of phoukas," said Eversleigh absently. "Have you met Mr. Gardiner? He is Miss Elizabeth's uncle."

"I have had that honor." Darcy shook Mr. Gardiner's hand. "He helped to heal my injured arm."

"Healing powers?" Eversleigh eyed Mr. Gardiner speculatively. "Interesting. He came here with Miss Elizabeth's mother. I removed the spells on her, and she is now in the drawing room becoming reacquainted with Aelfric. The rest of us are as you see us."

Elizabeth turned her face towards the window. Would he be able to tell she had been crying?

Darcy greeted Frederica, and now he was coming towards her. Surely she could keep her composure for a few minutes.

Even without looking at him, she could tell when he noticed the traces of tears.

"Elizabeth, what is the matter?"

His concern was her undoing. The tears started to pour out uncontrollably. Her shoulders shook as she choked back silent sobs.

The cushion on the window seat shifted as he sat beside her, and warm hands surrounded hers. "What is the matter? Is it your mother? Did Aelfric upset you?"

She could not get the words out, but Mr. Gardiner spoke for her. "Her mother is much changed, and the mother she knew is gone."

Darcy's arm came around her. "I am so sorry. Is there anything I can do for your comfort, anything at all?"

All she wanted was to be in his embrace, but how could she when she should not be allowing even this much in the first place? His love could never be a safe haven for her. One by one everything she had depended on had disappeared – her father, her idea of her family, her own past, and now even her mother – and she could not have Darcy without ruining them both. It was hopeless, and she was all alone. She stole the opportunity to rest her forehead on his shoulder and his arm held her more tightly.

"Forgive me," she managed to choke out, her words muffled by the handkerchief pressed against her face.

"Shh. There is nothing to forgive." In a voice only she would be able to hear, he added, "I want to be here when you need comfort."

If only she could allow herself to depend on that! But his words reminded her of where they were, and that Frederica, Eversleigh, and Mr. Gardiner were all witnessing her improper behavior. She had to find the strength to compose herself.

Slowly she straightened and took her hand from Darcy's. Missing its warmth already, she scrubbed the remaining tears from her face. "Lord Eversleigh, is there perchance a room nearby where I could retire briefly?" Her voice hardly quavered.

"Of course," Eversleigh said gently. "Just up the stairs and to the left. Perhaps Lady Frederica can accompany you."

Elizabeth hurried from the room without a word, not looking back at anyone. How mortifying to have lost her composure so badly, and to have allowed Mr. Darcy to take liberties in front of the others!

Frederica's voice said, "I think this is the room he meant."

It was a small bedroom, richly decorated, but the only thing Elizabeth cared about was the ewer of water and a basin. "Thank you. You need not stay. I only need to wash my face."

Frederica did not move. "Do you think I would be allowed to return? There is a reason Eversleigh sent me with you. Men never want women witnessing these scenes."

Elizabeth splashed water on her face. "What scenes?"

"Holding Darcy to account. There is no need to worry;

Eversleigh would not break the law by challenging him to a duel. Most likely they will settle it with their fists at Gentleman Jackson's."

Foreboding filled Elizabeth. "Settle what?"

"Oh, come now. Darcy's familiarity with you. Even your phouka seems to know all about it."

"No!" Elizabeth grabbed a small towel and scrubbed her face dry before running down the stairs and back to the library.

Eversleigh's voice was icy. "Just because I am part fay does not mean I can overlook this sort of thing, Darcy. Give me one reason why I should not pummel you into dust."

Darcy stared at his friend in shock. "What?"

"It is a good question," said Mr. Gardiner grimly, "although I believe I should be the one asking it."

Good God, they were talking about his behavior with Elizabeth. "I was simply offering her comfort, nothing more."

"And only a fool would believe that was the first time you have touched her." Eversleigh's scorn was clear.

Elizabeth burst into the room. "Stop it! He is not at fault!"

"This is not a matter for women," Eversleigh grated. "Pray be so kind as to leave us, *shurinn*."

"No! You listen to me, *shurinn*." Elizabeth sounded furious. "Darcy is not at fault. He made me an honorable offer, and it is not his fault I could not accept him, nor that I allowed him to comfort me."

At least her rage was not turned on him. "Elizabeth, I can handle this." Bad enough that the situation had arisen. He did not require a woman to defend him.

Elizabeth ignored him, continuing to glare at Eversleigh.

Silence weighed heavily for a minute before Eversleigh said

tightly, "In that case, you must accept him."

Darcy held his breath. Could this be enough to convince her? She always listened to Eversleigh, damn him.

Elizabeth looked heavenward as if for inspiration. "Do you think it is a good idea for him to marry a woman rumored to be a witch who refuses to be bound? How will the Collegium feel about that, especially when they have concerns about him already, and his uncle and aunt have just been revealed as sorcerers? And the life of that sorceress aunt was saved by that self-same witch at Darcy's express request? If we lived in a different world, a world where there was no shame in a woman using magic, perhaps I could marry him. But the world will not change, no matter what Lady Matlock may hope, and we must pay the price."

Eversleigh turned his face away, clearly considering what she was saying. Finally he said, "It is true that Darcy is not in a position to protect you by marrying you, and it might well put you at greater risk by doing so. But he can still damage your reputation. You must be more careful. Avoid each other's company."

Darcy glared at him, seething. If Eversleigh agreed with Elizabeth that their marriage was impossible, they were probably right.

"I must ask one more question," said Mr. Gardiner coolly. "Viscount Eversleigh, what is your relationship to my niece that you would risk your own safety to defend her reputation?"

Eversleigh looked completely unflustered. "Aelfric is my half-brother, and he would expect me to defend his sister's honor."

"Your half-brother as well? Interesting." Mr. Gardiner looked thoughtful.

It was easy for them to look unconcerned. They had not just had every hope torn away from them. Darcy stood jerkily and bowed to Elizabeth. "Miss Elizabeth." He did not trust himself to say anything more, so he walked out of the room, out of Eversleigh's house, and out of Elizabeth's life.

When Mrs. Bennet paid an unexpected call to Matlock House, Elizabeth had the presence of mind to suggest a walk in the square to take advantage of the fine weather. Frederica had already met Mrs. Bennet, but Elizabeth would prefer to keep her away from Lady Matlock until she knew more what to expect from her mother now that the binding spell was gone.

The fretful look that had characterized Mrs. Bennet all these years had vanished, replaced by a certain confidence. She even dressed differently now. The excessive lace and ribbons were gone in favor of simpler lines with an elegant cut, although she clearly still preferred bright colors. Mrs. Gardiner must have taken her to a milliner. Poor Mrs. Gardiner, to have to accustom herself to a new sister-in-law!

"I hope I am not imposing by calling on you," her mother said as they crossed the street into the square.

"Not at all. I hope Jane and Mary are in good health."

"Yes, and so are your aunt, uncle, their children, and most likely all of their servants. The weather is lovely for this time of year, although the clouds on the horizon look ominous. Now that we have covered the weather and everyone's health, may we move on?"

This was definitely not the mother Elizabeth knew. "You will be quite a surprise to everyone at Longbourn, not to mention Meryton."

"Some of them, no doubt, will think I should be bound again."

"I hope they will not." But Elizabeth could understand why they might. She herself would be happy for her new mother to turn back into her old self. "What did you wish to discuss apart from the weather and everyone's health?"

"First of all, I appreciate your assistance in having the spells removed. Had you done nothing, I would likely have lived under them the rest of my life."

"I am glad to have been able to do it. I wish I had realized you were spellbound sooner, but I was unaware of it until Uncle Gardiner said something to me about how different you were before you had children."

"It did not pass my notice, though, that you went to great lengths to get the spells removed, and as soon as that was accomplished, you fled. Your uncle tells me you do not even plan to return to Longbourn."

"I always planned to return to Matlock House after calling at the Gardiners, so it was hardly fleeing to do so. You did not need me; you had Jane, Mary, and my uncle. I do find your new speech rather disconcerting, though, as if you are a puppet and someone else is speaking your lines."

"You forget, Lizzy, how much time I spent among the fay. I recognize your strategy – you said three true things without addressing my point."

Elizabeth would need to remember that she could not fool this woman as easily as she once had. "Once you were free, Aelfric was naturally your first priority. I was glad to bring you together, but he is usually angry with me about something. Mary was already furious with me, and doubtless is more so since she has seen how much you were changed. I am no fonder than anyone else of being in company with people who are angry at me, and I had accomplished what I came to do. As for returning to Longbourn, that is not about you."

Her mother studied her. "I did not want any more children after Aelfric. Every pregnancy, every childbirth simply reminded me that I had, as I thought then, caused my son's death by my own irresponsibility. I did not want to care about any of you. Jane was an easy baby and caused very little trouble, but you were more difficult."

"I already know this part," said Elizabeth sharply. "I cried all the time, got into mischief, and ruined your favorite handkerchief. If this is to be another litany of why I am your least favorite daughter, I have no interest in hearing it."

Her mother winced. "I would not have said those things if I were in my right mind, although the handkerchief incident stung. It had been a gift from Oberon. As for the rest, your behavior was your nursemaid's problem, not mine. Your trips to Faerie were what I could not forgive. I could no longer quite remember Faerie, but I knew it was a place I wanted to go, and almost every day Bluebird came to take you there. When you stopped going there a few years later, I was even angrier that you did not appreciate the privilege you had."

"I stopped because Oberon decreed that I must."

Mrs. Bennet frowned. "Aelfric did not mention that to me."

Elizabeth shrugged. "He may not know. I do not remember much of that time."

"Titania must have been furious."

"She was. She still is, for that matter." Elizabeth paused. "Do you plan to return to Faerie?"

Color rose in her mother's cheeks. "No. The Sidhe love youth and beauty. I want Oberon and Titania to remember me as I was, not as I am now. Someday I might go there just for a few minutes to breathe the air again, but only if I were sure no one would see me."

"You still have Aelfric," said Elizabeth uncomfortably.

"Simply knowing he is alive is a great relief. You lifted an enormous burden from my shoulders with that news. I cannot begin to tell you how much that means."

"But why did you think you had caused his death?"

Her mother's face fell, making her look like her old querulous self. "When I saw that he was Sidhe, I knew he must never leave my side until I could take him to Faerie. To most people he would be an abomination, and to your father he was proof that he had been cuckolded. Most men would smother such a baby in the cradle. But I was so tired and so weak after childbirth, so I let the wet nurse take him just for a little while. I never saw him again. I had known better than to do that. To this day I cannot understand why I allowed it."

"Perhaps that was when my father set the spell on you."

"Or it was just my weakness." Her expression was anguished. "Even now, knowing he is alive, I despise myself for it."

"Did you think my father had killed him?"

"Yes," she said bleakly. "It was what any other man would have done. I am still surprised he allowed him to live."

Horrified at her mother's calm acceptance that her father would have killed Aelfric, Elizabeth asked, "Why did you remain at Longbourn when you thought your husband had murdered your child? My uncle would have taken you in."

"I had treated your father very badly. I knew I was increasing, and I intended to pass off Oberon's child, whom I assumed to be mortal, as his. How could I blame him for wanting to dispose of the evidence that I had been unfaithful to him? He could have punished me for what I had done or even sent me to an asylum to live out the rest of my life, but he never said a word about it. How could I have left him then?"

"You do not consider the binding spell a punishment?"

Her mother sighed. "Lizzy, you do not understand. That is what men do when their wives have magic. They have them put under binding spells. I do not like what he did to me, but I would not have expected any less. I deserved it for what I had done and to prevent me from doing it again."

Her mother had changed, but Elizabeth had nothing in common with this woman, either. "If you choose to forgive my father, I cannot stop you, but pray do not expect the same from me. Will you be returning to Longbourn, then?"

"Yes. I wish to see Aelfric once or twice more before I go, since it will be more difficult for us to meet at Longbourn where your father will be watching me. I do not want to hurt him again."

Elizabeth did not care about her father's pain. "Does he know you are no longer under the binding spell?"

"I wrote him and told him so, but, as you know, he rarely replies to letters. We will no doubt discuss it once I am back. But I am also worried about you. You look wan, and you have lost weight."

This was a new experience, both that her mother would notice her mood and that it would worry her. "I am simply overtired. Lady Matlock insists that I attend events that go on half the night, and I have never been able to sleep late in the morning as everyone in the *ton* seems to do." It was no one's business but her own that the loss of any future with Darcy kept her awake and in tears long after the household was in bed.

Her mother looked at her keenly. "Perhaps you should tell Lady Matlock that her schedule is too much for you."

"Perhaps I will." It was beyond disconcerting to be listening to this woman who looked like her mother but sounded so little like her. "It must be very different for you at Gracechurch Street now. I hope the changes are not too trying for Jane or Mrs. Gardiner."

"Jane, as always, is certain it will all turn out well. Mrs. Gardiner sometimes stops short when I say something, and then she laughs and goes on. But what of you? If you do not return to Longbourn, where will you go?" To her credit, Mrs. Bennet sounded genuinely worried about her.

"I have not decided. I may return to Rosings. Miss de Bourgh has said I am welcome there as long as I wish to stay or to work as her companion. My uncle Gardiner has offered me a home as well, but I worry about causing harm to the family's reputation or causing a rift between the Gardiners and my father."

"You sound very unconcerned about your future."

"That is because I am unconcerned. I am waiting to see how various things turn out over the next few months, but I know I will not be left without a home or food. If nothing else, I imagine Viscount Eversleigh would help me."

"Elizabeth Bennet, do not tell me you have an improper relationship with Viscount Eversleigh! Has he offered you *carte blanche*?" Her mother sounded horrified.

Elizabeth could not help laughing. "What an imagination you have! Viscount Eversleigh would help me because he takes his duties as my *shurinn* seriously, and he would not let me starve."

"You are *shurinn*? But how?"

Aelfric must not have told her. Perhaps her mother could keep a secret now, but Elizabeth would not wager on it. "I am not at liberty to tell you that, but I assure you that he has no improper intentions at all towards me." Her mother would be able to figure it out given a little thought, but it would be better to leave it uncertain.

"That is good. I would not want any more scandal right now. Yesterday Mr. Bingley left his calling card for Jane while we were out. I came here today in case he called again. It will be easier for Jane if she does not have to explain the changes in me."

"Mr. Bingley? That is good news indeed." And it could not be coincidence that Bingley had called only a short time after Darcy said he would speak to him. At least she knew he was thinking of her. The thought warmed the frozen waste of her heart a little, but it could change nothing. Apart from the revel, she doubted she would ever see Darcy again.

"Georgiana, I would like to speak to you for a few minutes," Darcy said.

The girl stiffened. "Did I do something wrong?"

"Not at all. This is more about me."

Georgiana set tentatively on the edge of her chair. "About you?" She sounded dubious.

"Yes. A situation has arisen which may force me to leave England for a time. I –"

"May I go with you?"

"I am afraid not. I will be with the Army in Portugal. I hope none of this will come to pass, but I want plans in place in case it does. I just met with my solicitor, and he is drawing up papers that declare Richard to be your guardian while I am away. He will also be responsible for Pemberley. If for any reason I have not returned within five years –"

"Five years?" Georgiana quavered. "Oh, no!"

He forced himself to forge ahead. "I think it unlikely, but we must be prepared. After five years, the revenues from Pemberley will start to be paid into your account, with Richard as trustee until you marry."

Tears began to roll down her cheeks. "What did I do?" she whispered.

Why must she always blame herself? He moved to sit beside her and put his arm around her shoulder. "Georgie, you did not do anything. Nothing at all. It is because of trouble in the Collegium. There are some men who were determined to prove I have been misusing my powers, and someone has been trying to make it look as if I have. Viscount Eversleigh, who is now Master of the Collegium, knows I did not do it, but until I can prove it, I must go away."

"But why would they do that?"

He shrugged. It would be better to leave George Wickham out of it. "They dislike me." It sounded like a very weak reason for them to start a vendetta against him. He could not understand it himself. Most men who befriended Wickham could not be bothered to do anything that took much effort.

"Does it have something to do with George Wickham?"

Damnation, how did she guess that? "These men are friends of his, and that is why they dislike me. Somehow I will resolve this, but it may take time, and that is why I must leave."

Georgiana's shoulders trembled, but she said nothing. Her stillness reminded Darcy of how he often felt when controlling his powers.

Abruptly he asked, "Georgie, do you have magic?"

Her eyes darted back and forth as if the answer might be written on the walls. "Women do not have magic," she whispered.

"Actually, they do. Our father was a mage and our mother was a mage's daughter, so it would be more surprising if you had no magic than if you did." Why had he never considered this before?

She licked her lips. "I never use it. Never."

"Would you like to learn to use it?"

Her eyes widened. "That would be wrong."

"Some people think so, but I do not. Cousin Frederica has learned to use her magic, and Cousin Anne is starting to as well. Even Lady Catherine has magic, though she misused it."

Georgiana looked down. "I do not know."

"Perhaps you should take some time to think about it. I am sure Cousin Frederica would be happy to teach you."

"Could... Could you teach me?"

Darcy sighed. "The rules of the Collegium do not allow me to instruct a woman. It is a foolish rule, but I agreed to abide by the rules when I joined the Collegium."

"Oh. It does not matter." But obviously it did.

How could he explain it to her when he did not understand it himself? God, he hated it when Georgiana pulled away into herself like that. If only Elizabeth were here. She would know what to say.

As clearly as if Elizabeth had been whispering in his ear, he knew. She would ask him why he was still a member of the Collegium if he disagreed with them. And she would not think it a good reason if he said it was because his father and Lord Matlock had expected him to be.

He would not be looking to flee the country if it were not for the Collegium. Why was he part of it?

"But I plan to resign from the Collegium, and after that is done, I will be able to teach you." He could not believe he had said it.

"You will?" Georgiana's eyes were shining. "Thank you!"

# Part Five

# Wild Magic

# Chapter 14

When the ladies at Matlock House retired to the drawing room after dinner, Lady Matlock produced a piece of fine notepaper. "I received this shortly before we sat down to dine, and it concerns the two of you. Would you care to hear it?"

Elizabeth sent up a silent prayer that it would not be yet another invitation. She had already attended more soirees, Venetian breakfasts, and musicales than she cared to remember. At each one, she had been introduced to so many people she could hardly recall their names, but most of them either preferred their friends of longer-standing or spoke exclusively to Lady Frederica about balls Elizabeth had never attended. Lady Matlock had carefully introduced her to a number of marriageable gentlemen, but none of them could compare to Darcy, and he was not an option.

"Yes, Mama," said Frederica.

Lady Matlock unfolded the paper. "It is from Viscount Eversleigh. After the usual niceties, he says, 'I pray you will be so kind as to inform Lady Frederica and Miss Bennet that tomorrow morning I plan to walk through Hyde Park to visit some mutual acquaintances with a fondness for nature. In case the young ladies might be inclined to an outing, I will call at Matlock House after breakfast to see if they would honor me with their company. Our marigold-loving friend has been asking about them, and I promise not to bore them with discussions of horses.' I understand the significance of marigolds, but the horses are more mysterious."

"He is hinting that he will not expect me to spend time with my horse-mad brother," said Elizabeth. "I think I must go. I promised Titania that I would return and stay with her for a time, and this is a good opportunity." And it was the excuse she had been looking for to leave Matlock House. It was hard enough knowing she could never have Darcy without being thrust into the bosom of his family where she was forced to hear his name frequently and had to pretend she did not care. In Faerie, no one would take it badly if she seemed sad. Perhaps she could tell Bluebird about her woes.

"We would be sorry to see you leave us," said Lady Matlock. "You are very welcome to stay. Frederica has enjoyed having another young lady here rather than the usual male procession of mages and her brothers."

"You have been everything that is kind and welcoming, your ladyship, and I am very grateful for your hospitality. I have been fretting over my promise to Titania. I especially do not want her to feel I have forgotten her, especially when we have the revel coming in a few weeks."

Frederica nodded. "Perhaps I should stay there for a few days as well."

Elizabeth held her breath. She liked Frederica very much, but she needed time away from Darcy's family. Time to heal.

"Nonsense," said Lady Matlock. "You may pay a call to Titania, but I expect you to return here afterwards. I need your help in planning the revel."

"Yes, Mama," said Frederica with a sad lack of enthusiasm.

"There is a faerie ring in Hyde Park?" exclaimed Frederica. "How can it possibly remain hidden in such a crowded place?"

Eversleigh said, "It is between two of the paths. You have probably walked past it a dozen times and never noticed it. Miss Bennet, can you tell where it is?"

Elizabeth closed her eyes and let the air play over her face. She pointed to the southwest. "Over there. I can sense them, but I do not know how. Mr. Darcy once said that he thought he knew every inch of the grove at Rosings, but he had never seen the glade with the ring until he was led there. Now he sees it easily."

"Lord Eversleigh, have you heard anything from Darcy of late?" asked Frederica. "We have not seen him since the day you removed the spell from Mrs. Bennet. He sent a note telling us there was more trouble with the Collegium."

Elizabeth silently blessed her friend for asking the question she could not.

"The Board of Inquiry has re-opened his case, but so far nothing has happened," said Eversleigh, carefully not looking in Elizabeth's direction.

"Why can you not simply stop the Board of Inquiry? You are Master of the Collegium," said Elizabeth determinedly.

"Acting Master, and no, I cannot. Neither the Master nor the Council of Mages can intervene in Boards of Inquiry. They have to be independent in case the leaders of the Collegium are suspected of sorcery. Otherwise there would be no method to remove a sorcerous Master." Eversleigh sighed. "No one ever expected to see inquiries misused this way."

Frederica folded her parasol. "My father grumbled about Darcy's Board constantly. He was furious with them."

"I know. But Darcy seemed well enough when he accompanied Lord Matlock and me to Faerie two days ago. I assume you have heard about that visit?"

Frederica sighed dramatically. "Repeatedly and in great detail, but my father did not mention Darcy was there. He is always touching the ring Oberon gave him as if he cannot believe it is on his finger."

Eversleigh laughed. "I am not surprised. I do not think he cared if either Darcy or I were there after he spoke to Oberon. Darcy appeared in relatively good spirits, though part may have been that Faerie relieves the pressure of the elements on him."

Elizabeth looked away. Thoughts of Darcy had been keeping her awake at night and haunting her days, and he was in good spirits? Did he not feel the pain of their separation? Her throat grew tight with unshed tears.

"Miss Bennet, if you were not my *shurinn*, I should have said that you seem in relatively good spirits," said Eversleigh with a degree of exasperation. "I do not have the same insight into Darcy."

She glared at him. "You are becoming altogether too good at this."

"What are you talking about?" asked Frederica.

"Nothing," said Elizabeth firmly. "I am looking forward to spending time in Faerie where nothing ever changes and there are no surprises. Well, fewer surprises," she corrected. Aelfric had been a surprise, but it was the mortal world that kept turning upside down until her life was completely unrecognizable. What had happened to Elizabeth Bennet of Longbourn, the country gentleman's daughter who loved her father and looked down on her mother, who lived in a country free of sorcerers, and who despised Mr. Darcy and feared any mage who might be part of the Collegium? She should certainly not be walking through fashionable London with an earl's daughter and a viscount who was also Master of the Collegium, on her way to hide her broken heart in Faerie. It had been so much easier to be that country girl.

"That is one of its advantages," Eversleigh agreed.

"I wish I could stay there, too," grumbled Frederica.

Elizabeth said kindly, "The revel is only a fortnight away, and then you can visit Faerie to your heart's content." And she would have a fortnight of peace and quiet in the meantime.

Two hours after bringing Elizabeth and Frederica to Titania's bower, Eversleigh found Aelfric in the stables saddling one of the Sidhe horses. "Going for a ride?"

"They need exercise. Apart from the hunt, they are hardly ridden now that we no longer ride through the mortal world. It is much easier to travel through the rings."

"I have been speaking to our father."

Aelfric developed an intense interest in the silver rivets of the bridle. "What did you discuss?"

"Many things, including the upcoming revel, but mostly I wished to discover the truth of the rumors that you had influenced him into the war on the mortals. The rumors made no sense to me. While you might wish for war, I could not see our father following your advice. I gather he has spent little time with anyone but you recently."

"That has been his choice," Aelfric told the bridle.

"He has begun his decline, you know," Eversleigh said gently. "He should be stepping down, not starting a war. Why have you allowed it to progress so far?"

Aelfric leaned his forehead against the horse's head. "He is not far into the decline. There is no reason he cannot rule."

"He is dragging Faerie into a pointless war because he is becoming volatile and angry. You must know this, with all the time you spend with him. It makes me wonder if you have been hiding his decline by taking responsibility for his war."

"I do not want to lose him so quickly," said Aelfric, his voice low. "He will not wish to see me once he goes into retirement. I always knew you would not live long. Now I will be losing both of you, and I will be left alone. The other Sidhe see me as a child. If being a Sidhe means watching everyone you care about die while you still have centuries to live, I wish I had been born mortal."

Eversleigh laid his hand on Aelfric's arm. "Until today, I always assumed our father would outlive me, still hale and hearty when I am growing old and frail. I do not like discovering that is not true. You are not alone in this."

"You do not know what it is like here when you are away. I have no one apart from him."

Eversleigh leaned back against the stable wall. "Brother, have you ever wondered why the other Sidhe are so fond of mortals? Why they seek out mortal poets and lovers, and why Titania lavishes her affection on mortal children?"

"Foolishness, that is why," said Aelfric bitterly.

"Mortals, being short-lived, give affection freely, especially mortal children. They do not wait a century or two to judge whether you are worthy of their respect. The Sidhe are cautious. How many of them seem to truly care for each other? Parents and children, yes, but even couples who claim blood right live separate lives. When did you last see our father show particular warmth to Titania? He respects her, and he is not unkind to her, but they have been pursuing the same quarrel for ten years, or is it fifteen? There is no hurry to resolve things when you live for centuries. And what was the quarrel about? Titania losing one of the mortal children she favored."

"But I do not like mortals."

Eversleigh chuckled. "Except for me, Colonel Fitzwilliam, Darcy, Libbet – you have liked almost every mortal you have met of late. What Sidhe apart from our father has ever shown you the sort of casual acceptance Colonel Fitzwilliam did?"

"But mortals die," Aelfric said bleakly.

"Yes. I will die long before you. But you will have my children, grandchildren, and my grandchildren's grandchildren. There is a sort of immortality in that."

"But you have no children."

"As my mother reminds me at every opportunity! But I will someday." Someday when he had managed to forget Frederica Fitzwilliam. "You will have Libbet, too. I hope she will provide you some comfort and company when our father chooses to retire from society."

"Are you going to tell him he should?"

"Yes, although with a heavy heart. He would say it is my duty. I will also speak to Titania."

Aelfric picked up the curry comb and began to brush the horse. "Perhaps I should join you when you speak to our father." He did not meet Eversleigh's eyes.

"Good. That will do him honor."

"You have taken marvelous care of Augustus," Elizabeth told Bluebird. "His fur is so silky and shiny now. I am glad I did not have to leave him alone at Rosings while I was in London."

Bluebird scratched the tabby cat under his ears. "We have been happy to have him here, and Titania has grown fond of him. Now we can all be together."

Elizabeth said, "He seems happy here, though it is a mystery how I came to have a fay cat who lives in the mortal world with me and a mortal cat who lives in Faerie. I think they are as confused where I belong as I am!"

"You belong here," said Bluebird firmly, wrapping her arm around Elizabeth's shoulders.

"I do not seem to belong anywhere else, now that Longbourn is lost to me," said Elizabeth ruefully.

Bluebird looked up at the entrance to the bower. "Prince Evlan is back already! Titania will not be pleased to lose Marigold Meadowsweet so soon. It is good you are staying."

Elizabeth frowned. "Something is wrong." One look at Eversleigh's face was enough to tell her that much, even before he walked straight past them to sink to his knees before Titania. He said something quietly to her.

Titania looked puzzled but shrugged. "Away, all of you! I would speak with Prince Evlan alone. Libbet and Marigold Meadowsweet may stay if they wish."

Elizabeth glanced at Bluebird before moving forward to stand near Eversleigh. Somehow it felt right to be beside her *shurinn* in a time of difficulty.

When all the sprites and dryads had vanished into other parts of the bower, Titania said, "I am always glad to see you, Prince Evlan, but what is so important that we must speak privately?"

"When was the last time you were alone with Oberon?" Eversleigh's usual flowery compliments seemed to have vanished.

Titania pursed her lips. "It has been quite some time. We are quarreling, as you know, so we are only together in public."

"Have you noticed a change in him?"

The Faerie queen covered her eyes with one hand. "A change? Oh, no. Do not tell me there is a change."

"I met with him earlier today. He is irritable and distrusts everyone. This war on mortals appears to be part of it."

"Not the decline, I beg you! Perhaps he was simply out of spirits today."

"I fear it is more than that. Prince Aelfric has known for some time and has been attempting to hide the changes, as very young Sidhe are apt to do. I plan to speak to my father tonight, but I thought it only proper to inform you first."

Titania picked restlessly at the embroidery on a silk pillow. "I will go to him now and attempt to resolve our quarrel. I would not have him leave us with a quarrel between us." Her voice quavered.

"If you are able to resolve it, that would be a kindness."

"It should be simple. I will tell him that he is forgiven now that Libbet has come back to me."

Elizabeth's eyebrows shot up. How had she entered into this mysterious discussion?

"Was Libbet the child he took?" Eversleigh sounded surprised.

"Of course. He found Aelfric and Libbet playing together. He did not wish Aelfric to attach himself to a member of his human family, so he sent Libbet away and blurred her memories. I was particularly angered since when he took her mother, he said I could have her first child, but that turned out to be Aelfric. Then he brought me her second child, but she was terrified of Faerie, so I had to wait for Libbet, and he took her away, too."

Elizabeth froze. The reason Oberon had altered her memories was to keep her away from Aelfric? And the queen had been quarreling with him for years as a result? It was inconceivable. Elizabeth instantly resolved that if the king wished to keep her away from Aelfric, she would somehow become a friend to her despicable brother. How dare he?

"But now my Libbet is back. I hope you will bring your own children to me, sweet Libbet. I have always had a particular fondness for your family. My mother's brother fathered your grandmother, so you are like my own children."

"I..." Good heavens, how could she begin to answer all that? "Honored lady, I do not expect to have children, but if that should change, I would be pleased for you to meet my child."

"Not have children? Why not?" Titania sounded as shocked as if

Elizabeth had threatened to murder someone.

Elizabeth would never grow accustomed to Sidhe frankness. "I do not expect to marry, so I will not have children."

Titania's delicate winged eyebrows drew together. "But what of the man you are always thinking of? I have sensed your desire for him."

How utterly mortifying! Had Titania truly perceived her improper feelings for Darcy? How could she refer to them in front of Eversleigh and Frederica? If only she could sink down into the soft moss until it closed over her head!

Frederica said in an amused voice, "As a rule, mortals consider their desires to be a very personal matter, and we never speak of them."

"How very odd mortals are! Does that mean you and Evlan have never spoken together of it either? And he was so pleased to see you dressed as one of us!"

"I must insist we leave this topic," said Eversleigh, his voice strained. "I came here to speak of the king."

Titania's face fell. "I had forgotten for a moment. I wish I could forget it again."

Elizabeth wished she could forget the entire conversation. How could she ever look the other two in the face again?

"I am sorry to bear such sad tidings," said Eversleigh.

"I must go to him." Titania's silks swirled around her as she hurried from the bower.

Frederica's face was flushed. "I wonder if I shall ever grow accustomed to the quick comings and goings among the fay."

"One does become used to their mercurial nature and their disconcerting frankness," said Eversleigh, but he did not look at either woman. "There are few secrets in Faerie. I am surprised Aelfric was able to keep one this long, but I suppose it is because the other Sidhe pay little attention to him."

"I thought Titania has had many mortal followers over the years.

How can she be so unaware of what subjects embarrass us?" asked Elizabeth.

Eversleigh said ruefully, "Mortals who come to Faerie are often seeking to escape society's rules. They are attracted by that same openness."

"Were you?" asked Frederica abruptly.

"I visited here as a child, and I simply accepted the rules here were different. It never seemed odd to me. Sometimes I miss the frankness of Faerie in our mortal world where so many people wear false faces and hide their motivations behind shields of secrecy."

"That kind of frankness would make it impossible for sorcerers to hide their work," said Elizabeth. Since Frederica still appeared distressed, Elizabeth changed the subject. "What is this about Oberon entering the decline? How do you know?"

Eversleigh hesitated. "Forgive me. I do not feel comfortable answering that before I have spoken to Oberon. But..."

"But what?"

Lines appeared between Eversleigh's brows. "I had not known he was the one who interfered with your memories. That is very odd. It suggests the disturbance of his mind has been going on much longer than I believed, and he was simply cunning enough to hide it."

"But he is the king," said Frederica. "Did that not give him the right to do it?"

He turned a pained look on her. "The right, perhaps, but Libbet is his *shurinn*. He should have not been able to bring himself to harm her."

"He did more than blur my memories," said Elizabeth abruptly. "He did something to make me wish to stay away from Faerie."

He frowned. "What do you mean?"

Elizabeth rubbed her hands together, suddenly cold despite the warmth of the bower. "I have always loved to explore. I cannot see a footpath without having to discover where it leads. I explored every path near Rosings, even in the short time I was there. Bluebird gave me my talisman and told me I could go to Faerie whenever I wished, but I never did. It is completely unlike me. Until I drank Titania's Faerie wine, I had no desire at all to come back. The only reason I returned the first time was that I was desperate for a refuge."

Eversleigh drew in a deep breath. "You have known that all this time, *shurinn*, and never said anything of it to me?"

She shrugged helplessly. "He is your father. I did not wish to make you think ill of him."

He seemed to look off into the distance, but there was no distance inside the bower. "I should have spent more time here. I might have seen it sooner and saved us from this war."

"He deliberately kept knowledge of the war from you, so it would not have helped if you had been here," said Frederica. "I do not understand how it came to be your role to tell him of his decline when you have been absent much of the time."

"I am not the ideal person for this duty, but it falls to kin or close friends to speak the truth. Aelfric and I are his closest kin. Aelfric is young for this duty, and it is a great loss to him, more so than to me. If I may dare to say it, this is a time when he could benefit from having a sister."

"One he barely knows and whom he dislikes?" asked Elizabeth dubiously.

Eversleigh's brow wrinkled. "He does not dislike you, not at all. He likes you."

"Then why is he always furious at me?" exclaimed Elizabeth.

"Perhaps he does not know how to act towards a sister. Among the Sidhe, siblings are often hundreds of years apart."

She could not see how that made a difference, but there was no point in arguing about it. "Is it true Titania and Oberon have been quarreling for years over me? What is so special about me?"

"Nothing." Eversleigh paused. "That did not come out as I meant it. You are special in many ways, but in this case, you were likely only the pretext. They often quarrel, and as I understand it, Titania was displeased that Oberon finally had a Sidhe child when she did not."

"She seems to have taken this news about Oberon very calmly. Will it not be a great loss to her?"

"The Sidhe do not grieve long over those who have died, perhaps because they have grown accustomed to losing mortals they care for. They think mostly of the present, and at least for the Sidhe, there is rarely a strong emotional bond between them. They save that for their human followers."

"How sad!" exclaimed Elizabeth.

"Perhaps it is difficult to remain close to one another for hundreds of years at a stretch," said Frederica.

Eversleigh nodded. "Titania will likely be distressed for a time, though. From the standpoint of our relationship with the fay, I am glad you will be staying here, Libbet. If Marigold Meadowsweet would be willing to consider doing so as well, it could be beneficial. I would like Titania to be thinking of the effect on mortals when she chooses the next king."

"She chooses the king?" Frederica sounded shocked.

With a dry smile, Eversleigh said, "Things are different here. The king is chosen by the queen, and often they have no particular affection for one another. Oberon and Titania with their blood right are the exception, and most of the fay would be happy to avoid a similar arrangement in the future. It is widely held that Oberon and Titania's frequent quarrels are owing to their blood right. It might even be true."

"If Titania chooses a new king, will he choose the new queen when she goes into her decline?"

"No, but I cannot tell you who does. If you ask any fay, they will tell you the moon chooses the new queen, but if you ask what that means, they simply seem perplexed at such an odd question. It is most frustrating."

"But how could we influence Titania's choice of the new king? Surely she would have decided that long ago," said Frederica.

Elizabeth shook her head. "They do not think that way. They make decisions when they need to be made, with little forethought, and they rarely reconsider them."

Eversleigh nodded. "I have rarely been so frustrated as the time I attempted to explain what an engagement was to my father and a few other Sidhe. It is inconceivable to them that a man would decide to marry a woman and then dawdle for weeks or months before actually doing it. They would likely flag down the nearest clergyman and be married within minutes of the proposal. As for the calling of the banns, that makes no sense to them at all."

Elizabeth giggled. "You explain their point of view too well. Now I will always see engagements as foolish dawdling!"

Frederica said suddenly, "I will remain here, Lord Eversleigh, if you are willing to explain to my mother why I am doing so when she expressly told me not to. It might help if you offered to bear any needed messages. With the revel coming up so quickly, she will wish to discuss plans with me."

"For this cause, I will even brave Lady Matlock's displeasure. How much harder can it be than telling the King of Faerie that his time has come?" Eversleigh said lightly.

Even if she had not been his *shurinn*, Elizabeth would have seen the pain underneath Eversleigh's words. There was nothing she could say that was not a foolish platitude. But he was her *shurinn* and they were in Faerie where the rules of propriety did not apply. She embraced him. It felt odd, and quite unlike embracing Darcy, but it also felt right.

He returned the embrace and held her for a long minute. "I must go and make ready to speak to Oberon. No dawdling for weeks about this kind of thing either."

"Godspeed," said Elizabeth, and Frederica echoed her. They both watched after him as he walked away.

"I cannot believe it is real," said Frederica in a small voice. "I cannot imagine a world where Oberon is not king of Faerie."

"Nor I," said Elizabeth. "But everything is so confusing here. Sometimes I feel as if I have double vision. With one eye I see the shocking sight of a country miss boldly embracing a peer of the realm, and with the other I see her providing natural comfort to her grieving *shurinn*. It makes me feel as if my head is spinning like a top."

"It does not matter. I assume you will be marrying him."

Elizabeth turned and stared at her. "Where did you get that astonishingly incorrect idea?"

Frederica lifted her chin. "Perhaps because you embrace him, and you are so often together. He is so protective of you, and then there is this *shurinn* thing."

"I have no romantic interest in him, none at all," Elizabeth declared with exasperation. "*Shurinn* are close to each other, but it is the closeness of brother and sister, only intensified. I could embrace him precisely because I knew he would not take it the wrong way. Did you not hear what Titania said about the two of you? He would do almost anything to protect me from harm, but I am not the one he desires."

"Oh." Frederica looked away. "Who is the man you are always thinking of? Is it Darcy?"

"That does not matter, except that it is obviously not Eversleigh! And what is more, Eversleigh would have found a great deal more comfort if you had been the one to embrace him."

The dryads were starting to drift back in, bringing a halt to the discussion, but Frederica looked thoughtful for some time afterwards.

Titania returned after a short time, looking somber and seeming to want little more than to stroke Elizabeth's hair. When a sprite announced Eversleigh and Aelfric, Titania stood, rising to her full height. Silence descended on the bower.

Aelfric and Eversleigh stopped in the middle of the bower and remained there, as if they were actors awaiting their entrance. The fay around them began to whisper as they realized something was amiss.

Titania said in a clear voice, "Princes, have you news for us?"

Eversleigh bowed his head. "Prince Aelfric and I have spoken with Oberon. He has left, and there is no king in Faerie tonight."

Gasps and sobs came from around the bower, but Titania looked utterly calm. "Had he any final words?"

"Great lady, Oberon in his wisdom knew why we were there before we said a word. He told us it was his time, and he gave each of us his blessing. Then he left King's Hall and walked away without looking back. His name will be sung through the ages as one of the greatest of the Sidhe."

"You have performed your duty with honor, Prince Evlan and Prince Aelfric. You are fortunate to have had such a father. Now I must be alone with the moon." Her head held proudly high, Titania glided out of the bower.

Elizabeth whispered to Frederica, "I should go to Aelfric. I will return when I can."

"You look exhausted," Elizabeth told Eversleigh the following day when he came to the bower.

"Too many trips through the rings in a short time, and too many worries," he said. "I hope you are not becoming ill. You sound hoarse."

"Do you see Marigold Meadowsweet sitting by the queen and reading to her, with a rapt audience of dryads? I brought *The Mysteries of Udolpho* with me yesterday to read while I was here. Titania saw it and asked me to read a passage aloud. They had never heard of a gothic novel. Every time I stopped reading she begged for more. We tried having one of the dryads read it, but Titania claims that only a mortal can bring the correct feeling to it. We have been reading for hours."

"Is there any chance of a break in the story where I might be able to speak to Titania?"

"I will ask her."

A few minutes later, Titania waved away her sprites and beckoned Eversleigh forward.

Eversleigh went down on one knee in front of Titania but did not sink back on his heels. "Great lady, might I beg a moment of your indulgence?"

Elizabeth watched him suspiciously. Why had he knelt? Kneeling would be for a mortal queen. It might have been a mistake, but Eversleigh did not make mistakes of that sort.

"Of course, Prince Evlan. How may I be of service to you?" Titania's face was drawn.

"Great lady, I would speak to you not as my father's son, but as a mortal, one of some consequence in the mortal world. You will soon be making a decision of great import, and I have information which might be of some small use to you, if you will allow me the presumption of sharing it."

"Granted." With only the slightest expression of amusement, she said carefully, "Lord Eversleigh."

He bowed his head. "Great lady, out of loyalty Libbet has withheld from you certain details of her return to Faerie. There was another Sidhe involved, one of several Sidhe who are unhappy over the war with mortals. He learned from her that mortals no longer remember the Great Treaty. He hoped to employ Libbet and her friend Diarcey as go-betweens to educate mortals about the importance of the groves. Not knowing of your previous connection with Libbet, he wished her to tell you how little the mortals know. That is one thing I wish to tell you: that there are Sidhe who oppose this war." He paused. "The second matter is more delicate."

"Continue," said Titania.

"It is generally believed that Prince Aelfric encouraged my father in making war. I am of the opinion that Aelfric deliberately fostered this belief in order to hide our father's increasing irritability and impulsive behavior. Aelfric would not thank me for telling you this. I honor my father and my brother, and I would happily lay down my life to protect either of them, but I also believe this war to be misguided and dangerous. Mortals need education, not a war in which both sides will lose." He bowed his head.

"I see. Who is the Sidhe who met with Libbet?"

"Great lady, if you command it, I will tell you, but I prefer not to break a confidence."

Titania held out her hand to Elizabeth. "Come sit with me, my Libbet."

Elizabeth obeyed. At least Titania did not seem angered that she had never mentioned Cathael to her.

Titania stroked Elizabeth's arm. "It was Aislinn who brought Libbet to me. What Sidhe would Aislinn ally herself with? It could be Celynon, or Fionn, or Cathael, or ... Ah, it is Cathael, I see."

How had she guessed? Eversleigh's expression had not altered in the slightest.

"My poor Libbet, you cannot hide your reaction from me. Do not fear; I have no intention of harming Cathael."

It was so easy to view Titania as caring only for the pleasure of the moment that Elizabeth had forgotten she was also the woman who had ruled Faerie for centuries. The touch of her power was light, but it was there nonetheless.

"One last thing, Prince Evlan," said Titania. "These books Libbet brought – are there more of them in your mortal world?"

Eversleigh's lips turned up in a smile. "I believe there are."

"You must bring us all of them," the queen decreed.

He bowed. "I will bring you all I can carry."

Frederica said in a sweet, if slightly scratchy, voice, "Prince Evlan, do you not wish to take a turn reading aloud? You would bring such feeling to the role of Valancourt."

Titania made her decision faster than any of them expected, calling together all the Sidhe in the great clearing. She gave no reason for it, but it was not difficult to guess.

Lady Frederica Fitzwilliam craned her neck to see what was happening. She was not accustomed to being outranked and did not enjoy being in the back of Titania's retinue while Elizabeth stood beside the queen. She raised herself on tiptoe to get a better view of the lines of Sidhe men, each dressed in black and silver armor, Oberon's colors. The Sidhe ladies, all in silver, sat grouped to the side. Beyond the Sidhe, the clearing was crowded with lesser fay. Only the tall dryads and elves were visible; all the others were hidden behind the Sidhe.

She wanted to be able to relate every detail of the event. It would not occur again during her lifetime, nor her children's or grandchildren's time. Apart from Elizabeth, and perhaps Eversleigh if he was here, she would be the only mortal who could tell this tale. It was a heavy responsibility. No matter how long the ceremony lasted, Frederica intended to remember every detail.

She felt a sense of pressure behind her. It was Eversleigh, of course. She could always tell when he was nearby.

"Good morrow, Marigold Meadowsweet." He swept her a bow. There was something about how he said her fay name, as if he enjoyed the taste of it.

"Good morrow, Prince Evlan. I wondered if you would be here." She could play the game of fay names as well.

He nodded towards the dais where two silver filigree thrones sat side by side. "Is it the naming, then?"

"It must be. She has not said as much, but Titania gave Libbet a crown to carry on a silken cushion."

"It has only been two days. She has not wasted any time." Eversleigh sounded as calm as ever, but his eyes betrayed his worry. "Has she given any hints whom she may choose? So much depends upon it."

"Not a word. She has spoken privately to four Sidhe men, including your Lord Cathael."

"She likely only wished to speak to him about the war. He would be an improbable candidate for King; he is not of sufficient stature among the Sidhe."

"Titania also interviewed both Libbet and me separately, not at all in her usual manner, asking in great detail about mortal knowledge of the fay. I was also quizzed on the magic of mages and the history of magery. Can you imagine how the Collegium would receive the news that Titania learned everything she knows of magery from a mere woman?"

He smiled slightly. "Your father would be proud of you."

Frederica was less certain of that. "I hope so. Last night Titania went alone to the clearing to consult with the moon. She did not tell us what the moon may have said." As if the moon could say anything at all.

"It is a good sign that she asked Libbet to bear the crown. She would be unlikely to show so much public favor to a mortal if she intended to allow the war to continue."

"Is Aelfric here?"

"In line with the other Sidhe. I think he would have preferred to be with us."

Frederica wondered just whom he meant by "us." She glanced up at the overcast sky. "How will Titania know when it is noon? The Sidhe do not have timepieces, do they?"

"No. They eschew metal devices, apart from those made of silver and gold. Perhaps she just knows."

Silence fell over the clearing as Titania mounted the dais, followed by Elizabeth bearing a silken pillow with a gem-studded circlet resting on it. The queen's own delicate crown sparkled with diamonds as she stood in front of the thrones. As if she were unaware of the crowd before her, she took the circlet from the pillow and held it high in the air, her face turned up to the sky.

The expectant silence continued. Titania stood perfectly still, her raven tresses swaying gently in the breeze. A narrow shaft of sunlight burst through the clouds, setting the circlet in Titania's hands ablaze, and cut a line through the clearing.

Titania looked out over the lines of the Sidhe. "Lord Cathael, come forward."

Frederica could barely see Lord Cathael's form with the sunlight reflecting off his armor. He stepped out of line and strode to the dais, mounting the steps to stand before Titania. His face was pale, even for a Sidhe, and a muscle beside his mouth twitched. Despite his interview with Titania, he clearly had not expected this.

Without a word, Titania reached up and placed the diadem on his head. They both turned to face the crowd. Titania took his hand and raised it with hers. "Behold your King!" she said in a voice that carried throughout the clearing.

Cheers and stamping of feet met her announcement. The armor of each of the Sidhe shifted from black and silver to Cathael's colors of gold and sea green.

A shiver went down Frederica's spine. It was the end of the age of Oberon and the beginning of something new.

Titania and the new king sat in the thrones and conversed quietly as their subjects began to leave the clearing.

"That is all?" Frederica demanded of Eversleigh. "Choosing a king for the next few centuries, and that is all? Our coronations go on for half a day."

"The Sidhe do not like to waste time," said Eversleigh. He was smiling broadly and looked years younger.

"You are pleased with her choice?"

"I barely know Cathael, but the outlook for relations between mortals and fay has brightened substantially. Titania could hardly have made it clearer that she intends an end to the war. I am delighted." He shook his head as if unable to credit it. "Not only that, I finally have an answer as to how the moon picks a new queen."

"What do you mean?"

"Did you not see her name Cathael moments after the sunbeam struck him?"

"Surely you do not think she would have named whatever Sidhe the sunbeam happened to fall on?"

"I do not think it was that random. Last night Titania communed with the moon, and today at midday the sunbeam struck one of the four Sidhe she was considering. I have not the least idea how it could be possible nor what it means, but it is real. And I thought nothing about Faerie could astonish me now!"

His smile made him seem even more appealing than usual, and she was standing too close to him. Elizabeth had said he wanted her, but could she believe it? Abruptly she asked, "Why did you offer for me? You had never paid me the least attention before."

He tore his eyes away from the spectacle on the dais. Looking at her searchingly, he said slowly, "I had always dreaded marrying because I thought I would have to hide my Faerie connections from any woman high-born enough to be a suitable match. I thought any society lady would be horrified by fay behavior if I ever brought her here. Then I walked into Titania's bower and found an enchanting creature who fit into Faerie as naturally as she did in a London drawing room. I wanted you." He paused. "Dare I hope this means you have reconsidered?"

Frederica froze. He wanted her. Was that enough?

"Never mind," he said. "If you will excuse me, I must have a word with Aelfric before he leaves."

"Of course," she said hollowly. Was she glad or disappointed he had not waited for her to answer?

"You have a caller, sir. A Miss Darcy," said Eversleigh's butler.

Eversleigh lifted his head. "Are you certain it is Miss Darcy and not Mr. Darcy?" He had been expecting Darcy ever since receiving that odd letter of resignation from the Collegium. Not that it was completely unexpected, but he would have expected Darcy to tell him of it in person. But what would his sister be doing here? The girl was not even out yet, if he recalled correctly. She should not be making calls, especially not on single men.

"Sir, it is a young lady," the butler said disapprovingly. "She wishes to speak to you privately."

Most odd. What reason could she possibly have? Perhaps she was concerned about her brother. "Send her in. And station a maid at the far end of the drawing room where she can watch me." He could not see her for long in any case. He should already be on his way to Rosings for the revel.

"Very good, sir."

Eversleigh straightened his cuffs. If any other young woman made a request like this, he would assume it was an attempt at entrapping him into marriage. He could not believe it of Darcy's sister, though. Darcy had said she was timid.

"Miss Darcy," the butler announced.

She did not look as young as he had expected; her figure was fully formed. Perhaps he should not have dismissed the idea of entrapment so quickly. She curtsied stiffly, her face ashen.

"Miss Darcy, how may I be of service to you?" He tried to sound fatherly.

"I... I know I should not be here, but... I have a question." She stared at the floor.

"Is this concerning your brother?" he prompted.

"No. Yes. Mostly no."

If it was not about Darcy, what could it possibly be? "What is your question?"

"Is there a way you can tell if someone is under a sorcerer's spell?" The words rushed out quickly, as if she had prepared them.

Had Darcy told her of their suspicions that sorcerers might still be among them? "Are you afraid your brother is under a spell?"

"No, not him. Can you do it?" Her eyes were huge.

"It is possible, but I have never done it. We have no sorcerers in England." Apart from Lady Catherine de Bourgh, of course, but she was safely imprisoned and warded. "If you are worried that Sir Lewis de Bourgh might have put a spell on you, even if he had, it would have died with him."

"You do not *know* of any other sorcerers in England," she said quietly.

Why did young girls have to beat around the bush so much? "Perhaps you could tell me what you are so worried about."

She chewed her lip and opened her mouth as if to speak, but no words came out. Her hands clenched. "Oh!" It was a cry of frustration.

He had been missing the obvious. Young girls were imaginative. She must have read too many gothic novels about sorcerers. "I truly believe you have nothing to worry about. Girls often have these fancies. I think it would be best to send for your brother –"

"No! Can you not simply do it?" she begged.

"It is not a spell that can be done casually, and you will not even tell me why you think you need it."

She drew a handkerchief from her reticule.

Oh, no. Not tears. Anything but tears.

But she did not cry. She folded her handkerchief in half with trembling fingers, and then folded it over itself lengthwise. Grasping the resultant strip of fabric by the ends, she laid it across her face.

Across her mouth, to be specific. Like a gag.

"Are you saying the spell will not allow you to speak about it?" But she had just told him about it! No, she had not – she had asked if he could determine whether someone was under spell, not if she was. Clever girl. He should have expected as much from Frederica's cousin.

She nodded fiercely.

Now what was he supposed to do? He still had no evidence of sorcery, and he was reluctant to use the spell which could expose her innermost thoughts to him. "Can you write the answers?"

"No. I have tried."

Blood wards had worked to block sorcery at Rosings Park. He had no blood wards here, but perhaps... "I have an idea. There is a set of wards I use when practicing a new spell. They keep magic from escaping in case the spell goes out of control. Perhaps they can also block magic getting in. That might release you from the spell temporarily."

He took four black pawns from the desk drawer and waved her to a chair. He set one pawn to the north of her, one to the south, and then east and west. Crouching down, he touched his forefinger to the north pawn and spoke the words of the warding spell, feeling it flicker to life.

"Miss Darcy, does that change anything?"

The girl clasped her hands to her face and the words began to pour out of her. "Oh, God forgive me! A man wanted to elope with me. He put his hands on my neck and started speaking Latin. He said it was Latin love poetry, but it did not sound like poetry. After that I agreed to the elopement even though I did not want to. I could not say no. My brother discovered us before we left, and he frightened the man away, but later he started sending me notes whenever my brother was out of town asking me where he had gone and what he was doing, and I had to answer them. I tried so hard not to, but my hands would not obey me." Tears began to run down her cheeks.

For once he did not mind the tears. They were nothing compared to the reality of knowing there truly was an active sorcerer living in their midst. "Who is the man?"

She dabbed at her eyes with her handkerchief. "His name is Wickham."

"George Wickham?" he asked sharply.

She nodded. "Do you know him?" she asked anxiously.

Eversleigh sat down hard. The pieces fit together all too well. Wickham wanting to know Darcy's whereabouts so he could choose the locations for his dry wells. Wickham possessing the sorcery to force his friends to persecute Darcy to the point of unreason. There was still the matter of the missing water mage, but that could wait.

A living sorcerer. Why had he ever wished to be Master of the Collegium?

He had to do this properly. "He was once a member of the Collegium. Thank you for telling me. You are very brave. I believe you, but now I do need to check you for the presence of sorcery. I will need to touch your..." He almost said neck, but that was what Wickham had done to her. "Your wrist." He would have to use wild magic that way, but after all the other rules he had broken in the last few weeks, what was one more?

Silently she pulled off her glove and held out her wrist.

With his fingers on her pulse, Eversleigh closed his eyes and saw himself sailing through an ocean, a bright red ocean, in an ancient trireme. The current pulled his boat forward, and the wind was at his back. A green island loomed ahead. He landed the boat on a rocky beach and disembarked into a garden. Some of it was neatly planted, some of it grew riotously, and some parts were shrouded in mist.

There it was, a snake slithering between two rosebushes. With a lightning speed he did not possess in real life, Eversleigh grabbed it behind the head and drew its fangs. The snake screamed and slithered away. Eversleigh stared after it for a moment before returning to his ship. He pushed off into the ocean... and was sitting in his study with his fingers on Miss Darcy's wrist.

... and holding dripping snake fangs in his other hand. Sorcerous snake fangs. With an oath, he jumped up, ran to his desk and dropped the fangs in the top drawer, slammed it shut and turned the key. He wiped the remaining venom off his hand with his handkerchief and poured half a bottle of brandy over his palm for good measure, heedless of the mess. His housekeeper was going to kill him.

He had not expected any of that. There was a reason they called it wild magic.

"What was that?" Miss Darcy's voice quavered.

"That would be rather complicated to explain, but I did something that may weaken the spell."

"Can you not remove it?"

He chose his words with care. "I could, but it might damage your mind. There are better ways of dealing with that." Like asking Aelfric to help, or killing George Wickham. He was not usually a bloodthirsty man, but the latter sounded quite appealing at the moment.

"I do not mind the risk. I cannot stand having it in me."

"I mind the risk very much indeed. We will keep you safe until it can be removed. First, I am going to take you home, and we will explain this to your brother. He can set up wards like this for you."

"He is not there," she said in a small voice. "He left this morning for Portugal to serve with Wellington."

"He did what? Never mind; I heard you." He could hardly leave a young girl under a sorcerer's spell without protection, especially with the sorcerer still free. Lord Matlock was her uncle and could defend her better than anyone, but he was at Rosings preparing for the revel. "Whose care did Darcy leave you in?"

"He made my cousin, Richard Fitzwilliam, my guardian, but he is at Rosings."

As were Frederica and almost everyone he could trust with the situation. Except Aelfric, who would remain in Faerie until the revel actually began.

"Miss Darcy, I think I had best take you on a journey. Has your brother spoken to you about his trips to Faerie?"

# Chapter 15

It was the same glade Elizabeth had danced in on her first night in Faerie, the one where she had met Aelfric and her life had changed. Now the fay gathered there prior to making their grand entrance at the revel.

"Do you think we should rescue Mr. FitzClarence?" Elizabeth asked Frederica. Not that the young mage seemed to desire rescuing as he gaped at beautiful Titania, who in turn was trailing the tips of her long fingers along his jawline. Mr. Harbury, the poet, languished at her feet, his lips shaping lines of verse. The third of Titania's young gentlemen was making a valiant attempt to maintain his air of fashionable ennui, but he kept leaning closer to the Faerie Queen before recalling himself and pulling away. Titania seemed delighted with her new attendants.

Frederica flicked back one of the diaphanous silk veils which draped her close-fitting bodice of cream-colored silk. At least the bodices of their dresses were modest enough; the skirts which provided a bare modicum of decency were translucent. Bluebird had flatly refused to wear the under dress, leaving her legs fully visible. Titania had taken some persuasion to wear extra silks to minimize the chance of her skin showing.

"I suppose I should make sure it goes no further, at least not before the revel," said Frederica reluctantly.

"Do you mind if I remain here?" Elizabeth had just spotted a familiar figure coming towards them.

"If you wish." Frederica's silks rustled around her as she walked away.

Elizabeth caught her breath at the sight of Darcy. She had been bracing herself to see him at the revel, but here he was now, and it was as if all those weeks of pain and longing vanished in a moment. But something was wrong. He should be in evening dress, not a greatcoat and travelling boots.

He stopped beside her, his expression somber. "Do not worry. I will not embarrass you."

"Mr. Dar –" She broke off and corrected herself. "Diarcey, your presence does not trouble me at all. Is something the matter? I did not expect to see you until the revel."

"I will not be attending the revel. I am leaving." He spoke with heavy finality.

Her heart began to pound. "I do not understand. What are you leaving?"

"England. I am on my way to Dover. I sail for Portugal on the morning tide, and I do not know when, or if, I shall return to England. I came here because I could not leave without saying goodbye."

No! He could not leave. "You are going away?" Her voice trembled.

"Yes. I must."

"But why?" Then she realized the truth. It was because of her, because of the impossible situation they were in. She forced herself to remain calm. "My apologies; it is none of my affair. You must wish to speak to Marigold Meadowsweet."

"No. It is better if her family remains unaware until I am gone. It is Collegium business, and I want my uncle to be able to say honestly that he knew nothing about it."

"The Collegium is sending you away? I do not understand." But at least it was not because of her.

He looked away. "The charges I faced at the Collegium have been raised again. This time they have decided I am guilty, and the Board of

Inquiry has sentenced me to binding. Rather than submit, I have resigned from the Collegium and will be taking a position with General Wellington in Portugal."

"No!" She wanted to make his words disappear. She could not bear it if he went off to war and left her behind. "How could they decide you are guilty when you did not do it?"

"The judgment is not fair. No sensible man could look at the so-called evidence and call it anything but rumor and coincidence. Unfortunately, these particular three mages want me to be punished, and I doubt they care whether I did it or not. They are on my trail already. I had to sneak out the kitchen door of my house to avoid them. If I did not have the ability to use the faerie rings, they would have caught and bound me already."

She shivered. "Could you not simply stay out of their reach by using the rings? You could travel back and forth between different parts of England and they could not track you." At least he would be safe from the dangers of war.

He shook his head. "I will not be a fugitive in my own country, and I still would not be safe. Somewhere there is a powerful mage who actually is responsible for the dry wells, and he is working with my enemies. It is safer if I simply leave."

"Can nothing be done to stop them?" Despair welled in her throat.

"I have tried. Eversleigh plans to bring it up for review at the next meeting of the full Collegium, but that is not until next winter."

Next winter. Anything could happen by then. Tears burned her eyes. "Why do these men hate you so much?"

He shrugged. "It is old news. George Wickham is their friend, and I caused him to be expelled from the Collegium. Wickham is skilled at exacting revenge. This is a very potent one."

"Wickham?" She had a sudden memory of Wickham at the dance

her first night in Faerie, in this very grove. What had he said? Something about the prince being helpful to him in matters pertaining to someone they both disliked. At the time, she had thought he meant someone the prince also disliked. But Wickham would have still believed that she disliked Darcy. She clapped her hands to her cheeks in dismay. "Oh, how could I have missed it? Tell me again, quickly, what it is they say you did."

Darcy looked surprised at her question. "There have been a number of cases where wells have mysteriously run dry, always on the land of someone I have disagreed with or disliked, and always when I was staying in the same vicinity. Only a water mage could cause that to happen, and I am the only known water mage powerful enough to do so."

"I know who could do it," she said darkly, her breath coming quickly. "Come with me. We must speak to Aelfric immediately."

He held back. "I have been seen by too many people already, and I must leave at once. The Board of Inquiry will have realized I am headed to Dover, and I cannot afford to let them get there first."

Elizabeth caught at his hand. "Speaking to Aelfric is more important than you can imagine. If you have any faith in my judgment, I beg you to trust me."

He hesitated. "If you wish, then."

How had she failed to see it until now? Elizabeth silently cursed herself for missing the obvious. That first evening she had been so shocked by the discovery that Aelfric was her brother that she paid little attention to what had come before. Oh, foolish, foolish mistake!

Aelfric stood on the opposite side of the clearing. He was speaking to a gnome, but Elizabeth could not bear to wait until he was done. After all, the Sidhe were always abrupt to the point of rudeness, were they not? She would be just as abrupt and rude.

"Aelfric," she interrupted. "Pardon me, but I must speak with you immediately."

He looked mildly annoyed but did not seem to find her behavior surprising. "What is the matter?"

"George Wickham told me you were his liege lord." Behind her she heard Darcy draw in a sharp breath.

"That is correct."

"Did he ask you to make certain wells in the mortal world run dry?" Elizabeth held her breath waiting for his reply.

"Yes, but it is not a matter for public discussion. He wished it to be secret."

"I am afraid it must be discussed publicly. Did he tell you why he made such an odd request?"

"It was something about revenge on a mage who had mistreated him. I paid little attention."

Elizabeth's hands bunched into fists. "George Wickham is a liar. That mage did not mistreat him at all, but Wickham's revenge has been very successful. That mage is Diarcey, who was named by your own father. Because people believe he caused those wells to run dry, he has been sentenced to be placed under a binding spell."

Aelfric glanced uncomfortably at Darcy. "I am sorry for that, but as my liege man, Wickham was entitled to ask a service of me. There are doubtless two sides to the story, and I would have known if Wickham were lying."

"Oh, I am certain he found a way to speak the truth in a misleading way! Aelfric, you cannot allow Diarcey to be punished so harshly for something you did," she pleaded.

"Sister, you clearly did not understand the nature of the bond between liege lord and liege man. I owe him my loyalty."

Elizabeth stamped her foot. "You cannot do this! What of your loyalty to me? I claim blood right." It was a shot in the dark, but it was all she had.

"Libbet, of course you have blood right, and if Wickham's actions were harming you, then my responsibility would be to you. But you claim they are harming your friend. He has no relationship to me, so my responsibility to Wickham takes precedence." He spoke with an artificial patience as if explaining something obvious to a young child.

"Harming him also harms me! If you do not agree to tell the truth about what you have done, I... I will leave England with him this very night and you will never see me again." She did not dare look at Darcy.

Aelfric hesitated. "I am sorry for it, but I am bound by the code of the Sidhe. You should not leave with him, *tiarinn.*"

It should have made her want to obey him, but instead it gave her a wild feeling of recklessness. "You have no right to stop me from leaving with him, *tiarinn.*" She put heavy sarcasm on the last word. "You are the one who is forcing him to flee. You have chosen to ruin the man I love."

"Libbet, I am your kin. He is not. You should listen to me."

"You may be my kin, but I will never forgive you for this, not ever!" Why could Aelfric not see that Darcy was more than kin, that he was part of her?

That was the answer. It was right in front of her. With every ounce of strength she possessed behind each word, she said, "I claim blood right."

"Libbet, I have already explained that your blood right does not apply –"

"Not to you. I claim blood right to Diarcey." She would make Darcy into Aelfric's *shurinn.*

Aelfric drew in a long breath. "You do not understand what you are saying."

"Yes, I do, and I mean it." But she did not actually understand it, except that it would force Aelfric to protect Darcy. She would do whatever she had to for that.

Aelfric had reached the limits of his patience. "You cannot simply claim blood right on a whim. This is utter foolishness."

"It is not a whim. I claim blood right. Diarcey, do you deny it?"

Darcy's face was a study in confusion. "Er...no." It sounded more like a question than an answer.

"There you are." Elizabeth raised her chin. "I have claimed blood right, and he does not deny it."

Aelfric's shoulders slumped. "You truly mean to do this?"

"Yes." After all, if Aelfric was against it, that might mean it was a good idea.

Aelfric's scowl made his Sidhe features ferocious. "Very well. If you do this, I will cease supporting Wickham and will tell anyone you wish about my part in it. Are you satisfied?"

A tremendous weight lifted from her shoulders. "Thank – I am happy to hear it."

He still looked displeased. "Titania must still perform the rite."

"Naturally." Hopefully the rite would be simple and painless. She still had a long evening ahead of her, with a great deal depending on it.

"And it must be done now, if I am to break my word to my liege man over it."

Elizabeth raised her chin. "I am ready. Let us go to Titania this minute."

She dared not speak to Darcy while Aelfric could see. What must he be thinking of her? Would he be angry when he discovered what she had done?

Aelfric stalked up to Titania. "Libbet has claimed blood right to that man." He pointed to Darcy.

Titania examined Darcy, her gaze moving slowly from his head to his feet and back again. "A fine choice, my Libbet. I hope he is worthy."

"He is." Elizabeth's throat constricted. Watching Titania gave her an excuse not to look at Darcy.

"Come, stand in front of me, both of you and hold out your right hands – no, not that way, palm up." She drew out a small silver dagger.

Good heavens, what did this rite consist of? Was this a terrible mistake?

With a lightning quick movement, Titania drew the dagger's point over her own palm. Blood welled out of the cut. Titania held her hand over Elizabeth's outstretched palm and allowed several drops of her blood to fall into it. The fay blood sizzled and sparked in Elizabeth's hand, but she felt no heat, only the tingle of magic.

Titania repeated the procedure with Darcy. "Place your palms together, face one another, and turn twice widdershins."

It was a strange imitation of a formal dance. Elizabeth's eyes locked with Darcy's dark ones as they slowly turned. The heat of his hand against hers, the fay blood meeting between them, was shockingly intimate. What was he thinking? And why was she suddenly so dizzy? The sparks dancing around their hands were traveling up their arms. Something was flowing into her, something foreign and strong.

Why had she not realized the rite would include a spell? She might be changed afterwards. Was the spell even safe for mortals? Everything was spinning around her, and Darcy was the only solidity in her world.

Twice widdershins, and Elizabeth stumbled to a stop.

"Blood right is sealed." Titania clapped her hands. "More wine, to drink to my Libbet!"

Suddenly there were wine glasses in everyone's hands. Elizabeth held Darcy's hand, still dizzy, as they drank a toast.

But something was wrong. She could feel it inside her. Eversleigh needed help. Then she heard his voice.

"Aelfric!" Eversleigh staggered towards them, accompanied by a mortal girl.

"Georgiana! What are you doing here?" cried Darcy.

Eversleigh ignored him and grabbed Aelfric's sleeve. "Aelfric, this is Miss Darcy. She has a snake in her head. Can you take it out?" His speech was slurred.

Aelfric turned piercing eyes on Miss Darcy. "If she wishes, but what has happened to you?"

Miss Darcy wrung her hands. "He was well when we left his house, but he has grown more and more ill, yet he refused to stop."

"I defanged the snake." Eversleigh barely managed to get the words out. "I held the fangs here." He held up his hand. It was bright red, streaked with black.

"Evlan, you should have left it for me," Aelfric scolded. "Libbet, will you take him to Titania for healing?"

Elizabeth grasped Eversleigh by the elbow, offering what support she could despite her dizziness. "What snake was this?" she asked him as they approached Titania.

"A spell. Sorcery."

She gasped. "Lady Catherine put a spell on Miss Darcy as well?"

Eversleigh swayed. "Not Lady Catherine. Another sorcerer. Fellow named Wickham."

"Wickham, a sorcerer?" she exclaimed. Then Titania was before them, so she said, "Great lady, Prince Evlan has been injured by dark magic. He is in grave need of help."

Titania wasted no time. She took his hand and studied it. "My poor boy. You should not attempt such strong magic." She held his hand in front of her face and blew gently on his palm.

Eversleigh blinked. "Oh. That is better." He looked at his hand as if wondering who it belonged to. "Better, but I am so sleepy." He collapsed on the grassy bank and his eyelids began to droop.

Darcy demanded, "Georgiana, what is all this about?"

The girl opened her mouth but no words came out. She scrunched her face in concentration and finally said, "I... cannot... say...

it."

Aelfric, seemingly undisturbed by this, asked Miss Darcy, "Would you like me to remove the snake now?"

"Oh, yes. Oh, yes!"

He cupped her cheek tenderly, gazing into her eyes. She swayed slightly. Aelfric stepped back, a slender black snake in his hand and an expression of revulsion on his face. He dropped the snake and ground it into the grass with his boot heel. The grass burst into flames that leaped up quickly, flickered, and died. "Is that better?" he asked.

"So much better," the girl whispered. "Lord Eversleigh said I must not thank you, but I will never forget what you have done for me." She yawned.

Behind her, Elizabeth watched the proceedings with a look of shock.

Darcy caught Georgiana as she crumpled. "What did you do to her?" he demanded.

"I removed the snake. She is unharmed, merely asleep," said Aelfric.

"What is this snake? I do not understand."

Aelfric's mouth twisted. "It was dark magic. I do not wish to speak of it. I must cleanse myself now." He strode away.

Darcy wanted to run after him, but he could not leave Georgiana. He carried his sleeping sister to the edge of the clearing and lowered her gently to the ground.

"That..." said Elizabeth in an awed voice, "That was very wild magic."

"But what did he do?"

"Dark magic is what the fay call sorcery." She hesitated. "Just before Titania healed him, Eversleigh told me Wickham had cast a spell on your sister."

"Wickham again? It cannot be. He is a liar and a cheat, but not a sorcerer." But a sinking feeling of uncertainty filled him.

"Eversleigh sounded certain, but he is asleep now as well."

Darcy scowled. "I wish that brother of yours were more inclined to ask questions before he acted."

Titania called out, "Come, it is time!"

Elizabeth's eyes grew large. "The revel! I must go. But you..."

He did not like it. He did not like any of this, but he knew she was right. "I will remain here to watch over my sister."

She bit her lip. "Will you still be here when I return? You will not leave?"

His sister was unarousable, Wickham was a sorcerer, he himself had just undergone a fay spell no one had bothered to explain to him, and he could still feel it tingle through him. He could even feel Elizabeth's distress at leaving him.

He could not help himself. He pulled her to him and kissed her.

"Libbet!" called Titania. "We must go!"

He released her reluctantly. "I will be here."

Elizabeth touched her fingertips to her lips, looking dazed.

"Go now," Darcy said. Or he would not be able to let her leave at all.

Elizabeth was glad to be able to hide in the rear of Titania's train as they began their journey to Rosings Park, entering the faerie ring three at a time. Her lips were still burning from Darcy's kiss, and the rest of her was reeling from everything else that had happened. And he had kissed her in front of everyone. Not that anyone in Faerie would care, especially after they had claimed blood right, but she was still shocked at herself.

"Well, that was interesting," said Frederica pointedly as they arrived in the glade at Rosings. Several elves carried torches to light their way.

"Which part of it? I do not even know what you saw." Elizabeth knew she must be blushing fiercely.

"I could hardly miss the part where you claimed blood right. Titania did not seem surprised."

Elizabeth flushed. "Titania knew. Not who he was, but that he existed. Remember that day she told us about our desires?"

"How could I forget?" muttered Frederica. "I have never been so embarrassed in my life."

Titania held up her hand and the group halted at the edge of the grove within a cloud of inky shadows. Strings of colored lanterns revealed the crowd of revelers in the formal gardens ahead of them. "We are to await our cue," said the queen.

Elizabeth shook her head in a vain effort to clear the cobwebs out of it. This was the moment they had been working toward, and so much depended upon it. Would the guests flee screaming into the night as she feared, or would they welcome the fay as Lady Matlock and Frederica hoped?

Lord Matlock mounted a well-lit podium in the garden and clapped his hands for silence. "Ladies and gentlemen, I thank you for attending our moonlit revels. Tonight is a very special occasion, one that none of us will ever forget. You have seen our actors from Drury Lane presenting a tableau of Queen Titania's bower from A Midsummer Night's Dream, a representation of that time, centuries ago, when the fay walked among us and we counted them as our friends. When we began our dark ages, fighting among ourselves and fearing the unknown, the fay quietly retreated into invisibility. We were left with only the old tales and reflections of past glory in plays and novels.

"Today we are more civilized than our forebears. We speak to each other rather than fighting. We have learned to appreciate poetry, art, and all that is beautiful. This has not gone unnoticed among the fay.

Tonight it is my very great honor to welcome back the denizens of Faerie to our lands."

The handful of dryads and elves in the crowd who had posed as guests suddenly dropped their glamour to reveal their true selves. Audible gasps and shrieks surrounded them. Furtive voices whispered everywhere, and at least one lady appeared to swoon. Other guests backed away from the fay.

Lord Matlock held up his hands for silence. "A few of the fay folk have already joined us, but I pray you to welcome our guests of honor. Titania, the Faerie Queen, and her attendants, Prince Aelfric of the Sidhe and Lady Aislinn of the Sidhe."

Each of the Sidhe stepped out of the shadows as they were named. Titania came forward on Aelfric's arm as Elizabeth, Frederica, and the others fanned out behind them. Lady Matlock, stationed prominently in front of her guests, dropped into a deep curtsy.

The guests buzzed nervously. A few followed Lady Matlock's example, but most hesitated or backed up. Titania glided forward in silence towards the prepared bower, nodding regally first to one side and then the other.

At the tableau of the bower she waved her hand at the actors playing their Shakespearean roles. "Begone," she said in her warm, chiming voice. The actors scattered in apparent panic. Lady Matlock must not have warned them about this part of their duties.

Titania waved her hand again and an elaborate silver filigree throne appeared in the center of the bower. Her three mortal swains gathered on the hillock around her as if they had spent their entire lives lounging in a rustic bower. At least that part came naturally to Elizabeth, much more so than appearing in public with her hair loose and twined with flowers. Frederica took her place by Titania's feet, her legs curled under her and her golden head leaning against Titania's knee. No doubt it looked very picturesque to those who were unaware she had been instructed to take that place to prevent any guest from coming too close to Titania.

"I would like to meet some of these mortals, especially if it is two or three at a time. I am unaccustomed to crowds." Titania appeared to be speaking to her attendants, but her voice spread farther than a mortal's would.

A few brave souls came forward, but most of the crowd held back and a few even scurried away. Lord Matlock joined his wife and Lady Jersey in an informal receiving line just outside the bower.

Lord Matlock laughed at something a ruddy-faced man said to him. "My friend, if you believe my magic could create one tenth of this spectacle, you vastly overrate my abilities. My abilities are nothing to theirs. You should have seen Prince Aelfric the first time I met him, calmly conjuring a table full of real fruit out of thin air." His voice seemed unnaturally loud in the silence.

The ruddy faced man said to Aelfric, "Is that true? Do you have the power to conjure things?"

Aelfric smiled politely and produced an apple on his outstretched palm. "For you."

Elizabeth hurried to his side and said to the stunned man, "The fay dislike being thanked."

"I..." The man looked up from his astonished inspection of the apple. "What do I say, then?"

"They do not mind being told what we think of their actions." She could hardly believe she was being so forward with a perfect stranger, one who was no doubt far above her in rank, but she could not allow him to upset Aelfric when her brother was on his best behavior.

"I am amazed. I have never seen such a thing." The man held the apple gingerly.

"Why did the fay seek me out?" said Lord Matlock in a carrying voice to another guest. "They did not. It was sheer coincidence. My son and daughter happened to become acquainted with that dark-haired young lady over there, Miss Bennet. She is Prince Aelfric's sister and one of the very few mortals with the ability to visit Faerie. She took my daughter to meet Queen Titania, who kindly invited her to join her retinue. My Frederica is the one at the Queen's feet."

Lady Matlock appeared beside the ruddy man. "Your Grace, you look as astonished as I felt when I first met one of the Sidhe. They are remarkable, are they not?"

"Remarkable, yes, indeed." He still looked dazed as Lady Matlock ushered an older couple and a young lady up to Aelfric.

"Prince Aelfric, may I present Mr. Watts, one of our mages, and his wife and daughter, Mrs. Watts and Miss Watts?" said Lady Matlock.

Mr. Watts eyed Aelfric skeptically. "You claim to be a Sidhe?"

"Father, please," murmured Miss Watts, her color rising.

With perfect composure, Aelfric replied, "No, I do not claim to be a Sidhe. I am a Sidhe."

Elizabeth whispered to Aelfric, "Flowers for the ladies."

Aelfric obediently produced two white roses. He handed one to Mrs. Watts, and then stroked the petals of the second against her daughter's cheek before giving it to her. "Beauty for the beauty," he said.

Miss Watts appeared enthralled.

Next came the Earl and Countess of Wisley, who received an apple and a rose, followed by an elegant older lady. Elizabeth held her breath. Older mortals were still a novelty to Aelfric, making him unpredictable.

Lady Matlock said, "Permit me to present Mrs. Clapp, a dear friend of Lady Jersey."

Aelfric studied her for a moment and said, "The showiness of the rose is not for you. You have the resilience and strength of our smaller, but no less valued, delights." He produced a nosegay of buttercups and cornflowers. "They will not wilt."

"You have a silver tongue," Mrs. Clapp said with just a hint of tartness. "But you have chosen my favorites. The young ladies will need to keep a clear head around you!"

Aelfric's patience astonished Elizabeth as he met guest after guest. She had never seen him like this. Was he following instructions from Eversleigh? She hoped he could maintain it, especially since most of the guests were still eyeing them suspiciously from a distance.

She had known it could not be this simple to introduce the fay into mortal society. She prayed it would not turn into a disaster.

"Oh, dear," murmured Lady Matlock during a brief pause. "Perhaps you should return to the queen. Sir Walter Holmes's daughter is sitting beside her and taking down her hair. Sir Walter will not be pleased."

Titania's entourage had indeed increased by two young ladies. A handsome man in evening dress was painting the scene. Had Lady Matlock arranged for a painter? Elizabeth had never heard of such a thing at a society entertainment. She smiled when she realized the painter's easel was made of silver filigree.

Titania held her hand out to Elizabeth as she approached. "Here is my Libbet. She must be in the painting, too."

Frederica looked up at her from her position by Titania's knees. "Mr. McKee told the queen he wished he had his paints so he could record this historic scene."

"It will be my masterwork," said the unmistakably dazzled painter.

Titania nodded regally. "I have not yet renamed him. I wish to see his painting first." She turned back to meet another guest brought to her by Lady Jersey.

It was a relief to sit down on the ground by Frederica. Elizabeth was exhausted, and the most challenging part of the night for her was yet to come.

A starry-eyed girl with a crown of daisies said, "I cannot believe this. In Cornwall, where I grew up, I saw the fay all the time, but that the queen herself should invite me to join you! Do you think she will permit me to return to Faerie with her?"

Frederica nudged her elbow. "Titania has invited Rowan and Honeysuckle to join us." She added in a whisper, "Miss Butler and Miss Holmes."

"She would be delighted, I am sure," said Elizabeth. "You are Rowan?"

"That is what the queen says. Everyone in London says my true name, Jennifer, is odd simply because it is Cornish, so I am glad she gave me a new one. But how do you dare to wear your hair down?"

The elegantly dressed Miss Holmes, now Honeysuckle, shook her loose tresses. "Think of it as a costume ball. I like the freedom of it."

"But people are staring at us!"

"Pay them no mind. Let them stare and see that we are not afraid," said Miss Holmes.

Frederica grabbed Elizabeth's arm, her eyes wide. "Stand up, all of you, this second," she hissed frantically. "He is here, though Lady Jersey did not expect him. And Eversleigh is not! He was supposed to deal with him if he came."

"Deal with what?" Elizabeth struggled not to trip over her silks as she stood up.

Frederica leaned over Titania and said urgently, "The Prince Regent is here. He acts in the King's name." She swallowed hard and whispered, "He is very fat. Do not say anything about that." She dropped gracefully into a full court curtsey and bent her head.

The Prince Regent? Good heavens! Elizabeth did her best to imitate Frederica, who had the advantage of having been presented at court in her first Season, but the narrowness of her underskirt and the uneven ground made it difficult. With her head bowed, she peeked through her lashes to see a large number of boots coming towards them.

"Prince Aelfric, you should stand with Titania." It was Lady Matlock's voice. "Where is Viscount Eversleigh?"

Aelfric said, "He is in Faerie, healing from an injury caused by dark magician – what you would call a sorcerer."

"Another one?" Lady Matlock sounded exasperated. "Well, I suppose I will have to do it myself, then. Queen Titania, the Prince Regent has requested the honor of an introduction to you."

Titania's silks floated as she stood. "You must rise, all of you. He has his retinue, and you are mine."

Startled, Elizabeth raised her head. At Lady Matlock's nod, she rose from her curtsy, attempting to keep her wobbling to a minimum.

Lady Matlock said briskly, "Let us have your dryads directly behind you, with the mortals and sprites after them."

"Libbet and Marigold Meadowsweet will walk with my dryads." Titania's voice did not leave room for argument.

Her legs weak, Elizabeth obeyed, not even objecting when Bluebird took her by the hand.

They stood far enough back that she could not make out the words that passed between Titania and the Prince Regent, but from their voices, it seemed to be a cordial meeting. Elizabeth could barely believe she was in the presence of royalty. He looked just like the caricatures she had seen.

Her legs were starting to feel stronger when Lord Matlock approached the royal party. His hearty voice carried well. "Your Royal Highness, we have a special entertainment planned to celebrate Queen Titania's visit, and we would be deeply honored if you would permit us to present it to you."

"What sort of entertainment is it?" The Prince Regent eyed the dryads hopefully.

"It involves three young ladies. Among the fay, all women

perform magic, and they find our ban on ladies employing magic to be barbaric. I tend to agree, especially now that I have learned what accomplished young ladies can do with magic. My daughter, Lady Frederica, my niece, Miss de Bourgh, and our dear friend Miss Bennet will join together in delighting us with an illusion of the King's Hall in Faerie. It will be unlike the flat illusions you have seen in the past. With this illusion, you will be able to walk through it and experience it from all angles just as you would if you actually travelled to Faerie."

Prinny's response was clearly in the affirmative.

Elizabeth wished she could hide somewhere, but she reluctantly stepped forward with Frederica towards the spot where Anne de Bourgh was waiting between Lord Matlock and Titania. The idea of performing the complicated illusion in front of half the *ton* had been intimidating enough. Adding the Prince Regent to the audience made it terrifying.

Titania said softly, "Libbet, child, your gift is still unsteady from the blood binding."

What was that supposed to mean? "Perhaps, but I cannot step back from this now."

Anne took hands with Frederica on one side and Elizabeth on the other. "Let it begin."

Elizabeth did her best to ignore the audience, focusing her attention on building the illusion, first creating a mist and then solidifying it into the vaulting ceiling of living wood of the King's Hall. She felt Frederica building the opposite side, while Anne channeled power to both of them. She adjusted her construction to bring out the fine details of the gargoyles and to make the falling water from the fountain glisten.

But part of her ceiling was turning back into mist. She forced her attention there to repair it, but then the fountain slowed and the grassy floor began to fade. The sounds around her began to disappear, and something was wrong with her feet. This had not happened when they had practiced it. Surely she could not fail now in front of this august audience and the Prince Regent himself!

Then she felt Aelfric's power buttressing her own, supporting her ceiling and walls, tweaking a detail here and there. The flowery scent of Faerie air wafted past her. The entire illusion strengthened and became more solid as Prinny and his retinue walked through it. Somehow, with Aelfric's help, Elizabeth was able to hold her part of the illusion for the interminable minutes until Anne said, "It is done."

Gratefully Elizabeth let the illusion dissolve into mist. What was wrong with her? When they had practiced building the illusion, it had been challenging and draining, but she had been able to maintain it.

"Libbet," said Frederica in an odd voice, "why are you standing in a puddle of water?"

Elizabeth looked down at the water that rose to her ankles. It did not spread across the level ground to Anne and Frederica. There was no denying it was unnatural. Her feet were soaking wet. "Perhaps it is something Mr. Darcy did."

"But he is still in Faerie with his sister."

And she was at the revel in front of the Prince Regent with water clinging to her feet and ankles. She could not simply walk around that way! What had Mr. Darcy said about dealing with water, that he told it what to do? It was worth a try. Feeling utterly foolish, she looked down at her personal puddle and said, "Leave me and sink into the ground."

The water obeyed.

"I feel very strange," she said.

Bluebird materialized beside her. "You should have listened to Titania, Libbet. This was too much for you."

"But I did it before. I am certain I will be fine if I can only sit down for a few minutes."

Frederica looked at her worriedly. "Unfortunately, that is the one thing you cannot do." She tipped her head in the direction of the Prince

Regent.

Bluebird's steadying arm came around her. "I will support you."

Elizabeth allowed herself to lean against Bluebird. At least her part of the evening was done.

Only a few guests were still lingering when the servants brought out a new table of food especially for the fay guests. The dryads, sprites and elves descended on it with a frightening alacrity, while Titania's swains fought for the privilege of bringing her a plate.

Frederica said to Elizabeth, "Just look at my mother and Lady Jersey. They are going to be perfectly insufferable about what a success this evening has been."

"They deserve it. I thought it would be an utter failure at first, but once the Prince Regent showed his approval, everything changed. I had not thought it possible that it would turn out so well."

Frederica stifled a yawn, looking as tired as Elizabeth felt. "I am glad it is almost over. It is more enjoyable attending an event like this when one is not part of the entertainment."

"I will have to take your word for it since I have never attended anything like this. But I must speak to your father before we leave. He will want to know what happened earlier, and it does not seem likely that either Darcy or Eversleigh will be in a position to tell him."

"I suppose so. He should be in the Italian Garden. Mama sent him there when she decided the crush was becoming too much for him."

"He looked like he was enjoying himself immensely," said Elizabeth. But Lady Matlock did have reason to worry about her husband's health, so perhaps it had been wise.

Aelfric set down his plate of food, a true sacrifice for one of the fay. "I will accompany you. I do not like you walking about alone when

413

there has been dark magic afoot."

Elizabeth considered telling him it was unnecessary, but she was too tired to quarrel. "Very well."

Without the colorful lanterns, the Italian Garden was darker than the park where the revel was held, but the full moon made it light enough to see. Lord Matlock sat on a bench overlooking the parterre, a single lantern at his feet.

"Did my wife send you to check on me?" he asked. "I assure you my heart is ticking away just as it is supposed to, and there is no cause to worry."

"I am glad of it, though I did not come here at Lady Matlock's behest, but to tell you of certain discoveries we made just before the revel." Elizabeth drew a deep breath. "It appears George Wickham, formerly a member of the Collegium, has taken up sorcery, and he convinced Aelfric to make the wells go dry. Aelfric is prepared to tell everyone that he, not Darcy, was responsible for the dry wells. Wickham cast a spell on Darcy's sister, too, but Aelfric has removed it. Lord Eversleigh was injured by the spell, and he is recovering after being healed by Titania." Good heavens, she sounded incoherent.

Aelfric frowned fiercely. "Wickham was responsible for the girl's snake?"

"That is what Eversleigh – Evlan – told me." She had forgotten Aelfric had not been present to hear that part.

Lord Matlock had grown still. "I think you had better tell me this story from the beginning."

After she finished relating all that had occurred, Lord Matlock mopped his forehead with his handkerchief. "I had hoped we were past our sorcery problems when my sister was sent away," he said with unusual quietness. "Richard had the right of it."

"I wish that had been an end to it, too." What else could she say?

Aelfric said calmly, "You need not worry about Wickham. I will kill him."

If he was expecting an argument from Elizabeth, he would be in for a disappointment.

Before Lord Matlock could comment, four men approached them from the direction of the house. The leader carried a lantern and was in a Rosings footman's livery.

Lord Matlock sighed. "Why do I think this is going to be more bad news?"

Aelfric faded back into the shadows.

The footman halted in front of them. "Lord Matlock, Mr. Biggins is here to see you."

The earl's eyes drooped, and he murmured to Elizabeth, "From Darcy's Board of Inquiry."

Elizabeth stiffened. These must be the men hunting for Darcy.

Lord Matlock stood and said affably, "Mr. Biggins, it is always a pleasure to see you, but as the bard said, our revels now are ended, and I believe you were not on the invitation list."

"I am here on Collegium business, Matlock. The Board of Inquiry has made a decision. Under Collegium law, Darcy must submit himself for binding. He has fled from us, and we have reason to believe he may be here."

"I have always wondered why our founders chose to invest such power in Boards of Inquiry," Lord Matlock remarked. "Perhaps they assumed the members of such boards would strive for justice rather than acting out of personal spite. Still, we make do with what we have. In this case your judgment will have to be suspended. There is new evidence in the case which exonerates Darcy."

Biggins scowled. "New evidence must be presented properly. We will bind Darcy now, and should this supposed evidence change our judgment, he will be released."

Matlock shook his head gravely. "I fear that would be a poor choice on your part. Darcy has resigned from the Collegium and can no longer be required to submit for judgment, and tonight he is under the protection of mages far more powerful than you – and I do not refer to myself."

"We have listened to you long enough, Matlock. He must submit now."

"And I say you must listen to the new evidence now. Prince Aelfric, might I be so bold as to impose on you to make certain explanations to these gentlemen who want to bind Darcy? Gentlemen, this is Prince Aelfric of the Sidhe." Lord Matlock leaned back, clearly preparing to enjoy the spectacle as Aelfric stepped out of the shadows.

Biggins's face twisted in fear at the sight of the Sidhe. "I do not know what game you are playing, but stay out of our way."

Aelfric put his hand on the sword at his belt, the one that had not been there five minutes earlier. "You will not bind Darcy or harm him in any way."

The men stiffened. Aelfric's appearance could be an illusion, but his voice was clearly not that of a human. "You cannot stop us."

"I most certainly can. Your judgment is mistaken. Darcy may be the only mortal able to control the waters, but it is child's play for any of the Sidhe."

The three men jumped backwards as a jet of water fountained up in front of them. "In this case, I – oh, not you as well!" Aelfric's voice turned peevish.

"What is the matter?" asked Elizabeth anxiously.

"They have snakes in their heads, too. All three of them." Aelfric sounded disgusted by this turn of events.

"Snakes?" asked Lord Matlock, baffled.

Elizabeth leaned close to him and said softly, "He means they are under a sorcerer's spell."

Lord Matlock's head snapped in her direction. "Are you certain?"

he breathed.

"Aelfric seems to be certain."

"That would explain why they have been so unreasonable." He studied the three men before turning back to Elizabeth and murmuring, "I do not like these odds, even with your friend Aelfric here."

Neither did Elizabeth. If any of the men had sorcery at their command, it could be disastrous. As it was, they were watching Lord Matlock closely. Did they realize they had been detected? Would they try to stop her if she went for help? But perhaps help was already at hand. She looked hard at Aelfric and thought as loudly as she could. Danger! She imagined the sight of the men in blindfolds. Again and again. Danger! Blindfolds. Danger. Blindfolds.

Aelfric shot her a bewildered look, shrugged, and gestured towards the men – who were now blindfolded, bound at hands and feet, and gagged.

Lord Matlock's eyes bulged at the sight. "What?"

Aelfric said apologetically, "Libbet seemed to think you wanted them that way. I will free them if you wish."

"No, I like them that way very much," wheezed Lord Matlock. "I thank –"

Elizabeth kicked his boot.

"… I mean to say you are a very useful fellow to have around."

"The gag was my idea. That rude one in front was preparing a snake spell for you, and I was tired of hearing him speak."

"So was I," said Lord Matlock. "Libbet, my dear – pardon me; I meant to say Miss Bennet. Would you be so kind as to inform the mage with Queen Titania that I would greatly appreciate his immediate assistance? Darcy as well, as I assume he must be lurking somewhere hereabouts. I would do it myself, if I thought I could stand up without bringing on another heart paroxysm." He looked paler than he had the time Elizabeth had healed him, and this time her magic was too depleted to help.

"Gladly." Elizabeth bobbed a curtsy and set off for the part of the garden where Titania's retinue remained. After a few steps she picked up her skirts, heedless of showing her ankles, and began to run.

Darcy took off his greatcoat and laid it over Georgiana's sleeping body. He had once again failed to protect her from Wickham. Her expression, even asleep, was pained. And all he could do was to try to keep her warm. He had failed her in so many ways.

Wickham, a sorcerer. It was still a struggle to believe, but in hindsight he could see the beginnings of a pattern. He had missed the signs.

A dryad glided up to Georgiana's other side, carrying silken blankets and a pillow. Without looking at Darcy, she spread the blankets and gently placed the pillow beneath her head. The dryad brushed her fingertips over Georgiana's closed eyelids.

Darcy felt the prickle of magic. "What are you doing to her?"

The dryad finally looked up at him. "It is to give her sweet dreams," she said in a low, melodious voice.

Darcy glanced down at Georgiana's face. She was smiling a little now and the look of pain was gone. He felt a wave of thankfulness towards the dryad, but it left him tongue-tied. What could he say when he was not allowed to thank her? "Your gift is a generous one."

The dryad nodded and glided away. How did they move so smoothly?

Everything had been such a chaotic rush. It had been an ordinary day until Hobbes had brought him Biggins's calling card. There was only one reason Biggins would call on Darcy, and that was if the Board of Inquiry had decided against him. The news that he had two other mages with him only confirmed it. Darcy had grabbed what money he had at hand, escaped out the kitchen door under the concealment of illusion, and fled to Faerie.

A rush of wind struck his face as a bird flew a few feet away from him. A white raven, of course, who circled back to him, cawing frantically.

He was too tired and worried for this. "What is it, Pepper?"

Darcy put up his arms to defend himself as the raven flew straight at his face.

Pepper gave an exasperated caw and changed into a cat. She bit into his trousers and yanked at them.

"Pepper, I cannot go with you this time. I must stay with my sister."

This time Pepper's teeth reached his skin.

"Ow! Devil take it, Pepper!"

Pepper yanked at his trousers again.

Darcy held up a hand. "Just wait." He stood up and waved to the dryad who had helped him. When she came closer, he asked, "Are you able to understand the language of phoukas? She wants me to go with her, but I cannot leave my sister."

Pepper released his trousers and meowed.

The dryad nodded. "She says Libbet is in danger and needs you. Your mother's brother is near death." She paused to listen again. "There are dark magicians, and only fools left to fight them. Libbet is frightened." She looked up at Darcy. "If you wish, I will watch over the girl. She is safe here."

"I...you are kind." And suddenly he knew it was true. He could feel Elizabeth's fear as she leaned over his uncle and whispered something to him. How in God's name had that knowledge come to him? "Can you take me there, Pepper?"

Elizabeth was out of breath when she reached the bower. "Lord Matlock requires... Help. Sorcery. He is ill." The young mage FitzClarence did not hesitate, dashing off in the direction she pointed.

Titania grasped Elizabeth's arm tightly.

"No, I must return to him," Elizabeth gasped. A moment later she and Titania were somehow standing at Lord Matlock's side, and Elizabeth's arm felt as if it had been yanked out of its socket.

Lord Matlock's hand was pressed to his chest as he spoke weakly to Aelfric. "If I do not survive this... tell my son... tell him you are to have your pick of the horses in my stables. They are the finest in England."

Titania leaned over Lord Matlock. "You are ill?"

"My heart," he wheezed.

"I can help you," said Titania.

"If you wish. I suspect it is too late." His normally ruddy face was white.

Titania laid her hand on Lord Matlock's cheek and gazed into his eyes. After a moment, she beckoned Elizabeth to her and put her other hand on Elizabeth's cheek. "Mortal hearts are different from ours. I must see yours to know how his is supposed to work."

A tickling heat built up in Elizabeth's chest and sweat broke out on her forehead. What was one more bit of magic running through her?

Titania began to sing, a wordless melody that seemed to wind itself in and out of the air. FitzClarence arrived, chest heaving, with Darcy just behind him. How had he known to come?

Aelfric held up his hand to stop them. "The queen is healing Lord Matlock."

"And those men?" Darcy gestured to the bound mages.

"They have snakes in their heads," said Aelfric matter-of-factly.

Mr. FitzClarence peered at the blindfolded men. "Is that not

Biggins?"

"It appears to be," said Darcy grimly. "What happened?"

"Snakes," said Aelfric, as if surprised he had to repeat himself. "That one in front was building a snake spell for Lord Matlock."

"Snakes?" Mr. FitzClarence sounded baffled.

"Sorcerer's spells," said Darcy.

Elizabeth's eyelids were growing heavy. Would it be rude to sit on the ground? She was so tired, and the ground looked so very appealing. She sat, put her head on her knees, and slept.

Titania finally stopped her song. "He will live. His heart is different now, neither entirely mortal nor fay, but it will do what is needful."

"We are in your debt, great lady," Darcy said. Perhaps the queen of Faerie could help with this new problem as well. How could he ask her without making a demand? "I will need his advice for dealing with these men who have been practicing dark magic. I do not know what to do with them."

She gave him a sympathetic look. "I wish I could help you, but I am not permitted to interfere in mortal conflicts. I will leave Libbet with you. She needs you." And she vanished.

What the devil was he to do now? The three mages, either sorcerers or in thrall to sorcery, were struggling against their bonds and trying to shout through their gags. Elizabeth, Lord Matlock, and presumably Eversleigh were still in their deep sleep from healing. Why had Elizabeth needed healing? Had someone hurt her? He could not afford to think about that.

If only he had some idea what had led to this situation! But everybody who knew what had happened was unconscious. It was as if A

Midsummer Night's Dream had magically turned into Hamlet, with sleepers scattered about the stage in place of dead Danes.

Well, everybody except Aelfric, who might or might not understand any part of it, with his wild talk of snakes. He said nothing had been wrong with Libbet but could not explain why Titania had healed her. His highest priority seemed to be waiting for Lord Matlock to awaken so he could ask him about his horses.

"Are there any other mages here tonight?" Darcy asked FitzClarence, who was visibly trembling at the thought of facing sorcery.

"I saw Watts earlier, but he has left already," said FitzClarence. "I was told to pay attention to Titania, not to the guests."

"What of Lady Frederica?"

"She went somewhere with Miss de Bourgh after the Prince Regent left."

The Prince Regent? Darcy raked his hand through his hair. Three possible sorcerers and a mage who was still wet behind the ears. This was not promising. A few days ago, the responsibility to deal with the situation would have been his, but he had resigned from the Collegium. "FitzClarence, with Matlock and Eversleigh incapacitated, and those three suspected of sorcery, you are the senior member of the Collegium here, at least until we find Richard Fitzwilliam. It falls to you to decide what to do with our guests."

"Me?" squeaked FitzClarence. "You are senior to me."

"Unfortunately for you, I resigned from the Collegium two days ago, largely because of the antics of Biggins and the rest of his Board of Inquiry. They have placed me under proscription for misuse of my powers." At least sorcery might provide an explanation for their outrageous behavior towards him.

Aelfric said, "If that refers to the dry wells, he did not do it. I was responsible for those."

"I do not believe Darcy has done anything wrong, but I have no idea what to do," said FitzClarence. "If I truly am in charge, then... then I ask *you* to take charge of them, Darcy."

Damn it. Eversleigh and Lord Matlock would expect him to do it, too. "Aelfric, you said the one man was making a snake. The other two – are they sorcerers as well or only enslaved to a sorcerer?"

Aelfric shrugged. "I cannot tell unless they attempt to use a spell. I only noticed the snakes because they were so startled."

A fine time for Aelfric's near omnipotence to fail! "Is there any other way to tell?"

Aelfric considered this. "You could ask the phouka. She might know."

Pepper! Compared to FitzClarence and Aelfric, Pepper was a veritable pillar of dependability, but she had disappeared into the night after leading him here.

"Pepper, I need your help," he called to the empty air, scanning the sky for a white raven in flight.

Pressure against his ankle made him look down. "Pepper! Good cat." He squatted down to be closer to her eye level. "Pepper, we have a problem. Those men who are tied up – at least one of them is a sorcerer, a user of dark magic. Can you tell me if the others are sorcerers or just under a spell?"

Pepper meowed, stretched, and strolled leisurely over to the men.

FitzClarence looked discreetly appalled. He must have thought Darcy had lost his mind, talking to a cat.

"She only looks like a cat. She is a phouka." When Pepper turned her head to glare at him, Darcy added hastily, "Or she is a cat who is also a phouka. I am not certain of the details."

"Her eyes do not match," whispered FitzClarence nervously.

Pepper sniffed at one of the unknown men and turned her face away as if displeased by the smell. She repeated the process with the second man. When she came to Biggins, she sniffed one side of his head, walked down the length of his body, sniffed his trousers, and sank her teeth into his leg just above his boots. Biggins's body jerked, but his shriek was muffled by his gag.

Darcy would not have thought a cat could look disgusted, but Pepper did as she trotted back to him. "Let me see if I understand. Biggins is a sorcerer, but the other two are not. Is that correct?"

Pepper began to purr.

"That is worthy of even more fish." Darcy straightened. "Gentlemen, I believe our best course of action is to confine these men in a safe place until Eversleigh is able to examine them. The dark cellar at Rosings Park should suit them admirably."

# Chapter 16

"Darcy, what are you doing here?" Eversleigh's voice, still thick with sleep, interrupted Darcy's reading.

Darcy closed his book and set it on a side table. "At last! I was starting to wonder if you would ever wake up."

"How long has it been?"

"A day and a night. You fell asleep after Titania healed your hand. Aelfric dealt with Georgiana's snake, and she fell asleep, too, so there has been no one to answer my questions. Then things became truly exciting – in all the wrong ways."

"But how did I get here? I remember being in Faerie."

"Aelfric brought you back to Rosings, but Titania insisted on keeping Georgiana until she awakes. What in God's name happened to her?"

Eversleigh sat up and stretched. "She was under a spell placed by George Wickham. Nothing too serious; she simply had to tell him where you were going every time you left London. That solves the mystery of how someone could know all about your travels even when you tried to keep it secret."

Darcy scowled. "Wickham has become more trouble than I ever thought possible, and that is saying quite a bit. Now we are up to four sorcerers – the late Sir Lewis de Bourgh, Lady Catherine, Wickham and Biggins."

"Biggins is a sorcerer as well? Damn."

"I am afraid so. He is locked in the wine cellar, blindfolded and bound, guarded by Richard Fitzwilliam, two footmen, and a very self-satisfied cat. Of course, according to Aelfric, Biggins is also under a sorcerer's spell, presumably Wickham's. Biggins's two cronies are bespelled and locked up. And now they are your problem." Darcy forced himself to stop before he started tearing his hair out. It had been a very stressful day.

"Good God, what happened while I was asleep? How did you discover he was a sorcerer?" Eversleigh was wide awake now.

"Apparently Aelfric announced it to his face. You may be able to get a clearer story from Aelfric; he just tells me things like 'snakes are slippery.' Lord Matlock and Elizabeth are both in fay-induced sleep as well, so that is all I know. I have never felt so out of my depth in my life."

"Darcy," said Eversleigh distinctly, "I think you had best start at the beginning and tell me everything that has happened."

Darcy glared at him. "What does it mean when a woman claims blood right to a man?"

"Could we save the discussion of fay etiquette until we have dealt with the sorcery?" Eversleigh sounded exasperated.

"No, it cannot wait." He had already waited a night and a day for this answer, and so much depended on it.

"If you insist, it is the fay equivalent of marriage, although there is also an element of adoption and some exchange of magical power. Now can you tell me what happened?"

"Fay marriage? Is it irrevocable?"

"Yes, it is lifelong, and why is this so damned important?"

Darcy allowed himself a foolish grin. "Because Elizabeth claimed blood right to me shortly before you arrived and collapsed at our feet."

"Elizabeth claimed blood right? Good God. I have never heard of a mortal doing that before."

Darcy shrugged. "She was trying to force Aelfric into saving me from being bound. It seemed to work." He was going to have a very interesting discussion with Elizabeth when she finally awoke.

"How did Aelfric come into this? Never mind. Just start at the beginning, if you value your life."

"In the beginning, God created the heavens and the earth, and presumably he created Faerie as well," snapped Darcy.

"Darcy, I am not –" He halted, his eyes widening as he stared at the door in shock. "Lady Frederica?"

Good God, what was Freddie doing here? And in her nightgown!

She rushed to Eversleigh's bed. "You are awake! Thank God! But are you well?"

In a much gentler voice than he had used to Darcy, Eversleigh said, "I have never been better in my life than I am at this moment."

"You!" Frederica spluttered. "You… Do you know how worried we have been? What were you thinking to try such risky wild magic? You could have been killed!" She punctuated each statement by striking his shoulder with the side of her fist.

"Frederica –"

"Did I give you leave to use my name? After all you have put me through?"

"Marigold, then –"

"Stop it! You do not know what it is like not knowing if – mmph." She broke off as Eversleigh stopped her complaints in a most ungentlemanlike manner. The bed creaked as he pulled her to him.

Darcy glared at the oblivious pair. What was wrong with everyone at Rosings Park? He ought to stop them, but then there would be yet another fight, and he was tired of fighting. With a sigh, he picked up his book and held it directly in front of his face, so close that the print blurred.

He would give them five minutes to resolve their difficulties, and then he would step in. What could happen in five minutes, after all? But wait – they were already in a bed. Only three minutes, then. And in their nightclothes. No, he would give them one minute.

Lady Matlock's voice dripped ice. "I see I will not receive any assurances from Viscount Eversleigh about my husband's health tonight. I believe I will return to my bed, and I hope that when I awaken in the morning, this will prove to be nothing worse than a very bad dream."

Darcy's book fell out of his suddenly frozen hands. Lady Matlock, clad in a seemlier dressing gown, stood in the doorway glaring down at her hapless daughter.

Frederica disentangled herself from Eversleigh. "Mama, it is not what you think –"

"It most certainly is exactly what I think." Lady Matlock turned to leave but tossed out one parting remark. "Darcy, I am ashamed of you. You at least should know better."

"Me? I was not the one tearing propriety to shreds!" he said in disbelief, but she was already gone. Lady Matlock liked to have the final word. "At least I did not walk out of the room and leave the two of you alone."

"Pity," drawled Eversleigh, but a smile touched his lips.

"I knew you would stop us," Frederica announced. "But do not worry. Mama is not truly angry."

Darcy said dryly, "If you leave this room continuing to insist you are not engaged, we will see an eruption that will put Vesuvius to shame."

"Oh, well, then," said Frederica.

Eversleigh grinned and pulled her to sit beside him, his arm remaining around her shoulders. "Good. I am glad that is finally settled. But as utterly delightful as this topic is, I believe Darcy was about to tell me something extremely important about sorcerers in the wine cellar."

Frederica came to Elizabeth's room several hours later. "Good, you are awake, too. Poor Darcy has been up in the boughs snapping at everyone and looking ready to explode. He has been frantic over you and attempting to deal with all the sorcery while not being able to ask for help from anyone in the Collegium. The worst is when he has to ask your cat to tell him whether someone is a sorcerer. Poor Darcy, reduced to taking orders from a cat!"

"I imagine he would not like that," said Elizabeth as she pulled a comb through her hair. "I understand his worry, though. First Sir Lewis, then George Wickham, and now Biggins were all members of the Collegium. If the Collegium has hidden three sorcerers, how many more may be among its ranks?"

"Eversleigh is already planning an emergency meeting of the Collegium, though I cannot imagine how he will explain to them that Aelfric must look in each one's eyes and Pepper has to sniff them. My father seems unable to sit still long enough to worry about it."

"Is your father well? I was certain he was dying in front of me before Titania came. It was so much worse than the attack he had before, and my magic was already depleted."

"My father?" Frederica rolled her eyes. "He is driving my mother mad. Titania apparently made his heart into something halfway between a Sidhe and a human heart. Somehow this also ended up giving him boundless energy and a mischievous sense of humor. It is a little frightening."

"I wonder if she did anything to my heart. It was a very strange sensation. But she would probably not change anything without asking me first." Elizabeth flexed her sore arm. "I would not have minded if she had fixed this, though. How is Anne de Bourgh?"

Frederica's expression grew sober. "She has been helping my mother to receive the constant stream of callers from London, but it has been difficult for her to have a sorcerer in the house. It brings up too many memories, she says."

"Why are they calling? Simply to meet Anne?"

Frederica's face brightened. "Our revel was a grand success. Everyone claims they were delighted with the fay from the moment they saw them, and Prinny himself praised our illusion-building and said he would like to see more of it. No one will dare call you a witch when the Prince Regent has approved your use of magic! But the reason they are coming here is that every hostess in London wants to invite the Sidhe to their own soirées. Since they do not know where to leave calling cards for them, they come here. The poor *ton* has no idea how to deal with beings who do not follow their rules. A few ladies have even asked how they can arrange for their daughters to learn to make illusions. Anne will be pleased about that."

"Dare I ask what has been said about the blood right ceremony?" She suspected Darcy would have discovered its true meaning by now. He would have every reason to be angry with her.

"Not a word. Darcy has been silent as the grave on the subject. To be fair, he has had a great many distractions. I still cannot believe you did it."

"I am shocked by it myself. Naturally, I will not hold Mr. Darcy to any commitment."

"But you did it to save him!"

"He never asked me to save him, especially not in that way. Bluebird said the binding was why I could not keep up my part of the illusion with you and Anne. If Aelfric had not stepped in to help, I would have embarrassed us all."

"It was very strange to feel his magic as part of it, though Anne seemed to like it. I find it disturbing, though, that a Sidhe can join a spell without having to touch the person casting it. What if we do not want their help?"

"You need not worry on that account. Aelfric could only do it because of his blood right to me."

"This blood right business is very confusing. I am glad no one can claim it to me."

"I do not blame you. And now I have three men with blood right to me – Aelfric, Eversleigh, and now Darcy. *Tiarinn*, *shurinn*, and *eliarinn*, though that last one was rather rash on my part, to say the least."

"Do you regret doing it?"

"No." Even if Darcy was angry, she was glad she had been able to offer him protection. Part of them would always be joined, even if she never saw him again. But his kiss had given her hope.

There was a knock on the door. "Enter," said Elizabeth.

Darcy stood in the doorway, his eyes fixed on her with indecipherable look. He walked slowly towards her.

Good heavens! He was in her bedroom. This was beyond improper, even with Frederica there.

Without taking his eyes from Elizabeth, he said, "Freddie, you may go now. I want to be alone with my *eliarinn*."

He knew. Sometime between the revel and this moment, he had learned the meaning of claiming blood right.

"Certainly," Frederica said brightly. She closed the door behind her.

Elizabeth's heart began to pound as Darcy continue to advance towards her. "I know you did not understand what blood right entailed. I will not hold you to a commitment you entered into unknowingly."

"It hardly matters whether you do, because I certainly intend to hold you to it, and the bond cannot be broken," he said conversationally. "Have you tried to use magic since that night?" He stopped less than a foot from her.

She took half a step backwards. "Only for the illusion at the revel."

He held up his hand and rubbed his thumb against his fingertips.

Blue flame emerged from his thumb, just as it did when she made flame. "You see what has happened to me? I imagine the same has happened to you. There is water in that basin. Tell it to spill over the edge."

"I have no power over water." She had never seen him like this.

"Try anyway."

Silently she told the water to spill. And it did, just as it had listened to her at the revel. "Good heavens!" No wonder her magic had misbehaved. She had some of Darcy's magic, and he had some of hers.

"Good heavens, indeed. Now close your eyes and tell me what I am doing with the hand I have behind my back."

"How could I... Oh, very well." She closed her eyes and thought about his hand. Suddenly she could feel it – from the inside. Her eyes flew open. "You have your fingers spread."

He produced his hand, and his fingers were indeed spread. He stepped forward until their bodies were almost touching. "Do you still believe it is possible to choose not to hold me to the commitment?" He seemed intent and demanding at the same time, hunting her like a lion stalking a gazelle. Was he displeased with her?

She moistened her dry lips with her tongue. "I did not expect that to happen. I assumed it was more of a legal connection, and I had no way of knowing Aelfric would break with Wickham that night anyway."

"You said you loved me. You said you would leave England with me. You claimed blood right to me. There is no going back." He placed his hands on her shoulders, but instead of pulling her towards him as she expected, he steered her backwards one step at a time. "If I had known what it meant, do you know what I would have done?"

The back of her legs came up against the bed, causing her to sit down with a thump. "What?" Why was her voice so high?

He placed his hands on the bed on each side of her hips and leaned over until she could feel the warm rush of his breath on her face. "I would have done it anyway," he whispered.

His lips descended on hers. As his mouth moved across hers, unleashing a tide of desire, he bore her backwards until her head was on the pillow. He scooped her legs up onto the bed and then he was above her, propping himself up on his elbows with his legs trapping hers.

Elizabeth rallied one final bit of rationality. "Why are you behaving this way?"

His smile had something feral about it. "Because I have noticed that whenever you take a step towards accepting me, you run away afterwards. I want to make it clear your running days are over."

Joy flooded her. She wound her arms around his neck. "Who says I want to run? After all, I was the one who claimed blood right."

His eyes flared. "So you did, *eliarinn*." He brushed his lips against the side of her neck and trailed his tongue up to her ear. "And I did not deny you," he whispered before turning his attention to the sensitive notch between her collarbones.

With a whimper she arched herself towards him, desperate to feel his body against hers, and he obliged by lowering his body to meet her own. She could feel the pressure of him through every inch of her, and it still was not enough. She clasped his head between her hands and brought his lips back to hers.

She had longed for this so much since that night in the Dower House sitting room and had despaired of ever feeling it again. And it was even more – so much more contact, and this time she could feel the reflection of his pleasure in her response. It made her even more shameless, running her hands down his back as his kiss devoured her.

That ache she remembered started building again deep within her, making her writhe beneath him. Oh, she needed more! And this time there was no need for guilt or shame, and she could drown in the pleasure of his hand caressing her neck, her shoulder, her arm – had he pushed her dress off her shoulder? Yes, and now he was bringing his mouth to that tender skin...

The knock on the door barely registered to Elizabeth through her sensual haze, but Darcy must have noticed it. "Go away!" he called.

"Fitzwilliam Darcy, I am going to count to ten, and then I am opening this door." Lady Matlock sounded furious.

"I should have locked it," muttered Darcy as he helped Elizabeth pull up the shoulders of her gown. They both scrambled off the bed.

Elizabeth attempted to straighten the rumpled counterpane, but it was hopeless. Instead she sat down firmly in the middle of it to cover the evidence. There was nothing to be done about the disheveled state of her hair.

The door opened to reveal a frowning Lady Matlock. Her husband stood behind her, looking more amused than annoyed.

"There is no reason for concern." Darcy bit out the words. "Elizabeth and I went through the Faerie equivalent of marriage just before the revel."

"That is not my equivalent of marriage," said Lady Matlock. "Darcy, you will find a horse, ride to London, and return with a special license. Now."

"There is no point," Elizabeth said, acutely conscious of her swollen lips. "I am not of age, so it would not be valid."

"In that case, Darcy will also have to call on your father and get his permission," said Lady Matlock severely.

"My father is more likely to lock me in the attic than to give his permission," Elizabeth said. "Convincing him may not be a quick process, and I am not willing to speak to him about it at present."

"Then we will just have to keep you apart until he gives it," Lady Matlock stated firmly.

Darcy made a noise that could only be described as a growl. "Come, Elizabeth. We are leaving."

"Where do you think you are going?" Lady Matlock demanded.

"To Faerie, where everyone agrees we are married," snapped

Darcy.

"Nonsense," said Lord Matlock cheerily. "There is no need. I can fix this." He left and a moment later came the sound of footsteps bounding down the stairs.

Lady Matlock placed a beringed hand over her eyes. "One hesitates to even wonder what he means. We will wait for him in the drawing room, though. Not here."

They found Eversleigh, Frederica, Anne, and Colonel Fitzwilliam already in the drawing room, each with a knowing smirk. Elizabeth's cheeks burned. Frederica must have told them all why she had sent her parents to Elizabeth's room.

A quarter of an hour later Lord Matlock strode into the drawing room and dropped two papers in Darcy's lap. "Signed and sealed. That should take care of it."

Darcy read through the top paper and shook his head. "I do not know why you think it will help to have a letter from you granting your permission for Elizabeth to marry me. You are not her father."

Lord Matlock settled himself comfortably in a large armchair. "Second letter."

Darcy did not bother to look at it. "Tell me you did not forge her father's signature."

"I did better than that. I adopted her." Lord Matlock looked smug.

Elizabeth's jaw dropped. "You cannot just adopt me!"

"Of course I can," said Lord Matlock. "I told you I would fix it, and I did."

Elizabeth looked at Darcy. "That cannot be legal, can it?"

"Perhaps, if your father does not challenge the adoption."

"He would not dare," said Lord Matlock. "By the time he could, you will have been living as husband and wife. Too much scandal, and what judge is going to believe that an impoverished country gentleman with six daughters refused to give his permission when the Earl of Matlock wanted to adopt one of them?"

"Five daughters, and you ought to be careful, my lord," Elizabeth said archly. "I might decide I like being an earl's daughter better than getting married."

Darcy and Lady Matlock spoke in unison. "Absolutely not."

Lord Matlock guffawed. "No worries there. You would never agree to be in my custody for a second longer than necessary. Darcy will ride to London tonight, get the special license first thing tomorrow morning, and we will have you married before dinner. Tonight we shall drink a toast to this very short engagement."

"And to celebrate having a new daughter for a few hours," said Eversleigh. "Not to mention having claimed blood right. Did I tell you Titania is extremely excited about it? She says your children will be *tiarinn* to her, which will make the two of you her *shurinn* as well."

"*Tiarinn*? But that means shared blood kin. Our children would not have any of Titania's blood," said Elizabeth.

Eversleigh's mischievous look intensified his resemblance to the Sidhe. "You were bound together by Titania's blood, and apparently that gives something to your children. Your offspring may have interesting magical powers."

Darcy took Elizabeth's hand and intertwined his fingers with hers. "I have not had the chance to mention this to you yet, but if any of our children turn out to be elemental mages, I would want them to spend part of their childhood in Faerie. For years I dreaded having children and watching them suffer as I did. Even when I wear a ring of fay metal, there is still enough elemental pressure to be difficult for a child. In Faerie they would have a chance to be ordinary children."

Elizabeth batted her eyelashes at him. "Allowing my children to spend time in Faerie? How would we ever get Titania to agree to that?"

Frederica and Eversleigh laughed, but everyone else, including

Darcy, looked puzzled. Elizabeth explained, "Titania has been asking for my children to visit her already. I believe she would settle for any child I could find on the street."

Lord Matlock's old look of curiosity was back. "How did Titania's blood come into this? Tell me about this binding."

"We are still discovering for ourselves what it means," admitted Darcy. "Here is one effect of it." He rubbed his thumb and fingers together and produced fire.

Lord Matlock leaned over to examine the flame. "Fascinating. How did you do that?"

"It is Elizabeth's wild magic. Some of it transferred to me in the binding, and she now has some control over water."

"Really?" Frederica eyed Eversleigh assessingly.

Lord Matlock pulled over a chair. "You must tell me about it this minute."

The butler announced, "Miss Darcy and Mr. Alfred."

"Georgiana!" Darcy jumped to his feet and embraced his sister. "You are awake! Are you well?"

She smiled tremulously at him. "I am perfectly well. Prince Aelfric has taken such good care of me."

"Aelfric did?" Darcy sounded surprised.

Aelfric held out both hands to Darcy. After a moment Darcy grasped Aelfric's wrists, his expression confused.

Eversleigh pointed a finger at Darcy. "You owe me an apology for all those times you told me *shurinn* is not a real bond."

Darcy's jaw worked, but he said nothing.

Eversleigh turned to the others with a gleeful look. "Darcy has just discovered that his reaction to Aelfric has changed now that they are *shurinn*. I would venture to guess he cannot bear the illogic of it."

"Of course *shurinn* is real." Aelfric sounded astonished anyone would think otherwise. He gripped Eversleigh by the wrists, kissed

Elizabeth's cheek, and sat down beside Anne and kissed her. On the lips.

"I am sorry to have stayed away so long," Aelfric told Anne. "My *shurinn*'s sister needed care."

"That had to come first, naturally." Anne appeared completely unperturbed.

Aelfric looked up as he noticed the complete silence in the room. "Is something the matter?" he asked.

Anne spoke before anyone else could respond. "Aelfric has become a frequent visitor here of late. And none of you are to say even one word about it. Not one single word." It was a clear warning.

Lady Matlock might have said nothing, but her expression spoke volumes.

Anne turned back to Aelfric. "Your timing is excellent. We have just learned that Elizabeth and Darcy are to be married tomorrow afternoon, and I am sure Elizabeth would like for you to be present."

"Married?" Aelfric's forehead wrinkled. "But they have already pledged blood right."

"True," said Eversleigh. "But in the mortal world, everyone expects a man and woman who are lovers to have words of marriage spoken over them. People would be cruel to Libbet if she and Diarcey did not go through the marriage ceremony."

"Oh. Then she must do it." Aelfric still appeared concerned, though. "Anne, should we have a ceremony? I do not want anyone to be cruel to you."

For once, Anne's air of certainty slipped. She chewed her lip for a moment. "Let us speak about this later."

"That is a very gentlemanly offer, Prince Aelfric," said Lady Matlock approvingly. "Some women are married to sailors who are absent for long periods of time, so it would not be unusual that you are not always here."

Miss Darcy's previously happy expression had disappeared, and she appeared to be blinking back tears. Elizabeth reviewed in her mind what had been said recently and hurried to the girl's side. "Miss Darcy, I am so glad you could be here, even though this wedding tomorrow is but a patched-up business. When Lady Matlock discovered a few hours ago that your brother and I went through a bonding ritual in Faerie, she was insistent that we must marry immediately." She leaned closer, whispering in the girl's ear. "To be honest, this wedding is not completely legal, so your brother and I plan to have another proper wedding at a later date. This ceremony is purely to appease Lady Matlock."

"Oh." She seemed to breathe easier. "That explains it. I could not see why it was happening so quickly."

"Neither can I!" She needed to distract the girl before she realized her brother had already made the commitment without telling her first. "What did you think of Faerie?"

"Oh! It was wonderful. Even better than I had imagined it. I only awoke a few hours before we came here, but Queen Titania was so kind to me. I have never seen anyone like her! Can you believe she invited me to visit her again? She called me her Woodlark because she said my voice was silken like the lark's."

"Oh, no," groaned Colonel Fitzwilliam. "Not another name. I can barely remember one name per person. It is too much for me to manage two different names to be used in different places, and one world where it is rude to thank someone, while in the other it is rude not to thank them!"

"Fay names make more sense than mortal names," volunteered Aelfric. "Evlan and I call you Dubheach, which means black horse."

Colonel Fitzwilliam clutched his hands to his head.

Darcy returned the following morning with a special license in hand. "They accepted my uncle's letters and gave it to me," he told Elizabeth. "Whether it is legal or not is a different matter."

With an arch look, Elizabeth said, "It is more legal than the blood right ceremony."

He smiled in a way that sent heat rushing through her. "I cannot argue with that."

"I told you I would fix it," said Lord Matlock smugly.

"Let us not forget it is more Christian," said Lady Matlock frostily. "I will make arrangements for a clergyman to come here this afternoon."

"Thank you," said Darcy. "Mr. Cox, the vicar of Chiddingstone, might be a good choice. He helped to counsel the servants here after Lady Catherine's sorcery was revealed, so he will not be as shocked by the situation as some might. Mr. Collins of Hunsford would not be appropriate. He is not permitted to come to Rosings Park."

Lady Matlock nodded. "Very well." She swept from the room.

The butler announced, "Mr. Debenham."

A slender, dark man in his mid-thirties entered the room and bowed. "It is a pleasure to see you again, your lordship, Darcy, Miss de Bourgh."

Lord Matlock rose to his feet. "This is a pleasant surprise, Debenham. I have been wishing for your presence. When did you return from Ireland?"

Debenham said coolly, "I reached London two days ago and began hearing rather alarming reports from here. I thought I might offer my assistance."

"Kind of you! Miss Bennet, may I introduce you to Mr. Debenham of the Council of Mages? Miss Bennet is Darcy's intended."

Debenham bowed over Elizabeth's hand. "A pleasure. Darcy, I must have missed the notice of your engagement. My congratulations."

"Thank you. The engagement has not yet been announced," said

Darcy.

Debenham eyed Elizabeth. "You are a fortunate man."

"He is indeed!" said Lord Matlock. "Come to the library, and I will tell you what has happened. Your assistance will be most timely."

"I am eager to hear about the recent events," said Debenham. "Perhaps Darcy could join us, as I understand he witnessed much of it. Is Eversleigh here as well?"

"He is somewhere about the grounds, walking with my daughter. He can join us when he returns. Aelfric, you have a unique point of view on recent events as well. Permit me to introduce you to Mr. Debenham."

Debenham's eyebrows rose. "A Sidhe? The details of your entertainment are true, then. I have not known how much to credit the wild stories I have heard."

Aelfric gave a cold nod of acknowledgment but said nothing.

With a regretful look back at Elizabeth, Darcy followed his uncle and the others to the library.

"Debenham is here?" exclaimed Eversleigh when he and Frederica returned from their walk. "Excellent. Now we can make some decisions."

"He is in the library with Lord Matlock, Darcy, and Aelfric," offered Elizabeth. "You might want to rescue Aelfric. I do not think he liked Mr. Debenham."

"I suppose I should join them." He turned to leave, but his way was blocked by a grim-faced Colonel Fitzwilliam standing in the doorway, his arm pressed across his stomach.

"Sorcery," the colonel rasped. "Bad. In the library, I think." He could barely choke the words out.

"What?" cried Frederica.

His face ashen, Eversleigh made a hushing gesture. "Voices down.

Are you certain?"

The colonel nodded slowly. "That stench. Unmistakable."

Eversleigh seemed deep in thought. After a moment he shuddered. "They are using iron on Aelfric. Elizabeth, can you sense what is happening to Darcy?"

Elizabeth closed her eyes and reached out with that special sense. She gasped. "He is unconscious. There is something covering his face, something rough." She jumped to her feet. She had to go to him.

"Stop," said Eversleigh. "You must all leave. This very minute. Go out the kitchen door and seek Titania's protection."

Frederica's eyes were wild. "I will not run away. They need our help!"

"Do you think I do not know it?" Eversleigh's voice, while quiet, was harsh. "You cannot fight a sorcerer face to face. He will bespell you and use your power as his own. Miss de Bourgh will testify to that. By escaping, you weaken him, and you remain free to help rescue the others later. Go!"

"But you are staying!" cried Frederica.

"Only because I can remain invisible for at least half an hour. I will learn what I can in that time, and then I will join you. Now go!"

Elizabeth grabbed Frederica's hand and tugged at her. "Come, Frederica. You, too, Anne. Especially you."

Frederica asked Eversleigh desperately, "Will you find my mother and send her?"

"If I can." Eversleigh flickered out of sight.

Elizabeth cast an anguished glance over her shoulder towards the library as she hurried Frederica and Anne along. What had they done to Darcy? Colonel Fitzwilliam brought up the rear, stumbling occasionally as he fought a bout of nausea.

They took the servants' staircase down to the kitchen. Fortunately no one questioned them as they paraded through to the outside door. Elizabeth longed to tell them to run as well, but that could endanger their own escape, and none of the servants possessed magic to be misused. Still, it felt wrong to abandon them.

Colonel Fitzwilliam's color began to improve once they were past the kitchen gardens. "We must go around the rose garden. The library windows look out on it."

They were nearing the grove when the ground heaved under them. Elizabeth staggered and bumped into Frederica.

"Darcy must have awakened," said Colonel Fitzwilliam with grim satisfaction. "Look at that." He pointed towards the lake, where water shot out in jets towards the house. The ground still thrummed under them.

Anne cupped her hands by her mouth and blew. Three whirlwinds sprung up in front of her and raced towards the house. "That may help him."

"Oh, no!" cried Frederica. "We forgot about Georgiana! She is still in the house."

Colonel Fitzwilliam raked his fingers through his hair. "We will have to hope Eversleigh finds her. Now go!"

"Can we go into the grove safely? Will the trees fall?" asked Elizabeth.

"It is safer than staying here!" snapped the colonel.

Elizabeth shivered. "Let us go, then."

"You and your friends must remain here," said Titania instantly when Elizabeth explained the reason for their flight. "No one will hurt you here. Dark magic is a terrible thing."

"You are generous, great lady," said Elizabeth. "I do not wish to bring any trouble to you, but one of the dark magicians, a man named

Wickham, is half fay and can travel through the rings."

Titania's nostrils flared. "How do you know this?"

"He had sworn allegiance to Aelfric. None of us knew he used dark magic."

"At least he will protect Prince Aelfric, then."

Elizabeth shook her head miserably. "He is a liar and a cheat. If he sees an advantage to abandoning Aelfric, he will do it without hesitation."

Titania beckoned to one of the dryads. "Go to King Cathael. Inform him that there is a mortal dark magician with the power to travel through the rings."

The dryad bowed her head and left.

"I cannot interfere with events in your world, Libbet, but we will defend our own," Titania said. "There is someone here who may wish to help you, though." She raised her voice. "Albion, my love!"

A disheveled Mr. FitzClarence appeared in the archway to a private section of the bower. "Great lady?"

"My Libbet has brought ill tidings from your world. You should help her."

Darcy swam back to consciousness as an acrid smell made him gag. His head throbbed and his eyes would not work. No, something was pressing on his eyes. A blindfold, that was it. His hands were tied behind his back and something sharp poked into his throat.

"Ah, I thought that might bring you back to us." It was Debenham's self-satisfied voice. "I would advise against trying to drench us or knock down the house before you have heard what I have to say. I have a knife at your throat and will not hesitate to use it."

Sorcery. Elizabeth. Damn it, he needed to be able to think. "It is your life as well as mine," he said hoarsely.

"You are not in a position to make threats, my friend." Debenham sounded amused.

Darcy coughed, making the knife dig into his skin. "Not a threat. I have a death curse, if you recall." And he needed to set it. Debenham, Biggins, Wickham, all must die if he did. He made a little twist in the words in his head, just as his father had taught him. There, that was done.

"Ah, I had forgotten that little detail about elemental mages. I always assumed it was a myth."

"Then this is your chance to find out." Darcy had always had his doubts about it, too, but this was not the moment to admit to it.

"It is no matter. I can always knock you unconscious before I kill you." The pressure of the knife eased.

"Too late. I already set it." Darcy coughed harder, but his throat would not clear.

"A pity," said Debenham coolly. "You force me to consider less gentlemanly options, such as reminding you that your lovely intended is our prisoner, and I will make certain she pays the price for any misbehavior on your part."

Elizabeth! Darcy's stomach clenched in fear, but he could not afford to let Debenham see that. "I suppose it is hardly surprising that a man who will stoop to using sorcery would not hesitate to harm an innocent woman."

Debenham chuckled. "Darcy, Darcy. Sorcery is but a tool, just as magic is. When changes are needed, we must use the tools at hand."

The blindfold tightened briefly and then fluttered to the floor. Darcy blinked hard to clear his vision. He was still in the library, although now books were scattered about the floor, and a small table was on its side. Across the room from him, Lord Matlock wore a blindfold. Definitely bespelled. Aelfric was nowhere to be seen.

Debenham tugged on the bonds tying Darcy's hands. "Do not get any clever ideas simply because I am kind enough to give you this small freedom. The wards around you are not the weak blood wards you are accustomed to. A mere touch of these ward lines will shred your flesh. Only your flesh, not anyone else's. I set them using your blood. They will block any spells you cast."

It hardly mattered. He could not think clearly enough to talk, much less concentrate enough to cast a spell. His hands came free. Darcy rubbed his wrists as his fingers tingled. If the wards were indeed that strong, only someone with stronger magic could remove them. "Where is Prince Aelfric?"

"Imprisoned where he can do no harm."

"What are you planning?" It was blunt, but Darcy's pounding head kept him from thinking of a subtler way to ask.

Debenham's cold smile sent shivers down his spine. "I had not intended to move so quickly, but you could not be allowed to introduce the Sidhe further into our affairs. Having Matlock, Eversleigh, and you all in one secluded location was too tempting to pass up, and then you handed us a weapon against the Sidhe in the form of Prince Aelfric. Once we have taken a few more mages to give us their power, we will be ready to use Lord Matlock's connections to reach the Prime Minister and the Prince Regent."

"I see." Taking over the government, then. Damn. He had hoped their ambition did not stretch that far. If Debenham discovered how much power he could steal from Anne de Bourgh, he would be nigh unstoppable.

"I will hope you will come to your senses with a little time to reflect on what I can offer you. If not, imprisonment seems the only option." Debenham shrugged, as if it made no difference to him one way or another. "If I cannot use your power, you have little value to me. Think about it. Come, Matlock." He turned on his heel and walked out of the room, with Lord Matlock trailing behind him.

It made Darcy's gorge rise. He could not afford to worry about his uncle now, though. The only thing he could do was to find out how much the wards limited him. He told the lake to make quiet ripples and felt it respond. Good. His elemental magic still worked. He tried a spell to open one of the books on the floor outside the wards. Nothing.

Now the frightening part. He extended his senses towards Elizabeth. At first he could not find her, and his heart tried to pound out of his chest, but then her warmth stole over him. He could feel her relief at his presence. She was unhurt, thank God. He tried to sense where she was, but the effort made his head pound enough that his ability to reach her slipped away. She was safe, and that was enough for now.

"It has been far longer than half an hour!" exclaimed Frederica for at least the third time. "They must have caught him."

"Eversleigh has the good sense to hide if his invisibility slips," said Elizabeth tiredly. She had no energy to spare for worry about Eversleigh. He was likely safe. Darcy most certainly was not. Nor was Aelfric.

"Not if he were injured," argued Frederica.

"Leave off, Freddie!" snapped Colonel Fitzwilliam. "If he is captured, he will be in precisely the same position as our father and mother. Father survived being bespelled once, and he will do so again."

A dryad told Titania, "Prince Evlan seeks an audience."

"Thank God!" Frederica cried.

"Bring him to his friends," Titania instructed.

Eversleigh looked pale and exhausted, but otherwise unharmed. Colonel Fitzwilliam held out his hand. "Replenishment?"

Eversleigh merely nodded. The colonel took his wrist, and gradually Eversleigh's color began to return.

"What did you find?" demanded Frederica.

"Nothing good. That is enough, Fitzwilliam. Save your energy.

We may need it more later."

The colonel removed his hand. "Tell me if you change your mind."

Eversleigh nodded and sank to sit on the moss. "FitzClarence, I did not expect to see you here."

The young mage blushed. "I was visiting Titania when these four arrived. Naturally I offered my assistance."

"I thank you. We will need all the help we can get." Eversleigh rubbed his hand over his forehead. "Debenham is indeed a sorcerer. He has two other enslaved mages who are feeding power to him. They have released Biggins and the others. Wickham is apparently on his way."

"My parents?" asked Frederica, her voice now steady.

"Lord Matlock is bespelled. I could not tell whether your mother is or if she is merely cooperating for your father's sake. Debenham and Biggins could not manage to put a binding spell on Darcy, but they had the servants subdue him physically. He is tied, blindfolded, and warded."

"And Aelfric?" asked Elizabeth hesitantly.

"He is imprisoned in the wrought iron pergola. They were tearing down one section of it to block off the ends. Either they did not try to bespell him or, more likely, their efforts failed."

Elizabeth shook her head. Poor Aelfric, caged like an animal. "Why do they want him? Surely they must realize that holding Aelfric makes every fay their enemy."

"They plan to use him as a hostage. Historically, those sorcerers who do not die a natural death have been killed by elfshot. They think having Aelfric will keep the fay from attacking them."

Colonel Fitzwilliam looked up. "Will it?"

Eversleigh snorted. "Hardly. The Sidhe would never allow mortals to dictate to them. Unfortunately, that means Aelfric is at great risk."

"Unless we get rid of the sorcerers first," said Colonel Fitzwilliam.

"There are three of them? Debenham, Biggins, and Wickham?"

"That is all we know so far, and their spellbound mages, including Lord Matlock. I know little about what sort of magical abilities Biggins or Wickham have, but Debenham is both powerful and skilled. He will not be easy to defeat now that he is using sorcery." Eversleigh looked grim. "He casually used a spell to repair some of the damage Darcy's earth shaking did to the house, rebuilding walls that had collapsed. I have never seen such power in a mage."

Anne stalked across the small bower as if she could not remain still. "If there is only one sorcerer, I can unmake his eyes as I did with Sir Lewis. But only one, and afterwards I will be so weak I could be captured easily."

Colonel Fitzwilliam raised his head. "My father said you unmade Sir Lewis entirely, and they buried an empty coffin."

"Hardly! I am good at unmaking, but no one could be that good. I unmade his eyes along with most of his face. I did not know how to limit it to just his eyes."

The colonel's brows knitted. "I am certain that is what he said."

"You might have misunderstood, or perhaps Lord Matlock had some reason to want you to believe I had unmade him. It does not matter."

Frederica looked up. "He may have been trying to justify the decision to bind her. But if you only unmade part of his face, what killed him? Did he bleed to death?"

Anne came to a halt, her expression puzzled. "I do not think so. There was almost no blood. It was very strange. I do not know what happened. I fainted, and when I awoke, they told me he was dead."

"Perhaps your unmaking reached his brain, and that killed him. It does not matter. Still, if you could blind Debenham, we would have a better chance, even if it did not kill him."

Eversleigh said, "It may come to that, but first we need a plan.

Fitzwilliam, you are our military man. Will you walk with me outside?"

Eversleigh and Colonel Fitzwilliam returned an hour later, their faces grim.

Frederica pounced on them immediately. "What have you decided?"

"We cannot defeat the sorcerers in open battle, even if we rally dozens of mages to our cause, so we must look at other alternatives." Eversleigh looked directly at Elizabeth. "We need to rescue Darcy."

"What about my parents?" asked Frederica.

"I am sorry to say Darcy has to be our first priority. The one thing we have learned is that sorcerous spells do not work on Darcy. Lady Catherine failed with her obedience spells. Debenham and Biggins have failed to bind him. If Wickham had been able to bespell Darcy, he would have done so long ago."

"Perhaps sorcery does not work on elemental mages."

"That was my first thought, but Lord Matlock was able to bespell Miss de Bourgh. Still, the important thing is that Darcy is invulnerable to sorcery. That makes him our most powerful weapon. We need him. Without him, our chances of defeating the sorcerers are much lower."

Elizabeth was not going to argue with a plan to rescue Darcy. "What will we need to do?"

"I am making a plan to free him," said Colonel Fitzwilliam. "I am still working out the details, but I am inclined to believe it is possible for us to do it." He gestured to indicate their small group.

"How can six people possibly do anything against a sorcerer?" Frederica asked dispiritedly.

"We are not six ordinary people," said the colonel. "Anne has extraordinarily strong magic. As a source, I can supply even more.

Eversleigh is one of our best spell-masters. And three of you are women. Debenham will assume none of you have any magic to speak of, so he will underrate you. Even more important, any military strategist will tell you that communication is the key to winning battles, and Eversleigh and Miss Elizabeth can convey things to each other without being in the same place."

Eversleigh nodded. "Normally we can only sense strong sentiments, but we can plan that certain sentiments mean one thing or another."

"With that ability, we can divide into groups," said the colonel. "One group can set up a diversion while the other rescues Darcy. We will need certain things we cannot get in Faerie, though, so I will go to London to obtain them. I doubt Debenham has had a chance to set up people to watch for us, but I will stay away from Matlock House in any case."

Eversleigh said, "I will also go. I need to do some research about sorcerous binding spells in the Collegium library. We will not return until tomorrow morning lest we over-use the rings. We cannot afford to be without that ability."

"What about the rest of us?" asked Elizabeth, her voice steady.

Eversleigh eyed Frederica. "My preference would be for the ladies to remain here. You cannot help us buy guns, you would not be allowed into the Collegium library, and it would be easier for us if we do not have to worry about your safety. FitzClarence, we could use your assistance if you are willing. You would be able to go to our houses for items that might be useful to us."

"I am happy to do whatever I can," said FitzClarence.

"I have a task for the ladies to perform here," said Colonel Fitzwilliam. "My rescue plans are likely to include passing you off in the dark as elves. We will need appropriate clothing and a few bows and arrows. I would like to make the rescue attempt tomorrow night."

"Libbet, I need your help as well." Eversleigh frowned. "In order for the rescue to work, we need Darcy to remain alive until tomorrow night.

Colonel Fitzwilliam scowled. "We have little control over that when he is in their hands."

Eversleigh rubbed his forehead. "I believe he is in more danger from himself than from Debenham, and that worries me."

Elizabeth shivered. "What do you mean?"

"If I know Darcy, he will be plotting a way to kill Debenham using the elements. Flood, fire, or earthquake – any of those could kill Debenham, but Darcy would die with him."

"He would not do that!" Frederica cried. "It would kill my parents and his sister, too."

Eversleigh exchanged a look with Colonel Fitzwilliam. "If I saw a chance to kill the sorcerers at the price of my own life and those of Lord and Lady Matlock, I would do it without hesitation," he said gently. "Your father would do the same, as would your brother or FitzClarence. We have all studied the history of sorcery and the evil it creates. Our lives would be a tiny price to pay to prevent another reign of sorcery."

Colonel Fitzwilliam said, "Our father would do it if it meant killing all of us and everyone he has ever known."

Frederica lifted her chin. "Are you saying Darcy should kill them all?" Her voice shook.

Eversleigh slowly shook his head. "If I could be certain the sorcerers would die, yes, I would want him to. But we do not know if Debenham and the others have defenses against fire, water, or falling stones. What if Darcy reduces Rosings Park to rubble, but the sorcerers are left standing there unharmed? If it were me, I would try it anyway, but Darcy is more valuable than I am. If we lose the one man who can withstand sorcery, our chances to defeat Debenham will be lower."

"Far lower," grated Colonel Fitzwilliam. "Almost nonexistent."

"Unfortunately, I am unable to tell him to wait," said Eversleigh. "Libbet, do you think you could tell him not to fight back through your bond?"

"I can try," said Elizabeth shakily. "I have never attempted a specific message. I wish I had more experience with this."

Darcy. She pictured him in her mind, and suddenly he was there. Warmth, love, and gratitude dissolving into fear. Trapped and helpless. She thought as loudly as she could. *Wait for us. Do not fight. Wait for us.*

Her sense of him began to slip away. She pounded her fist on her thigh in frustration.

"Well?" asked Eversleigh.

"He feels trapped. I cannot tell if that means he is locked up or something else. He seemed glad to be connected to me, but he is grim, perhaps dreading something. I tried to tell him to wait, but I do not know if he could hear me." She opened her right hand and gazed at her palm. Blood right. "I will keep trying."

"It is reassuring he is still alive and well," said Eversleigh. "Perhaps he is not planning something at all, or he may know something that tells him it is useless. I feel rather grim myself, so I am not surprised he does."

But Elizabeth felt it was more than just that, and fear ate at her stomach.

# Chapter 17

Darcy massaged his aching neck. He had somehow managed to sleep in his chair for an hour or two, but he was paying for it in stiffness. At least the morning sun had made an appearance outside the library window, freeing him from the long hours of darkness with no escape from his thoughts.

There could be no good resolution for him. Of his very few choices, all were bad, and the most dignified seemed to be to accept his captivity with apparent calm, even if it meant pretending to read a book that could not begin to hold his interest. It was preferable to burning the house down without any guarantee he could burn Debenham with it.

When Biggins came in wearing his customary smirk, Darcy merely glanced up at him and returned to his book.

"Now, now, Darcy. No point in ignoring me. I am doing you a favor this time."

Perhaps the earth was flat, too. "How kind of you."

"Lord Matlock has been fretting about your well-being and has convinced Debenham to allow him to talk to you. Ten minutes, no more."

Now he had Darcy's attention. Peering behind him, he could see Lady Matlock holding the arm of her blindfolded husband. "You are in luck, Biggins. As it happens, I am quite at leisure to receive visitors."

Biggins stepped back to allow the Matlocks to enter. Lady Matlock led her husband to an armchair. "The chair is right behind you, my dear. You may sit."

"Never thought you would have to lead me around like a helpless baby," grumbled Lord Matlock. "I hate this."

"I know, my dear," said Lady Matlock. "We all do. But here is Darcy, and he appears unharmed."

"I am indeed unharmed." A few bruises hardly counted as harm. "And you?"

Lord Matlock made a hissing sound. "Disgusted with myself and under a control spell, but that is all." His hands were linked by a short rope, giving him some ability to move them. It was more freedom than Darcy had expected him to have.

"The control spell prevents you from removing the blindfold, I assume."

"Debenham is too clever to resort to that. He told me if I made any attempt to remove the blindfold, they would blind me."

"I am glad they did not do that." Darcy had assumed Debenham would already have blinded his uncle.

Lord Matlock scowled. "Debenham wants to use as few spells on me as possible. Apparently each spell reduces the amount of power he can draw from me. An interesting fact about sorcery, if we survive long enough to document it." His voice dripped bitterness. "How have they treated you?"

"I cannot complain of discomfort. Debenham set blood wards around me to stop spells, and there is always a guard here, but I have a comfortable chair and they bring me whatever books I request. It could be much worse." It would only last until Debenham realized Darcy would never cooperate, so he should enjoy the comfort while he could.

"Do the wards stop your elemental magic?"

Darcy shook his head before realizing his uncle could not see him. "No, but it makes no difference. I can only control water and earth, and those are no danger to Debenham and little use to me." Would Lord

Matlock understand his silent message?

His uncle sat perfectly still for a moment. "Yes. It is a pity you cannot control fire, but there is no point in wishing for what we do not have."

It had taken several hours for Darcy to realize that his failure to use fire the previous day had left Debenham with the impression he had no power over it. Now that Darcy knew Elizabeth and the others were safely away, he was waiting for his chance. Once he had Debenham close enough, he would set him and everything around him afire. Innocent lives would be lost – the servants, his aunt, his uncle, and his own – but far worse would happen if Debenham consolidated his power. He had to do it soon, too, before Wickham arrived. Wickham knew he controlled fire.

Darcy said, "Debenham seems to be hoping he can convince me to join him, so he treats me well. I do not know if he truly believes he can change my mind, or if he is simply making the best of it since he can neither bespell me nor kill me."

"Ah, yes," said Lord Matlock with the first sign of his old self. "The elemental mage's death curse. How very useful it is, even when not employed."

"I assure you I have already chosen the curse and set it to take effect on my death, even if I am taken by surprise." If Darcy were certain enough that the old stories of the death curse were true, he would be making efforts to force someone to kill him solely so the three sorcerers would die with him.

"I wish Debenham would kill me," Lord Matlock said. "At least that would be an honorable death rather than watching everything I fought for being destroyed."

"My dear, we must not despair," said Lady Matlock. "I may not be clever, but I know there is always hope."

Lady Matlock, not clever? She must be hiding her abilities, too.

Lord Matlock's hands clenched into fists. "Even if we miraculously escape another reign of sorcery, my legacy is destroyed. I wanted to be remembered as a scholar and a mage who protected England from sorcery. Instead my name will be cursed for generations as the man who let sorcerers come to power, even when they were right under my nose. My own brother-in-law and sister, sorcerers. I appointed a sorcerer to the Council of Mages, and if Debenham had not been in Ireland at the time, I might have made him Master of the Collegium instead of Eversleigh. I all but paved the way for them."

"You had no way of knowing. They hid their sorcery well," said Lady Matlock gently.

"Oh, there were signs. Small ones, now that I look back on it, but the signs were there, and I missed them. Would that I had died before discovering how badly I failed in my duty."

"You trusted Debenham," said Lady Matlock. "You could not spend your entire life suspecting everyone and watching for the slightest hint of deception."

"Why not?" roared Lord Matlock. "That was my responsibility!"

Darcy wished he had consolation to offer. No one had suspected Debenham, but his uncle was right. He was the one who would be blamed for this. "Sorcerers are always deceitful. Honorable men have fallen victim to them time and again throughout history. You hold yourself to an impossible standard."

Lord Matlock grimaced. "It was hubris, nothing more. I was my father's second son and therefore destined to lead the Collegium. When my brother died and left me the earldom, in my pride I thought I could manage both positions – Master of the Collegium and Earl of Matlock. Instead the Collegium had only half of my attention. I should have resigned as soon as I inherited."

"My dear, you will always manage to find some way to blame yourself. The fault lies with Debenham, not with you. We can do nothing now. I only wish I knew if Frederica and Richard were safe."

Finally, something Darcy could help with. He had managed to reach Elizabeth, enough to know she was in Faerie with the others. "I am not worried about them. I am somehow certain, in my heart, that they are both safe and with Miss Bennet."

Lady Matlock's eyes closed for just a moment, but she gave no other sign of the relief she must be feeling. "I hope you are correct, but you know how I fret."

"Naturally. I would worry, too. That was why I stopped fighting Debenham. He threatened to harm the ladies, and I had not yet realized they had escaped." Darcy was still blaming himself for that.

Lord Matlock finally stirred himself to speak again. "If Debenham tries to influence you by threatening me, you should not give in to him."

Darcy almost smiled. "I know. He has already tried threatening to hurt both of you. I told him you would spit on my grave if I cooperated with him to spare you."

"Good," said Lord Matlock. "You are absolutely correct."

Biggins said loudly, "That is enough." He nodded to the footman. "Help Lord Matlock back to his room and be sure to lock the door."

After Lady Matlock led her husband out, Darcy noticed a scrap of paper on the chair she had sat upon. It was out of reach, outside of the wards holding him. But if he could only distract the guard for a minute, he might be able to produce a breeze to blow it to him.

He prepared himself carefully, organizing the wind currents in his mind. He held up the book he was reading. "Pardon me, could you bring me the second volume of *Plato's Works*? It should be on the third shelf in the corner." As the footman obligingly turned his back to look for the book, Darcy told the air to blow. The wind picked up the paper and wafted it to the floor beside him. Darcy grabbed it and stuffed it inside his book. The breeze had been stronger than he had intended, and several other papers had fluttered to the floor. If he managed to live through this experience, he would make a point of practicing his control of air more.

"This one?" asked the footman.

"That is the one."

The footman brought him the book, picked up the blown papers, and started to close the window.

"Leave it open," said Darcy. "I like the fresh air, even if it becomes breezy in here." And it would leave an opening in case a white raven might want a way inside. Not that he thought any rescue possible against a sorcerer as strong as Debenham, but he needed to hold onto a ray of hope. He opened his book to the page with Lady Matlock's note. It was upside down, but he managed to shift it surreptitiously while pretending to cough. She had written in tiny letters that were hard to see.

*My husband is considering doing something rash which is destined to fail. If something rash is to be done, you would be more likely to succeed. You have our blessing, regardless of the outcome for us. God bless you.*

Darcy swallowed hard. It was no more than he had already planned, but this absolved him of the guilt he felt over it. It was decided, then. The next time Debenham came into the room, Rosings would go up in flames.

Elizabeth solved the problem of obtaining elf clothing by asking Bluebird for it. Having discharged that task in something under five minutes left her with endless hours to fill. She reached out to Darcy regularly, hoping a sense of her presence would provide some slight relief. It was perhaps the only thing that kept her from running mad. She took turns reading aloud to Titania and later took a long walk to distract herself, but mostly she remained in the private corner of the bower with Frederica and Anne since Titania was not fond of sad faces.

But through it all, she felt an ache in every inch of her body, nauseated by the idea of Darcy imprisoned. Eversleigh had told her the sorcerers would not kill him. She believed him, but the sick taste at the back of her mouth came from the thought that Darcy might prefer death to indefinite imprisonment by sorcerers. Then her chest felt hollow at the thought of never feeling his arms around her again. Oh, why had she denied him for so long? They might at least have had a little joy before this happened.

Anne and Frederica talked together in low voices, but Elizabeth could not bring herself to take part. How could they not resent her when the welfare of Frederica's parents and Aelfric were put second to Darcy's? It seemed so unlikely that a rescue could work. She dared not let herself believe in it.

Eversleigh's reappearance with Colonel Fitzwilliam in the midafternoon brought an end to the waiting.

"The rescue will happen tonight," said Colonel Fitzwilliam. "Eversleigh found the spell he needs to counter a sorcerous ward, and I have arranged for guns and fireworks to be delivered to a hidden spot just outside Rosings."

"Fireworks?" Frederica asked dubiously. "How is this going to work?"

"The guns are for our first distraction. I will be firing them off by the groundskeeper's cottage. Debenham will send out any available servants to find out what is wrong, but he will not risk himself. The fireworks are for our second distraction, where we pretend to be fay folk attempting to rescue Aelfric. That will bring out the sorcerers. Then Eversleigh will keep himself and Anne invisible while they find Darcy, take care of his guard, and break the wards."

"That would be a fine plan, except for the part where Elizabeth, FitzClarence, and I have to convince the sorcerers we are an entire fay army," said Frederica.

"That is where the fireworks, illusions, and magic come in. Ah, FitzClarence, you are back! Well done." The mage was accompanied by Jasper Fitzwilliam.

Frederica gasped, "Jasper? What are you doing here?"

"I asked FitzClarence to bring him," said the colonel.

"Have you run mad?" hissed Frederica.

Jasper, the youngest and least regarded of the Fitzwilliam family, did not seem to hear her, or perhaps he was just accustomed to his family's disdain. But he was not sporting his usual cocky grin, presumably because of the seriousness of the situation. "You wanted me?" He sounded dubious. "FitzClarence says you want to rescue Darcy, but I don't know what help I can be."

Richard clapped his arm. "You are the perfect man for the tasks I have in mind. First, I need you to get the groundskeeper at Rosings drunk, and after that, I need you to make four people in the dark look like an attacking army of the fay using fireworks, noise, and whatever magic Miss Elizabeth, Frederica, and FitzClarence can produce."

Jasper's face cleared. "Is that all? That will be easy."

Was Rosings under attack? God, Darcy hoped so, but he could not tell what was happening outside in the dark. Flashes of light illuminated the window, and inhuman howls and ululations sent shivers down Darcy's spine. Damn the wards that held him in place and kept him from the window! "Can you see anything?" he asked his guard who was peering out. Not that he could rely on what his guard reported, but it was better than nothing.

"Hard to say. Flying balls of fire and lots of colored lights over on the other side of the garden."

The other side of the garden? That must mean near the pergola where they were holding Aelfric. The young Sidhe could not use magic himself when he was surrounded by iron, so it must be someone else. Was it the fay trying to rescue Aelfric?

None of this made sense. First there had been random gunshots somewhere near the lake, and then this. Bright lights and shouts, accompanied by deafening bangs. Fireworks. Why would the fay be using fireworks?

His hands ached with the desire to help the attackers. He would use anything – a gun, a sword, even his bare fists. But all he could do was to sit in this thrice-damned chair.

He heard rustling, and suddenly his guard collapsed to the floor. "Are you hurt?" Darcy asked.

"Hush." It was Eversleigh's voice, sounding as if he were only a few feet away, but the room was empty.

Darcy swung his head from side to side, but he could see nothing. Had captivity sent his mind running mad?

"He is unconscious." Anne's voice came from the direction of the window where the guard lay.

They were not there, and then suddenly they were. Sick relief filled Darcy. "What are you doing here?" he whispered.

Eversleigh squatted by one of the stone carvings used for the wards and studied it. "Rescuing you." He held out his hand near the ward but did not touch it.

"What is happening outside?"

"A distraction. Debenham and Biggins are out there now. This is a blood ward?"

"Made using my blood," said Darcy. "Debenham says the wards will cut my flesh to shreds but they do not seem to affect anyone else."

"Can you break it?" Anne asked Eversleigh.

Eversleigh nodded. "I can manage the spell if you can supply the brute magical force."

Of course. Debenham's sorcery was far more powerful than Eversleigh's magery. Anne's power should be enough to break it, though. At least he hoped so.

Eversleigh said to Anne, "When I point to you, pick up the ward and carry it toward the corner. It will be hard to pull."

Anne nodded. "Ready."

Eversleigh began to chant the words of ward breaking. When he reached the conclusion, he pointed to Anne.

She stooped to pick up the ward and froze in place, an expression of horror on her face.

"What is the matter?" asked Darcy urgently.

"I cannot move my body, only my head. Nothing happens when I try." Her whisper was agonized. "It is his magic. My father's."

"No, I assure you, Debenham set the wards," said Darcy. "Perhaps he worked with your father so his magic seems similar."

"Not similar." Anne was breathing quickly. "It is the same, I tell you!"

"It cannot be. You unmade Sir Lewis."

"No, I did not! I do not know why Lord Matlock said I did. I unmade his eyes, and when I woke up, they said he was dead."

Eversleigh muttered a spell. "Can you move now?"

"No." Tears leaked down her cheeks.

"Forgive me." Eversleigh attempted to move her arm, but it did not budge, not even as Eversleigh's face turned red and perspiration broke out on his forehead. "No use."

There had to be a way to free her. "Anne, can you unmake the ward?"

Anne closed her eyes. "No. It is as though nothing is there."

What had Debenham done? And why was his magic like Sir Lewis's? The notebooks, the ones in Sir Lewis's study. What had been in the last one? Sir Lewis had been testing ways to control another man's body. His last notebook had shown some slight success.

That notebook had been filled. All of them had been. Why had he never realized there must have been another notebook with his last notes? He was a fool.

"Well, well, well." Debenham stood in the doorway. "Having a party, and you did not even invite me?"

Eversleigh winked out of sight.

"Impressive trick, Eversleigh, but it will do you no good." Debenham closed the door and leaned back against it. "All I need to do is wait for the servants to return. They will be able to find you by touch, and you cannot stay invisible forever. Your little diversion would have worked so nicely if I had not set the wards to alert me if anyone touched them. Sorcery can be so very useful."

Darcy was helpless, and so was Anne. But Eversleigh still had a chance. He would not be able to break open the window and escape before Debenham could stop him, but perhaps Darcy could help. He pictured the window hinges in his mind and set a tiny intense fire burning inside them, feeding the fire with his own energy.

"Nothing to say for yourself, Darcy?" Debenham drawled.

"I was trying to decide whether I should call you Debenham or Sir Lewis," Darcy said coolly. "It must be pleasant to be back at Rosings Park after all these years."

Debenham started at that, but quickly regained his composure. "I do not know what you mean."

Darcy encouraged the fire inside the hinges. If he could keep Debenham distracted a little longer, Eversleigh might be able to push the window out. "If that is how you prefer it, but I knew Debenham years ago, and you are not that man."

"People change with time, Darcy."

Hotter, hotter. "If you are truly Debenham, where did we first meet?"

"I have met thousands of people over the years. I do not recall most of them."

Was that the smell of melting metal? "What college did you attend at Cambridge? Surely you can remember that."

Debenham's eyes narrowed. "This is a stupid game, and I am done with you."

So it was true. The bottom seemed to drop out of Darcy's stomach. "Does Biggins know the truth about you? What would he think if he knew you could not remember your college?"

"I was at Trinity, you fool!" Debenham's face was turning a mottled red.

"A good guess, given how large Trinity is, but Debenham went to Corpus Christi. Are you not going to release poor Anne from your ward? That looks like a very uncomfortable position."

"You will not whisper a word about this to anyone, Darcy. I cannot kill you, but I can make you wish I had."

"I have no doubt of that." The threats meant nothing to Darcy but a way to buy more time. "How does it work? Does any part of Debenham's mind remain?"

The sorcerer shrugged. "I neither know nor care."

"A pity. I did like the man – at least before this." Fire. Fire in the hinges.

"Spare him your pity. He was already learning sorcery when I met him." He turned his attention to Anne. "The little girl has grown up, I see. I should thank you for falling into my trap. Your power will be very useful, and there is unfinished business between us. You cost me a great deal."

Anne did not respond.

"You remember how to remain silent, do you? Good. But be warned your little trick will not work twice. If you destroy these eyes it will be but a minor inconvenience. My own body still lives, and I can use it to take control of one of the others. But where shall we begin, you and I? An eye for an eye, perhaps?"

The window fell away with crash and the sound of shattering glass. Smoke curled from the broken hinges.

Debenham rushed to the window and stared out. "What the devil!"

An invisible hand opened the door to the library. Eversleigh must have escaped.

"Damn him!" Debenham raced to the door and dashed out.

"Kill me." It was Anne's voice, just above a whisper.

Darcy was speechless. "I..."

"I beg you! I know what I face, and he will want revenge on me." Her voice was agonized.

Anne knew what Sir Lewis was like better than he did. "But..."

"Quickly! Before he returns! There will not be another chance."

In her position, he would want to die, too, and he had spent hours trying to devise ways to kill the sorcerers using his powers. But death was irreversible. "I cannot. I am sorry."

"Then I will do it myself!" She created it a tiny whirlwind directly in front of her, hovering in front of her face. At first nothing happened. She could not move, and her face was blocked by the whirlwind that was sucking the air from her lungs.

Longer and longer. How long before she lost consciousness? Darcy's hands ached to reach out to her, but the wards blocked the way. How could she do this to herself? And why was he holding his own breath?

The whirlwind vanished. Anne's head hung limply, her skin chalk white. But after a moment she sucked in air, her color slowly returning.

Of course; she could only keep the whirlwind going until she lost consciousness, and then her body would insist on breathing again. He let out a deep breath, but his chest ached for what she would suffer.

She raised her head, blinking her eyes. "Dear God, no," she whispered hoarsely. "No."

"I am sorry." What else could he say? Helplessness sent bile into his mouth.

"Darcy, I beg you, help me. Otherwise I will have to use fire, and I do not want to burn." Her voice shook with horror.

God, no. How often in the last day had he imagined dying by fire? His mouth was dry. Which was worse, allowing her to bring herself agonizing pain before the relief of death, or putting out the fire and condemning her to torture?

"Damn you, Darcy." Anne looked straight at him as the hem of her skirt began to burn. She was going to do it.

He could not allow it. He grabbed the ewer of water they had given him for washing and threw it on the flames, calling extra pond water to douse the remains. "Not that way, God have mercy!" He glanced around desperately. The basin. That would do it. He piled up three books, set the basin on top, and used another book to push the pile through the wards until it was just below her chin. He told the pond water to fill it to the brim. "Do the whirlwind again. When you lose consciousness, your face will fall in the water." And she would drown.

"Thank you." Her voice dropped. "Tell Aelfric... No, nothing."

The air began to swirl again, trying to suck the water from the bowl as well as stealing Anne's air. It took all of Darcy's control to keep the water still. At least it kept him from thinking about what was about to happen.

The whirlwind died away again. This time water sloshed over the edge of the basin as Anne's face fell into it. He could tell when she inhaled water, and he knew what she would be experiencing if she still felt anything. He had ended up breathing in a lungful of water several times before he learned to control his magic. It was a painful, choking feeling. He looked away, unable to bear to watch.

Finally there was a thump as her body toppled to the floor. That had not happened when she was unconscious earlier. That must mean... Her head was facing away from him, so he could not see her face.

Debenham reappeared and stopped short at the sight of Anne's limp body. "What happened?"

"She has elemental magic. She drowned herself." And he had helped her.

Debenham rolled Anne onto her back. Water dripped from her open mouth. "I need help in the library!" he shouted. He glanced up at Darcy and snapped his fingers.

Black spots danced before Darcy's eyes. His ears began to ring, and the world slipped away.

Elizabeth tried to keep panic at bay by counting the others as they arrived beside the faerie ring at Rosings. Frederica, Jasper, and Richard Fitzwilliam. No sign of FitzClarence, but Titania had given him his own talisman to travel to Faerie, and Eversleigh could help Anne.

"Wait!" A girl's voice called out. "Take me with you, please!"

Frederica's head snapped around. "Georgiana?" she asked in disbelief.

Darcy's sister hurried into the glade. "Freddie? Why are you dressed as an elf?"

"Never mind that," said Elizabeth. "Into the ring, quickly! We can talk more in Faerie." Elizabeth touched her stone and the ground dropped away. The familiar flowery scent of Faerie surrounded her.

Frederica hugged Georgiana. "We have been so worried about you!"

"They never found me. I saw all of you racing away from the house, so I knew something was wrong. I heard the servants talking about the sorcerer in the cellar being freed, so I hid in a closet until night-time and then crept out of the house. I spent all day here hoping someone would come, but I hid when it grew dark. When I saw all the lights, I thought it might be the fay, so I ran to the grove."

"Clever girl!" said Frederica.

"Hold a moment," said Elizabeth sharply. "Colonel, do you feel anything unusual about her?"

The colonel frowned. "No jellied eels. She is not bespelled."

Elizabeth let out the breath she was holding. "Good."

"What happened back there?" the colonel demanded. "Why did you stop us? Did Eversleigh free Darcy?"

She waved them out of the ring. The others might be needing it. "I do not know. Eversleigh told me to run. Something was very wrong." The despair and fear behind the preplanned signal still resonated in her. Of course it did; Eversleigh was still feeling it, so she did as well. "Did FitzClarence hear my whistle?"

"No idea," said Jasper. "He had gone behind some trees with his bow."

Elizabeth felt the thrum of power from the ring and turned to see Eversleigh arrive. Anne was not with him. She ran towards him, her hands held out. Frederica was right behind her.

Eversleigh held up a hand to stop her. "Do not touch me, or I will break into a thousand pieces." He sounded remote, like a stranger.

"What happened?" asked Frederica.

Eversleigh closed his eyes tightly as if he could not bear to look at them. "It was a trap. We got in with no problem, but as soon as Anne touched the ward, she became unable to move. Debenham caught us there. I tried to turn both of us invisible, but it did not work on Anne any longer, no matter what I did." His throat bobbed as he swallowed.

"What did Debenham do?" Elizabeth did not think she wanted to know the answer.

"Debenham is really Sir Lewis. He is still alive, and somehow he took over Debenham's body. Anne knew."

"Dear God," Richard whispered.

"Where is Anne?" asked Frederica.

Eversleigh wiped the back of his hand over his mouth. "She... Oh, dammit." He took Richard Fitzwilliam's arm and led him a short distance away.

A few minutes later the colonel trudged back to them, his face ashen. "He asked me to tell you. He managed to stay in the room when Debenham thought he had escaped. Anne was at Debenham's, that is to say Sir Lewis's, mercy, and she was the one who had blinded him. He...well, never mind what he said he would do to her. She begged Darcy to kill her, and when he would not, she took her own life."

Frederica collapsed to her knees, burying her face in her hands. Georgiana's face was ashen.

Numbness spread through Elizabeth. It could not be real. She would not let it be real, but the tight pressure within her chest would not go away.

The colonel continued, "That is not all. As Eversleigh was making his escape, he saw them carrying FitzClarence into the house. Bad enough any of us were captured, but he is a direct connection to the royal family. They can use him to get to his father, the Duke of Clarence, and he is Prinny's brother and the king's son. God above, why could they not have taken me instead?" His despairing voice seemed to cut the air.

Darcy must be beyond horror. Elizabeth could not imagine what it would do to him to watch his cousin kill herself. She reached out to him with that special sense. It was hard to hear him over Eversleigh's despair, but finally she found Darcy. He was unconscious. That was probably a blessing.

But what were they to do now?

A short time later, the somber group huddled in their private corner of Titania's bower. The failed rescue attempt had exhausted them all. Frederica had told Georgiana what little they knew, and now Georgiana sat next to Colonel Fitzwilliam while Frederica had Eversleigh's arm around her shoulder. Neither of her brothers even raised an objection. None of them had the heart for conversation, but no one wanted to go to sleep.

Finally Jasper Fitzwilliam spoke. "What next?"

Eversleigh sighed deeply. "Debenham does not know of your involvement in this, so you can go back to London whenever you wish, although eventually he will round up anyone with magic to bolster his own. While I was in London, I told my solicitor to look for a house in an isolated part of Scotland. I will purchase it under a false name and convert some of my funds into gold. We cannot stay in Faerie forever, and we will need a safe bolthole."

Frederica raised her head from his shoulder. "Surely you are not giving up?"

"I will never give up, but I have accepted there will be no quick victory. This is going to be a long struggle. We need time to find allies and to watch for weak points. To do that, we will need money and a safe place to retreat."

Elizabeth could not look at him. "What about Darcy?"

"If Anne de Bourgh could not break his wards, none of us has a chance. Debenham will not kill him, not while he has the death curse. Sooner or later he will set up some sort of prison for him. Our chances of rescuing him may be better when he is no longer surrounded by sorcerers."

"But my parents –" Frederica began.

Richard said heavily, "He is being realistic, Freddie. We need to retreat and lick our wounds until a better time."

"But in the meantime, the sorcerers will be consolidating their power!"

"We cannot win now," said Richard. "There is no point in throwing our lives away."

"What would our father say?" Frederica asked.

Eversleigh made a sound that might have been a distant relative of a laugh. "He would say Scotland is not far enough, but it is as far as I am willing to go. All of you are welcome to join me there if you wish. Libbet, I hope you will consent to come with me as my sister."

Elizabeth did not think her voice would work, so she merely nodded. It made more sense than any other option when Debenham knew she was betrothed to Darcy.

In a choked voice, Frederica said, "I suppose the Church of Scotland can perform a wedding as easily as the Church of England."

Eversleigh squeezed her shoulders silently.

Jasper sprang to his feet and began to pace. His brother and sister paid no attention. Elizabeth supposed it was a surprise he had sat still this long.

After a few minutes of frantic pacing, Jasper brought his hands together in front of his face. "I have an idea."

His brother said wearily, "The last thing we need is one of your crazy ideas."

Frederica turned her face away from Jasper.

With an irritated huff, Jasper squatted down next to Eversleigh. "Sir Lewis is controlling Debenham's body from his own, right? Magic is weaker with distance, so Sir Lewis's body must be very close. If we can find his body, we can kill him. Debenham would lose his sorcerous powers, and then...then we can decide what to do next. What do you think?"

Eversleigh said slowly, "It is an interesting thought. Even if we cannot kill him, we might learn more about how Sir Lewis operates."

"An interesting thought?" the colonel retorted. "It's a bloody brilliant thought. Jasper, for all your mad ideas over the years, this one makes up for quite a lot."

"It does?" Jasper sounded surprised.

Newly invigorated, Richard said, "We need to make a list of places he could be. Sir Lewis would want to keep his body secret from the others, so it is unlikely to be in the main house or the dower house. But the outbuildings... The stables are likely too busy, but are still a possibility. The threshing barn, the dovecote, the oast houses, the gatekeeper's lodge. We can rule out the gamekeeper's cottage since we were just there."

"Not the dovecote," said Georgiana in a small but steady voice. "I hid there after dark, and it was empty."

"Wait," said Eversleigh. "How will we check all these places? I cannot keep up this pace of invisibility, even with your replenishment."

"We can go after dark," said Colonel Fitzwilliam.

"Too dangerous," said Eversleigh. "They will be watching for us."

"This one is mine," said Jasper with a grin hardly in keeping with the circumstances. "No one there knows me. I can wear the laborer's clothes I used for the groundskeeper, and I have the local accent down. No one will suspect me."

"Until you get distracted," grumbled Richard.

Jasper's eyes flashed. "You can say anything you like about me, but the one thing I can do well is to copy an accent and play a role. I did it with the gamekeeper, and how many times have I fooled guests at Matlock House into thinking I was a stable boy?"

"It's true," said Frederica. "Jasper is a natural mimic."

"How will you get inside the buildings?" Richard was still far from convinced.

"I do not need to. I only have to discover which of those buildings is being guarded. That will be the one."

"Promise me you will not try to do anything more by yourself," Frederica pleaded.

"I promise," Jasper snapped. "Just because I can't use magic doesn't mean I can't do anything at all."

Confused, Elizabeth asked, "Why do you say you cannot use magic? You were doing it beautifully earlier."

Jasper grimaced. "I have magic, but it is for spell-making, like my father. If I could remember the words for a spell for ten minutes it might even be useful, but my memory is like a sieve."

"How do you suppose you were making all those magic fireballs, then?"

He shook his head. "You were making the fireballs. I just threw them for you because I could get them further."

"What do you mean? That was how it started, but I was not making them fast enough for you, so you started making them yourself." What was wrong with him? Did he have problems with his memory, too?

"I don't even know how to make fireballs! I tell you, my magic is useless!"

So that was it. Elizabeth even managed a ghost of a smile. "You wanted more fireballs, so they appeared. That was wild magic, the same kind I have, and yours is very strong."

Jasper looked taken aback. "Wild magic? What is that?"

Eversleigh said, "It is instinctive use of magic, without recourse to spells."

"You mean I can do magic without spells?" Jasper's voice rose on the last words. "Why did no one ever tell me?"

"I doubt anyone realized," said Elizabeth soothingly. "Your father knew almost nothing about wild magic before he met me. He would give anything to be able to use it himself, but he has spent too many years casting spells." She almost added that Anne had wild magic, too, before she remembered Anne would never be using magic again.

"Will you show me more? Right now?"

Nothing could be done about finding Sir Lewis's body before morning, and Elizabeth would run mad if she spent those hours brooding about Anne's death and Darcy's captivity. Perhaps she could even do a little good while she distracted herself. "Certainly. Let us go outside the bower, though."

Frederica did not even ask to watch.

Darcy yawned, but it was pointless to even think about sleep. Even with his eyes open, he kept seeing the image of Anne's face falling into the basin of water and hearing the thump of her limp body falling to the floor. Closing his eyes only made it more vivid.

Had he done the right thing? Should he have helped her? Could he have somehow talked her out of it? Damnation, how many times was he going to keep asking himself these same unanswerable questions! It did no good to think about what he would have wanted if he faced imminent blinding and being placed in a sorcerous binding spell. Imagining her dilemma just made his stomach churn. Instead, he said yet another prayer for her soul, asking God to forgive her for taking her own life. No point in asking for forgiveness for himself; he could not yet make himself repent of his actions. He could still do one thing for her, though, and that was to keep her name clear of the stigma of suicide. Without any other witnesses to her death, he could say it was a misplaced spell.

He had considered her liaison with Aelfric to be foolhardy and reckless, but now he was glad of it. At least she had that brief happiness.

The door opened and Debenham walked in. "Out," he said to the guard, jerking his thumb back over his shoulder.

The guard scurried away. Debenham closed the door behind him.

It was easier to think of him as Debenham. If he thought too hard about Sir Lewis living in Debenham's body, his stomach might rebel and bring up the remainder of his dinner. Taking over a man's life was an unimaginable crime.

Debenham pulled up a chair and sat facing Darcy. "Your friends seemed to have a very accurate idea of where you and Prince Aelfric were."

"Apparently so."

Debenham narrowed his eyes. "How did they know?"

"You would have to ask them that. I did not waste their time with questions." It would have been a good response to make to a Sidhe – true but misleading.

"Come, come, Darcy. I imagine you have some idea."

Darcy shrugged. "You want ideas? Perhaps they bribed a servant for the information. Or it could have been Eversleigh. You saw him turn invisible. Maybe he has been peering in the windows. He might be standing right next to you now for all I know. Perhaps Prince Aelfric has some fay method of silent communication and was able to tell the fay where he was. Choose whatever theory you like best."

"Eversleigh is an interesting possibility. I am impressed he can conceal himself so well. I can do so, too, but it requires sorcerous power. But who is to say Eversleigh has not availed himself of the same power?"

Darcy gave a scornful laugh. "I think not."

"One never knows. You have been taken by surprise by sorcery already, I would guess."

He inclined his head. "Indeed, it was only a few months ago that we learned you were a sorcerer. Sir Lewis, that is. You hid that well."

Debenham looked pleased. "I know. Matlock sent me a groveling letter to apologize for having missed the signs. It was most amusing."

"No doubt. I have been curious how you managed your disappearance, though. How did a blind man find a way to make himself disappear with his notebook and enough money to live on? The servants must have seen you, if nothing else. Lady Catherine never reported discovering a theft." Perhaps he might discover some useful nugget of information.

Debenham chuckled. "You are missing the obvious, my friend. Lady Catherine arranged my disappearance. She took one look at my ruined face and decided she would rather have a dead husband than a blind and disfigured one. She was willing to give me anything I asked, as long as I vanished."

Lady Catherine had a great deal to answer for. "Why did you agree to leave? It was your house and your money."

"It was an opportunity to devote myself to my research. Not be interrupted by long dinners, callers, estate business, bah! And I did not want to be pitied for my affliction. I knew I would have eyes again soon enough, so Sir Lewis had to appear to die in any case. That was as good a time as any."

"So you left?"

"After a few weeks of recovery in the attic." Debenham smirked.

But still, blinded mages could not perform magic. "How could you do spells without your eyes?"

"Good luck, or perhaps good planning on my part. I had a servant whose mind was already under my control, and I learned quickly how to see through his eyes. It is astonishing how much progress one can make when truly motivated."

"I suppose you practiced on the servants until you found Debenham. Or were there others in between?" The words left a foul taste in Darcy's mouth.

"A few. I needed to become proficient before I tried it on a skilled mage, one with powerful enough magic to accomplish my goals."

Now the question Darcy really wanted the answer to. "How long have you been Debenham?"

The sorcerer took a moment to think. "About eight years. Since poor Debenham had that odd apoplexy. He was never the same afterwards, you know. Even his speech sounded a little different. Everyone was very sympathetic and congratulated me on my miraculous recovery. I moved to Ireland before anyone started asking questions about the odd gaps in my memory, and I have stayed there ever since, apart from brief visits for Collegium business. Those meetings were very useful for recruiting other sorcerers. And that fool Matlock never saw what was going on under his own nose! I am half-tempted to tell him the truth, but there is no point in taking the risk."

Darcy leaned back in his chair. "Yes, I imagine you are eager to keep Biggins and Wickham in the dark. Otherwise they might not be so cooperative if you try to take their bodies."

"Precisely. And you will not tell them, Darcy." Debenham's smile was a threat. "You know now what I am capable of."

"If you think I care about what horrible fate awaits either Wickham or Biggins, you could not be more mistaken."

"I knew you were not a fool, Darcy."

Why was Debenham revealing so much to him? Surely he could not think Darcy would ally with him, after Anne's death and knowing that he was a stealer of bodies. And while he might be telling his secrets, he did not act like someone wishing to gain Darcy's trust.

The answer came to him abruptly. Sir Lewis had not been able to tell anyone his story since he left Rosings all those years ago. He wanted to boast of his achievements and show how clever he was. Well, if he wanted to talk, Darcy would give him that chance. Sooner or later, the information might be useful, and it was not as if he had anything else to do. "I have a question, purely to satisfy my own curiosity. What do you hope to do when you take over the government?"

"I do not plan to take it over, just to ensure that certain decisions are made. I have no desire for the work of ruling the country and fighting wars."

"What do you want, then?"

Debenham smiled, his eyes dilated. "Apart from riches? Repeal of the laws against sorcery. I refuse to spend the rest of my life hiding my talents. I have great plans for England."

Darcy shuddered inwardly. The man was out of his mind. England would pay an enormous price for his insanity, and there was not a damned thing he could do to stop it. "You will have to accomplish them without my help."

The sorcerer shrugged, his eyes narrowing. "As you wish, although you may yet see the foolishness of your ways. But that is enough for tonight. Sleep well, Darcy."

As if he would ever sleep again.

It was well past midnight when Wickham strolled into the library that had become Darcy's prison. "Well, well. The omnipotent Darcy, brought low at last."

Darcy had known Wickham would not be able to resist coming to gloat, but after watching Anne die, it seemed like pointless pettiness. "So it would seem," he said indifferently.

"I had not expected the pleasure of a true conversation with you since you were supposed to be under a binding spell. I knew you would hate that, even more than I hated being expelled from the Collegium. I should not be surprised, since my spells never worked on you, either."

"It would have been so much simpler for you if they had worked. You would not have had to go to all the trouble of setting up the dry wells and bespelling the Board of Inquiry." Let Wickham see he had not been fooled.

Wickham laughed. "So, you guessed that much."

Darcy shrugged. "I had an enlightening conversation with Prince Aelfric about you."

Wickham clasped his hand to his chest in a pretense of surprise. "You have had dealings with Faerie? I am shocked."

"I am certain you enjoyed tricking him into helping you. Tell me, as his liege man, do you feel even the slightest guilt over his current predicament?" Darcy had tried reaching his senses out to Aelfric once, thinking that since they were now *shurinn*, it might work. He had connected, but Aelfric had been too blindly angry to notice.

"Not at all. He was useful to me as a conduit to Oberon, nothing more."

Oberon? How had Oberon come into the picture? "No doubt you found ways to use him as well."

"Of course. He never questioned all my hints that mortals were deliberately trying to destroy the groves. His little war did not go as far as we had hoped, but one cannot have everything. Perhaps I should visit him again and see if he is more receptive."

Wickham had been the force behind Oberon's distrust of mortals? And he was unaware Oberon had gone into retirement. "What did you hope to gain from that?"

Wickham smiled. "Debenham thought it would distract the government and the Collegium from looking for sorcerers. No one seemed to care, though. Did he mention to you that he has promised me Pemberley?"

Bile burned Darcy's throat. "I cannot say I am surprised, except that you are settling for so little."

Wickham employed his familiar, charming smile. "I have never been particularly ambitious, you know. As long as I have revenge on you and all the money and women I want, I do not care who runs the country. Perhaps I will look up dear Georgiana again. She does not share your invulnerability to sorcery, you know."

It would only encourage Wickham if Darcy showed him any emotion. "I know. As you say, we cannot have everything." Darcy yawned ostentatiously. "Debenham's generosity to me does not go as far as a bed, but I sleep well enough in this chair. I could wish for a better selection of books, but I can only blame Lady Catherine for that."

"You do not fool me, Darcy. You detest being powerless to stop me, but you should have thought of that before you took advantage when I had no power. Now the tables are turned." He made a mocking bow. "Do sleep well, Darcy. I certainly shall." He left with a jaunty wave.

Darcy finally let himself feel the fury choking him. Damn Wickham, and damn him again for knowing his every weak spot. But at least he had said nothing about Darcy's ability with fire. Either he was too lazy to bother thinking out the implications, or he assumed Debenham had taken care of it already.

Not that it mattered now. Burning down Rosings would not kill Sir Lewis, so there was no point. Now Darcy had no options at all.

The next morning, Jasper Fitzwilliam set off cheerfully for Rosings before dawn dressed as a common workman with a talisman to work the faerie rings in his pocket, but he took all the good spirits in the group with him. By the time the sun was well up in the sky, Elizabeth had begun to worry. The outbuildings at Rosings were not far apart, and it should take less than half an hour to visit them all.

Frederica picked at the fabric of her skirt. "I wish we had not let him go." Her voice trembled.

"Jasper? He will be fine," said Colonel Fitzwilliam a little too heartily.

"You cannot know that. He is so easily distracted." A tear rolled down her cheek.

Elizabeth said, "He knows how important this is, and he will not let us down. He has some new skills, too. Last night, when neither of us could sleep, I taught him how to cast illusions with wild magic."

"Could he actually do it?" asked the colonel sharply.

"As if he had been doing it all his life. I would have said wild magic ran in his blood rather than spell-making, and quite powerfully. He will be a force to reckon with when he has more experience."

"It starts as the same thing," said Eversleigh.

Frederica burst into tears. Her brother had his arm around her even before Eversleigh reached her.

"He'll be back soon. You will see," said the colonel.

She buried her face in her handkerchief. Between sobs, she managed to choke out, "He is my little brother. That man has already taken our parents, Darcy, and Anne. I cannot bear it if he takes Jasper, too."

The tears that were now never far from Elizabeth's eyes threatened to escape. She stood up jerkily and walked out into the main area of the bower, where Titania was listening to a dryad playing the harp. How could the dryads and sprites seem so carefree in face of this looming disaster? But sorcerers in the mortal world would have little effect on their lives. Unless they cared about Aelfric, no one they loved was at risk.

Eversleigh spoke from beside her. "When I visited my solicitor, I added a codicil to my will. If I do not survive this, you will receive a lifetime allowance, enough that you need not worry about having a roof over your head or food to eat."

Elizabeth turned to him in surprise. "That is generous of you, but quite unnecessary. I do have family who will support me." At least for the time being, and if they could do so safely. Just two days ago she thought to be the mistress of Pemberley, and now she might have no home at all.

"I did it for my own peace of mind. I can face the prospect of death with a little less cowardice if I know the people I care about will be taken care of."

"I would very much prefer that you do not die." Her breath caught on the words.

"Ah, but only a fool would deny that it is a real possibility, not least because I might, like Anne de Bourgh, find myself in the situation where the cost of saving my life is too high."

There was no answer to that. "What of finding Sir Lewis's body? Do you think that can work?"

"Finding his body? Yes. Killing him? No. Sir Lewis is not a fool. He will have his body well-guarded. We could not reach Darcy through his wards. Would he defend his own life less?"

Elizabeth bit her lip. "What about a gun? Can the wards stop a bullet? Or protect from a fire?"

"His wards are beyond my understanding. And we may never find out where he is. Jasper Fitzwilliam should have been back by now."

Across the bower, Titania gasped. "I will return shortly." She swept out of the bower.

"What was that?" Eversleigh asked.

Elizabeth shrugged. "I do not know."

But Titania was already returning. "Prince Evlan, Libbet, come with me."

Elizabeth exchanged a puzzled glance with Eversleigh as they followed Titania out of the bower. The Faerie Queen led them off the usual path into a stand of trees.

Oberon stood in the middle of it.

Eversleigh stiffened. "Honored father."

"Where is Aelfric?" Oberon bit out the words.

"He has been taken prisoner in the mortal world by dark magicians, three of them. He is trapped in an iron structure at a place called Rosings Park."

"What has been done to recover him?"

Eversleigh said, "My mortal friends and I attempted a rescue last night, but we failed. I still hope to defeat the dark magicians, who also hold two mortals of your acquaintance, Lord Matlock and Diarcey. Fighting so many dark magicians at once may be beyond our powers, but we will not stop trying while they hold Aelfric prisoner."

"Show me," commanded Oberon.

Eversleigh stepped forward and bowed his head. Oberon laid his palm on Eversleigh's forehead. The two stood like statues for a long moment. Removing his hand, Oberon vanished without a word, leaving them in silence.

"What is he going to do?" asked Elizabeth hesitantly.

"Who can say?" Titania turned away as she spoke and returned to her bower. The conversation was clearly over.

"If I had to guess," said Eversleigh slowly, "I suspect he plans to offer himself in exchange for Aelfric. He would do anything to free him."

"But then he will be a prisoner."

"He might be able to trick his way out of it. Debenham is no match for Oberon's cunning, even in his decline. But Oberon no longer cares what happens to him. His life is already over." Eversleigh looked grim. "This was a major violation of Sidhe rules. After they retire in their decline, they never see or speak to another Sidhe."

"He must love Aelfric very much," said Elizabeth. Poor Eversleigh, having to trade his father for his brother!

"If you and I can sense Aelfric's pain, Oberon must feel it ten times more. Nothing less could have brought him out of retirement." Eversleigh rubbed his forehead. "I hope he can free him. But we might as well return to our own planning. I doubt we will hear from Oberon again." There was a dreadful finality in his voice.

# Chapter 18

Wickham strode into the room followed by four retainers. "Up, Darcy. You have a special visitor, a dear old friend of mine. He refuses to come inside the house, so you must go to him. Each of you take one of the wards. Do not let them touch your skin, only your gloves. Darcy, you walk in the middle."

"A visitor?" Darcy did not expect it to be a pleasant surprise since Wickham sounded so pleased by the news. Darcy would not give him the satisfaction of showing any fear, so he simply walked between the ward-bearing servants. Would they be able to stay close enough to the original positions of the wards for the boundary to be maintained? If a side was stretched too far, it might break, and he would need to seize his opportunity. The servants walked with military precision, though. A benefit of sorcerous control, no doubt.

Outside the bright sun made his eyes water. There was movement at the far end of the lawn, but he could not tell who it was. His guards led him past Debenham, Biggins, and their minions towards the visitor.

Darcy's eyes widened. It was Oberon, his crown glinting in the sun, prowling across the lawn like a predatory panther. But Oberon was no longer king, was he? Eversleigh said he had gone into retirement because he had grown too irritable and impulsive. Yet here he was, looking every inch the king. An angry, impulsive Sidhe king.

Darcy stopped when the servants set the wards down. Only then did he notice Lord Matlock standing in the middle of the lawn, his shoulders sagging, his stocky form casting a long shadow in the morning sunlight. Wickham returned to stand beside the house with Debenham and Biggins.

Debenham called to Oberon, "You can see they are both unharmed. Now, what are your terms?"

Oberon's upper lip curled. "My terms are thus: I will perform no magic on any mortal, nor cause physical harm. Should any mortal attempt to harm me, that same harm shall befall each of you, but twice trebled." Oberon strode between Darcy and Lord Matlock to stand before a terrified looking servant. The Sidhe held out his arm. "Pinch me."

The servant's mouth worked, but no sound came out.

"Pinch me!" Oberon's chiming voice echoed and rebounded.

The servant obeyed. Oberon did not flinch, but Debenham cried out in pain. Wickham and Biggins clutched at their arms.

Oberon turned back to the sorcerers. "Guard my safety as you would your own. An arrow or bullet from a mortal hand will have the same effect."

"Do you guarantee not to kill us if you remain safe?" Debenham's voice carried, but it was not as even as usual.

"I have said so." Oberon might have been speaking to misbehaving children.

"For our terms –"

Oberon interrupted Debenham. "I do not wish to hear your terms yet." Instead he stalked towards Darcy, all golden power, a world apart from the simple scribe Darcy had met in Faerie. His eyes seemed to pierce straight through him. "You will bear witness, and you will tell my sons." It was unquestionably a command. Oberon turned on his heel without waiting for a response.

What was he supposed to witness? Had Oberon gone mad?

Now Oberon stood in front of Lord Matlock, but neither of them spoke. Lord Matlock fingered the gold ring on his hand. They must be speaking through the ring spell.

Oberon pointed at the ground. A large fiery circle sprung up in the grass around the two men. His voice oddly amplified, Oberon said, "Anyone who crosses that line will die."

The sorcerers conferred agitatedly among themselves.

Lord Matlock's blindfold vanished and a small snake appeared in Oberon's hand. He dropped it in the grass and crushed with his heel, just as Aelfric had done for Georgiana. Had he removed the spell on Lord Matlock? It would make no difference. Debenham would merely cast the spell again.

Oberon spoke to Lord Matlock in a conversational tone just loud enough for Darcy to hear. "Bright magic's circle has no beginning nor end."

Lord Matlock replied, "Mortal blood and fay shall bind."

"Dark magic blights the circle and all within."

"Mortal blood and fay shall bind," repeated Lord Matlock.

It sounded like a blood magic spell, but for what? To free Aelfric? Surely there must be a simpler way. Did Lord Matlock know Oberon was no longer in his right mind?

Oberon continued to speak, but his voice was low enough now that Darcy could only make out scattered words. Something about fay and mortal souls and withered hearts turned to stone. Lord Matlock's responses grew longer each time, and he stood tall once again.

Magic began to gather around them. Darcy could feel the vortex of it tugging at him, a pull so strong he could practically see the power of it. The circle of fire grew wider and brighter.

Oberon raised a silver knife, his expression exultant. "To this I spill my heart's blood." With animal-like grace, he slit his throat. Blood fountained from the wound onto the ground. He wore a frightening, otherworldly smile as he slowly sank to his knees and fell into the pool of blood.

But blood continued to pour as Lord Matlock dragged a matching silver knife across his own throat. His effort was less graceful and more horrifying. His lips moved in a silent prayer as his blood mingled on the ground with Oberon's, but he looked no less triumphant.

The sunlight suddenly became blinding. A crash louder than any thunder reverberated from every direction. The air seemed to shatter like glass as the earth shifted, knocking Darcy to his knees.

Lord Matlock crumpled to the ground beside Oberon, the flow of blood from his throat slowing to a trickle. The fiery circle flickered and faded to nothingness.

Stunned, Darcy could only stare at the bodies of his uncle and Oberon. A sapling no taller than his knee was already growing between them.

They had made a Great Spell together, the first since the time of Julius Caesar. It was beyond belief. The last Great Spell had sundered Faerie into two parts. What had this one done?

Nothing. Nothing had changed. His uncle and Oberon were dead, and Debenham, Wickham, and Baggins were still standing, seemingly unharmed.

Debenham strode forward, stopping just short of where the circle of fire had been. He snapped his fingers and pointed to a servant. "You there. Walk across the line."

The man's feet moved forward, but clearly against his will.

Debenham gave a sharp cry and pressed his fist against his chest. "What?" he gasped. He bent forward, his face screwed up in agony, and collapsed to the ground.

The wards surrounding Darcy sputtered and vanished. Debenham had been the one to set them. If the wards were dead, Debenham must be, too.

Biggins rushed forward. "Carry him inside! Fetch a doctor and –" His face turned ashen. His eyes huge, he reached out a hand and tumbled forward.

Darcy's mouth fell open. The Great Spell had worked. It had changed the laws of magic. Employing a sorcerous command spell was now a death sentence. Oberon and his uncle could not destroy sorcery itself, but now the choice to use sorcery would be a fatal one.

Wickham backed away from the scene with an expression of horror. He turned and bolted for the stables.

Darcy almost ran after him but stopped himself. There was no reason to chase him. Wickham was no longer a threat. He could be dealt with later.

"Mr. Darcy, sir." The butler's voice was unusually timid. "What should we do?"

A Great Spell, two dead sorcerers, a dead Sidhe and a peer of the realm, and the butler thought Darcy would know what should be done? "Free Prince Aelfric and ask him to come here." Aelfric might know something about how to handle the aftermath of a Great Spell. He could not possibly know less than Darcy did.

Elizabeth jumped as the earth seem to shiver. A bell tolled somewhere. No, it could not be a bell, because the sound came from all directions at once, echoing and re-echoing. The air took on that sharp tang that often followed lightning strikes. "What happened?"

"Magic of some sort. Powerful magic." Eversleigh held up a hand as if to test the air. "More than that I cannot say. Not sorcery, though."

Titania turned her face up to the sky with a plaintive, keening wail, an eerie fay version of a wolf's howl. Her face was lined with grief. "Oberon!" She ran from the bower.

Eversleigh jumped to his feet and followed her.

Frederica gave an exasperated sound. "Could he not have taken one second to tell us where he was going?"

Elizabeth closed her eyes and reached out her senses to Darcy. Something had changed for him. "Darcy is free. Something has astounded him, but he feels no danger now."

"Are you certain it is safe? Could it be a trick?"

Shaking her head, Elizabeth said, "Darcy thinks it is safe, and he cannot lie to me through this bond." At least she did not think he could.

"Let us go, then!" Frederica exclaimed.

Georgiana stood and shook out her skirt. "Where are we going?"

"Rosings," said Elizabeth with sudden certainty. "The Great Lawn." She should be more worried, but somehow she knew Darcy wanted her in that particular spot.

They emerged in the faerie ring in the grove. Colonel Fitzwilliam held his knife expectantly, as if it could guard them against sorcery. "Wait here," he told Georgiana. "I will come to get you if it is safe."

Georgiana nodded.

Elizabeth could feel Darcy's call more clearly now. She picked up her skirts and set off at a run through the grove, clambering past downed branches, around the Italian Garden and the west wing of the house. She skidded to a halt at the sight on the Great Lawn. Frightened servants huddled together on the steps of the house. The bodies of two men lay ignored in front of them. Were they dead? At the far end of the lawn, figures knelt in a ring around a sapling standing in a cloud of mist. Titania and Aelfric sat back on their heels in the fay manner. Eversleigh knelt in the human way beside Darcy. Brownies, dryads, gnomes, and even a few redcaps began to appear, joining those who knelt. Only Lady Matlock stood, her posture rigid.

Darcy, apparently sensing Elizabeth's presence, looked over his shoulder. He said something to Eversleigh before standing and striding towards Elizabeth.

"What in God's name is that?" Colonel Fitzwilliam demanded as he caught up to her.

"Mama looks unhappy," said Frederica warily.

Elizabeth had eyes only for Darcy. She ran to him, unable to control herself any longer. His arms closed around her, warming the frozen void within her.

Darcy pressed his cheek against the top of her head for all too brief a moment. Without releasing her, he said, "Richard, Freddie, wait. There is something I must tell you." Tension coiled in his body.

Elizabeth stepped back. Only a little, and she kept her hand on his arm because she could not quite bear to let go.

"Your father and Oberon performed a Great Spell to put an end to sorcery." Darcy's voice was rough.

"A Great Spell?" Frederica said haltingly. "But that means..."

"Yes," said Darcy. "They are both dead. They gave their lives to banish sorcery from our world. We are honoring their sacrifice."

Frederica gave a gasping cry. Colonel Fitzwilliam's face froze.

A Great Spell. Elizabeth dropped her hand from Darcy's arm. His first duty now was to his bereaved cousins.

Slowly they walked down the lawn together, Frederica choking back tears. When they reached the circle, Colonel Fitzwilliam silently knelt beside Lady Matlock. Frederica hesitated before going to her mother's other side and kneeling in the fay manner. Her shoulders shook with silent sobs. If Lady Matlock noted the arrival of her children, it was not obvious.

Elizabeth looked back over her shoulder at the house and froze, a shiver running down her spine. Could she be seeing correctly? She whispered to Darcy, "Eversleigh told us your cousin Anne was dead."

He gazed down at her with a sober expression. "It is true."

"But look!" She pointed at the portico where Anne stood in the doorway.

Darcy's eyes widened, and he took off at a run. Elizabeth followed him at a slightly more sedate pace, reaching them just as Anne pushed herself out of Darcy's embrace. "Good Lord, Darcy, what is wrong with you?"

"I thought you were dead!"

"I thought so, too," said Anne testily. "But then I woke up a little while ago. I hid until I realized the house was empty, and...what in heaven's name is going on out here?"

Elizabeth left Darcy to make the explanations as she hurried down the hill to tell Frederica and Richard the news. And there, kneeling beside Richard, was Jasper, looking completely disreputable in his laborer's clothes and reeking of ale, but alive.

"He must have brought me back somehow and used a spell to keep me unconscious," Anne told Darcy. "The last thing I remember is getting dizzy as the whirlwind stole my breath."

The image of Anne's head falling into the bowl of water wrenched at Darcy's chest. "Then you must have awakened when Debenham died, and his spell along with him."

Anne frowned. "Debenham is dead, but what of Sir Lewis? Could he have survived the death of Debenham's body?"

"Good God! I had not thought of that. Where would his body be?"

"How would I know?"

"Pardon me." How could he have missed that possibility? Darcy strode down to the spell circle and grasped Richard's shoulder. "I am sorry to disturb you. Did Eversleigh tell you Sir Lewis was in Debenham's body? We need to find Sir Lewis's body and make certain he is dead. Can you help me?"

Richard's eyes widened, and he scrambled to his feet. "We had been trying to do that already. Jasper, did you find him?"

"In the old oast house, with half a dozen guards. They wanted me to bring them ale, so I did. They would not talk about what they were guarding, but it has to be him."

Lady Matlock turned her head to them, her expression frozen. "Did you say Sir Lewis?"

"Freddie can explain," Richard said distractedly. "We must go."

The oast house was not far away. Darcy, Richard, and Jasper reached it in a few minutes. A cluster of guards stood in front of it, but they were arguing with each other, not guarding it.

One of the guards looked up as they approached. "Who are you?"

"I am Fitzwilliam Darcy. Debenham is dead and I am in charge now."

The guard touched his forehead. "Glad someone is. We don't rightly know how we got here. Sounds odd, I know, but that's the way it is."

"Explanations can wait." Richard reached for the door latch.

Darcy pulled him back. "I will go in first. His spells do not work on me." He strode into the oast house. It was dark inside, but he could easily make out the slumped figure in a chair. The upper half of his face was a ruin of craters and scars. The horrific sight made him gag.

Trying not to look at his face, Darcy put his hand on Sir Lewis's chest. Nothing. No heartbeat, no breathing. "You can come in. He is dead. It is over." Over. Thank God!

Richard was the first to enter, a pistol in each hand. He must have taken them from the guards. At Sir Lewis's corpse, he raised one pistol and shot him point blank through the chest. Switching hands, he sent a bullet from the other pistol through the sorcerer's head.

Darcy turned his head away from the sight. "He was already dead."

"I know," said Richard. "I wanted to make sure he stayed that way this time."

"Good." It was Anne's quiet voice coming from behind him.

"Come out with me," Darcy said. "You do not want to see this."

"Yes, I do." Anne stepped past him and stared down at Sir Lewis's body, her lip curled in disdain.

Elizabeth was waiting for Darcy outside the oast house. "I know I should not be here, but I am not yet ready to let you out of my sight."

Darcy took her hand. "I could not agree more."

Richard emerged and handed the pistols back to the guards. He took a step towards them and stopped suddenly. "Oh, God. I forgot about Georgiana!"

Darcy's skin prickled with fear. "What happened to Georgiana?"

"Nothing," said Elizabeth quickly. "Your cousin told her to wait in the grove while he made sure it was safe here, but then we found out about the Great Spell and forgot everything else."

Poor Georgiana must be frantic. "I will fetch her," Darcy said. "You stay with the others."

With a trace of her old archness, Elizabeth said, "Did you not hear me say I will not let you out of my sight? I am coming with you. Do not worry; I am certain that in ten or twenty years I might be willing to be separated for a matter of minutes."

Even after these horrible days, she had the same power to enchant him as always. "If you are expecting a complaint for me, you will be waiting a long time." He leaned down and brushed her lips with his.

More fay arrived throughout the afternoon, including many of the Sidhe. King Cathael was one of the first to appear. For all their tendency to immediate action, the fay seemed to believe they should simply remain beside the Great Spell, so the mortals did the same. The tree continued to grow visibly.

As the sun finally dipped below the horizon, Titania stood and asked, "Are we all gathered now?"

It was hard to answer without knowing who she thought should be there in the first place, but there were enough murmurs of assent that Titania seemed satisfied. Her silver dagger appeared in her hand. "Now we will honor Matlock and Oberon by binding their spell." Titania glided forward into the circle, stopping just short of the mist covering the bodies. She lifted her knife and slashed her palm, holding her hand out so drops of blood fell into the mist. "I give my blood to bind. Titania, *eliarinn* to Oberon." She walked back to the others and handed the dagger to Lady Matlock.

Lady Matlock studied the dagger, as if uncertain what she was to do with it. At Titania's gesture, she stepped up to the mist, hesitated, and cut her fingertip. "I give my blood to bind. Eleanor, wife to Matlock."

As Lady Matlock exited the circle, Eversleigh claimed the dagger from her and followed suit. "I give my blood to bind. Evlan, son to Oberon and friend to Matlock." He brought the dagger to a startled looking Colonel Fitzwilliam.

The Colonel might have been surprised, but his military bearing showed as he marched forward and cut his hand. "I give my blood to bind. Richard, son to Matlock."

Aelfric awaited him. "I give my blood to bind. Aelfric, son to Oberon."

Eversleigh whispered in Frederica's ear.

She raised her eyebrows but stood and took the dagger from Aelfric. Her chin up, she walked forward and cut her finger without hesitation. "I give my blood to bind. Frederica, daughter to Matlock."

Eversleigh was beside Elizabeth. "You are next."

Elizabeth stared at him. "I? But I am not a relation."

"You are *shurinn* to Oberon, and through Darcy, you are kin to

Matlock. Go."

Elizabeth took a deep breath and took the dagger from Frederica, trying not to think of the bodies beneath the mist. She opened her palm, but at the last minute switched to her forefinger. It would be embarrassing if the blood did not flow. The dagger was unexpectedly sharp and she cut deeper than she had meant to. "I give my blood to bind. Libbet, *shurinn* to Oberon and kin to Matlock."

Her finger stung. She looked to Eversleigh who jerked his chin towards Jasper. Elizabeth took a few careful steps towards him, once again dizzy, much as she had been following their claiming of blood right. Darcy caught at her elbow as Jasper said, "I give my blood to bind. Jasper, son to Matlock."

Eversleigh said quietly, "You are next, Darcy."

"I give my blood to bind. Darcy, nephew to Matlock, and named by Oberon."

Miss Darcy was waiting for her brother. Eversleigh frowned and whispered to her but she shook her head. "I want to," she said.

Darcy looked reluctant to hand the dagger to his younger sister, but she reached up to take it from him, and he did not resist.

Miss Darcy's voice was so quiet Elizabeth could not make out her words. She flinched when she cut her finger.

Titania took back the dagger from her. "Are any other kin present today?"

Anne de Bourgh shook her head firmly. Apparently she believed Lady Catherine's story and did not consider herself related to Lord Matlock.

When no one responded, Cathael strode forward, a new knife in his hand. Instead of approaching the mist, he shed blood at the compass points: north, east, south and west. "I am Cathael, King of Faerie, and I ward this spell. Let no creature intending harm pass these wards." The lines between his wards glowed softly golden.

Titania followed the same path and added her blood at the four points. "I am Titania, Queen of Faerie, and I ward this spell." The lines brightened.

Eversleigh agitatedly whispered to Mr. FitzClarence, who was shaking his head. Eversleigh gave him a firm push forward. "The fay do not care about illegitimacy. They care about royal blood," he hissed.

Nervously FitzClarence came forward, his hands shaking. He had to cut a second finger to get enough blood for the final ward. "I am Henry, grandson to King George, and I ward this spell." The glowing lines flared. FitzClarence staggered as he walked away.

Cathael raised his arms. "The Great Spell is bound and warded. Let the names of Oberon and Matlock live forever in blessed memory." His words echoed and re-echoed.

A chill went down Elizabeth's spine.

An odd pressure had begun to weigh on Darcy's shoulders. "Elizabeth, will you stay with Georgiana for a few minutes?"

"Of course. Is something the matter?"

"No, simply something I had forgotten to tell Eversleigh and Aelfric. I will return shortly."

He found Eversleigh and Aelfric standing with Cathael. "Pardon me for interrupting. There is something I need to tell Oberon's sons. Just before casting the Great Spell, Oberon came to me. I did not know what he intended to do, but he commanded me to bear witness and to tell his sons what I had seen." The weight vanished. Oberon must have put magic into his command.

"You witnessed the spell?" asked Eversleigh in surprise.

Darcy had forgotten none of the others had been there at the time. "Yes. The sorcerers and some of the servants did as well, but I was the closest. Biggins had brought me there because Oberon demanded proof that I was unharmed."

Aelfric's gaze turned towards the tree. "I wish to hear it, but this tale does not belong only to us."

"You are correct," said Cathael. He strode to the edge of the circle and clapped his hands for attention. "I have just learned that Diarcey, nephew to Matlock and named by Oberon, stood witness to the Great Spell. Would you hear his tale?"

An affirmative chorus arose from the gathered fay.

"Damn it," muttered Darcy.

"Sorry, my friend," said Eversleigh. "It is expected. Tell everything, every detail you can remember, no matter how irrelevant. The color of the grass. The clouds in the sky. What the servants were wearing. Paint a picture." He took Darcy's elbow and led him to Cathael.

Darcy raked his hand through his hair. He hated speaking to a crowd. "Must I?"

"Yes."

A bright glow appeared over his head as he stood next to Cathael, illuminating Darcy's face. Good God, how was he supposed to do this? He cleared his throat. "I am new to bearing witness, so I hope you will permit Prince Evlan and King Cathael to remind me of what is necessary to tell you." His voice sounded strange to him. One of the Sidhe must be amplifying it to make it carry.

There was murmur of assent.

Cathael said, "Start by telling us who you are."

That should not be too hard. "I am Diarcey, nephew to Matlock and named by Oberon, and I am an elemental mage. I was captured by the dark magicians –"

Cathael made a hissing noise. "Who is your father? Where were you born? How did you come to Faerie?"

Good God. This was not going to be quick. "I am the son of

George Darcy, also an elemental mage, and Lady Anne Darcy, sister to Matlock. I was born in the north of England." What else? Surely they did not wish to know where he went to school. "My first lessons in magic came from my father, and later from Lord Matlock."

"Tell them what you told me, about learning to manage your elemental magic," said Eversleigh.

"What does that have to do with it?" Darcy whispered to him in annoyance. Did he really have to expose his most embarrassing childhood moments?

"It is part of your story," said Cathael firmly. "We need to know who is telling us this tale."

Darcy sighed in defeat. "It is not easy to grow up as an elemental mage in the mortal world. In Faerie I do not struggle with the elements, but in the mortal world, until I learned control of my skills, water would jump out at me, and I would start fires without intending to...." At least it became easier as he told it.

It was nearly a quarter of an hour before he reached his university years. Eversleigh gave him a brief reprieve, speaking in his place about the training of mages and the work of the Collegium, but he insisted Darcy tell the tale of Wickham's expulsion from the Collegium. Darcy managed to jump straight from that to the Board of Investigation. He was not going to tell the world about Georgiana and Wickham. That was not part of his story, but Elizabeth was, so he told of meeting her in Hertfordshire, his attraction to her and his rejected proposal, the boy bitten by the redcap, and the fear of fay attacks. It took another quarter hour to reach his first journey to Faerie.

He could not complain of an unappreciative audience. The fay, even the Sidhe, were listening with rapt attention. They murmured sympathetically at the tale of his proposal and laughed when he told the story of the gnome who made them ride to Cathael's keep, but it was a friendly laugh. Someone put a glass of faerie wine in his hand when his mouth became dry, and that helped, too.

Cathael told of Darcy and Elizabeth's appearance in his keep and learning the mortals knew nothing of the Great Treaty. The listeners reflected his surprise, and suddenly Darcy understood that the new king intended his story to educate the fay about the lives and beliefs of mortals. Somehow that made it easier, even though it seemed as if he would be talking half the night.

After it was finally over, Darcy collapsed beside Elizabeth and lay back in the grass.

"You must be exhausted," Elizabeth said softly. "You did very well, my love."

"I hope I never have to do that again. I feel singularly inobservant because I could not tell them the precise angle of the sun at the time of the Great Spell."

"For what it is worth, I feel as if I know you much better now." Elizabeth leaned down and kissed his forehead.

Georgiana's quiet voice seemed to come out of nowhere. "So do I, and I am glad."

At least some good had come of it.

Eversleigh squatted down next to him. "You have my deepest thanks. You did more tonight to help the fay understand mortals than I have managed in all these years."

"What happens now?" asked Elizabeth.

"The Sidhe and the lesser fay will keep vigil until sunrise, but they will not expect us to do so. They understand mortal strength is limited."

"Especially after the binding ritual. I can feel my magic shifting again." Elizabeth rubbed her arms. "I am worried about Mr. FitzClarence. It is hitting him hard."

"I am perfectly fine," said the young mage bravely, even though sweat poured off his forehead, his hands shook, and his face was ashen in the twilight. "Nothing wrong with me except that Prinny is going to murder me when he discovers I accepted a royal role."

"Unlikely, as he has no magic of his own, so he would have been unable to do it even if he had been here. It was sheer good luck that we had you." Eversleigh reached past Elizabeth to touch the back of FitzClarence's hand. "You are burning up with magic."

"You told me this would be the easiest assignment I would ever have, and look at me now," grumbled Mr. FitzClarence.

"How much easier can an assignment be than to flirt with Titania? I did not realize there would be sorcerers, a Great Spell, and blood bindings thrown into the mixture. You will have some interesting powers when this is over. If you were planning to be a minor mage, you may be in for a disappointment."

"Why is it so much worse for him?" asked Elizabeth.

"We merely shared blood to bind a spell, even if it was a Great Spell. FitzClarence created a shared blood ward with two Sidhe, and Sidhe magic is moving within him," said Eversleigh. "FitzClarence, I think you would be wise to remain in Titania's company for the next few days. She will be able to help you through this transition. I will speak to her about it."

"I certainly have no objection to that," said Mr. FitzClarence.

Elizabeth asked, "Lord Eversleigh, how did you know what to tell us to do in the binding ceremony? I cannot imagine you were aware of what happened at the last Great Spell."

"Hardly," said Eversleigh. "Fay ceremonies tend to follow a pattern, so I could guess what was coming once Titania began it. It was similar to what is done when one of the Sidhe is accidentally killed."

"Your years in Faerie have proved quite useful."

"It seems so," said Eversleigh. "And now, FitzClarence, let us go to Titania together. You can lean on me if you need the support."

FitzClarence nodded, clearly too exhausted to argue as he struggled to his feet.

"And then, *shurinn*, you will oblige me by sitting down next to Frederica or Aelfric and quieting that nervous mind of yours," said Elizabeth tartly. "You have been even more affected by the last two days than I have been, and you need to rest. It will do none of us any good if you collapse from weariness."

Eversleigh's mouth twisted. "Did Frederica ask you to say that?"

Elizabeth shook her head. "I fear it is simply obvious that you will not stop of your own free will, even when you should."

"Very well, *shurinn*. I will do so, since you insist."

After Eversleigh left, Darcy asked, "Does he have to obey you when you call him *shurinn*?"

Elizabeth considered. "No, but it is a reminder of the obligations we owe each other. If he had a compelling reason to disobey, he could do so. But if he simply does not wish to do what I ask, yes, he would be expected to listen to me."

"I used to wonder why you did whatever he asked. I thought it might bespeak an understanding between you, and I did not like it one bit."

"Oh, no. Simply *shurinn*." With an arch look, she added, "The same rules apply for *eliarinn*, but employ that power at your own risk."

Darcy whispered in her ear, "I would far rather have you willing than compelled."

Heat suffused Elizabeth's body. Tomorrow they would become one flesh, yet it seemed wrong to have such feelings when the bodies of Oberon and Lord Matlock lay yet unburied under the mist. Suddenly she stiffened.

"What is wrong, Elizabeth?" Darcy asked.

"Nothing." She did not want to be the one to point out the

obvious.

"It is not nothing. I can feel it."

Of course he could. It would take time to get used to this bond. "Nothing of import. I realized we cannot be married tomorrow after all, since you are in mourning for your uncle."

Darcy frowned. "There must be a way. My aunt insisted it must be done as soon as possible, and I am in complete agreement with her."

"It can still be soon," she said slowly, trying to bury her own disappointment. "But it cannot be the day after your uncle's death."

Darcy's nostrils flared. "I will speak to my aunt tomorrow." His tone indicated he did not intend to tolerate much delay.

A subdued group gathered for breakfast the next morning. No one appeared well rested. Although there had been no time to obtain mourning clothes, everyone had chosen to wear dull colors, greys and browns. Even the food seemed to be in mourning. Instead of the usual platters heaped with pastries, fruit, and meat, a paltry plate of toast and rolls sat on the sideboard.

Anne said, "I hope you will understand if service is somewhat lacking today. The staff are struggling to keep food out for the fay, and a few servants have fled out of fear of them. My housekeeper has recruited replacements in the village, but their inexperience shows."

That explained the limited array of breakfast foods. "Perhaps the servants will return after everything goes back to normal." Elizabeth helped herself to toast and jam.

"If they are frightened by Sidhe, it is better they leave," said Anne coolly. "Aelfric should not have to disguise himself when he is here."

It was definitely too early in the morning to discuss Anne's relationship with Aelfric, so Elizabeth said, "Did you see the tree this morning? The mist is gone, and the tree looks at least double the height it was last night." She did not mention that Lord Matlock's and Oberon's bodies had apparently disappeared along with the mist. She would rather have the Fitzwilliam family discover that on their own.

Anne buttered a slice of toast. "It will be a pleasant change. I never liked that view, anyway."

Lady Matlock swept into the room. "Good morning. I hope all of you slept well." She wore a dress of green striped muslin with gold trim and looked like a tropical bird alighting among a flock of sparrows.

Frederica looked accusingly at her mother's dress.

"That is a most unattractive expression, Frederica," said Lady Matlock. "You may wear mourning if you choose, but I will not. My husband had three great passions: spellcraft, a love of Faerie, and an absolute hatred of sorcery. Yesterday was the culmination of his life, not the end of it. I will grieve the personal loss I have suffered, but I will celebrate what he and King Oberon have done and be forever grateful my husband was given this extraordinary opportunity to create a living legacy."

"I am glad of it," said Anne. "I hate wearing black."

"I believe he would have agreed with you," said Darcy. "His final expression was one of triumph."

Lady Matlock nodded. "Thank you, Darcy. I am glad to know that. In the meantime, I have sent word to my eldest son of his father's death. Frederica, you will oblige me by beginning the study of defensive magic. I do not wish you ever to be in the position I was of knowing my magic might have helped to defend us, had I but chosen to learn to use it."

Frederica's eyes betrayed her shock. "Yes, Mama. As soon as I can find someone to teach me."

"Lord Eversleigh can teach you as soon as he has disbanded the Collegium."

Eversleigh choked on his coffee. "Well, I suppose that saves me the difficulty of breaking the news to you."

"It is hardly a difficult conclusion to draw. The Collegium's charter states its purpose as the prevention of sorcery, and that is no longer necessary."

Elizabeth was still trying to take in the radical idea of a world without the Collegium when Aelfric strolled in, sat down beside Anne and took her hand. "I just spoke to my father about you, and he was pleased to learn of our connection."

Anne tilted her head dubiously. "Your father?"

"Yes. Oberon is pleased."

A sudden silence descended upon the room. Elizabeth stared at Aelfric. What fay madness was this?

Eversleigh swallowed his last bite of food. "They can speak already? Excellent. There are several things I must ask Lord Matlock. Excuse me." He stood, tossed his napkin on the back of his chair, and left the room.

Frederica and Lady Matlock turned matching baleful looks on Elizabeth, as if somehow she ought to have an answer.

"Aelfric," Elizabeth said carefully, "I was under the impression that Oberon and Lord Matlock were, well, no longer alive."

"Of course they are alive," said Aelfric. "If they were dead, the spell would have died with them."

Elizabeth moistened her dry lips. "How can they be alive when they spilt their heart's blood?"

"Oak and ash, has no one taught you anything about Great Spells? Their blood and flesh have changed into the sacred tree, and they live within it."

It sounded impossible, but Eversleigh had not appeared surprised by the news. If Aelfric and Eversleigh both agreed on something, it most likely was true. "How can you speak to them if they are, um, within a tree? A tree has no mouth."

Aelfric shook his head, as if unable to comprehend her ignorance. "They can speak in our minds when we touch the tree."

Frederica said sharply, "They can recognize us?"

"Certainly." Aelfric reached for a roll. "They cannot focus on a conversation for long, but otherwise it is no different."

Darcy said slowly, "Eversleigh took us to the Great Spell in Faerie, and Lord Matlock talked to the tree there."

Frederica's chair scraped against the floor as she pushed it back. Without a word she ran from the room. Lady Matlock looked thoughtful.

Aelfric seemed unaware that his news had shocked anyone. "I am very glad to have my father's approval," he said to Anne. "That means he has no concerns about your parentage."

It might be true, but Elizabeth suspected Oberon's true concern was that his son should begin trying to sire another Sidhe as soon as possible. She took a sip of her coffee and eyed her remaining breakfast with regret. Frederica might well need a friend now. "If you will be so kind as to excuse me, I believe I should follow Frederica."

Anne shrugged. "If you wish."

How similar Anne's manners were to Aelfric's! Neither would ever learn the ways of polite society at this rate. Then again, Elizabeth herself might struggle with that now, given how readily she had accepted the notion of Lord Matlock and Oberon being transformed into a sentient tree capable of communication. Perhaps so many impossible things had happened of late that even this outrageously impossible thing seemed reasonable.

The oak tree seemed to have grown even since she had seen it out her window an hour ago. A carpet of poppies bloomed where they had spilled their blood to bind the spell. Elizabeth absently rubbed her thumb against the sore spot where she had cut her fingertip.

Frederica leaned against the tree trunk, her hands splayed against the bark and her eyes shut. Outside the wards, Eversleigh shook his head vigorously at something Titania was telling him. Cathael stood a short distance away, his posture soldier-like with his hands resting on the hilt of the silver sword, but without any threat in his stance.

More Sidhe and lesser fay had arrived during the night. How unfair it was that the Sidhe could remain so beautiful and flawless even after keeping watch all night! Elizabeth had slept in a bed, but even so, the weight of fatigue dragged at her.

Titania waved to her to join them. When Elizabeth reached her, the Faerie Queen said, "Libbet, you must help me convince this stubborn young *shurinn* of mine. I say he should claim blood right to Marigold Meadowsweet, and he will not oblige me."

Eversleigh said wryly, "I told her I have no objection to having blood right with her, but that the lady must be the one to make that decision, not I."

Titania pouted. "You are my *shurinn*, Prince Evlan, so you should follow my advice."

Which was more inexplicable, that Eversleigh was refusing a *shurinn* request from the Queen, or that Titania was involving herself in a personal matter of this sort in front of the spot where Oberon had slit his throat the day before? "Great queen, might I suggest a different approach? Marigold Meadowsweet can be stubborn and does not like it when any man claims something from her. She might deny Prince Evlan simply for making the claim. Perhaps you might suggest claiming blood right to her instead."

"A mere mortal cannot claim blood right to a prince of Faerie!" exclaimed Titania.

Elizabeth hid a smile. "Cannot or would not dare? In the mortal world, Marigold Meadowsweet is of high rank, and Prince Evlan is not a prince. If it is forbidden, there is nothing to be done for it, but if it is a matter of daring, I assure you that if she is agreeable to the blood right, she will certainly dare to claim it."

"I agree," said Eversleigh. "Nothing would delight her more than to flout custom."

Titania's tip-tilted eyes narrowed.

Elizabeth said hastily, "If nothing else, I pray you to allow Prince Evlan a chance to speak to her privately before taking such a step. It is his only chance at success."

The Faerie queen's anger seemed to dissipate as quickly as it had appeared. "Very well, but do not take too long about it." She turned away to speak to Cathael.

Eversleigh offered Elizabeth his arm and led her to the other side of the lawn where blankets had been spread on the ground for the comfort of mortals. She sat, and he sank down beside her.

He mopped his forehead with his handkerchief. "Good God! I have never resisted a *shurinn* request from a powerful Sidhe before. It was physically painful."

Elizabeth hid a smile. "I hope Frederica appreciates your sacrifice."

"As do I! But our understanding is still so fragile, and I dare not risk it, even to please Titania. I hope Lady Frederica agrees, though, since I do not know how much longer I can hold out."

"I am surprised Titania would be so insistent. My claim of blood right with Darcy must have put the idea in her head."

"It might have given her the idea, but this is a different matter. She knows we plan to marry, and she wants desperately to seal a blood bond between us before we conceive any children."

"My children with Darcy will not be enough?" How odd it felt to claim that as her future!

"Your children will carry her blood, but my children would carry both her blood and Oberon's. That is something she has never thought possible before."

And with Oberon dead, or at least turned into a tree, that desire would be powerful indeed. Titania did not like to wait. "I see."

"If she convinces Oberon to ask me as his *tiarinn*, I will not be able to refuse," he said gloomily. "May I depend upon you to explain to Frederica if that should happen?"

"I would have done so even without your request. And I will speak further to Titania on your behalf if necessary."

"You are the best of *shurinns*." Apparently the nearby presence of fay kept Eversleigh from expressing his thanks.

Darcy came up from behind them and sat on Elizabeth's other side. "Good morning."

How much more alive his presence made her feel! It was as if a spark passed between them when she met his intent gaze. "Good morning," she said, suddenly breathless. "We are waiting for Frederica, who is speaking to the tree."

"It does work, then?"

"It does," said Eversleigh. "I spoke briefly to Lord Matlock, and he agrees about disbanding the Collegium. We did not get much further before Lady Frederica arrived."

Just then Frederica stepped away from the tree. She spotted them and came to sit beside Eversleigh, the tracks of dried tears still showing on her face.

"Were you able to speak to him?" asked Eversleigh gently.

Frederica nodded.

Elizabeth asked, "Did he seem like himself?"

Frederica gave a quavering laugh. "Unmistakably. Who else could possibly be so smug?"

"Smug?" Elizabeth asked in surprise.

"Unbearably so. He says Oberon gave him no warning that he planned a Great Spell, and yet he still managed to compose a spell on the spot which sufficed. In English, no less, even though he had only ever written spells in Latin. He said he also made the boundary between our world and Faerie somewhat more permeable. He was smug about that, too."

"I wonder what that means," said Eversleigh.

"I do not know. He became distracted after that." Her expression became more somber. "I have the impression we will be finding more dead sorcerers."

"I fear so," Eversleigh said.

Across the lawn, Titania eyed them assessingly.

Elizabeth said, "Titania is very eager to speak to you, Frederica."

"To me?"

"Yes. See, she is looking at you."

"Well, then, I suppose I must go to her."

Eversleigh stood and helped Frederica to her feet. He watched after her as she walked away before sitting again. "Definitely the best of *shurinns*," he said.

She laughed. "If my children and your children are both *tiarinn* to Titania, will that make them *shurinn* to each other?"

He groaned. "I have not even figured out how the new blood tie between Oberon and Lord Matlock affects all the kinship, much less that."

"Performing a Great Spell together creates a blood tie?"

"A very strong one, apparently, as if they were now one person. I am more conscious of Colonel Fitzwilliam than I would expect." With a self-deprecating smile, he added, "I am always conscious of Lady Frederica."

Titania clapped her hands for silence. "My Marigold Meadowsweet has something to say," she announced.

Eversleigh's eyes widened. "Already?"

Frederica's voice rang out clearly. "As Matlock and Oberon have been joined in blood, let Matlock's daughter and Oberon's son be bound.

Prince Evlan, I claim blood right." She held out her hand towards him.

Eversleigh did not move, seeming frozen in place. Elizabeth pushed his shoulder. "Go to her, *shurinn*."

Finally he seemed to rediscover the ability to move, although it was without his usual fluid grace. He took Frederica's hand without hesitation, though.

Cathael said solemnly, "You do great honor to your fathers."

"Hold out your hands," said Titania. Once again she slashed her palm and let her blood drip onto their hands. "Palms together and turn twice widdershins."

As Frederica and Eversleigh began to move, Darcy's hand closed around Elizabeth's.

Darcy shook the hand of the alert young man in the clerical collar. "A pleasure to see you again, Mr. Cox. Thank you for coming to Rosings today. I realize it is somewhat inconvenient for you, but you will understand why I did not wish to ask Mr. Collins to preside at my wedding."

"Of course not." Mr. Cox's lips tightened. "His behavior has become something of an embarrassment to the local clergy. In any case, I am glad to come here. I have been hearing some odd rumors from Rosings Park."

"They are likely all true," said Darcy resignedly. "At least if they concern the fay and sorcery."

"I was surprised to notice the fay as I arrived. I have not been able to see them since I was a child."

"They have chosen to make themselves visible because of recent events. It is a long story, and a rather difficult one to credit. Perhaps you might wish to sit down while I explain." Darcy owed him the full story after his help with the servants when they discovered Lady Catherine's sorcery.

A quarter hour later, Mr. Cox's brow was furrowed. "Sorcery is the devil's work, and I rejoice that it will no longer taint our world. But I am shocked that Lord Matlock should be a suicide in contravention of God's law!"

"He did not commit suicide." Lady Matlock's cool but determined voice came from the door. "No more than a soldier who marches into a hopeless battle for the sake of his country, or, for that matter, Our Lord who permitted himself to be killed to redeem our sins. Lord Matlock did not wish to end his life, but he did so to save England from untold misery. That is not suicide."

Darcy jumped to his feet. "Lady Matlock, may I present Mr. Cox, the curate of Chiddingstone? He is the one I mentioned who offered support to the staff here around the question of Lady Catherine's sorcery."

Mr. Cox bowed deeply. "My apologies, Lady Matlock. I had not thought the matter through yet, but you are correct."

Lady Matlock acknowledged his words with a regal nod. "If we continue to have more contact with the fay, the church may face some challenges in determining how their magic can be accounted for within our Christian beliefs."

"Understanding more of God's creation can only enrich us all," said Mr. Cox.

"Perhaps we can speak of this more later. Eventually I would like to hold some form of service at the site of the spell. The wedding can take place there as well."

Darcy shook his head. "There are still many fay keeping vigil there. I would not wish to cause any offense to them."

"I agree with Lady Matlock." Mr. Cox's eyes had new fire in them. "The fay are heathen. It is to their benefit to observe a Christian service, even if it offends them."

"Exactly so," said Lady Matlock.

It was not worth arguing over. "Very well."

Darcy found Elizabeth by the Great Spell with Frederica, Eversleigh, Richard and Aelfric. "Are you ready, my love? The curate has arrived, and my aunt insists we must have the ceremony here by the tree."

Elizabeth looked up at him through her lashes. "I hope she does not think the tree will be able to see us."

Darcy's lips twitched. "I would prefer not to argue the point with her." He held out his hand to her, his heart filled with love for her.

Eversleigh said, "Can you wait a few minutes before starting?"

Darcy turned to Elizabeth. "I suppose there is no reason we cannot."

"Good!" Eversleigh hurried off towards the group of Sidhe keeping vigil.

"We may regret this," said Elizabeth with good humor. "I hope there will be no fay pranks."

"Ah, here is Mr. Cox," said Darcy. "Miss Bennet, may I present Mr. Cox, the curate at Chiddingstone? Mr. Cox, Miss Bennet is today's bride."

"It is a pleasure," said Elizabeth. "Thank you for coming today."

Mr. Cox bowed. "I am happy to be of service."

"Oh, dear," Frederica murmured.

"What now?" asked Richard darkly.

She gestured across the lawn. "Look at Eversleigh."

Eversleigh was speaking to Cathael, moving his hands to demonstrate a squared-off shape. Cathael replied, and several benches suddenly appeared facing the spell. Eversleigh shook his head and said something. Now it was two rows of benches with an aisle down the middle.

Mr. Cox's eyes were bulging.

"Is he trying to make it look like a church?" Elizabeth asked. "Who does he think will fill all those benches?"

"I have no idea," said Darcy. But the answer became readily apparent as Sidhe and lesser fay began moving towards the benches.

"This was not quite what I had in mind," said Mr. Cox quietly. "I suppose it will serve, though."

Eversleigh strode back towards them. "I hope that will be satisfactory," he said to Darcy.

Darcy raised an eyebrow. "Is there a reason you wish the fay to attend our wedding?"

Eversleigh grinned. "Not as such, but you showed great honor for fay traditions last night. They wish to show you the same respect by honoring your mortal tradition."

Lady Matlock appeared behind him. "If that is the case, we should do this properly. Richard, you will stand up with Darcy. Elizabeth, do you wish for Lord Eversleigh or Aelfric to give you away?"

"Why would anyone want to give Libbet away?" asked Aelfric. "You cannot give people away."

"It is a symbolic part of the ceremony," said Lady Matlock. "It would usually be performed by Elizabeth's father, but in his absence, one of her male relatives would take on the role."

"Then I should do it," said Aelfric firmly.

Elizabeth said tactfully, "Mr. Cox, may I present my half-brother, Prince Aelfric of the Sidhe? Could he perform that role even though he is not a Christian?"

Mr. Cox had gone rather pale. "I suppose it would not be a problem as long as he is respectful of our Christian tradition."

Lady Matlock nodded. "Who would you like to stand up with

you?"

Elizabeth peered across the lawn. "Is Bluebird here? She is my oldest friend."

Eversleigh cleared his throat. "*Shurinn.*"

Elizabeth turned to him with a look of mock dismay. "Oh, dear. Lord Eversleigh has already made up my mind for me. Who shall it be?"

He colored. "Titania performed your blood right ceremony. It might be seen as insulting to exclude her now."

Elizabeth laughed. "Very well, but you must ask her, *shurinn.* And quickly, since we know the fay do not like to be kept waiting."

"Titania?" Mr. Cox's voice quavered. "As in Shakespeare?"

"The very one," said Elizabeth with a smile.

As Eversleigh hurried back to the fay, Lady Matlock said, "If it is to be done quickly, let us all take our places, in as simple a manner as possible. Elizabeth, will you explain Aelfric's role to him?"

Within a few minutes, her ladyship had arranged it all to her liking and allowed the service to begin. Mr. Cox's voice only cracked once as he began to read the ceremony. Aelfric handled his duties with dignified aplomb, even when a white raven flew in and landed on Elizabeth's shoulder as they were walking down the aisle.

Afterwards, when Darcy and Elizabeth had walked up the aisle as man and wife, Darcy said hesitantly, "About the ring. I will get you another that will fit properly. I was so concerned about getting the license that I forgot completely about a ring."

Elizabeth held up her hand to admire the ring. "I am very happy with this one, and it fits perfectly."

"It cannot possibly fit you. Your fingers are much smaller than mine."

She extended her hand so he could see it did indeed fit. "Is it perhaps of fay manufacture?"

"Yes. How could I forget? Eversleigh gave it to me."

Cathael was the first of the fay to reach them. "Among our people, it is customary to give a gift on coming of age. Since that was not possible for you, I hope you will permit me to do so on this occasion." He took Elizabeth's hands and clasped his silver filigree cuffs around each of her wrists. They immediately shrank to fit.

"That is most generous of you. They are exquisite and will always remind me of the first time we met in your silver filigree hall." Elizabeth sounded oddly shaken.

"This is for you, Diarcey." Cathael handed him a silver dagger whose hilt was studded with rubies.

Darcy took it, since he had no idea what else to do. What did one say when given a gift worth a king's ransom? "It will be my great honor to wear such a royal gift." He tested the edge with his fingertip, having discovered during the blood binding that Sidhe knives were far sharper than any blade made of silver could possibly be.

"It is of dwarf manufacture. It will never lose its edge, and as long as you carry it, the elements will not trouble you and no harm shall befall you."

He could feel the magic tingling through it. An emperor's ransom, then. "It is a greater treasure than I deserve and almost as precious as the reward of peace between our people."

"It was a fortunate day when you stumbled into my keep. Without it, we would be at war and sorcerers would roam your land." He touched the coronet he wore. "It has led me on a most unexpected road." He nodded to them and walked away.

Elizabeth looked at the cuffs on her wrist. "I shall stop feeling guilty about not bringing a dowry to our marriage."

"Good. I do not care in the least about a dowry as long as I have you."

"That is not what I meant." She held one of her cuffs up so he could see the diamond set in it. It was the size of a wren's egg. "These should be in the Crown Jewels."

He smiled. "My question is how I can carry a magic jeweled dagger with my modern attire. We no longer wear dagger sheaths."

Elizabeth glanced down at his waistcoat. With a mischievous look, she said, "Most gentlemen may not, but it seems you do now. Perhaps you will set a new fashion."

Frowning, he followed her gaze and discovered that indeed there was a leather dagger sheath hanging down below his waistcoat. "How did that...oh, never mind. I will never become accustomed to Sidhe magic." He gingerly tucked the dagger into the sheath.

A few elves, dryads, and Sidhe also came forward to present them with gifts. Many of them gave a gift from nature – a perfect seashell, a rounded stone, a variegated leaf, or a flower. Darcy managed to follow Elizabeth's lead in admiring each of these as much as the occasional priceless gem or magical harp.

A scowling brownie stomped up to them and stopped in front of Elizabeth. "'Tis nae so bad, that." She jerked her head towards the Great Spell.

"I met you at the Millers' cottage, did I not?" asked Elizabeth.

"Aye." With a ferocious frown, the brownie thrust something into Elizabeth's hand before stomping away.

Elizabeth smiled. "From a brownie, that is the height of civility towards a mortal."

"What did she give you?" asked Darcy.

Elizabeth opened her hand. "It looks like a seed. A magical seed."

"What will it grow into?" said Darcy cautiously.

"I have not the least idea, but it will be interesting to find out."

Eversleigh joined them with Frederica on his arm. He pointed to

Elizabeth's wrist cuffs. "Did Cathael tell you the meaning of those?"

"No, and I do not feel any magic woven into them," said Elizabeth.

Eversleigh smiled dryly. "No magic, but silver cuffs are the traditional gift a Sidhe gives his daughter when she comes of age, and she wears them all her life."

"What do they give their sons?" asked Darcy.

"A silver dagger." Eversleigh pulled one out of a hidden sheath under his coat. "Oberon gave me this."

Darcy drew out the one Cathael had given him. "You will have to show me how to wear a dagger sheath properly. Does the gift have a particular meaning?"

"I would guess he is acknowledging a debt to you. It suggests you have the right to call on him for assistance in the future."

"Interesting," said Elizabeth, with a lilt of laughter. "I often find weddings a little dull. This one has been the exception."

"I think it was absolutely perfect," said Frederica.

Elizabeth gave her an arch look. "I agree. I think every bride should be given away by a Sidhe, attended by the Faerie Queen, and have a phouka on her shoulder."

Frederica sighed. "Being married at St. George's, Hanover Square is going to be so very dull in comparison."

"Ah, yes, there is that." Elizabeth took Frederica aside and lowered her voice. "May I say something extremely impertinent and improper?"

Frederica's eyebrows rose. "Pray do."

"You are aware the fay bring fertility to the mortal world. Today they have been very busy, especially during the wedding ceremony. We were surrounded by fertility magic. Every gift I was given was infused with it. Titania practically drenched me in it. I will be astonished if I do not conceive a child tonight. I can sense nearly as much fertility magic on you. I know your mother plans to delay your wedding until the Season begins, and...well, I also know how difficult it is not to consummate blood right even for a day. If you are hoping to take precautions against conception until your wedding, I must warn you they are very unlikely to be effective. Very, very unlikely."

"Ah." Frederica's gaze grew distant. "I thank you for the warning. I had best speak to my mother about the wedding date."

"If you can convince your mother to consult your father on this, I suspect he would support you. I imagine he has a better understanding of wild magic now."

Frederica giggled. "Oh, yes. Poor Oberon. Father must be badgering him mercilessly with questions."

"Thank you for not taking offense at my suggestion. I am not looking forward to speaking to Georgiana about this, nor trying to explain to my new husband why his little sister should be under armed guard around Sidhe men. They seem to be leaving her alone for now, but it cannot last."

"Poor Georgiana! Will you warn Anne, too?"

Elizabeth's lips twitched. "I will leave that to Aelfric to explain. Your poor mother might not be able to bear yet another hurried wedding."

"At least our children will be of an age and will be able to play together," said Frederica.

"How very practical of you," teased Elizabeth.

Eversleigh joined them. "About that wedding at St. George's, Hanover Square –"

"You need not worry, *shurinn*. I have already warned her," said Elizabeth.

Relief flickered over his face. "As I have said before, you are the very best of *shurinns*."

"I cannot believe the two of you can even speak together about these matters!" exclaimed Frederica, blushing.

Elizabeth smirked. "After you have spent as much time in Faerie as we have, you will find yourself just as unembarrassed. But there are limits to what I will say to other men, *shurinn,* so I am counting on you to explain matters to the Fitzwilliam brothers and Mr. FitzClarence."

Eversleigh bowed. "I have already warned them to direct their attention only to Sidhe ladies for the time being, and I do not believe either will have any difficulties with that. Fitzwilliam is already discovering his new popularity." He gestured across the lawn where Colonel Fitzwilliam stood between Aislinn and another Sidhe lady, each of them stroking his arm. He did not seem in the least distressed by his predicament. "Jasper disappeared a few minutes ago with a Sidhe lady."

"They must think they have died and gone to heaven," said Frederica.

Eversleigh wore his mischievous look. "They will soon discover heaven can be an exhausting place. Sidhe ladies have great difficulty conceiving children, and an unusually fertile mortal man will find himself very popular indeed."

Frederica clapped her hands over her burning cheeks. "I have not spent nearly enough time in Faerie to listen to this!"

"You may be relieved, then, to hear that Aelfric has used his very best glower to warn every Sidhe man here away from Georgiana." Eversleigh sounded amused.

"Thank God!" said Elizabeth.

Since Elizabeth appeared to be sharing secrets with Frederica, Darcy took the opportunity to approach the curate. "Mr. Cox, you are a courageous man. I must apologize. I had no idea you would be thrust into the middle of the fay like this. I know how shocking my own first experience with them was."

The young curate ran his finger under his clerical collar. "It was certainly unexpected, but I am glad of the opportunity to meet with our invisible neighbors. Viscount Eversleigh was kind enough to assist me while the fay were asking me questions about Christianity. I had not expected such curiosity from them. Of course, I have never before had the privilege of leading a service in front of a living miracle." He nodded towards the oak tree.

A miracle, indeed. "Have you always lived in Kent?" Darcy asked.

"No, my family is in Norfolk. I came here two years ago in response to an advertisement for a curate."

"One of my family livings in Derbyshire is currently vacant. It is not the most valuable of livings, but it is a respectable and secure one. If you might have an interest in it, perhaps we could discuss it further."

The curate's eyes widened. "I...Why, yes, I would be most interested in discussing it, whenever it is most convenient for you."

"Good. I expect to remain at Rosings for at least a few days."

"Lady Matlock has already asked me to return tomorrow to discuss another service."

Darcy wondered if his aunt was planning a memorial service or another wedding. She had not been pleased to discover Frederica had claimed blood right. "Tomorrow, then."

As sunset approached, the fay began to trickle away until there were only a pair of elves left standing guard by the Great Spell.

"What are they guarding?" Elizabeth asked Eversleigh.

"I have not the least idea," he replied. "They say this is how it is done, and that appears to be all the answer we will get. Miss de Bourgh, I fear your Great Lawn has become a sacred place to the fay, and you are likely to find them there frequently. I expect mages will also wish to visit the Great Spell."

Anne shrugged. "They are welcome. We almost never had guests at Rosings until my mother left, and now there are always people coming and going. I like it."

"If you continue to encourage your cook to put out food for the fay, there will be even more," said Eversleigh.

"Good. Aelfric says mortal food is what gives them vitality, but only if it is given to them voluntarily. I am willing to provide that."

"You might wish to consider replanting the lawn as a garden," said Elizabeth. "I suspect it has the most fertile soil in England now, and your gardeners may tire of having to cut the grass every day."

Anne appeared to consider this. "I would like a new garden."

Elizabeth felt a touch on the inside of her elbow that sent a trickle of heat through her. She did not even need to look to see who it was.

"I have arranged to have our dinner served in my room." Darcy's warm breath tickled her ear as he spoke quietly. "I have been sharing you with everyone all day. I want to have you to myself."

She looked up at him through her eyelashes with a teasing smile. "I hope that means we can go there now."

His eyes darkened with desire, sending a pleasurable fluttering through her insides.

At long last, they were alone together. Darcy looked across the small table at Elizabeth's fine eyes. His wife, his *eliarinn*, his Elizabeth. His for the night and forever, here in his bedroom.

He was determined to act as a gentleman tonight, wooing Elizabeth over dinner, even if every instinct insisted on making passionate love to her immediately. He would do this properly if it killed him. He would not think about sliding the blue muslin of her dress off her shoulder, revealing the flesh he had dreamed of for countless frustrated nights, nor what it would be like to feel her lithe body moving under his, her dark curls spread across his pillow as he made her his. No, he would not think about that. Not yet. He would show Elizabeth he could restrain himself.

Elizabeth picked up her wine glass and studied it, appearing engrossed in the reflection of the candle flame on the curved surface. She bit her lip.

He took her hand in his. Even that slight touch raised his desire to near-painful levels. "Is something troubling you?" he asked. "We do not need to hurry this if you do not feel ready." Of course, he might burst into flames if he had to wait much longer, but Elizabeth's comfort tonight was paramount. The tastes of her passion he had already experienced were intoxicating, and he would not allow a bad experience to taint her desire.

Her face cleared, and she smiled. "Oh, it is nothing like that! I am just thinking about what will likely happen after tonight. Did you feel all the magic pouring over us at our wedding?" She reached out and ran her finger along his cheekbone.

God, but her touch was a heady thing! He could feel the heat of it spread through his body. "It would have been hard to miss, but I could not tell what it was doing. It did not feel malicious." How could he think about magic when all his attention was on retaining his sanity for the next hour until he could decently take Elizabeth to his bed?

"It was fertility magic. A very great deal of it." She tilted her head with a teasing look.

Fertility magic? That was what the fay usually did in the mortal world, was it not? Then it hit him. "You mean the magic was for you and me?"

"Yes. We will not know for certain for some time, but it seems very likely that tonight you will not only make me your wife, but also the mother of your child." She seemed to be watching him with some anxiety. "I hope you do not mind it happening so quickly."

Elizabeth, carrying his child. He could practically feel his blood rushing through him. By morning his seed could be growing inside her. They would be bound together in every way. If he had been aroused by her before this, it was nothing compared to the desire now pounding through him.

"Mind it?" he somehow managed to say. "Quite the opposite."

How could he restrain himself now? The Sidhe believed in acting on their urges immediately, and he was bound to Elizabeth by Sidhe blood and magic. Perhaps it was time to do honor to that tradition instead of proper society manners. If the fay wanted Elizabeth to bear his child, he would oblige them. Immediately.

He stood behind her chair, plucked her wineglass out of her hand, and set it down. His finger trembled as it traced her soft skin just above the fabric of her dress.

"Mmm." She pressed against his touch like a cat.

Good God, how many buttons could fit on the back of one bodice? Tiny buttons that kept slipping through his fingers as he tried to undo them, but now the hidden flesh above her shift was beginning to appear. He could not keep himself from pressing his lips against each inch of newly-exposed skin.

Elizabeth gave a soft moan at his caress. "The fertility magic seems to be working already," she said, her voice husky.

He bent to nibble her earlobe and whispered, "If the fay want you carrying my child, would it not be rude to let anything stand in the way?"

"Terribly rude," she said with a breathy laugh, and rose. "I will assume I need not call for a maid to help me undress."

"Absolutely not." There were even more buttons than he had thought. Oh, to be a Sidhe who could wave his hand and make her dress vanish completely! There was only one thing to be done if he wanted to preserve his sanity. He grasped each side of the dress and yanked until the buttons gave way, revealing her shift and stays. One less layer to go.

She turned and wound her arms around his neck, her eyes smoky with desire. "I have been wondering how long it would take you to do that, *eliarinn*. You are not the only one who is impatient." She brushed her mouth against his.

Restraint be damned. He teased her lips apart and claimed the delightful taste of her. This close together, he could feel her desire washing over him and intensifying his own.

Elizabeth.

Much later, Darcy ran his fingers through Elizabeth's hair. "I hope you were not too shocked, my love."

Elizabeth giggled. "The feelings engendered were a surprise, but as for the rest – well, I have spent time with Titania and her dryads. One learns quickly not to be shocked."

"I suppose that is true." Darcy kissed the corner of her lips.

"Besides, I think both of us have grown accustomed to experiencing the unknown. Do you recall the first time I introduced you to Pepper in her raven form, before you had been to Faerie? You looked as if your entire world had tumbled upside down."

He smiled. "Birds are not supposed to meow."

"And now you ask my cat to identify sorcerers for you and you let my Sidhe half-brother pull snakes from your sister's head. Why, you barely blinked an eye when your uncle slit his throat and turned into a tree!"

"I did blink my eyes several times at that," said Darcy with mock austerity. "But you are right. Magic which shocked me a few months ago now seems almost routine. You had the advantage of knowing about it all your life."

"I had other things to learn." Elizabeth ran her hand down his chest. "I remember telling Charlotte once that nothing would ever change. Magic would always be forbidden to women, and I was sure you were looking for an excuse to put a binding spell on me. I could not have conceived of a time when the Collegium would disband or the Sidhe would come out of the shadows, much less that I had a brother among them. And the idea I could consider Eversleigh a friend when he was Master of the Collegium! Compared to those earth-changing things, your uncle turning into a tree was barely worthy of notice. Everything has changed, and I have no idea what tomorrow will bring. I cannot imagine a world free of sorcery and the Collegium where women are safe to use their magic." She sounded wistful.

"Our world will be different, at least for those of us with magic, but as long as I have you, I am happy."

"Good, since you cannot get rid of me." Elizabeth laid her head on his shoulder. "I wonder if anyone has ever been both married and *eliarinn* before."

Darcy wound his fingers in a lock of her hair. "I cannot say if there have been any in the past, but, as Lady Matlock asked Mr. Cox to return tomorrow, I think we will have company soon."

"Without a doubt." Elizabeth yawned, her eyelids drifting down. "I always did want to start a fashion."

# Epilogue

*One month later*

"It is not too late to turn around if you wish," Darcy said to Elizabeth. "I can go to Longbourn alone to speak to your father."

Elizabeth cast an amused look at him. "My wishes do not change the fact that we were married almost a month ago, and I have yet to mention that fact to my family. It cannot be put off forever, and if I do not go now, there will be no hope of forgiveness from Jane or my mother."

"Just from them?"

"I doubt my younger sisters will ever forgive me for revealing Aelfric's existence, so it hardly matters on their account," she said lightly.

"Of course, *eliarinn*." His tone made it clear he was not taken in.

Elizabeth sighed. "I am still not accustomed to having you see through my efforts to make matters light." It was in some ways the most difficult part of the *eliarinn* bond. She had never before realized how often she disguised her feelings.

"Do you regret telling them about Aelfric?"

Elizabeth looked down at her hands. "Sometimes I regret not telling my mother about him privately as I originally planned. My sisters would have been happier not knowing, but my mother likely would not have kept it a secret in any case."

"It was Frederica who forced the issue, was it not?"

"Her intentions were good. I do not think she understood that my family was not as liberal-minded as hers."

"Not all that liberal-minded. Lady Matlock has not yet forgiven her for the hurried wedding," said Darcy. "At least she is no longer angry at us."

"Did I tell you I asked Eversleigh why Lady Matlock did not seem affected by the blood binding? He laughed and said it was because she was a very good actress."

Darcy smiled. "He understands her well. I believe Lady Matlock could be hit by a bullet without wincing or changing her expression."

"It will serve her well in the coming weeks." London society was still in a dither over the events at Rosings Park. The revelation of the fay, sorcery, and a Great Spell in quick succession had been a shock, and more than one newspaper had flatly denounced it as a trick. A delegation of disbelieving mages had descended on Rosings to inspect the tree and interview everyone who had been present. Fortunately, it was hard to deny the evidence of a talking tree, nor could anyone ignore the reports from all over the countryside that people who had not seen the fay since childhood were now catching glimpses of them. "How was your meeting with Cathael this morning?"

Darcy smiled. "I am a sad excuse for an ambassador. I am much more in sympathy with Cathael's directness than the hemming and hawing of the Foreign Office. A meeting with Cathael takes ten minutes. The foreign office drones on for half a day."

"Was he angry they did not agree to have the groves replanted?"

"No, because I had warned him that nothing would happen quickly. We came up with a plan, though. He will tell the lesser fay to stop working around any destroyed grove, and he will send extra workers to the adjacent rings. When there is a circle of failed crops around each destroyed grove and the crops in the very next field are rich and thriving, the Foreign Office may be more willing to replant the groves."

Elizabeth laughed. "You are indeed a sad excuse for an

ambassador! You are consorting with Cathael against our government."

"Well, Cathael is right," said Darcy reasonably. "I explained to the Prime Minister that you could not have normal negotiations with someone who makes instant decisions and can sense any deception, but he seems not to understand. Cathael mentioned Titania has been missing you."

"How can she be missing me?" Elizabeth exclaimed. "Last week when I visited she had her two new followers, Rowan and Honeysuckle, not to mention Mr. McKee doing another painting of her, a poet she called Buckthorn, and, of course, Mr. FitzClarence. How many mortals does she need?"

Darcy leaned down to caress her lips with his. "None of them are you. She has known you all your life, not just a week or two. I am in full sympathy with Titania on this. No one else could take your place for me, either."

Darcy took Elizabeth's hand as the carriage turned into the lane leading to Longbourn. "Are you ready, my love?"

"No," said Elizabeth with a breathy laugh. "But I doubt I will ever be."

He brushed his lips over her knuckles, turned her hand over and repeated his action on the inside of her wrist.

She shivered. "You are trying to distract me!" she accused.

Darcy smiled, that slow smile she had never seen before the last few days. "Is it working?"

"How vain you are!" she teased.

The carriage drew to a halt. Darcy stole a quick kiss before the door opened. As he handed her out, he held her gaze warmly.

Elizabeth took a deep breath at the sight of her former home.

Had it grown smaller in her absence? She smoothed the silk of her skirt, a rose silk dress Frederica had given her. Elizabeth no longer felt like the same girl who had left Longbourn in March, so she had chosen to wear a dress that would make her look different as well.

The familiar butler opened the door, his expression changing from surprised pleasure to wariness. "Miss Lizzy!"

"Is my mother at home, Jenks?" asked Elizabeth in a businesslike manner.

"She is in the drawing room. Shall I announce you and... Mr. Darcy, is it not?"

"It is." Darcy handed him a calling card.

"No need to announce us, I think," said Elizabeth.

She paused outside the drawing room and drew a deep breath. "Very well," she said, more to herself than to Darcy, and walked in.

Mrs. Bennet jumped to her feet. "Lizzy!" She hurried forward to embrace her. "What a happy surprise! Oh, just look at you! If you try to tell me that this dress did not come from a London modiste, I will not believe you! And those beautiful cuffs! You look like a faerie princess."

Elizabeth, breathless from this enthusiastic greeting, said, "Your new style suits you very well." As she had in London, Mrs. Bennet wore a simple dress with only a small amount of lace and no flounces at all, but with elegant lines.

Jane appeared beside her mother. "Oh, Lizzy! I am so glad you have come! I received your letter but did not know where to write to you."

Elizabeth kissed her sister. "Once Mr. Gardiner told me you were engaged to Mr. Bingley, I could not stay away." It had been the final impetus for this trip, especially since Elizabeth wanted any unpleasantness with her father over and done before Jane's wedding.

"You will come for the wedding, will you not?"

"I would not miss it for anything!"

Bingley was shaking Darcy's hand. "It is good to see you, my friend."

Mrs. Bennet appeared to notice him for the first time. "Mr. Darcy, forgive me for allowing my pleasure at seeing Lizzy to overtake me. You are welcome to Longbourn." Her voice held puzzlement.

Impulsively Elizabeth took Darcy by one hand and her mother by the other, joining all their hands together so Mrs. Bennet's hand covered theirs. "Mama, Mr. Darcy and I have claimed blood right."

Mrs. Bennet's jaw dropped. "Blood right? You... and Mr. Darcy? Oh, my goodness! Mr. Darcy! I cannot believe it! You and Mr. Darcy! Oh, you have been a sly one, Lizzy! Blood right! Oh, my!" She fanned herself with her free hand.

Elizabeth laughed, for the first time seeing something of the mother she had known in this new Mrs. Bennet. She was improved even in her rapture, though: she had not said a word about Darcy's riches. "It happened rather suddenly, but I am glad you are pleased."

"Pleased? I could not be happier! Blood right! I suppose that means Mr. Darcy must have been to Faerie as well."

"I followed Elizabeth there." Darcy sounded amused.

"True, the first time he followed me there," said Elizabeth. "The second time, the king gave him the freedom of Faerie. And now Cathael, the new king, has asked the Prince Regent to name Darcy as the ambassador from St. James's Court to Faerie. The Sidhe have taken quite a liking to him."

Darcy flushed. "He asked for me because I am the only mortal man he knows well."

Mrs. Bennet clapped her hands together. "Ambassador to Faerie! How well that sounds. And you shall be an ambassador's wife!" Her face fell. "Or do I assume too much? Are you engaged?"

Darcy said firmly, "Mrs. Bennet, you need have no worries. We came here today so that I could ask Mr. Bennet's permission. If he is at home, I will do so right now."

"Certainly! Mary, pray show Mr. Darcy to the library."

"Good luck," Elizabeth told him as he followed Mary out of the room.

Lydia, who had been sitting with Kitty by the window, said sullenly, "You just wanted to be the first of us to marry, even if it meant marrying a man you hate! But it did not work. Jane will be the first."

Mrs. Bennet said sharply, "That is enough, Lydia. Apologize to your sister and go to your room."

Lydia's eyes flashed. "Sorry, Lizzy," she snarled. "I hate you!" She fled from the room.

Mrs. Bennet sighed. "It is a good thing you had the spell removed when you did. Lydia needs to be taken in hand, and I did not even realize it before."

Stunned, Elizabeth could think of nothing to say. For years her mother had encouraged Lydia's bad behavior. This change was overdue.

Jane said quietly, "Lydia dislikes the changes in our mother, and she blames you for it."

"I see," said Elizabeth faintly.

The butler announced Darcy's name as he entered the library.

Mr. Bennet stood to greet him. "Mr. Darcy, this is a surprise. I had not realized Bingley invited you to Netherfield."

What did Bingley have to do with it? Did he still think of Darcy only as Bingley's friend? "No. I came here today with your daughter Elizabeth. I would like your permission to marry her."

"Lizzy? You want to marry Lizzy? Is she here?" Mr. Bennet rose half way, stopped, and slowly lowered himself back into his chair.

"She is visiting with her mother and sisters to allow us time for this discussion."

His face grew cold. "I assume then that you are part of this business with the fay? I suppose you must be."

"I am. I believe at this point I am supposed to assure you that I hold your daughter in tender regard, which I do, and that I have adequate resources to care for her, which I also do. By the laws of Faerie, Elizabeth and I are already married, and we have been through a wedding service with a curate so we would be married in the sight of God and of English law. However, because of events beyond our control, I could not seek your permission then. I hope you will give it now."

"A fay marriage means nothing to me, but if Lizzy has her heart set on marrying you, I will not stand in the way." The words sounded bitter.

"Thank you."

"How much of this sad story do you know, Mr. Darcy?"

"If this sad story refers to binding spells and Prince Aelfric, I believe I know all of it."

"Tell me, of all the men you know, how many of them, if their wife were delivered of a Sidhe baby, would not strangle the infant in his cradle?"

"Very few, I imagine. You are to be commended for choosing not to do so."

Mr. Bennet removed his spectacles and set them on his desk. "It was not an easy decision, and I am rather tired of having Lizzy paint me as the villain of the piece because I attempted to keep my marriage intact."

"Having not been in your position, I cannot judge. Elizabeth is the one you need to convince. Incidentally, there is a slight possibility she and I may have a Sidhe child because we were bound together with Sidhe blood. I hope we do not, since I would not like to give up a child to be raised in Faerie."

Mr. Bennet's lips curled with distaste. "You will have to forgive me if I believe any fay ritual is meaningless."

Darcy inclined his head. "You are entitled to your opinions. In my experience, the ritual we underwent is quite binding, and in some ways more so than a traditional mortal marriage."

"You do not find mortal marriage binding?"

"It is different." Darcy closed his eyes and focused his attention on Elizabeth. "Right now Elizabeth is sitting in the arm chair next to the hearth. She has her right arm raised like this as she explains to her mother – I cannot quite catch it – no, it is about the wedding of Lady Frederica Fitzwilliam to Viscount Eversleigh. She is shocked at your wife's manner of disciplining your younger daughters, and she is pleased because she can feel my attention on her." He opened his eyes. "That comes with the fay binding of blood right."

"You gave up your privacy? I am glad to be spared that."

"Only when we choose to have it so. I can block her from seeing what I am doing when I wish for privacy."

"That will only be trouble. She will wonder what you were doing and suspect the worst."

Clearly there was no moving Mr. Bennet from his prejudices. "In any case, I thank you for your permission. I will rejoin Elizabeth now. I suspect your wife may have more questions for me."

"Perhaps I will accompany you."

"How has it been here since your return, Mama?" asked Elizabeth. "Are the neighbors acknowledging you?"

"Some still do. No one is aware of Aelfric's existence, only that I was spellbound. People who knew me long ago have accepted the change fairly well. Others, like that silly Lady Lucas, do not know what to do with me. At least it has stopped the gossip about your magic, since my situation is more scandalous. It will be a long time before the people of Meryton accept a woman with magic."

Her mother truly had changed if she now saw her dear friend Lady Lucas as silly!

"I am sorry there has been gossip about you," said Elizabeth. There had always been gossip about Mrs. Bennet, but before it had been about her lack of manners.

"It is nothing. Oh, Lizzy, I was so worried for you! All that frightening news about sorcery and Great Spells and mages dying, and I knew you were likely in the midst of it. I wrote to Matlock House asking for your whereabouts, and Lady Matlock herself sent me the kindest note, despite her own bereavement, that you were quite well and would no doubt contact me soon. But she did not tell me where you were, and that worried me even more."

"I did not mean to worry you. I was in Faerie while the sorcerers were at Rosings, but I returned as soon as they were dead. All I saw was the aftermath of the Great Spell. Most of the time since then I have been at Rosings relearning how to manage my magic without accidentally setting anything on fire. All of us who were present in the aftermath of the Great Spell were caught up in its magic, and Viscount Eversleigh would not let any of us leave until we mastered the changes. It was quite the magical muddle."

A shadow crossed Mrs. Bennet's face. "The newspaper said one of the sorcerers was a Mr. Wickham. We have all been wondering if that could possibly be our Mr. Wickham, but none of us could believe it."

"I fear it was him. He fled the country after seeing the other sorcerers die. He apparently thought sorcerers would be safe outside England, but the Great Spell did not stop at our borders. He died the first time he tried a spell." None of them had thought to consider what might happen outside England, but reports had come quickly of sorcerers dying across Europe. Italy was in turmoil after the loss of their ruling sorcerers, and there had been interesting rumors about sudden deaths among Napoleon's aides.

"Viscount Eversleigh – is he Aelfric's brother, then? I cannot think of another way you could be *shurinn*."

"That is correct."

Miss Bennet dropped her voice. "How is Aelfric? I have heard nothing."

Elizabeth smiled. "He is presently enamored of a young woman and is busy with her. There is no cause to worry."

"But he lost his father to the Great Spell..." Mrs. Bennet went silent. Even after all this time, she apparently was not indifferent to the memory of Oberon.

"Aelfric is as well as anyone can expect. Oberon had already gone into his decline, so Aelfric had lost him already." Aelfric was still badly shaken by his experiences with the sorcerers, but he would not thank her for sharing that information.

"Are you still living at Rosings?" asked Jane, clearly eager to change the subject away from Aelfric.

"No, I went to London a fortnight ago. Viscount Eversleigh, Mr. Darcy, and Colonel Fitzwilliam, Lord Matlock's son, had to meet with the Prime Minister and his cabinet to tell them about the sorcerers and the Great Spell. Aelfric was with them part of the time because Lord Eversleigh felt they would be more inclined to believe him in the face of Aelfric's evidence. Then they had to inform the Collegium, which was very difficult, especially after two more mages died while performing sorcery. Now the Collegium is disbanded, and Lord Eversleigh has started planning a new organization of mages." Most of the planning was being done by Frederica and Lady Matlock, but it was better not to mention that. "Darcy continues to meet with the Foreign Secretary about the new relationship with Faerie."

Mrs. Bennet frowned. "Where have you been staying? At

Matlock House?"

Elizabeth met her mother's eyes with a level look. She could not keep the fact of their wedding hidden forever. "I have a confession to make. Lady Matlock insisted on having an immediate marriage service after we claimed blood right. Lord Matlock managed to get us a license even though I was underage, but we decided we would not announce the marriage until after my father gives his permission." Her purported adoption by Lord Matlock was another thing better left unmentioned. "I have been staying at Darcy House, naturally. We came here as soon as Mr. Darcy could get away."

Mrs. Bennet clasped her hands to her heart. "Married already? Mrs. Darcy! Does that not sound fine?"

At the sight of Jane's shocked face, Elizabeth said, "I wish all of you could have been there. It all occurred so quickly, and the wedding itself was so unusual, that it is hard to believe it actually happened. Lady Matlock announced it would be happening, and ten minutes later I was standing before the curate! It was during all the madness after the Great Spell. Someday, when we have a great deal of time, I will tell you the entire story."

"Was Aelfric there?" Of course, Mrs. Bennet's thoughts had gone immediately to him.

"As my only male relative present, he gave me away. We had a remarkably understanding curate. We had intended to have a second ceremony in the usual manner in the Longbourn church, but, well..." She turned to her mother and whispered in her ear. "Two days later, Titania told me I was already with child." The idea of having another wedding when she would be three months along had no appeal.

"Already? Oh, oh, oh! Oh, my dear! Is it true? I am so pleased! I shall be a grandmother! And Titania herself told you? Such an honor! Oh, my!"

So much for keeping that a secret from her sisters until the ordinary time! "Titania said so, and I have no reason to doubt her, but it will be months before I show the usual signs." She had just started feeling a little queasy in the mornings.

Jane was the first to congratulate her and kissed her cheek warmly. Elizabeth took advantage of her closeness to whisper, "You must come to visit me in London. I have so much to tell you!"

Mary asked abruptly, "Is it true that Miss de Bourgh is opening a school at Rosings for women with magic?"

"That is her plan."

Her sister's knuckles whitened. "I would like to go there, if I may."

Mrs. Bennet's expression brightened. "A delightful idea, Mary! Just what I would do if I were your age."

Elizabeth said, "I can see no reason why you should not. I will ask Miss de Bourgh about it if you would like. I will likely be spending a good bit of time at Rosings myself as Mr. Darcy's younger sister is there." Georgiana had a long road ahead of her. Her undeveloped magic, suddenly augmented with Sidhe magic and elemental magic, seemed to be blossoming into new, unknown magical powers.

"Thank you." Mary ducked her head, looking as uncomfortable with maternal approval as Elizabeth felt.

A change of subject was clearly overdue. "Jane, I am longing to hear all about your wedding plans. The Gardiners knew nothing but the date."

Before Jane could even respond, Mrs. Bennet jumped in. "Is it true what your aunt wrote to me, that you took two of her children to Faerie?"

Elizabeth laughed. "I did borrow them for a day to soothe Titania. She has missed having mortal children to fuss over, and she needed the distraction after all that had happened. She was most taken with young Maddy and wants her to return. My uncle favors it, since he has been taken with the notion of selling fay jewelry to mortals." She glanced down at her wrist cuffs.

"Those are lovely cuffs. I always wished for some of my own, but they never gave them to mortals in my day." Mrs. Bennet looked more closely at the cuffs and her eyes widened. "Are those diamonds?"

"Paste," said Elizabeth firmly. If she had to wear them every day, she had no intention of allowing anyone to believe she was flaunting that sort of wealth.

"Still, they are beautiful," said Mrs. Bennet with a sigh.

"Cathael, the new king of Faerie, gave them to me on the occasion of my wedding, and I must wear them every day to avoid insulting him. A few ladies in London have ordered similar ones. I hope they will become fashionable, since it is difficult to explain them to people with no knowledge of Faerie. At least they fit over long gloves."

The safe chatter continued until the tea tray arrived, with Darcy and Mr. Bennet just behind it. Elizabeth was relieved to see a small smile on Darcy's face.

It was comforting to have Darcy beside her again, but her father's unusually grim visage made her stomach churn. What right had he to be angry? Her mother might have forgiven him, but Elizabeth was not ready to do so.

Mrs. Bennet gestured to the chair nearest her. "Mr. Bennet, do join us. I am about to pour the tea."

"I thank you for the invitation, but whether I stay or not depends upon Lizzy's wishes," said Mr. Bennet.

That was unexpected, not to mention treacherous. What could she say? That she wished him far away, and even more wished he would be the man she once thought he was? After so much time in Faerie, polite lies no longer sprang quickly to her lips.

Mrs. Bennet said reproachfully, "Lizzy, you may disagree with his choices, but he is still your father. You owe him respect and courtesy."

Fury choked her. How could her mother say that, after everything they had all suffered? She should not have come here today. But she managed to say, "I hope you will join us."

Darcy murmured, "Elizabeth, the tea."

The tea? He was concerned about tea? Then she realized the teapot was trembling as the water within it churned wildly. Quickly she chased her anger away as Darcy had taught her, focusing only on the moment and calming herself with slow breaths and happier memories. This was nothing more than a social call where they would share polite niceties.

The teapot stopped trembling just in time. Mrs. Bennet picked it up and began to pour.

Elizabeth waved farewell to the Bennets until they were out of sight, and sank back into the seat. "I do not suppose we could travel by faerie ring instead and send the coach back to London empty."

Darcy smiled sympathetically. "I do not think that would qualify as discreet usage. If other people knew how easily we could travel around the country, they would all be demanding the ability and would overwhelm the rings."

"I suppose so. I hope Jane will be able to accept my invitation to visit us in London. I hardly had any opportunity to speak to her, and my mother kept bringing the conversation around to Faerie, Aelfric and magic, leaving poor Jane out. So much has happened since I last spoke with her alone that I feel like we are practically strangers. How did it go with my father?"

"Well enough. He could see I was not feeling friendly towards him. He was not happy that I was also involved with Faerie, and he seems to feel misunderstood by us."

"By me, you mean."

"I told him he should explain himself to you, not to me, but I think I did start to see something of his position. What he did cannot be justified, but I can see better how his situation could have led him to make a poor decision. I am sorry. I do not mean to pain you."

Her throat tightened. "What did he say?" She was not sure she wished to hear the answer.

"He asked me what I thought other men would have done in his position, and..."

"And what?"

"I saw myself in his place. A young man, very much in love with his wife, just as I am, and excited to become a father. If, at the very moment I expected to have my child placed in my arms, I instead learned you had been unfaithful to me, had likely only married me to give your baby a name, and that the true father was a godlike being I could never compare to – I cannot even imagine how devastated I would be. And if you were proud and excited about this infant who just destroyed everything for me..." He shook his head. "Not to mention worrying about the scandal should anyone discover it was not just an odd-looking baby. He might have killed the infant. He could have sent your mother away to live alone in poverty, or even to an asylum. But he loved her enough to keep her with him, and he did what he had been taught to do when a woman meddled with magic. I would not have done that, but my father and my uncle told me all my life that binding spells were wrong."

Tears rolled down Elizabeth's cheeks.

Darcy quickly put his arms around her. "I am so sorry, dearest love! I should have said nothing. I beg you to forgive my clumsiness."

She buried her face in his shoulder, choking back sobs. "No, you were right to tell me."

"Even so, he should have asked another mage to cast the spell. It is forbidden to use spells within one's family."

"Eversleigh said my father had tried to remove the spell later, but failed. If so, why did he not seek out another mage to help him?"

"I can guess at that. He would have been too embarrassed to admit that not only had he cast the spell against the rules, but then he could not even remove it."

"It was easier just to drift away from the Collegium and do nothing," said Elizabeth bitterly. "He always chooses the easiest way."

"If the spell were removed, he would have had to explain to people why she was suddenly changed."

"Still, I have been unfair to him. I saw only what his actions had done to Aelfric, to my mother, and to me. Mama even said I was unfair to him. It was her actions that brought it all on."

"And his actions that kept it from ending," said Darcy. "If his embarrassment had not been greater than his desire to right his errors, this would have been over years ago."

"True. Neither of them is without fault. I suppose I should speak with him when we come for Jane's wedding." She snuggled closer to Darcy and slid her hand inside his coat to rest on his waistcoat.

"You seemed to do well with your mother."

"Tolerably so. I think she will be easier to deal with now that she is no longer so silly, but we may never have much in common. Even when it comes to Faerie, she idealizes it in a way I do not."

"You need see your parents no more than you wish. It seems we shall be busy between Pemberley, London, and Faerie. I am looking forward to showing you Pemberley. I think you will like it."

"As long as I am with you, I will be happy. I look forward to seeing Charlotte at Pemberley, too. I have so much more family now than I used to – your relatives, Eversleigh, and Aelfric. To think I disliked both of you so much when I first met you!"

He gave her an edgewise look. "You still get annoyed at Aelfric regularly."

"He often deserves it! But his heart is good."

The carriage slowed to a stop. Elizabeth peered out the window to see fields of grazing sheep. "Is something wrong with the carriage?"

"I do not know."

The footman opened the door and flipped down the steps. His expression impressively inscrutable, he said, "Mrs. Darcy's brother and her raven."

Pepper swooped past him into the carriage, transformed into a cat, and curled up on Elizabeth's lap.

Darcy stepped out of the carriage and gripped wrists with Aelfric. "It is generally easier to find people at the beginning or end of their journey, you know."

Aelfric scowled. "London is full of iron, and I have too many sisters at Longbourn. It is simpler to find Libbet wherever she is."

"Well, now that you are here, come sit with me," said Elizabeth, patting the bench beside her.

He picked up a covered basket and ducked his head low to step inside. "What an odd way to travel."

Elizabeth exchanged an amused glance with Darcy. "Is this just a social call, or did you have a reason for tracking us down in the middle of Hertfordshire?"

Aelfric thrust the basket at her. "Bluebird asked me to give this to you. She said it is for the baby."

Elizabeth pressed her lips together to stifle the laugh that threatened to emerge. "You do realize the baby will not be making an appearance until next spring."

Aelfric shrugged. "She wanted you to have it now."

"Very well," said Elizabeth resignedly. She opened the cover of the basket and exclaimed, "What is this?"

A black cat opened its eyes and stuck its head out of the basket. One eye was green and the other was amber.

Darcy laughed. "Another phouka? Is one not enough?"

"This one is for the baby," Aelfric explained patiently.

"I suppose every baby needs its own phouka," said Elizabeth in a droll manner.

Pepper meowed loudly in agreement.

"That is all," said Aelfric. "I will leave you to finish your journey in this odd contrivance. Oh, Libbet, Titania is asking for you."

"Good heavens, does everyone know?" asked Elizabeth.

Aelfric looked puzzled. "Yes, of course." He carefully stepped out of the carriage, looking disproportionately tall on the steps.

After the footman shut the door, the black cat crawled out of the basket and sniffed at Darcy's leg.

Aelfric's face reappeared at the window. "I forgot to tell you." He pointed at the black cat. "Bluebird says her name is Snowy."

# Glossary

**Note:** The Faerie creatures in this book are based on traditional folklore. Wikipedia has articles about each type of fay if you'd like to learn more. I've noted which terms are my own invention.

**Blood magic** – spells which are strengthened by shedding blood. My invention.

**Brownie** – a type of fay who perform chores for a particular household in return for a bowl of cream or other offerings. From British folklore.

**Collegium of Mages** – a society of mages that imposes rules on magic usage, run by the Council of Mages. My invention.

**Dryad** – a type of fay, dryads are tree spirits. Classical and German folklore.

**Elemental magic** – a type of instinctive magic that affects the elements, i.e. water, air, earth, and fire. My invention.

**Eliarinn** – a type of magical fay kinship similar to marriage that is established between two unrelated people. Titania and Oberon are an example of *eliarinn*. My invention.

**Fay, Fayfolk** – any of the many types of creatures who live in Faerie, including elves, dryads, brownies, redcaps, Sidhe, sprites, pixies, dwarves, phoukas and more. Traditional.

**Lesser fay** – all the fay apart from the Sidhe. Traditional.

**Mage** – a mortal magician, generally a member of the Collegium of Mages. My usage.

**Phouka** – a type of fay, phoukas are shapeshifters who can take the shape of a cat, fox, raven, horse, wolf, or human. They are usually dark. From Celtic folklore.

**Redcap** – a type of fay, redcaps are very small, have sharp teeth, and can be malevolent. From Border folklore

**Shurinn** – a type of magical fay kinship between two people who share a blood relative but are not otherwise related. Eversleigh and Elizabeth are *shurinn* because they have a half-brother in common. My invention.

**Sidhe** – the highest-ranking fay group that rules Faerie, they are ethereally beautiful and once rode through the mortal world seeking poets and other artists. From Irish and Scottish folklore.

**Sorcerer** – a mortal magician who practices dark magic, casting spells on people, rather than things. My usage.

**Tiarinn** – a type of magical fay kinship between close blood relatives. My invention.

**Widdershins** – in a left-handed direction, i.e. counterclockwise. Old Scottish word.

**Wild magic** – magic performed instinctively rather than by traditional spells. My invention.

**Note on fay genetics:** Since Faerie doesn't follow the same natural laws as the mortal world, I went to some trouble to establish breeding rules for fay that are completely impossible by our standards.

# Acknowledgments

I'd thought about writing a fantasy *Pride & Prejudice* variation for years. I owe thanks to many people for making this book a reality and hopefully worth reading, despite my lack of experience with fantasy. My greatest praise goes to Monica Fairview and MeriLyn Oblad for having the courage to tell me the original version still needed work. Really, I only hated you for a few days before I started appreciating you again! My thanks also to Nicole Clarkston, Nicola Geiger, David Young, Dave McKee, Susan Mason-Milks, Ana Martínez Ribeiro, Debbie Fortin, and Lori Orcena for making sure there would be fewer errors in the final book than otherwise. I could not have done it without them.

# About the Author

Abigail Reynolds may be a nationally bestselling author and a physician, but she can't follow a straight line with a ruler. Originally from upstate New York, she studied Russian and theater at Bryn Mawr College and marine biology at the Marine Biological Laboratory in Woods Hole. After a stint in performing arts administration, she decided to attend medical school, and took up writing as a hobby during her years as a physician in private practice.

A life-long lover of Jane Austen's novels, Abigail began writing variations on Pride & Prejudice in 2001, then expanded her repertoire to include a series of novels set on her beloved Cape Cod. Her most recent releases are the national bestsellers *Alone with Mr. Darcy* and *Mr. Darcy's Noble Connections*, *Conceit & Concealment*, *Mr. Darcy's Journey*, and *Mr. Darcy's Refuge*. Her books have been translated into seven languages. A lifetime member of JASNA, she lives on Cape Cod with her husband and a menagerie of animals. Her hobbies do not include sleeping or cleaning her house.

# Also by Abigail Reynolds

## The Pemberley Variations

What Would Mr. Darcy Do?

To Conquer Mr. Darcy

By Force of Instinct

Mr. Darcy's Undoing

Mr. Fitzwilliam Darcy: The Last Man in the World

Mr. Darcy's Obsession

A Pemberley Medley

Mr. Darcy's Letter

Mr. Darcy's Refuge

Mr. Darcy's Noble Connections

The Darcys of Derbyshire

The Darcy Brothers (co-author)

Alone with Mr. Darcy

Mr. Darcy's Journey

Conceit & Concealment

## The Woods Hole Series

The Man Who Loved Pride & Prejudice

Morning Light

Made in the USA
Middletown, DE
23 July 2019